A Fearless Memory

OIL KNIGHTS, BOOK 4

MARIE JOHNSTON

LE PUBLISHING

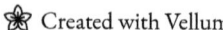

The only thing I coveted more than the old farmhouse next door is the guy who owns it. My best friend's brother.

I don't mean to give my hot neighbor a full peep show when my puppy locks me outside in nothing but a towel. Austen Knight pretends he didn't see *everything* and offers me an interior design job—help him renovate the farmhouse I've adored since I was a kid.

I'm a single mom trying to run a business in a small town. I can't be alone with Austen day in and day out without igniting rumors that could hurt the career I've worked so hard for. But I need the money, and he's leaving after the house is done and goes on the market.

Turns out, renovating with him is fun. Working with him is addicting. And I look forward to our cold beer together after a long day. When work turns to pleasure, I should put a stop to what we're doing, it's not professional, but I can't.

Austen reignites something in me that I left behind long ago. He's become so much more than my friend's brother and my neighbor, but he's going to be gone soon. Guys always leave in the end. I'll be a struggling single mom again, and he'll be nothing but a fearless memory.

One

VIENNE

The worst thing about having a hot neighbor was how often I caught myself looking out the window, hoping for a glimpse of that shirtless god. Too bad he's the brother of my friend. And the brother-in-law to two more. I treasure my friendships more than lusting after a guy.

I ripped my gaze away from my kitchen window and rinsed my coffee cup for the third time.

No shirtless god.

I wasn't in the market for a relationship, but I liked to *look*. And Austen Knight gave me oodles to look at. Tall, with longish dark hair, a devilish grin, and a sense of humor that showed me I didn't laugh enough in life.

He also exuded *here for a good time, not a long time* energy, which I needed to stay far away from. Crocus Valley, North Dakota, was a small town. I didn't need to give the contractors I worked with more opinions about what I did and with whom. My parents would have questions like *Wasn't that how it all started?* or *You think you're going to be the one to nail him down?* All of that wasn't enough to avoid the bachelor next door, then I had my teen daughter. None of my dating life needed to get back to Catherine again. Sex wasn't worth that drama.

"Mom?"

I jumped. The mug fell from my hands and clattered into the bottom of the sink. Crap. I'd been staring at Austen's back deck again. I rinsed my cup for a fourth time.

"Did I scare you?" Catherine giggled. My almost fifteen-year-old still found the most humorous situations were when I embarrassed myself, except for when her classmates commented on my dating life.

"Yes. I'm tired." Tired of ignoring our new neighbor in the house I coveted. "Are you leaving?"

"Yeah. I need to let Teddy out. Will you be here long enough to let him in?"

I hadn't wanted a dog. Being a divorced single mom who ran her own business while keeping a side hustle kept me busy enough. Then Austen's sister, Aggie Barron, got a puppy in at her animal rescue. A purebred Pembrook Welsh corgi, usually selling for well into the four figures, but not Teddy. He'd been born with a cloudy eye and a misshapen head. His little snout curved to the right and his left ear sat back farther than his other side. He hadn't been dumped, but Aggie hadn't been able to say no to his *cute wittle face* when the breeder talked to her about finding him a home.

I couldn't say no, either, and took him in, knowing the possibilities. The puffball with big ears and a bubble butt could have seizures. He might not live long. He might need his eye removed. He could be nothing but vet bills and heartbreak.

Except my other friend, Sutton Knight, Austen's sister-in-law once she remarried his brother Wilder later this summer, said she'd help out. After I saw the way Catherine dropped to her knees and gushed over the corgi, I took her up on the offer.

Catherine promised she'd take care of him. He was healthy—so far—but he was still a puppy, and the doggy duties somehow encroached on my time.

"Last time," I warned her. "You have to get up earlier and get him outside to potty and back in to eat."

She rolled her eyes in that *I knoooww* way teens did. "I can put food and water at the base of the deck."

Teddy's legs and body were currently too short for stairs.

I checked the time. I had a phone meeting in an hour, and I needed to shower. But Catherine had five whole minutes to walk to the school before her week-long volleyball clinic began. "Go ahead and do that. I'm working from home all day, so I can check on him."

"Thanks, Mom." She kissed my cheek, and once again, I marveled over how tall she'd gotten. We were almost at eye level, but when she wore her athletic shoes, she was taller. Her hair was a few shades lighter than mine and twice as thick. She'd pulled it back in double Dutch braids.

I went upstairs into the shower. I switched from mom mode to interior designer and mulled over the lighting options to talk over with the contractor who'd hired me for a house he was building. Jim didn't want to special order light fixtures, but the box stores wouldn't have what the clients wanted. I had to be careful how I talked to Jim. He was older and knew my dad, and he always brought up how I got my parents' car stuck in the ditch one Friday night. *Twenty* years ago. It wasn't like that was how I spent my weekend nights anymore.

The homeowners had asked for me directly, otherwise I might not have gotten the job. Cracking the small-town circle of contractors and good ol' boys had proven challenging, but I was slowly building a reputation.

Slowly.

A bookkeeping side gig was keeping this household afloat and siphoning my soul one reconciled account at a time.

The sound of barking came through the shower. I cocked my head. Teddy wasn't a barker, but the neighbor's dog, Dobber, took to barking like he was paid per woof. That neighbor wasn't Austen and gave zero fucks about people who worked from home or slept during the day. The boxer mix gave a ton of fucks and wanted everyone to know.

By the time I stepped out of the shower, Dobber was going wild. He was most likely excited by Teddy. If I didn't bring the puppy in, Dobber would make me sound unprofessional as hell on the phone. I'd do it as soon as I was dressed.

I squeezed the water out of my hair. Okay, I had to remember to tell my client about—

Bark, bark, bark.

Inhale, two, three, four. Exhale, three, two, one. I put my contacts in. I'd talk to her about the types of fabric we could use for—

Bark, bark, bark.

I couldn't think.

I'd bring Teddy and his food and water into the

mudroom. Dobber would settle down, and I could finish getting ready.

Wrapping a seafoam-green bath towel around myself, I scurried out of my bedroom, down the stairs, and through the back hallway. The door hung open with only the screen door closed. I'd have to remind Catherine to close it all the way. Teaching girls the safety aspects that came with being a woman, especially one who lived alone with her daughter, wasn't for the impatient. Catherine thought I overreacted half the time and teased me for how automatically I flipped the lock on the handle.

I opened the door. "Teddy, come on, boy."

The puppy was delighted to see me. He rushed up the bottom stair, his tongue lolling out of his weaker left side. He stared at me, his head tilted to the side.

Oh. His little legs.

Shoot. Maybe I should get dressed first. Did I have time?

Bark, bark, bark. Dobber held a steady cadence.

Heck with it. I tightened the lip of my towel and crept out, peering left and right. I stayed low, sidled down the stairs, grabbed the dog, and raced back, hoping my towel would stay in place.

Inside, I gave him some quick pets and situated him in the mudroom, where he had a little doggy pad and some chew toys. He didn't mind being inside, but he loved being outside, trotting parallel to the fence with Dobber. The louder Dobber barked, the happier Teddy was.

Dobber was mellower in the afternoons, and I had no calls planned after this morning's meeting. Teddy could play with his friend then.

I was about to shut the mudroom door but stopped. "Your food and water."

Could I get away with not being seen twice? Time was ticking, but I only needed a couple of seconds.

Keeping a hand at the clasp on my towel so I didn't accidentally show my boobs to any neighbors who couldn't quit spying out their kitchen windows like me, I crept out. I'd die if I flashed Austen, if he was even home. I bent my knees to grab the food dish without flashing my ass to Dobber's owners.

A thud made me jump. My frantic gaze jolted to the back door. I hadn't closed the mudroom door, and Teddy must've wandered out and knocked this one closed. *Always lock the doors. All of them, even the back door.*

"Shit."

Grasping the food dish, I straightened and raced up the stairs. I jiggled the knob. Locked.

The habit was so automatic I didn't notice I had flipped the doorknob lock.

Cold washed through my veins. The sun was shining, and it was a beautiful June day, but goose bumps spread across my skin. I had an important meeting. If I fucked up with the contractor, or worse, ghosted the call, I'd undo five years of hard work. I'd be a side-hustling book-keeper who lived child support payment to child support payment forever.

Inhale, two, three, four. Exhale, three, two, one.

The spare. Right. Yes.

I glanced around. No one had caught me in nothing but a towel. Yet. Unless they were looking out their window being a creep like me, but then I'd rather not know.

I went to the potted plant that held a variety of decorative rocks and found one that was a little more...plastic...than the others. It wasn't perfect camouflage, but I'd also been terrified to lock myself outside while Catherine was inside alone and so deep in her headphones she wouldn't know I was gone. I gripped the rock to slide the trapdoor open. A bird squawked and I fumbled the key.

The metal clattered on the deck floor and disappeared between the slats. "No, no, *no*."

The deck was a few feet off the ground, positioned over a bed of rocks. I gripped the flimsy hook of my towel flap, holding the rest of the fabric up. How was I going to crawl underneath the porch without mooning the neighborhood? Without hurting myself? And do it in time to be ready for my meeting?

I hopped from foot to foot. Those rocks would be painful on my knees, but to get to the key in the middle of the damn rock bed, I'd have to belly crawl.

Oh, god.

Inhale, one, two—fuckaroo.

I was descending into panic. Wasn't this what my ex used to chide me on? *You worry too much, Vienne.* One of us had to be concerned with being adults who could provide a home for our child.

I was still shifting from foot to foot and the seconds were ticking by. No way out but through, like my dad said.

Letting out a slow breath, I centered myself and took the few stairs down to the grassy lawn. I stayed on the soft portion of my backyard and judged which side was shorter. The lawn sloped, and I had more room to crawl underneath on the right, but I'd have to go a few extra feet. The other side had prickly bushes I'd have to wedge through. The branches looked like they were waiting to hook my towel.

Dobber watched me quietly.

"If you hadn't been so noisy, this wouldn't have happened."

He remained quiet, like a silent doggy apology.

You always gotta blame someone, Vienne. I envisioned my ex's words blowing away in a puff of smoke. He'd diminished everything I'd contributed to our relationship, but I was the one who got shit done.

Time to get to work.

I put a foot on the rocks. The river rocks weren't small, nor were they terribly big and pokey. So, not unbearably painful. I could do this. I took another step and my uneven platform shifted only slightly. Panic speared my chest, and I wobbled.

When I reached the edge of the deck, I crouched, trying to keep all my bits covered. My back was to Austen's house. Dobber was actually quiet, watching me, judging me as too useless to play with.

Join my exes, Dobber.

I gingerly got on my hands and knees. "Ouch." The back of my thighs caught a light breeze, and the towel rode even higher. Panic shot through me. Reaching behind me, I gauged how much ass I was flashing.

A door opened and shut. My heart stuttered, and I craned my head around.

Austen had stopped, his gaze on my backside, his knuckles white on the shaker bottle in his hand. He was shirtless, and his red basketball shorts covered less than my towel, but he was massively more concealed than me.

Normally, I'd appreciate his broad chest and those abs that rippled like a rushing creek, but my butt cheeks were waving around like a flag. Was my entire ass showing? My *labia*? I rolled to my side in mermaid pose, but the move pulled on my towel and the flap came loose. I barked and clutched both flaps in my hand. He didn't see my boobs, but god, what else had he caught sight of?

"You okay, V?" he asked, his voice gruff. Only he called me V. Usually, he made it sound akin to buddy or pal, but today, there was a thread of concern mixed with amusement and the shortened version of my name came off as...intimate. Familiar.

Embarrassed butterflies fluttered in my stomach, only to be smothered by humiliation.

He averted his gaze to the wooden fence at the back of my yard. I wasn't a voluptuous woman. He was probably wondering why I bothered with a towel. My *B* cups wouldn't be a handful for him, and my body type was more long-distance runner than burlesque dancer like his sister-in-law Tova. I wasn't often concerned about my appearance, but I'd been fearful of giving him a show while he couldn't look away fast enough.

I swallowed my humiliation. "I got locked out getting the dog's food, and I dropped my spare key. It's under the porch." My cheeks burned. I hated looking inept, and to do it in front of a guy I'd see regularly in my friend group because they were his family? Not my shining moment.

He nodded and glanced at my grip on my towel. Tension radiated through my body. *Please go inside so I can get my key in peace.* He did, pivoting to disappear into his house.

Oh. Okay.

Disappointment curdled in my belly. At least he didn't sprint during his getaway. I was carefully rolling onto my knees when the door banged open. I plopped back onto my hip, stunned to see Austen hop off his porch with a throw blanket tossed over his shoulder.

He crossed to the short chain-link fence between our yards and smoothly jumped over like a heavily muscled and absurdly handsome gazelle. He was next to me in seconds, and I shrank in on myself. Towering hotness. The smoky cedar of his aftershave surrounded me. The guy smelled better than my actual cedar deck. When I braved a direct look at him, I saw he hadn't shaved. My fingers tingled, wanting to stroke over the prickles, and I wondered how they'd feel scraping the insides of my—

He swung the blanket over my shoulders. "There ya go."

The move brought him closer to me. I was impossibly rigid. Improper thoughts and that aftershave—my vibrator could not handle the onslaught of lust cutting through my humiliation.

I could've melted into a puddle. He was sweet too? He'd been a flirt the few times I crossed paths with him at Knight family gatherings I had also been invited to. But I had recognized the general flirtatiousness. He probably charmed streetlights out of their bulbs. I wasn't special.

The thought doused a good amount of arousal. Not enough, but I remembered I was still in nothing but a towel and a throw blanket, and I had no clue what an eyeful he'd gotten.

I was afraid to let go of the towel, but I used one hand to keep the edges of the blanket tight around me. "Thank you."

"Allow me." He moved behind me.

I let out a squeak when strong arms clamped around me and lifted. "Austen." I lost track of the moving parts of my towel. Were my privates flapping in the wind again?

I kept the fabric secured under my arms and cinched the bottom of the blanket around me.

"Sorry. Just thought it'd be easier." His deep voice rumbled in my ear, but he didn't release me. I was surrounded by smoky cedar and fabric softener scents. "Are you steady?"

No.

I nodded.

He released me, and my world spun for one heartbeat.

Did I swoon?

Of course I did. Austen had been more chivalrous than my ex in the ten years I'd been married to him.

"I'll get the key. Where'd you drop it?"

I maneuvered around to keep the rocks from biting into my skin. "By the flowerpot next to the door. Are you sure?"

He grinned, all strong jaw and twinkling eyes. He oozed country-boy charm with the innate sexiness some men possessed just because they once put a uniform on. He no longer had hair neatly trimmed close to his scalp. He'd grown it out, like he couldn't be bothered with regular cuts, just like he didn't mess with shaving too much these days. The haphazard look shouldn't have worked so well on him, but it did. My heart stammered.

"I'm sure I'm stronger than that towel," he drawled.

My cheeks flamed. My hold was so tight on the blanket I was mummified. What had he seen when he walked out of his house? "Th-thanks."

His grin widened until it consumed me. I stood, waiting to be devoured by anything related to Austen, but he turned away and dropped down. Next thing I knew, he was belly-crawling under the deck.

"Doesn't that hurt?" I ducked to see how his big body fit under the planks.

"Nah, it's fine." The sounds of rocks scraping together filled the air. "Ah, I see it."

I jumped to the grass and used his distraction to arrange the plaid throw blanket around me a little better. He started to emerge, athletic shoes first, then a tapered waist with rippling muscles, and finally his head. He popped up like he belly crawled across rocks all day, every day.

He brandished the key. "All yours."

"Thank you, Austen."

His gaze darkened, but I didn't read into it. My nerves couldn't take more adrenaline. Desire and arousal would turn me into a mumbling mess for my important meeting.

I took the key, our fingertips brushing. More quivers raced around my chest wall. "Betcha didn't think this was how your morning was going to start."

His eyes heated and stroked down my body. "Definitely not what I expected."

What did he mean by that? The heat in my face stoked hotter. "So, um, thanks."

"You're welcome." He stretched the back of his neck. His pecs flexed, and the bulge of his biceps was unreal. I was riveted. "Hey, can I talk to you about the house?"

The house. He must not have seen everything I had to offer, but if he had, he wasn't interested in more than my professional opinion. A depressing thought, but for the best. I couldn't have a fling with the neighbor, and I wasn't looking for a relationship. "I have a meeting, but later?"

"Sure." He lifted his chin toward my house. This

time, the gleam in his eye made my pulse jump. "Hang on to the key this time."

ᚴ

Austen

"Fuck," I groaned, my release spurting between my hand to hit the shower floor.

I sucked in gulps of air until the tremors in my body subsided. The bliss of the orgasm faded against the pounding cold of the shower. I needed a new water heater. One of the many improvements on the list for the house.

The appliance was no problem. The rest of the improvements were what I had to talk to my sexy neighbor about.

When I'd woken up this morning, I'd gotten my protein shake ready and went out to the deck like normal to drink my breakfast and figure out what the hell I'd do on this little pet project I'd picked up before my big move to California. Then I saw her.

Not her face, oh no. What I saw would go in my spank bank for years to come. Round ass. Strong thighs. Pink pussy.

Fuck's sake. I couldn't get the image out of my mind. I'd had years of practice keeping my thoughts and emotions under control. Countless times I'd wanted to laugh my ass off in the middle of formation but had to hold it together. There'd even been times I was turned on and had to stay professional. Instances where I'd found fellow soldiers attractive or when one lush lieutenant I'd been with the night before had outright stroked my dick before a command meeting.

But today, I should win a goddamn award. I'd kept my erection from poking out of my shorts. Then I'd had to act like I was a happy helper and that I didn't want to push her back to her knees and plunge inside of her.

A shiver racked across my shoulders. "Shit." I turned the frigid water off and toweled myself dry. My dick hadn't been satisfied with a hand job after I was thinking about Vienne on her hands and knees again.

Bet her tits were perfect little handfuls too.

She was usually a bundle of energy that didn't have the time of day for me. She was friends with all my siblings and their significant others, and I was little more than their brother to her. I'd been her neighbor for over a month, and she'd hardly noticed.

But I'd noticed her. She was off-limits. All the other times I'd been around her, my stay had been temporary. Now that I lived next to her, I couldn't change that she was friends with my sister and two sisters-in-law. Those women would tear me apart if I messed around with Vienne, a single mom, and then sold the house and moved once I fixed it up.

I wasn't hitting her up for her opinions on the renovation because I wanted to get close to her. I really did need her help. I could do all the manual labor, but I had to be told what to do. A guy who'd worn the same uniform all day for twenty years, after eighteen years of jeans and cowboy boots, had a hard time dressing himself, much less picking out paint colors and wood trim.

When I was dressed in another pair of shorts with an old gray Knight's Arabians and Cattle Company shirt, I went to the kitchen. Attempt two at food. I'd missed lunch trying to forget the sight I walked out on and had worked in the basement, mopping and cleaning cobwebs out of the corners. When the dehumidifier wasn't running full blast, the mustiness crept into the rest of the house. None of my attempts to renovate would do any good if the smell and decay crept into every surface.

The surveyor had said the foundation was good, but I'd found a few cracks to seal. I would add more sealant around the windows outside and pile dirt around the foundation to keep moisture from pooling around the base of the house.

I opened my fridge. A whole lot of nothing. Fuck, I had to get groceries. Or I could go to Hummingbird's— again—and bullshit with Thelma. Thanks to my military retirement income and my meager inheritance, I could eat out when I wanted to.

Someone knocked. I rounded the counter, and out of the top window in the front door, I could make out the sharply styled dark hair of my oldest brother, Cody.

When I opened the door, he took in my damp, finger-combed hair and my outfit. "Did you just wake up?"

It was almost two in the afternoon. I gave him a droll look. "You know how I like my beauty sleep."

"Aggie got a couple of goats in at the rescue. Just so happens, the kids want a few goats, and I need fence put up."

I draped my arm on the doorframe. "Does Aggie realize she doesn't have to give her rescues to only family members?"

"Not until her family quits taking them. Wilder's coming over tomorrow, but I'd like to start today."

"You asked him first?" I mock pouted, but inside, I was a little sulky, not gonna lie. I would be in town for a little over two more months, but my oldest brother only asked in a pinch. Wilder might be just as jobless as me, helping at the family ranch once in a while, but he was always at Sutton's vet clinic installing or building something. I was fixing up the house, but I'd make time for family.

Cody only shrugged. "Not used to you being around."

Fair enough. Soon, I'd be gone again. "When do you want me out?"

"Whenever. We've got a lot of fence, and Grayson and Ivy aren't exactly experts." He glanced over and waved. "Hey, Vienne!"

The spike of lust was instant. I shouldered him out of the way and stepped outside. "You can get back in, right?" I grinned.

Pink dusted the apples of her cheeks. "I triple-checked."

She was dressed this time. Her black running shorts rode tantalizingly high on her thighs. She wore a tank top that showed off her toned arms. Only one necklace hung around her neck. Was her pulse fluttering under the thin chain?

"I owe you though. I was almost late for my meeting." She hugged a covered dish of something close to her. Underneath the bowl was my blanket. Her gaze shifted to Cody. "I locked myself out this morning. He helped me get into the house."

That view. I'd wake up every morning hoping to catch a glimpse of those sweet pink folds. Arousal kicked low in my gut. If I didn't quit picturing Vienne on her hands and knees, I would sport an erection in front of her and my brother.

I only had to behave for a couple of months. When I moved, I'd be working hot and heavy with a few old army buddies to start a new security firm. Dating would be back to the low priority it'd been most of my adult life.

"He is the family hero," Cody said, mostly because he knew I hated when I was recognized for my service. I appreciated their appreciation, but when it was directly on me, I never knew how to act, like when someone in Buffalo Gully paid for my dinner because they knew I was in the military. Or when I went to rodeos and they asked for active military or vets to stand. Not many guys were comfortable in those situations, and after growing up the middle kid of five, I wasn't accustomed to the attention.

"A real Knight," I joked. I'd need to polish my halo after feeling like a creep for how much I liked what I'd seen.

Vienne's soft laugh was reward enough for a lame play on my last name. "I, uh, made you something. As a thank-you."

My stomach chose that moment to growl.

Cody smirked. Of course, he'd heard. "In the nick of time. My bachelor brother is used to others doing the cooking. I bet he's wasting away."

I scowled at him. No, I wasn't eating at the dining facility three times a day, but that didn't mean I hadn't cooked for myself during the last twenty years. "You didn't have to. I was happy to help."

She rushed down her porch steps and across the lawn to my yard. "I'll drop this off quick. I didn't mean to interrupt."

"You weren't interrupting anything," I assured her. "Cody was begging for my help." My brother chuffed. I was never too old to get a rise out of him.

She crested the stairs of my porch, giving me a tight-lipped smile. "Thanks for letting me use the blanket." When she presented the dish, I took the meal and blanket from her hands. The bowl was cool. Through the plastic wrap, I could see shell pasta with bits of tomato and bacon.

"It's a BLT pasta salad. I took a chance that you eat carbs once in a while."

Carbs weren't what I was hungry for. "I'll eat your carbs."

The flush in her cheeks deepened.

"I'll let you two chat," Cody said, making his way down the porch steps. "See you later, Austen?"

"You gonna feed me too?"

He grinned. "Dessert's included."

"Then I'll be there."

"You going to the street dance tomorrow, Vienne?" he asked.

There was a street dance? I was always the last to know, but then I was usually the farthest away.

"I wasn't going to," Vienne answered, "but Catherine wants to go for a while."

"Tova would love to see you. Aggie's not going. Too soon after Tripp's birth."

I had another new nephew, and I'd actually been around when this one was born. Unfortunately, I had no idea what to do for siblings after babies were born. Did I bug them by going over there? Tova and Cody lived across the road from Aggie and her husband, Ansen, and my brother Wilder's soon-to-be wife-again, Sutton, was Aggie's best friend. They checked on her. Aggie's daughter, Ro, cried when she saw me. Stranger danger. I'd be in the way if anything.

I switched my attention back to Vienne. Her gaze was stroking across my chest, then jumped up to meet mine. The flush in her cheeks deepened.

Too bad everything about Vienne screamed commitment. She had a kid and a house and a job she'd built from the ground up, according to what Aggie said. Someone like Vienne would want something serious, and I wouldn't be around long enough for a commitment.

She gave us a small wave as she backed away. "You two have a good day."

"Hey, before you go—I wanted to hire you."

Her brows popped. "Oh." She fiddled with her necklace, the rest of her tense. "For what?"

"To help me with the house. That's what I wanted to talk to you about."

Cody nodded. He'd been the one to recommend Vienne. She hadn't done work for him, but I'd looked at her website. Professional. Her portfolio was good enough, and besides, the house renovation wasn't being done for me. I would sell as soon as I was finished. The profit would go toward the buy-in with my buddies to start the security company.

"Oh," she said again hesitantly. "I mean, it's almost too late in the summer to get the good contractors—"

"I'll be doing the work."

She squeezed the chain in her fist. "You?"

I held out my hands. "Boss me around."

Dismay filled her features. "I'm sorry. I don't have the expertise for an old place like this." Her gaze slid to the front door. A covetous look crossed her face, followed immediately by regret. "You'll have to find someone else. Thank you for thinking of me though. Um, keep the dish." She flashed another one of those tight smiles before she rushed down the stairs and cut over the lawn back to her house.

When she disappeared inside, Cody coughed. "Is that the reaction you usually get from women?"

"Not always." Not ever. I crossed my arms, my mind working around my disappointment. Had I pissed her off between her gifting me food and my request to hire her?

Cody clapped my shoulder. "Don't take it personally. You aren't in uniform anymore, and the women aren't falling at your feet."

"Funny, jackass." Rejection never knocked me down. I wasn't everyone's cup of tea. I was too country, too rigid, too easygoing, too tall, too much of an ass, too nice. Whatever the reason, I'd been let down because of it. But seeing Vienne rush from my steps hit differently. Her rejection wasn't just personal, it was professional, and I had no idea why.

Two

VIENNE

I'd survived the first encounter with Austen after possibly baring my all to him. After seeing Cody, I'd nearly run back into the house, but he'd seen me and I rallied. The salad had been delivered. The blanket was back with its rightful owner. And I'd survived yesterday.

I'll eat your carbs.

Was I the girl who'd take everything he said and make it dirty? I shook my head and concentrated on the invoices in front of me. The job with Jim was almost done. The clients were happy, and I had nothing else lined up after.

So, why'd I turn down Austen?

He'd been nothing but nice and respectful, but when it came to my endeavors, I was protective. I had Jim reminding me of the few times I was irresponsible as a teen. Okay, the few times I was busted, but still, I was in my midthirties. I had a daughter who liked to take dance lessons and play volleyball. I wasn't sure if she knew boys existed. In other words, she was the opposite of me.

Austen didn't know my past, and therefore, he couldn't hold it against me. But I loved what I did and I took my job seriously. I couldn't work with him if he didn't take me seriously. I also wouldn't know what he was like to work with until I was committed. It'd look bad if I started a job with him and then bailed. My reputation was on the line, and Austen was an unknown.

I would've loved to dive into that house. I knew exactly what I wanted to do, but I hadn't lied when I said I didn't have experience. The jobs we'd normally hire people for, he wanted to do, which would probably include refinishing hardwood floors, replacing bathroom fixtures, and removing countertops. I could research all of it. Actually, I'd been dying to learn those tasks, but right now I had to concentrate on building my business, not on taking roles of various contractors.

My phone rang, and my stomach dropped when I saw Dave's name. My ex-husband didn't call unless he knew it'd be a long text exchange otherwise. And it was usually a lengthy back-and-forth when we didn't agree on something related to Catherine.

I put him on speaker since Catherine was still at her volleyball clinic for the day. "Hi, Dave."

"Vienne, hey," he said like he was calling a client.

Tension knotted my back. He didn't schmooze me unless he was asking for something. "Catherine's not back yet. Were you trying to get a hold of her?"

"Ah, no. I wanted to talk to you about that volleyball camp the university puts on."

I faintly recalled Catherine mentioning it. "Okay?"

"Yeah, she got in."

"You applied already?"

"The deadline was the middle of May, and she was wait-listed." As if that was a good enough excuse to not talk to me first. "But good news—she's in. This'll be really good for her since she's talking about how competitive the clubs are getting."

"It's not competitive, it's favoritism."

His placating sigh put me on edge. "She needs to be good enough that it doesn't matter."

"Those Bismarck clubs cater to the local high school players. It won't matter how good she is when they want to give the open spots to their own players."

"Vienne..."

"Then there's the one client I did work for who said she felt like that one club discriminated against her kid. They just left a spot open on the roster and didn't let her play, even when the coach asked for her on the team. My client said maybe they should change their name to Corrupt Volleyball Club."

"That's just conjecture."

I rolled my eyes to the ceiling. If one of his friends said the same thing, he'd never consider having Catherine play for a club like that. He acted as if I didn't know how these things worked. As if I hadn't played from elementary school to college. As if I couldn't see who coached at the schools and also held top positions in those clubs.

But what did I know? I had only been a Division I athlete. I also monitored those clubs and saw when some rostered fewer teams each season because athletes probably went to other clubs or quit altogether.

"I don't want Catherine to lean on excuses," he said.

"And I don't want to waste time or money on clubs that are only interested in looks and status and not developing a wide range of players. I don't trust that self-serving mentality with my athlete."

A few beats of silence went by. I wasn't usually so adamant with him, he could out-stubborn a mule, but I was protective of Catherine and her volleyball experience.

He cleared his throat. "Regardless, this camp is an excellent opportunity if you don't mind her being gone for a little over four weeks. She could come down at the end of June and have her two weeks with us over the Fourth instead, then go to the camp."

"Us" was Dave and his new wife, Betti. Perfect Betti. Summer visitation with Dave and Betti was usually the last half of July.

Catherine would be gone a third of the summer. Loneliness tugged at my chest. She would be graduating in a few years. Then what? Maybe it wasn't a bad thing to ease myself into having her gone for longer periods of time. "Yeah, that'll work."

"Great. I went ahead and paid the fees, but I'll shoot you a message for half the amount."

"Wait—what?" Half the amount? A two-week camp? That wasn't going to be a small number.

"Vienne." His disappointment resonated over the line.

"Dave." I echoed his tone. I hated how passive-aggressive I got around him. "You could've given me a heads-up so I could've budgeted. This is pretty last minute."

"We'll be driving her every day. I don't expect you to kick in for that. But I thought she said you were getting more work in your little interior design gig."

My little gig. It didn't help my pride that I had no future projects on the horizon—and I'd turned down the one offer I'd gotten. "No, it's fine. Send me the info."

Shortly after I hung up, he sent me the amount. I had to set the phone down and consider how I was going to pull hundreds of dollars out of my ass. I glanced at the wall that bordered Austen's house.

Setting aside the towel debacle yesterday, why was I so resistant to the idea of working with him?

Because his family had become my pseudo-family. I didn't have sisters. My sister-in-law and I didn't have much in common, so we didn't talk a lot. My parents were...not unsupportive. Opinionated? Passive-aggressive? Disapproving of my life's choices?

If Austen and I didn't get along, I couldn't expect it not to spill over into my friendships. He was their brother or brother-in-law.

No. I'd have to find more work.

I dialed Jim's number.

He answered with a huff. "Olson's."

Olson's Contracting was just Jim and whoever could stand working for him. "Hi, Jim. I'm closing out all the invoices and wanted to touch base one more time." *Please offer me another job.*

"We're good, Vienne."

"Oh. Okay." *Just ask him for a referral.*

"Hey, uh, you did good, kid."

"I'm not exactly a kid anymore, Jim."

"Eh, I know. But Lacie and I go back a long way."

Lacie was in her fifties, and she'd been in the area for years. She was the go-to interior designer for contractors like Jim, but she was also established enough to take long vacations twice a year. Coincidentally, I booked more jobs during those times. "I know. She's good." Too good, dammit. "But if you know of anyone else I'd be a good fit for, let me know."

"You know what? I heard—uh, never mind."

"Oh?" Why would he pull back a referral when he said I did good?

"It's just..." His chuckle sounded nervous. "You know Dot Bentwood?"

"In the house by the golf course?" The place was a sprawling Midwest mansion, and it'd been the talk of the town when she and her first husband had built it fifteen years ago. Then she'd gotten the place in the divorce, which had centered the house in gossip once again. Now she was remarried.

"Yeah. She talked to me about some renovations she wanted done over the winter." When Lacie would be south during the cold season.

"I'd love to work with Dot."

"It's just, well, she don't even want to work with Lacie."

"Really?" I leaned forward, as susceptible to small-town chatter as much as the next person.

"She don't want no women coming and going from her house. I guess the mister works from home."

"She doesn't trust him?"

"You remember how she got divorced, right?"

I tried to recall the details. I was sure my mom had mentioned something, but I had been in the middle of my own marriage crisis when Dot got divorced. "No."

"The ex-mister was banging the housekeeper."

Now I remembered. Mom had said she didn't even know there were housecleaning companies in town when she relayed the story. "Right. It's coming back."

"She doesn't trust easy, but if I tell her that you'll only be there when I'm there and most of your work will take place in your home office, maybe she'll okay it? Not a lot of guys out there doing what you do."

Not in Crocus Valley anyway. "I'd really appreciate it. When would the job start?"

"October."

A sweep of relief went through me. I'd be fine until October. I had the bookkeeping job with Rudy's shop across the street, and it'd hold us over until then. "Thank you, Jim."

"Tell your dad I say hi."

"Will do."

After I hung up, I leaned back and rubbed my hands down my face. A job!

The prudent thing to do would be to take the offer Austen had extended, but for once, I wanted to enjoy the way my plans were finally coming together.

Austen

I hadn't gotten over the sting of Vienne's rejection. Something about the way she ran off my porch burrowed under my skin and festered. So the street dance was the last place I should be. Watching her dance with guy after guy, looking everywhere but at me, only confused me more. I'd upset plenty of women in my years, but I was never clueless about what I'd done. I was smart, and there were always signs. Vienne had given me nothing but a pasta salad and a fantastic view I'd like to see again and again.

I'd played it cool about what I'd seen so I wouldn't

scare her off, but maybe she was embarrassed anyway. The not knowing for sure might be killing her. Getting ignored by my sexy neighbor was doing damage to me.

Since I'd been here, I'd watched Vienne talk to Cody and Tova, Wilder and Sutton, and I'd overheard her ask them about Aggie. I'd received nothing beyond that damn thin smile.

I polished off my beer.

"Heya," a woman said from my left. "I'm Kya."

She was pretty. And young. So goddamn young.

Truth be told, she was probably in her mid to late twenties, but the twelve to fourteen years between us felt like a few decades. "Hi, Kya." I didn't care to introduce myself, but my mama taught me a few manners before she walked out the door. "Austen."

She grinned and revealed a dimple that made her look younger. "You haven't danced yet. Do you?"

"I've been known to take a spin." Cody and Tova were tearing up the pavement. Same with Wilder and Sutton. I'd been sulking into my beer, wondering why I hadn't given up and gone home yet.

She cocked her head like she wasn't sure if I wasn't getting her hints or if I was turning her down. "Okay..."

"Like right now?"

Her laugh was awkward. "Yes, please."

She seemed like a genuinely nice person who only wanted to dance. I stood from the picnic table, leaving my beer behind. Vienne was in the arms of some guy who looked closer to Kya's age. Disgruntled, I started to two-step to the beat of a fast country song.

The man Vienne was dancing with had his back to us, and I caught her gaze over his shoulder. I lifted my brows at her, and she reciprocated with that damn flat smile.

Her partner's ass had a worn round ring in the back pocket from a can of chewing tobacco. The thick belt around his waist was probably cinched with a belt buckle bigger than his head.

He wasn't her type.

What would that make me? I was a chew container away from being him.

Why did I care again?

"Austen?"

I snapped my attention back to Kya. She'd been talking to me, and I'd been staring at Vienne. "Sorry. I'm not myself tonight."

"I wasn't sure if I should even approach you," she admitted. "You've been eyeing Vienne like she's a doe and you're in a hunting stand in the middle of November."

Vienne was acting like a skittish deer, but only around me.

I wasn't that noticeable. Was I? "We're neighbors," was all I said by way of an explanation. Who else had noticed my acute attention? Had Vienne? Maybe that was why she was keeping her distance.

"Sure." Her smile was understanding. "Well, thanks for indulging me."

I gave her a quick smile. "Thanks for getting me off my ass."

She laughed, and I maneuvered us around a couple slow dancing their way through the upbeat song. "You're welcome. I just come to dance, but some nights, it's hard to find someone who doesn't think this is speed dating."

We finished the song and then Tova was tapping on my shoulder. "Sorry, Kya. Mind if I talk to my brother while Cody checks on the kids?"

I'd never tire of hearing Tova and Sutton call me a

brother. For a bunch of kids left to ourselves, we were expanding our network of loved ones.

"No problem, Tova," Kya said. "I figured I'd get one Knight brother on the floor while he was free. See you Sunday?"

"Of course. You're my favorite pole dancing class."

Kya laughed. "We're your only pole dancing class, but I'll take it."

Tova hauled me to the outskirts of the roped-off area for dancing.

She was small in my arms, and if I had any hope of leading this dance, I was mistaken. Tova probably only let Cody boss her around on the dance floor.

"To what do I owe the honor?" I hadn't been around much, but Tova had never singled me out to chat before.

"You into Kya?"

I couldn't get a read on her tone. "Are you warning me or warning me on her behalf?"

She shrugged. "Kya can take care of herself, and you're not her type."

"What about me isn't her type?" My question came out defensive, but I was feeling a little raw after Vienne's shunning.

"Your dick."

I barked out a laugh. Kya's speed-dating comment made sense. "Fair enough. So what's your angle, then?"

"Cody said Vienne turned you down."

I could've done without my oldest brother witnessing the rejection. I also wouldn't have missed Tova's pity. "I tried to hire her, but she passed."

"Did you do something to her?"

Only in my dreams, very vividly and explicitly. "I helped her into her house when she got locked out."

"Hmm... Then maybe it's okay," she muttered to herself as she ignored my lead and kept us moving around the fringes of the other couples dancing. "She might just be wary of you."

"Why?"

Tova pursed her lips. "It's not you, specifically. You're a good guy. We've given her no reason to think otherwise, either, but you are a single man, and she's been burned before."

The explanation helped the sting. If Vienne was gun-shy about men and I was only in town temporarily, why was Tova interested in how well Vienne and I got along? "Why are you asking about V?"

"Dr. Jake is trolling the crowd for an easy lay, and he's trying to get to her."

Anger seethed under my skin. I'd heard about the playboy veterinarian. His reputation with women in the area had driven a lot of clients Sutton's way when she'd opened her veterinary clinic in town. "Do he and V have a thing going?"

Tova sucked her bottom lip in. She didn't answer until resolve filled her eyes. "They did, and I didn't think it was serious, but she stopped whatever she had with him and hasn't quite been the same."

"How?" What'd the fucker do to her?

"I can't put my finger on it. She's just more subdued." Tova's grip on my shoulder tightened. "Don't tell her I said anything. I can trust you, right?"

"I had a top-secret security clearance if that makes you feel better."

"But you're not in the army anymore."

"You're right. I'm going to suddenly spew government secrets."

She laughed. "Point taken."

She craned her head around. I looked in the same direction. Vienne was dancing with a different rodeo reject, a guy a good decade older than her. I didn't know him. He could be her age, whatever that was, but I assumed she was younger than me. Another guy waited on the edge of the crowd, longneck in hand, his leering gaze on her. That had to be Doctor fucking Jake.

Tova growled. "I need you to cockblock him."

Surprise made me skip a step. My foot grazed Tova's boot-covered toes, and I got pierced by her stern instructor gaze. "Sorry," I mumbled. I had faced scarier first sergeants than her. "You want me to what?"

"Dance with her and keep dancing with her so Dr. Jake can't cut in."

"What if she doesn't want me to?"

"Seriously, what happened between you two?" she asked, her tone curious.

"When I tell you literally nothing, Tova, I mean it." The way Vienne overlooked me dented my manly pride each time.

She frowned. "Maybe we should abort mission."

I laughed. "Is that what this is?"

The song was winding down, and Cody was pacing the length of the picnic table, his bootsteps deliberate, looking almost as determined as Dr. Jake to get back to holding his partner in his arms. Seeing my brother dressed in jeans and a button-down shirt, like Dr. Jake and the rest of the guys at the street dance, was nice. When he dressed casually, it usually matched his attitude. He'd been uptight for far too many years.

She patted my shoulder. "I'm just trying to protect my friend's heart."

The strongest urge to do the same for Vienne rose inside me. She was prickly toward me, but she had to have a reason. More importantly, my family was worried about her. If Tova was concerned, Cody would be too. He'd been through enough, and I wanted to be of service during my short time in Crocus Valley.

"All right. Let me just see what I can do."

"You're a good guy, Austen."

Tell that to Vienne.

Tova said she had, and it didn't seem to matter.

Three

VIENNE

I should leave. Catherine had gotten bored and went home an hour ago. Not before she gave me the exciting news that the mom of one of her volleyball friends was forming a winter and spring travel team.

I liked the mom. We'd had several talks about youth athletics, how cutthroat it was getting and how grateful we were that our kids could play in small communities where it was a little more inclusive. I trusted her to run a good program. But we'd also talked before about how expensive sports clubs are. Aside from the fees, there was the cost of travel. My schedule was flexible, but my budget wasn't.

Still, if Dot would allow me to work with Jim, I'd be fine. That house was huge. The payday would be even larger. I'd interior design my ass off to make sure of it.

With some of the financial pressure reduced, I could enjoy my night. I loved street dances. I liked moving and talking and laughing, and okay, I would admit that it was nice to be a sought-after dance partner. Single women were outnumbered at these things, and I had my pick of partners to dance with.

But there was one choice I was avoiding.

Jake Burrows. He was after something. I could always tell by that look in his eye, and I'd fallen for it way too many times. No more.

I was about to ask a freshly divorced Eli Kent to dance when Jake blocked my path. "Vienne. It's been a while."

It'd been months. Four intentional months of avoiding him. My lonely heart and my ignored libido made me weak, but I refused to succumb to his practiced charm.

A wave of heat crowded in behind me. "Sorry, I've been waiting on Honey V all night."

Honey V?

Austen's voice registered a half a heartbeat before his big hand wrapped around mine, and he tugged me to the dance floor.

I blinked at Jake. His expression clouded, and he shot an annoyed look at Austen.

Relieved, I sank into Austen's hold. I didn't usually hug the person I was dancing with so close, but I needed the lifeline. I snuck a peek up at him. His face wasn't shaded by a cowboy hat or ball cap like many of the guys here. His hair was swept off his forehead but fell free as we moved.

His glare was aimed at Jake.

"Do you know him?" I asked, wondering just how much he'd heard.

"I know of him," he said darkly.

Cool relief flooded my body. At least one person in

town didn't know about me and the infamous playboy Dr. Jake.

Austen expertly maneuvered me around the other couples dancing, and I didn't have to worry about a thing other than enjoying a competent partner. An odd sense of protection surrounded me. I'd been dancing with other people all night, but they hadn't made me feel as cared for as I did now. He also won the badge for most muscled dance partner of the night.

"How do you know him?" he asked.

The question doused my contentment. Austen's jaw was tight, his eyes shadowed thanks to the fading sun. I was seeing the serious side of him that had always intrigued me. Usually, he was the jokester. The guy who always had a smile and a witty response. He gave his brothers grief all the time, and for the most part, it was fun to watch. This Austen was almost grim. Harder. For the first time, I could picture him being a career soldier.

Flutters detonated in my belly.

I liked light Austen. I could crave his broodier side. I was not traveling down this path again.

"Other than just living in the same town?" I tried the nonanswer, but Austen's gaze was shrewd. A dark brow cocked, and his hold tightened. He twirled us through two couples who were oblivious to who was next to them. I didn't think Austen was paying attention, his intense gaze was focused on me, but we didn't collide with other dancers.

"We had a thing," I blurted out. I'd rather he hear the juicy gossip from me. Catherine should've been the first to know I was sort of seeing Jake. Instead, the rest of town had pieced together my dating life. I would not have another conversation that started with *They told me to ask you if Dr. Jake has sex like an animal, Mom! Why would they ask me that?*

"He wasn't my boyfriend." I didn't need to explain, but I had to let Austen know my judgment wasn't that epically bad. I'd only deluded myself. Still, I couldn't let Jake take the blame for everything. He was at fault for failing at anything resembling monogamy, but he hadn't promised me he was a one-woman man.

"Is that why you're avoiding him? He wants to put a ring on it?"

I snorted. "He's famously allergic to monogamy." Austen's jaw hardened. Did he think Jake cheated on me? Technically, Jake hadn't. "He honestly didn't do anything wrong. I just can't see him again."

His gaze flicked to the side, presumably where Jake was standing. "He hasn't gotten the message."

"Probably because I never actually told him. I just quit answering his calls and messages." I didn't care to hear that he had no issue moving on. I witnessed it. As it was, Jake wouldn't be sniffing around if he hadn't tried other routes and been turned down tonight.

"For most guys, that's enough of a message."

"Austen Knight, you are supremely optimistic on behalf of your entire species."

He chuckled and relaxed under my hands. "Touché."

We danced without speaking for another minute. This was what I liked. Free movement. Someone else made the decisions about what direction we went in, and I could just be. A partner like Austen was rare. Other guys were plodding, and I couldn't blame them. Some didn't know how to lead their way out of a bathroom stall. And others were too rigid, too clingy, or too some-thing that ruined the experience.

I was Goldilocks, and Austen was just right.

The song wound down, but Austen didn't let me go. "Looks like he's waiting for you."

His observation gave me a reason not to pull away and cut the dance short. "He must've been shot down by everyone else."

"Now you're being too pessimistic on behalf of my species. You're not a last choice, Vienne."

I blinked at him as a warm glow ignited inside me. When was the last time a guy had said something so sweet to me?

Another song started, and he steered me around with his arm banded around my waist. I had no choice but to hold on, but also…I didn't want to let go. I peeked at him from under my lashes.

Had his jaw always been so defined? He was the brother who goofed off, but in private, he was different than I expected. Butterflies fluttered in my stomach. I liked this side of him, but at the same time, I was missing the easy part of him. I could use a laugh. A little more fun tonight. Since I'd seen Jake swagger into the crowd and order a beer at the wet bar, I'd been admonishing myself for thinking a few flings with him were worth the orgasms he could give.

"I've gotta ask one thing, Vienne."

Surprised, I glanced up. "Yeah?"

"Why were you avoiding me tonight?"

He'd noticed? I hadn't just been staying away from Dr. Jake. Keeping my attention off Austen had taken Herculean effort. I didn't think I'd been insulting, yet he sounded almost hurt. "I'm sorry. I thought you'd be upset I said no." My answer was a percentage of the truth.

"Why'd you turn me down?"

Guilt nearly made me stumble. It wasn't Austen's fault he made my pulse flutter or that I adored his house. "It's not personal. Really."

"Sure about that?"

The woman in me who just wanted to prove she didn't always make bad decisions reared her head. My reason was very personal. "It's not about you." He looked doubtful, and I didn't like thinking I let him down. He really had helped me yesterday, and he'd been a perfect neighbor so far. I'd give him a portion of the truth. "I have a hard time getting respect in my field and especially in my hometown. I didn't want to start working with you and find out you didn't want to listen to me."

His mouth formed a troubled line, making his lips a defined bow. I'd never dwelled on a man's lips. Now that I could trace a perfect outline, I wouldn't forget his. "I wouldn't disrespect you, Honey V."

"Why are you calling me that?" He'd only started tonight, and he'd done it in front of Jake, which I didn't hate.

"It fits."

No one would claim I was sweet as honey. Not my ex-husband. Not Theo, who I'd broken up with well before the Jake debacle. And probably not even Jake to get me into his bed. But Austen didn't elaborate, so back to the job he tried to hire me for.

"You wouldn't mean to. But you said you wanted to do the work yourself, and no offense, I don't know the quality you do. I don't know how you'll fight me if I don't agree with how you're doing the renovations— because it'll reflect on me when you sell the place."

"I can see that," he admitted. "I promise I'm easy to work with."

"I honestly don't have much experience working on old houses." There were several reasons I'd been too scared to accept the offer from Austen. Messing up a dream project was one of them. Lusting after the brother of my friends was another.

"I don't have plans to change anything structurally unless you have suggestions."

"That partial wall put in by the main-level bathroom does the whole kitchen and dining room area a disservice. I'll give you that advice for free." The wall had clearly been added when the '90s remodel was done, and it unbalanced the whole area. I couldn't believe the awful work when I'd first seen it after Tova invited me over when she lived there.

"Help me tear it down."

My two-step faltered. I'd never been invited to do some of the manual labor. It wasn't my place. I'd been relegated to mostly desk work. I was the idea person, but sometimes my fingers itched to destroy something and re-create it into something beautiful. "You'd really be okay if I picked up a hammer and tore into that wall?"

The corners of his jaw flexed. "I've had two decades of sexual harassment training, for one. And two—I've been working alongside women for twenty years. They've had to do everything I had to do. I would hope I'm the last one to give you hell for doing *manly* things."

"I'm sorry. I didn't mean— It's not always a gender thing. It's that some of the people I work with still see me as a precocious teen."

"Don't be sorry. You said it wasn't about me, and I need to listen."

He maneuvered me around another couple. I'd danced with the man before, and Kya was in my pole dance class. I gave her a nod and a smile. I felt like I owed Austen more. He'd been willing to give me a chance on a house that had once been the jewel of downtown and now was like any other aging farmhouse. I'd love to work on his home. Austen would be upset to know how much he should take my rejection personally. I said no, mostly because of him. "Full transparency, I'm a little afraid of how it'd be perceived."

A furrow formed in his forehead, then he nodded. "I see."

"Usually, I get hired by a company. Sometimes, the homeowners they're working for can request me, but that's not how I usually get work." Yet. "Regardless, there are a lot of people in and out of a place I'm working on. If it's just you and me?"

"I can see how rumors would ignite."

"You do?" I'd been prepared for his denial. He continued to surprise me.

He flashed me a smile, and I was afraid my panties would incinerate. "You forget I grew up in a small town with parents who fueled a lot of talk. It's not fun to walk around wondering what others are saying about you."

I was almost more disheartened to hear him say that. He wasn't arguing that he had to have me work for him. He wasn't negotiating, and he wasn't crestfallen. Why would he be? "Thanks for understanding."

"You bet."

And that was that. Was my decision the right one?

I could use the money. The volleyball camp. The traveling team this winter. Dave thought his child support should go to optional things like sports camps instead of back-to-school clothing for a girl who grew an inch over the last two months and would probably add another inch before August. I'd been through that discussion with him before, and it'd turned out as well as all our other disagreements.

So, yes, the money would be nice, but if I kept my reputation pristine until the job with Jim this winter, then I'd build a more stable career in the long run.

The song was winding down. I'd been through an unexpected roller coaster of emotions dancing with Austen, but I wasn't ready to quit dancing with him.

"Back to the Jake problem."

A spark of delight made me smile despite hearing Jake's name. We continued to dance through a new song. "What problem? After we're done dancing, I'll head home. It'll be fine. I won't succumb to his charm." I glanced toward the picnic tables. Jake was already chatting up another girl. Well. Wasn't that quick?

I was relieved. I *was*. But what a punctuation point at the end of my determination. How easy was I to move on from?

Austen's gaze lifted to where I had looked. Oh, good. He could see how quick it was for a guy to forget me.

"If you think that's charm, Honey V..." Austen's lazy smile sent a shiver tracing down my spine. "I'm sorry for the underwhelming experiences you've been getting."

"Yet he can talk her into a quickie in his pickup. He might even still try to hit on me before or after." I'd seen it happen before. My pride still smarted.

Tension rippled through his jaw, and his eyes narrowed. "What is it about him?"

I was too ashamed to admit why a shallow man like Jake had once wrapped me around his finger and made me think there could be more. I'd give Austen an abridged version. "He can make a girl feel like she's the only one."

"But she's not."

I shook my head, shame heating my face. "Nope."

The music wound down, and the first notes of a slow ballad began. If I continued to dance with Austen song after song, people were definitely going to speculate about us. Combined with being reminded of what a clueless Pollyanna I could be when it comes to guys, I would twist myself into circles if I kept dancing. "Thank you for interceding, but I need to get going. Catherine's home and I have an early morning." My morning date running numbers for another company.

"I'll walk you to the exit so he doesn't jump you."

"I'm sure he's— Oh." Jake was roaming the edges of the dance space again. The other woman must've turned him down. And he'd come to me. Like always. "I appreciate it."

"Did you walk here?"

I nodded and let him lead me toward the picnic tables. Six more blocks and I'd be at my house.

"I'll walk you home, then."

"You don't have to cut your night short for me." Should I refuse altogether? I'd just told him that people might talk about us, but then I'd also refused a job with him so we wouldn't be spending days together on top of him walking me home.

"I don't mind, V. I had nothing else to do, and honestly, no one's going to match your moves."

My steps stuttered. I doubt he meant it. "You can lay it on thick."

"Trust me." His eyes crinkled at the corners with a

hint of a smile. "One of the few things I learned from my mama was to two-step."

How could he be so sweet while showing no real interest in me outside of my work?

And did I want him to?

No. I told him we couldn't even work together because of the possibility of rumors.

But... Was I not his type? Was he used to women throwing themselves at him? Did he steer clear of single moms?

Did he see everything when I was on my hands and knees and was he revolted?

I did not care! I wasn't looking to start something—with anyone!—and I should be glad Austen wasn't being an intrusive neighbor.

He wandered next to me, giving nods to people who recognized him. We weren't arm in arm, but I noticed the speculative glances. I edged away just a few more inches, instantly missing his heat.

At least if they talked, I could honestly tell Catherine he did nothing but see me home like a good neighbor. Not every guy was after a booty call. Austen wasn't even after my booty.

When we reached his house, he continued until he was at the edge of my sidewalk. The chirps of crickets and frogs got lost in the buzz of the cicadas.

"Have a good night, Vienne." He was distant. Perfectly charismatic while holding himself aloof. Just like he'd been the other day when I'd gotten locked out.

"Thank you." *Thank you for being a nice guy.* Even if I chafed against it.

He walked across the lawn and took the stairs to his front door. He waited until I made it to mine.

The question that had plagued me since he found me locked out resurfaced. My face flamed. I was better off not knowing, and since he was being all chivalrous, he'd probably lie. But I had to ask.

"Hey, Austen," I said before he unlocked his door. *Here goes nothing.* But I had to know. How embarrassed should I be? "How much did you see? When I was..." God, my throat would rather close up than ask, yet it was better than wondering. "When I was looking for the key?"

His face was already shadowed from the porch light behind his head, but his eyes grew impossibly dark. "I saw everything, Honey V."

Four

VIENNE

The noise of the bar wasn't enough to crowd out my thoughts. I took aim at the dartboard. It was Thursday night, and even Aggie had come out to play a quick post-partum game. We were between dart leagues, but keeping our Thursday night girls' night was easier than changing our schedule. We congregated at a table by the dart boards, standing tall and proud against the dark wall.

This was the first time we were all reunited at the bar since Tripp had been born, and part of me had been afraid we'd break and everyone would go about their busy lives, leaving me behind.

Sutton was a busy vet who owned her own clinic. After she and Wilder said their vows, they had a consulta-tion scheduled with the fertility specialist in Bismarck. Tova had three kids, one was still a baby, and she taught dance. Catherine was usually one of her students, but my daughter wanted to get on the varsity volleyball team this year and had put a pause on dance until the winter. And Aggie had two under two at her place. My kid was a teen and mostly self-sufficient.

A moment of longing tugged at my heart. A familiar sensation, but one I hadn't had for a while. Even when I had dated Theo and thought we'd eventually get married, I hadn't envisioned having more kids with him. But there had been a time when I would've loved more kids.

Now I was the one with a teen and everyone was just beginning their motherhood journeys. I totally understood if our weekly meetups had to be halted, but a part of me panicked. I'd missed out on enough time with friends when I was a young mother, and I didn't want to miss out on more because I was nearing the empty-nest stage when I had so badly wanted that nest to be full for a little longer.

Without darts night tonight, I'd be at home avoiding a certain neighbor who'd answered one question honestly.

Everything. He saw *everything*.

What did that mean? Being on my hands and knees on the rocks wasn't the most flattering pose. Add in the full sunshine, and I highly doubted I looked my best.

When was my last wax appointment?

God. Everything. The relief I didn't have to look him in the eye, knowing he'd seen it all, almost smothered the mourning over not being able to work on the house.

I lobbed a dart and hit outside all the rings. "Shit."

"Good thing we're not competing," Aggie said. "We wouldn't stand a chance without our sharpshooter."

"Sorry. I'm off my game tonight."

Aggie adjusted her bra straps, not caring if anyone saw. She was nursing, and she'd been here for an hour and a half. She joked her letdown clock was ticking, and she'd have to get home for another feeding. "Want to talk about it?"

This was what I had missed with friends. Growing up in Crocus Valley, I'd had my friend group. For college, we'd all scattered. I'd gone to Denver, where I could be a city girl among all the offerings of outdoor life. Once upon a time, I had my own volleyball passion. That had lasted less than two years after moving to Denver. I'd become a newlywed mom in a city full of people I didn't know. I'd made a few mom friends over the years, but none of them had lasted through the divorce and the move.

Now I had people to talk to, and they were all Austen's family. I wanted to discuss him and how unbearably attracted to him I was. How I didn't want to be. And how it didn't matter anyway. Oh, and that time I showed him my cooch. Could someone commiserate the embarrassment with me?

Since they knew something was bothering me, and since I didn't care to get into the *Jake is an asshole* conversation again, I'd tell them a modified reason. "Austen wanted to hire me to help update the interior of his house."

"That's great," Sutton said and grinned. She was the only woman, other than me, who was drinking a hard cider. The two nursing moms stuck to regular seltzer. "You love that place."

"I said no."

Three pairs of shocked eyes stared at me. Maybe the "Jake is an asshole" conversation would've been better. I didn't think how telling them I wouldn't work with a guy who was important to them would come off.

"Why?" Aggie asked.

"He wants to do the work himself and have me for guidance. You know how that'd look?" None of them nodded as if they understood. "After Catherine got so much shit about me and Jake?"

Comprehension dawned, and they all nodded.

Aggie shook her head, frowning. "That's not fair that you miss out on a great project because a bunch of kids couldn't be nice."

"It wasn't just them," I clarified. "Their parents were probably the ones talking about my sex life." I'd been humiliated that day Catherine came home. How many times had I gotten groceries and the clerk knew I'd been with the playboy vet? Had she pitied me?

"That shouldn't be your problem," Aggie stressed.

Tova tapped her slender fingers on the table. "Can't you talk to Catherine about it? Let her know Austen wants to hire you, but you know people might think you're sleeping with him and you don't want her to get upset."

I threaded my lower lip between my teeth. I hadn't thought of discussing the work with her. Besides, depending on when he wanted me to start, she'd be gone for a month for the volleyball camp and time with her dad. "I guess I could, but what if—"

"You're hot and single, Vienne," Sutton said. "The Knight brothers are good-looking. No matter what, people are going to talk just because you're breathing the same air in the same zip code."

True. I slumped. The past was bitch-slapping me, and I was retreating. A young Vienne wouldn't have cared. I knew I missed a good opportunity, but had it been for no reason?

Aggie put her hand on my arm. "It's not too late. Austen hasn't mentioned hiring anyone. Talk to Catherine and call him."

Tova nodded. "I know how much you wanted to get your hands on that place. You're a good mom, Catherine knows that, but not one damn person should slut shame you."

"It wasn't slut shaming as much as people questioning my judgment." Which I'd done enough myself. The whole situation hadn't been a good look for a solo interior designer trying to be taken seriously in a community that knew I forfeited a scholarship when I got pregnant and dropped out of college. "And, of course, the hard time Catherine got because of it. But I'll talk to her." Then I remembered the everything part and I winced.

"Uh-oh," Aggie said. "There's some other reason Catherine won't go for it?"

"Catherine? No." My body grew hot. More embarrassment? A hot flash? Definitely not arousal. "Teddy shut the door on me when I went out to get his food dish. I got locked out and dropped the key between the deck slats." I took a deep breath. "I was only in a towel because the neighbor's dog, Dobber, was barking while I was in the shower."

Tova gasped. "You got locked out in nothing but a towel?"

I screwed my face up. "Oh, it gets worse. I was about to crawl under the porch, my ass hanging out in the wind, when Austen came outside." Telling someone about the humiliation would lessen it, right?

Tova's mouth dropped open. Aggie's gaze grew wide. Sutton snorted, tried to smother her laughter, but kept giggling.

I pressed my fingertips to my forehead. "He saw it all," I groaned. "It was awful."

"I'm sure he didn't." Aggie snapped her mouth shut at my look.

I dropped my hand. "Nope. I asked him."

Tova chewed her lip. "Was this before the street dance?"

Why'd she sound so scared? I nodded.

She glanced away. "I'm so sorry. I asked him to cockblock Jake. I didn't know..." Her mouth twitched.

"Go ahead and laugh, I'm almost there. It definitely wasn't my best look."

"He's a guy," Tova said, snickering. "I'm sure he was quite content with the view."

"He pretended like I was covered head to toe. My crotch did not stagger him."

Sutton snorted again and covered her mouth with her hand.

Aggie's shoulders shook. "I'd die. I'm sorry, Vienne. So embarrassing."

"Em-bare-ass-ing." Sutton chortled.

I gave her a fake glare, but laughter was bubbling up inside me too. Grateful I told them, I could finally see the whole debacle for the absurd moment it was until Tova's comment registered. "You asked him to cockblock me?"

She shook her head. "Not you. Jake. He was at the street dance with his sights set on you, and Austen was just sitting around except for when Kya dragged him out."

I'd been envious of Kya. I knew she wasn't interested in him, but she still got to know what being in his arms felt like.

I'd gotten to find out too, but at the time, I hadn't

known. My imagination happily filled in, and yet I hadn't been close to how nice it was to actually dance with him. To talk to him. To have him be in control.

If Tova hadn't stepped in, I wouldn't know. But also...he wouldn't have asked. Any last hope remaining shriveled. "Thank you."

"I was afraid I overstepped," Tova admitted. "But you should be able to have a good time without Jake hitting you up."

I had a better time when I thought Austen was dancing with me out of his own free will. "Thank you. And I didn't know Austen got the full view until after the dance." I shouldn't have asked.

"He could've lied. That's one of those times it's okay to fib." Aggie wrinkled her nose. "Why didn't he?"

I lifted a shoulder. Yes, he could've told me what he knew I wanted to hear, but he hadn't, and my respect for him notched up. My crappy exes were probably to blame. Any man who faced a touchy subject without flinching made me take notice.

Aggie slid off the stool. "My boobs say it's time to go. Next week?"

I pushed away from the table. "See you guys then."

I was threading my way through the bar when I saw Rudy. I gave him a nod and stopped at his table to say hi. He was my boss, in a way. The small engine repair company was only one of his businesses I did the books for. The guy owned five different repair shops in three separate towns.

"Hiya, Rudy."

He grinned, and the apples of his ruddy cheeks glowed red. I knew all the numbers of his business, but I was always surprised this guy was an entrepreneur. I was as guilty of falling for small-town stereotypes as anyone else. The dirty overalls he never changed out of went with his perpetually messy hair and he had the red, glassy look of someone on their second bottle of champagne when he hadn't touched more than his pot of coffee all day. His wife called him Red, but he was a mostly gray blond now.

"Vienne!" He clapped me on the back, nearly sending me face-first into the middle of his group. His wife beamed at me, and I thought I recognized the other two as his daughter and her husband. "You know Maddy and Chris, right?"

When I nodded, Maddy smiled. "Hi, Vienne. No hard feelings?"

"About what?" I turned my attention to Rudy.

He adjusted his grungy ball cap and coughed. "I haven't told her about that yet, Maddy."

My stomach was slowly sinking to my toes. The only thing Rudy would talk to me about in that tone was bookkeeping. "Is this how I'm hearing I'm fired?" I joked. *Please don't fire me.*

"I'm not firing you," he said in a regretful way that said I was out of a job. "But I won't renew the contract with you at the end of the year. Maddy and Chris are moving back to Crocus Valley. She's taking over for me, and Chris will be doing the books."

"Oh. Oh, well, that's good news." Which absolutely sucked for me. It'd take three to five accounts to replace Rudy's gig. "Retiring then?"

"Yeah. The missus tells me it's time." His grin was genuinely happy, taking the sting off.

I still hurt, but the panic was mine. I put too much reliance on a job I wanted to be temporary, and when it lived up to its role, I wasn't ready. "We'll work out the kinks so it's a smooth transition."

"I told ya," he said to his daughter and son-in-law. "She's a good one." To me, he said, "I'll put in a good word about you to guys I know."

"Uh, thanks. You know, I don't think that it's necessary. I'm not sure I'll have time." *Shut it, Vienne.* I couldn't. As much as I needed the income, I couldn't wither away waiting for jobs to come my way in two different professions. What if I struggled to find work in both areas? That'd be demoralizing.

No. Ready or not, I was all in interior design.

"Good to hear." He thumped me on the back again. Even sitting down, the guy was easily able to reach the middle of my shoulders. "I knew there'd be a day you'd be too busy for my little project."

My smile had to be as weak as my joy felt. I was happy for Rudy and his family. I also wished I really didn't have the time for his job.

I said my goodbyes and went to my car, grateful I could play it cool when I was disintegrating inside. What was I going to do? I couldn't start the New Year with no work. If I saved, then I could weather a few months, but if Catherine was on the travel team? We'd have normal fees and then all the traveling expenses.

I could bill Dave like he was doing to me. The muscles in my shoulders knotted. I hated to anticipate the conflict.

When I pulled up in front of the house, I stared at Austen's place. The solution was staring me in the face. If the job offer was still open.

I could save all the money I earned from Austen's project. It'd be enough to pay for the travel team and an emergency fund. The house would be put up for sale, and I would be able to get my name out there.

My reputation would have to stay pristine. I'd be working closely with Austen.

He'd never made a move on me. Nothing said he would, just because I gave him paint samples and showed him a bathroom redesign. I was getting way ahead of myself. He'd been nothing but courteous and respectful. After our talk while dancing, I was confident working with him would be a good experience.

My friends' suggestion came to mind. I had to talk to Catherine first. I'd check that worry off my growing list.

When I got in the house, it was quiet. I heard the familiar thump of a ball coming from outside. She was in her loose pajama bottoms and an old Denver Zoo T-shirt of mine.

I leaned out the back door. "Hey, can I talk to you for a sec?"

"Sure." She didn't look at me but continued bumping and setting the ball over her head all the way to the deck.

"Good control."

That earned me a brief smile. "Thanks."

When she was inside, I led her to the kitchen. While I filled a glass with water from the fridge door, I launched into my talk. "Austen wanted to hire me for work on his house."

She had the ball under one arm, her feet set wide apart, and was swaying from side to side, full of restless energy. It was almost nine p.m. and I was ready to crawl between the sheets. "Okay?"

"I said no after the Jake debacle."

She stopped moving and her eyes went wide. "Why would you do that?"

That wasn't how I expected her to react. I thought she'd nod in understanding. "So you don't get crap again from your classmates."

"Mom."

"Catherine."

She rolled her eyes. "Austen is, like, nice and stuff. Everyone knows what Jake's like."

Didn't that make my judgment sound awful? "He's nice too."

"He's nice to get into your pants. Austen's not like that."

"Austen doesn't want in my—" I shook my head. Not the conversation to have with my fifteen-year-old. "You sure it's okay? If it's not too late and he hires me, I'll be coming and going from his place, and you know what a big mouth Rudy has."

He was great to work for, but he went to Hummingbird's once, if not twice, a day. More news got spread in the diner than in the town's weekly newspaper. He'd be how everyone learned I was at Austen's house all the time. I'd casually mention I was working with my neighbor the next time I talked to Rudy.

If Austen still wanted to hire me.

"It's one thing if the rumors are true, Mom, and you were doing Jake." She shuddered.

I scowled at her. I would've rather she hadn't known, but at least she thought I was fucking around. While many parents would have a problem with their kid witnessing that, I didn't. I'd rather she thought I slept with who I wanted when I wanted instead of knowing I settled for a man I knew wouldn't treat me the way I wanted. "Well, I won't be sleeping with Austen."

"Gross." She tossed the ball up and bumped it lightly. "Not in the house."

She smirked and went back outside. I peered out the kitchen window. Austen wasn't on his deck. I didn't have his number, and I didn't want to bother any of my friends to get it.

I smoothed my hands over my jeans shorts and went out the front door. With my shoulders squared, I marched to Austen's front door and knocked. The light was on behind the living room blinds.

The door opened, and my mouth went dry. Austen's hair was hanging over his forehead, giving him a bad-boy edge I'd never seen on the usually clean-cut man. But mostly, his lack of a shirt always left me tongue-tied. At least I was dressed this time. He had on jeans, and his feet were bare. The way he looked should be forbidden, yet it was a shame he stayed home and no one saw those hip ridges.

"V?" He had a longneck in one hand, but he snapped his fingers with the other. "You want your dish back. Excellent pasta salad, by the way. Didn't make it more than one meal." He stepped back to turn. He liked my food?

"No." I'd told him to keep the dish anyway. "That's not what I'm here for."

The thought that he liked something of mine delighted me. Left me shining like the midday sun. But he also wanted to hire me. That should feel better.

It wasn't my designs he was putting his mouth on.

My heart kicked against my ribs. Back to business. "Is the job offer still on the table?"

He propped a forearm on the doorframe. "I haven't found anyone else with the availability I need."

For once, I was glad launching my business was a struggle. I had a lot of open days on my calendar. "I'm just wrapping up a job, but if you want to send me your thoughts and what you have planned, I can start working on some ideas." I stuffed my hands into my pockets, and his gaze dropped to my legs. "That is if you're still interested."

He slowly lifted his gaze to mine, but with that hair shadowing his eyes, I couldn't figure out what he was thinking. Did I imagine the heat?

In a blink, he was back to congenial Austen Knight. A lazy half grin curved his lips. "You're hired."

Five

AUSTEN

After I emailed Vienne at her official Design by V email the week after the street dance, she replied to say she could start at the end of June. Until then, we'd nail down the details of what she'd do, what I'd do, and the sequence of the tasks we'd tackle.

I'd get a few days to get a hold of myself. To convince myself I'd be nothing but professional. I wouldn't make the fears she'd confessed to me come true.

That was before I told her the truth. Why'd I tell her I saw it all? No girl wanted to hear that from their neighbor.

Yet when she'd asked, she hadn't been laughing about the situation. Her cheeks had been beet red, and even with the streetlights and the fading rays from the late summer sunset, I'd caught the anxiety on her face. I wouldn't have been able to lie to her at gunpoint. The truth had seemed important, and the way my neighbor kept her distance from me, I would've felt like a giant douche if I wasn't transparent.

Didn't mean I was above stroking a few out to the memory of her on her hands and knees. I couldn't be doing that shit if we were collaborating on the house. She had to feel comfortable working alone with a guy she barely knew. I had to quit getting hard-ons when I was around her.

Besides my bodily reaction, I had more to prepare for.

Now, it was Monday, and I'd been pestering her with messages since last Thursday. What tools and supplies did I need? She listed some of the basics for stripping carpet, like a scraper and a staple remover, but said not to buy new. She could find some to use if she didn't have them.

As for repairing and polishing hardwood, she said she'd have to see the condition of the flooring first. I'd had to run to Buffalo Gully to raid the ranch of their extra tools beyond the hammers and screwdrivers I'd been using. My youngest brother, Eliot, had bitched the entire time. *Why'd you drive three hours to get tools? Aren't you rich off your government retirement?*

I was doing okay. More than good, and thanks to my meager inheritance, I was doing just fine. I could buy a rolling toolbox and fill the whole thing up. But I hated waste, and Eliot hated stuff, so it worked and gave me something to do other than fantasize about my neighbor.

The doorbell rang.

"Fucking finally." Email wasn't as good as the real thing.

Vienne was coming over to help me plan what I could work on until she was able to start.

I opened the door, and she frowned at what I was wearing. While I was in my postretirement basketball shorts and old, gray Knight's Arabians and Cattle Company shirt, she was in worn blue jeans, athletic shoes, and a tank top that showed off impressively toned arms. Her turquoise eyes were still stunning behind her black-framed glasses.

"Good thing you're not doing any demolition today," she said.

"A real man tears shit up in basketball shorts."

"A real man would gouge some skin off his leg if he did that." Her no-nonsense expression didn't waver as she entered the house. "We're going over the changes we plan to make first and then the timeline. Once I get your approval, I'll put in the order for the appliances and get measurements for the flooring and the cabinets. And then you might want something that protects you better than shorts."

I grinned. I didn't mention her tank top wouldn't offer any more protection. She might cover up, and I quite liked seeing her toned arms and a tease of her cleavage. "Is that an order?"

"It's a strong suggestion. If you hurt yourself, it's going to be a pain to find contractors who can do the work before you go do whatever it is you're going to do."

The reminder I'd be leaving hung over us. I moved into this house planning for a temporary stay. I'd wanted a side project while waiting for the start date to arrive. I'd done a lot of work on the place, and I had a lot more to do. This was the first time I wished I had planned for a longer stay.

Instead of boring her with the details of where I was going and what I'd be doing, I nodded. "Yes, boss. Lead the way."

Since she was all business, I gave her free rein. For

the next four hours, she covered her contract, her fees, and then quizzed me on color swatches and preferred manufacturers. She already knew the house, and it was like her thoughts for the last however many years poured out.

"How long have you had these ideas in mind?" I asked. She might've come up with all her plans over the weekend, but I didn't think so.

The pink spots were back on her cheeks, and she drummed her fingers. Vienne was a fidgety person, but she wasn't wearing her bracelets or necklaces. She'd come to work. "My mom designed the house I grew up in after this place."

"It had to have looked better than it does now." The house itself wasn't in bad shape. The cosmetic changes over the years—along with the half-hearted remodel almost thirty years ago—hadn't done the bone structure of the place justice. A strong, solid farmhouse shouldn't look wimpy and cheap inside.

She nodded. "My parents' ranch is outside of town. Mom was so happy to build a real house, but the old owner would never show her the inside. So it's just the look. Inside was all based on necessity since Mom had no inspiration. When he remodeled, she was heartbroken. I guess I always imagined what the inside would look like. When Tova showed me..." Her mouth tightened. "It's a travesty. This house could've been a historic home in Crocus Valley, but it's lost its character and is just another run-down, downtown home."

"Good thing it's got you." My stomach started protesting a delay of lunch. I'd run a couple of extra miles this morning, hoping I'd keep my mind away from picturing Vienne on her hands and knees. My morning protein shake burned off hours ago. "How about we begin with lunch?"

Her excitement dimmed. "Lunch?"

"V, we've been working without a break since eight. It's after noon."

She looked around like she was remembering she was on a stool at the island. When she'd been reviewing paint and stain colors, she rushed through the house holding her paper samples so I could form a picture in my head. Then, she had perched on her stool and scribbled notes.

"Wanna go to Hummingbird's?"

"Oh." She stiffened. "No, I have food at home."

"Not as good as Hal's pancakes."

She softened and smiled. "He is an amazing cook, but I need to take advantage of working close to home and eat lunch there."

Was it a money thing? "My treat."

She shuffled her samples, taming them back into the envelopes she'd separated them in. "Thank you for the offer, but you're going to be paying me enough."

"I went from eating with everyone in the army to no one. You'd be saving me from another boring lunch by myself."

A smile played along her lips. "You used to eat with everyone?"

I nodded. "I still did almost every day, even toward the end, but I was used to the noise with four siblings, a mom who complained about having to feed us all the time, and a dad who yelled about how long we were taking at the table to get out of work."

"That's awful, Austen." She'd listened right through my light tone and heard what I actually said.

I hadn't meant to rip the Band-Aid off my past. "It's

normal. I saw a lot of drama during the last twenty years that puts any of those times to shame."

"My family dinners were chaotic, but usually because I was arguing with my mom and brother."

"I take it since you're an interior designer, your brother's going to take over the ranch?" Eliot was the youngest Knight brother, and he hadn't been able to leave as soon as the rest of us. I often thought he got stuck with taking over Knight's Arabians and Cattle Company, just like Cody got saddled with the oil well part of the business since he was the oldest. Aggie was younger than Eliot, but Barns had blocked her out of everything, taking his anger at Mama's absence out on her. Wilder and I got to choose our paths.

"Yes, he's partners with Dad now."

"You didn't want to be?"

"Did you?" she countered, almost defensively.

Taking over her family's ranch must be a touchy subject. Was it for me? I'd never thought of it. "I would've been just another worker. Nothing about that place would've been mine. Eliot was willing to wait out Barns's life expectancy. I wasn't."

Surprise crossed her face at my callous comment. "I'm not wishing for my parents' life expectancies to shorten—"

"I didn't mean—"

"I know you didn't," she said softly. "I've heard stories of your mom and dad. It's okay, Austen. My parents are...nice...but I left for college and then I didn't finish college. I got pregnant with Catherine, married Dave, and then Dave wanted a divorce, so I came back home. To them, I just generally don't finish what I start.

Taking over the ranch, if I had been interested, was never on the table."

"What about your business?"

She exhaled and lifted her hands, then let them drop. "You're the biggest client I've ever booked."

"Nice. I like to be the biggest."

She laughed. "You make that sound dirty." She pushed off her stool. "Thank you for the offer, but I'll eat at home. I have the other job I need to wrap up—" She snapped her fingers. "That reminds me. Are you planning on doing an open house when you put the house up for sale?"

"I don't see why not."

Her gaze jumped around the room, giving me a glimpse of her nerves. She danced her fingers around her collar like she was searching for a necklace. "Good. Great."

"Why? Is it critical?"

"No, it's just... It'd be a good advertisement for me." She was almost sheepish.

"We'll absolutely do an open house. We can make it a joint thing. You can be here to answer any questions on the changes we made."

Relief crossed her face. "Great, thanks, Austen. In the next couple of days, I'll put in some orders for this project. Tomorrow, I'll be back with an estimated time-line and what we can work on based on that."

And just like that, she was gone. I didn't even have time to puff my chest about the open house thing. I was astounded by how well she put distance between us when our bedroom windows were right across from each other.

I was having my afternoon beer on the porch. I thought I'd be working all day, but Vienne had presumably holed up in her home office and was making calls, ordering paints and appliances. I'd messaged her asking what I could start on. My task was ripping out carpet and cleaning the floors underneath.

I'd finished removing carpet in one upstairs room already. The work didn't take long when it was just me. I had prepared for delays, but apparently when it was just me and I didn't have soldiers fucking up underneath me, constantly yanking me away from other duties to deal with issues, I could get shit done quickly. If I messed up, I fixed the problem and moved on. Independent work was refreshing.

Was I ready to go back to working with three guys? We'd each have a say in how we ran our security business, but we'd also have client demands. Since they were paying the bills, we'd return to having limited say as we did in the military. How often would I get pulled away from my job to put out figurative fires left and right caused by others?

But what else would I do? I was lucky. I got out of the service, and I had a place to go. I had career aspirations. I had connections that would help me start a company. Others got lost in the shuffle or even lost in the change.

I wasn't one of them.

The back door of Vienne's house opened and a fuzzy, large, baked potato with a honky tonk bedonkadonk waddled out.

"Hey, Teddy," I greeted him when he made it to the edge of the stairs.

Catherine banged out the door after him. She tossed her volleyball onto the lawn and carried Teddy down the steps. She wore a ratty gray shirt that nearly went past the hemline of her navy-blue volleyball spandex. Her socks were pulled up to her shins, but her feet were stuffed into slides. Looking at her, I could pick apart what her dad might look like. He must be taller since Catherine was taller than Vienne, especially with those puffy sandals on, but probably not as tall as me. Catherine's hair was also lighter than Vienne's highlighted dirty blonde, and she had double braids winding down the sides of her head.

As soon as she hit the base of the porch, she tossed a volleyball up and set it to herself. "Hey, Austen."

"KitKat." I set my beer on the outdoor table and took the steps down to my lawn. Standing across from her, I wiggled my fingers. She set the ball toward me. I set it back. We continued to volley. Sometimes after a hit, she practiced the dance moves Tova taught her, but at other times, she was in full volleyball mode.

She reminded me of young, fresh-out-of-school soldiers I'd worked with, only she was more mature than over half of them. But still, I was familiar with the younger crowd, and talking to Catherine was nostalgic. Her age group was brave and courageous. They looked at the world through a different lens than me, but they could also be their own worst enemy and do the stupidest shit until you wondered how they dressed themselves in the morning.

I missed that.

"Heard you're going to a volleyball camp," I said as I lobbed the ball back at her.

She returned my effort with a bump. I sidestepped and tapped it to her.

"Yep." Her attention was on the ball. "My dad got me in. I fly out next week."

"Nice."

"I'm usually only gone for two weeks in the summer, but it'll be a month this year."

A month. How was Vienne dealing with that? "Damn. I was going to hire you to mow the lawn."

She caught the ball. "How much you paying?"

"Twenty." I didn't dislike mowing. The lawn was small and didn't take long, but I'd heard Catherine arguing with Vienne about new volleyball shoes last night through their kitchen window. I'd been sitting on the porch since the weather had cooled off in the evening, and I'd been sweaty all day replacing the water heater and working on the basement. Vienne had told her daughter that her dad expected them to foot the bill for half the camp, so the new shoes would have to wait unless Catherine's dad bought them while she was there.

Catherine narrowed her eyes and juggled the ball from hand to hand. She swept her gaze across the lawn. "I could get two rounds in before I leave."

I'd mowed a few days ago, but we'd gotten a solid night of rain and the grass had really grown. "Deal. Just buzz over when you do yours."

She scowled and set the ball toward me. "Mom can mow."

I lobbed it back. "I'm not hiring you and leaving her with more work."

Her frown deepened, and she returned the hit. "I don't get paid to mow our lawn."

I laughed, keeping our peppering going. "I didn't get paid to work cattle and get my ass kicked by ornery horses either. But you can bet I still had to do it."

"Working cattle's fun."

"Not when your dad's screaming at how you're doing it." The urge to point out lessons to young soldiers was apparently still with me, only I had switched to youth volleyball players.

"Grandpa isn't like that."

"Good."

She hesitated with a bump. "Your dad was that bad?" The ball almost didn't make it to me, but I returned it.

"He wasn't that good."

"My dad would never yell at me."

Was he around her enough for her to find out? Or was I jaded from Barns? "That's good. You have a good mother too."

She huffed out a breath. "Yeah, she's good," she said noncommittally.

I set the ball back. She had an awesome fucking mom. "My mama packed her stuff and walked out on five kids."

Catherine missed the ball. The puppy was sniffing at a bug and nearly got taken out. "Crap, Teddy. I'm sorry." She picked Teddy up and covered his head with kisses. "He's going to be so big when I get back. I asked Mom if I could bring him, and she wouldn't let me."

"Your dad would be okay with him?"

Her expression shifted. The answer must not be an easy yes. "His new wife hates dogs. So, your mom just, like, left and never came back?"

"Pretty much." From her aghast tone, my lesson had sunk in. She needed to give her mom a break. "We gonna pepper the dog back and forth or what?"

She made a scandalized sound and hugged Teddy hard before putting him down again. I laughed. Of course I was kidding, but she was fun to rile up.

Vienne popped her head out the back door. "Catherine, time for dinner." Her gaze landed on me, and her expression went from interested mom to closed-off interior designer. "Austen, hi." She brushed a hand down her yellow shorts like she was testing how long they really were.

I should've lied and told her I hadn't seen a thing. She was already skittish around me. Nothing like the confident family friend from when I'd visited my siblings before.

Catherine hung her head back. "I just got outside with Teddy."

She swung her vivid gaze toward her daughter. "Teddy can stay out. He'll be fine."

Teddy had his curved snout buried in the rocks. He popped his head up when he heard his name.

I wasn't going to be the creepy neighbor hanging out by the fence and eavesdropping—not when it was hard to avoid through open windows. I started for the house. "Thanks for playing ball, Catherine."

"What about Austen?" Catherine asked.

What about me? I glanced at Vienne over my shoulder. She cocked her head at her daughter.

"We should invite him for dinner." Catherine's question had the innocence of a kid who thought the world should work around her. "It's rude otherwise."

I could bow out. Save Vienne from making excuses. If she wanted a dinner guest, she wasn't jumping around at the idea it was me. But I waited.

Vienne inhaled a measured breath. I could almost see the count in her head. One, two, three... "Austen, do you have a hankering for a roast that might be medium rare to well done, depending on which part you get and runny mashed potatoes because I got a little heavy-handed with the milk?"

Some of my tension unwound from around my gut.

She was worried about food presentation? She should've seen some of the shit I'd had to eat over the years.

Whatever she served was better than chow hall food. "I happen to have a hankering for just that. I can bring a dry, store-bought cake over that's one of those 'seemed like a good idea at the time' purchases."

She laughed. A real, unguarded smile pulled at her lips. "Bring it over so we can have a well-rounded, not-quite-right dinner."

Grinning, I jogged into the house and got the cake from the counter. I also grabbed a six-pack from a local brewery I'd picked up when I was running errands earlier.

I didn't hop the fence. I went to her front door and knocked.

"Come in!" Catherine yelled.

I cataloged the place as I walked through to the living room. The layout was similar to mine, but the whole house was narrower, with fewer bedrooms. Her interior was much more modern and chic, done in earth tones with pops of color I never thought would work. The house had been through the same '90s to early aughts remodel. Light fixtures hung from the ceiling that didn't match the look of the house. Doors had been swapped out, and even the flooring had been laminated over.

I hadn't missed the pop of excitement in Vienne's eyes when I suggested she could help me with the physical work. She was dying to do more than superficial styling, but I doubted she had time as a single mom with a growing business.

I found the kitchen easily enough, passing through a dining room that faced the road and my house, not tucked in the middle of the floor plan like mine. The living room was on the other side and the kitchen was bigger, taking up most of the first floor except for some smaller rooms by the back door. Her home didn't have the office on the first floor like mine.

Vienne was finishing setting a third place at a small table in the dining room. The top was half cluttered with the same binders and paint samples she'd brought over the other day. Was the table her office?

Her food, mediocre as she claimed it was, smelled amazing. I didn't like to cook for one, but I'd been to my brothers' and Aggie's places. With the warmer weather, we'd had more cookout food. Nothing like roast and mashed potatoes.

"Don't tell my siblings I'm not eating Knight meat." I held up a beer to offer to Vienne.

"This might actually be a Knight roast. Tova gave me some she couldn't fit in her freezer." She considered the drink I gave her for a moment. Her loose knit top was falling off one shoulder. She wore a pink tank top underneath. No necklaces were around her neck, and she only wore a few bracelets. She took the bottle from my hands. "I've been to this brewery a few times."

"I heard it was local. I haven't gone yet though." It was hard to beat the back deck on a calm summer night. I actually bought the six-pack because it was called Summer Sunset.

She waved her hand at the rest of the beer. "I can throw those in the fridge."

"I'll do it. You cooked. Sit."

She stared at me a moment before she nodded.

When I was done, I slid into a chair at the end opposite Vienne. Her lilacs-in-bloom scent was stronger. Was this her spot to work in? "I promise not to splash gravy on your stuff."

"You're the one who'd face the consequences. I'm ordering paint color tonight, and you'd end up with beef-gravy brown on the walls."

Catherine took the spot between us. Vienne shoved dishes around with the same frenetic energy she did everything else. The jangle of her jewelry was quieter. I liked that she wore less around me. I didn't care, only that the smaller amount indicated her increased comfort with me.

I concentrated on the food so I wouldn't be caught creeping on the host. The potatoes weren't too runny, considering I hadn't had real mashed potatoes that weren't prepared from flakes for a couple of decades.

"It's good," I said after swallowing a savory piece of meat. Vienne gave me a look that said I didn't have to pretend. "Seriously. I don't cook much. I never did since it was always just me."

"You've never been married?" Catherine asked.

"Catherine," Vienne said on a sigh.

Her daughter shrugged, uncaring how personal her question was. "He doesn't have to answer."

"That's not the point," Vienne countered.

"Uh, your mom's right, but I don't mind. No, I've never been married, and I don't have kids."

"Why not?"

Vienne huffed again. I admired her coping skills. Barns would've lashed out, not caring how badly we were cut by his words. "It's okay—for me. Just remember, not everyone will be as cool."

I caught the almost eye roll as Catherine chewed. Vienne's gaze was on me, studying me.

Unsure if I said something wrong, I answered Catherine. "I moved around a lot. Never wanted to drag a family along." My standard answer caught in my throat, landing differently than when I usually said my reason out loud. I'd had an entire career that had included a lot of cool shit and a lot of not-so-cool stuff, but here I was, not much further than when I'd left Montana for the army at eighteen. "But, you know, it worked for some guys. For some guys, it didn't."

"Hmm." Catherine's mind was working. "Where all have you lived?"

The tension in my shoulders eased. I could answer this. "Missouri, Colorado, North Carolina, Georgia, Colorado again, and Maryland."

The girl's eyes rounded. "You really did move around."

"I like not being tied down." Usually, I said that with ease, too, but today, it left a sour taste in my mouth. "One more main move, then I'll have a home base and travel a lot for work." For some reason, I avoided Vienne's direct stare.

"Which place was your favorite?" Catherine asked.

None. "Colorado, but only because it was close to home."

"Have you been to war?" Catherine's tone carried a hint of humor, like she didn't think it was a serious question.

I lifted my gaze to Vienne's. Her eyes held no humor, but the curiosity was ripe. She wanted to know about me. Nosy neighbor or interested woman?

"Yes," I answered.

"Wait." Catherine planted her hands on either side of her plate. "Seriously?"

"I was deployed five times."

"Oh, crap. Sorry."

I shrugged her sympathy off. Getting deployed sucked, but I'd left my time in service doing a lot better mentally and physically than a lot of people I'd served with. That didn't mean those deployments and what I saw or did over there were easy. I could swap stories with another veteran for hours, but not with a teen who wasn't wearing a uniform. "I'm still finding sand everywhere," I joked.

She laughed. Vienne smiled, but her gaze went through me like she sensed everything I wasn't saying. Like she knew I didn't like anywhere I was stationed. All I had found was more loneliness while surrounded by people. Could she tell I didn't cook for myself because it was goddamned depressing that I was one of the few career soldiers I knew who'd never been married? My choice was deliberate after seeing the shit shows that went on around me.

But sometimes, I was a little envious of the hot mess.

The rest of the meal went by quickly, topped off with the underwhelming clearance cake that could've used some of the moisture from the potatoes. Vienne started gathering her plate and silverware.

"I'll help clean up," I offered. I was an unplanned guest. "Catherine can show me where everything goes, and I'll show her I can do dishes better than her."

Catherine was buried in her phone, but she jerked her head up. "We have a dishwasher."

"Prove it."

I earned another teen eye roll, but she was smiling.

Vienne got up, holding her plate in one hand and grabbing the glass dish with the roast in the other. "You really don't have to, Austen."

"It's the least I can do. Those runny potatoes were worth it."

She laughed again. "Stop it. They were not."

I was finally getting a glimpse of the real her. "You clearly haven't been subsisting on what the government calls mashed potatoes."

She smiled, and I took the plates from her hand, enjoying the surprised look I got from it.

"If you keep being such a conscientious guest, we're going to have to invite you over more," she joked, then her smile froze like she worried she'd asked me out when she didn't mean to.

I only grinned. "A standing invite. I like it. What sold me? The beer or the offer to clean up?"

"The cake."

I laughed.

"Mom!" Catherine called from the kitchen. "Can we do a fire tonight? With Austen?"

I held my hands up. "I swear I didn't bribe her to get you to feed me all night."

Vienne's lips twisted into a wry smile. "Sure. If he wants to stay."

Oh, I was staying. Catherine was already digging out the ingredients for s'mores, and I started loading the dishwasher.

She held up a package of Hershey bars. "Wanna do the firepit?"

Vienne carried in the food. I took those dishes from her too. "I can do the fire at my place if you don't want to mess with the pit."

She propped a hand on her hip and eyed the chocolate. "No, but I might take you up on your fire-making abilities."

"Mom hates starting a fire." Catherine's shit-eating grin told me she asked because I was here and could do the fire when her mom might've otherwise said no.

Aggie had once told me Catherine was a s'mores fiend. That'd probably been her goal all along when she'd asked me to dinner. "Let me finish the dishes and then I'll be your personal fire-starting caveman."

Catherine did a little dance, then rushed out the back door, calling for the puppy as she went.

"Go on out," I said to Vienne. "I can figure out the dishwasher, and I'll be right there."

"Austen...you're supposed to be a guest."

I straightened and smiled at her. "I can't give you a reason to kick me out now, can I?"

Six

VIENNE

The fire crackled, and it was almost midnight. My eyes were dry. I needed to take my contacts out. I blinked to moisten them. It was getting late.

Teddy had long been put to bed. The fluffy puppy had collapsed by my chair and started snoring. Catherine was having too good of a time for me to call it for the night, but I would have to be the adult and put both of us to bed. Still, the evening had been pleasant. More than nice after getting a surprise guest for dinner.

A guest who'd done the dishes.

Austen was considerate. Helpful. Was he always like that, or were manners bred into him? I knew his family, so I knew the answer, but he was somehow always more than I expected.

Catherine took the fire poker and spread out the smoldering logs. Not much light was emanating off them, and it'd been a while since Austen had added a new log.

I had soaked in the smell of campfire and would need a shower. Same with Catherine. I stretched my arms high over my head. I'd tossed on a hoodie. The days were warm, but the June night had been cool enough to need a fire and a sweater. "Well, hon," I said to Catherine. "You can use the shower first."

"Aww." She pouted, then a yawn broke through.

Austen chuckled. "You're going to be a zombie volleyball player tomorrow. Last day of the clinic?"

She nodded, and fading firelight bounced through the loose strands of her braid, creating a messy halo around her head. "I fly out Monday, and that camp starts the week after. Oh, Mom—remember I'll need new volleyball shoes before camp starts."

Those damn shoes were becoming a power struggle between me and Dave. "Make sure you let your dad know." I'd already told her that, but she wanted the easy way out, which was me. "You'll have time to shop for them before the camp."

"All right." She strung out her reply. "You know what he's going to say."

"I'm well aware, but I'll talk to him."

She gave me a small smile. We'd discussed some of the issues between me and her father. I hadn't been brutally honest, but I also didn't believe in hiding family drama. I didn't make Dave the villain, but I also refused to shoulder all the blame. She was old enough to be sick of his bitch sessions about expenses when his house was three times the size of this one.

After she gave me a good-night kiss on the cheek, she rushed into the house. "Night, Austen. Thanks for the fire."

"I only wielded the lighter. Y'all supplied everything."

He was surprisingly humble. With the rest of his family, he was usually joking or making light of what he did in the army. Mostly, it had seemed like he had one foot out the door. He might be ready to leave, but he paid attention while he was around.

He gave Catherine a hard time but wasn't mean or critical like my ex Theo had been. Austen also remembered the smallest details, like all of Teddy's possible medical issues. Catherine's favorite dance steps. And the different projects I'd worked on in and around town, the ones I'd spoken about with his family when we'd all been together.

"Thank you," I said after Catherine disappeared inside. I should get up. The graham cracker boxes and marshmallows needed to be cleaned up, but the night was quiet. Traffic drifted in from the highway, and town was filled with the songs of crickets and frogs.

"More peaceful when that repair shop is closed," Austen murmured. His long legs were stretched in front of him, and he hooked his hands behind his head. I was sitting beside him, but I was able to admire the V his torso made. I could appreciate how his wide shoulders tapered to his waist and his muscular thighs.

I swallowed and looked away. "Yeah, it is." Rudy liked to work with his overhead doors open all summer.

His business was quiet now, and all the lights were off. I didn't have to worry about him seeing Austen at my place. Firepits were what neighbors did. I had nothing to justify.

"Whatdya have in store for me for tomorrow?" He sat up and propped his arms on his knees. "Wait—you're off the clock. Forget I asked."

He really was that thoughtful. No wonder I had a

hard time not obsessing over him. I wasn't planning to get involved in a relationship, but that didn't stop my instinct from trying to point out perfect partners. What Little Miss Hormonal didn't recall was that Austen was temporary, and my commitment to singlehood was steadfast.

"Keep waging war on that awful carpet, soldier."

"Yes, ma'am." He laughed. "Why aren't we painting first?" He held his hands up like he thought I might get offended. "Just curious. I'll follow your lead no matter what."

Pleased he trusted me more than anyone else I had worked with, I smiled. "In case we damage the paint taking the carpet out, or bringing new flooring in, depending on the hardwood situation."

Another deep chuckle vibrated between us. "My hardwood situation is on point. What can I say?"

I laughed, but heat curled through my body. "I can actually stop over tomorrow. I finished the other project I was hired for, and I'm caught up on my bookkeeping stuff." I was just waiting on word from Jim on whether Dot would allow me to be the designer.

"You jump in whenever. You know where I'll be."

I was acutely aware of his location at all times, unfortunately. "Thank you for tonight."

His expression turned curious, and I was caught in his dark gaze. The dying embers of the fire reflected in his brown irises. "What about tonight do I have to be thanked for, Honey V? You fed me, then let me hang out at your firepit while feeding me again."

"You helped clean up and got the fire going." I held up my empty bottle of Summer Sunset he'd gotten. "And you brought beer."

"I did the bare minimum. That many assholes let you down?"

"Yes." I rolled my lips in. The answer came too easily.

He reclined in his chair, but this time when he stretched out his legs, he cocked his body toward me. "I've heard about Jake." His gaze flicked up to the light from the upstairs hallway that shone over the backyard. "What about Catherine's dad? You, of course, can tell me to shut the fuck up anytime."

"No, it's fine." And it was. We were just talking. I wasn't venting. He was like a neutral third party, and I'd never had a chance to discuss Dave with someone who wasn't a friend and, therefore, anti-Dave. Mostly, it felt like everyone was pro-Dave. Or at least anti-divorce like my parents. "We were young. Since I got pregnant and dropped out of school to save on daycare, he was our primary income. We lacked a balance in the relationship from the beginning."

"Meaning he thought you had to do everything else because he worked." He shook his head. "What about that guy you were seeing when you first met Aggie?"

"Theo?" Aggie might have been blunt when she mentioned Theo if he was memorable enough that Austen asked about him. "He was...like dating a dishrag."

He barked out a laugh. "I know the type."

"How? And how are you so understanding?"

"What do you mean?"

Exactly my point. He was clueless about what he was doing right. To him, he was being himself. Good thing I'd sworn off guys, or thinking about him leaving would hurt. "I mean, I feel like you wouldn't hound your ex to pay for fifty- to seventy-dollar volleyball shoes. If your kid needed them, you'd buy them."

"I'd like to think so."

"Well, Dave wants to be in control, but he can't be with Catherine. When he wanted to quit having kids, he said we were done. Didn't matter what I wanted. When he hated being expected to treat me like an equal instead of like his maid and daycare, he worked more, which made it really hard for me to finish my degree. And when I told him I wanted to open my own interior design business, he divorced me." I shrugged. "If I was bringing in part of the income, then I might want more say in how we spent our money."

"Holy shit. He sounds like a dick."

"Yeah, he can be. He's a good dad, mostly. And his new wife is everything I wasn't. Compliant. Perfect. Calm."

He grunted like he didn't agree with something, and I didn't dare ask what. "What about the dishrag guy?"

"Theo thought I was Cruella de Ville after I told him I wanted to do something once in a while. He said that if we were going to stay together, I'd have to work on my attitude."

Austen was mid-drink from his bottle and he sputtered beer. When he recovered, he swiveled his incredulous look toward me. "Work on your attitude? Did he really say that?"

"He sure did." I thumbed the label on my beer. I couldn't believe I was about to tell Austen something I hadn't confessed to anyone. Theo lived in the neighboring town, and our circles didn't usually overlap. "Technically, *he* broke up with *me*. I told him I'd work on my attitude all night long since he never wasted time worrying about my pleasure in bed."

A cough escaped Austen. "Jesus."

I smothered my humiliation. I'd bared everything to Austen, and he hadn't told anyone. Might as well open up my insides. "He couldn't understand why my world wasn't blown apart when he thrust for a few seconds and climaxed."

Austen didn't snicker like I expected. His intense gaze was on me. "And Jake?"

After tonight, I'd never have to worry about Austen being interested in me. He was getting full Vienne Ives. He hadn't known pre-married Vienne Wagner. She was a badass. "Jake has a certain reputation. After Theo, could you blame a girl?"

He gave a small shake of his head.

I actually blamed myself a lot. "And I started to..." So embarrassing. "Catch feelings. I was playing darts one night, and when I was leaving, I saw him getting out of the back of his pickup. I thought it was weird. Then he helped a girl out of the back seat who was fixing her skirt. I didn't even see him leave with her, but he'd been having a drink twenty minutes before."

"He was fucking around on you?" Austen's growl sent shivers down my spine.

"No. Like I said at the street dance, he never made promises. Never told me I was the only one he was sleeping with at the moment. We weren't exclusive. But I'm so— It's not— I thought I could handle it, and I couldn't." I rimmed my fingers around one of the bracelets I'd kept on. I'd cried all night after what I saw. "I was so damn naive. And I'm so done with relationships."

"It's not naivety to expect someone not to hurt you." His low growl smoothed over some of the lingering hurt.

"See? That's what I was asking." I pointed at him. "How are you so understanding?"

His Adam's apple bobbed, and he stared into the dying fire. "I was an officer and people expect army officers to be making decisions about war—positioning troops, supplies, movements, you know?"

I didn't, but I nodded. I'd seen enough military movies to have my own stereotypes. "That's not what happened?"

"It did, but there's a lot more. The daily reality is like herding cats and then counseling them afterward. I'd have privates marrying the first girl who looked at them twice and then lose everything in a divorce a year later. They'd be clueless about what happened. I'd have NCOs with pristine careers and the shittiest personal lives. And when those personal issues spill over and affect their job, leadership often steps in. Then there were the other officers. Clearly, not every soldier has a fucked-up relationship, but also, our way of life can amplify the issues. I've heard it all. There's only so many times someone can hear the same reasons for why their wife left before you think... that many wives can't be wrong, especially when your female soldiers are making the same complaints as the civilian wives."

"Is that why—" I was getting way too personal. "Never mind. I got after Catherine for being too nosy."

"I'd never tell you to shut up." His warm gaze landed on me. "You were going to ask if that's why I never married?"

I nodded. "Sorry. It's not my business."

His chuckle was dry. "I've been all up in your business, V."

"To be fair, you didn't ask to be flashed that morning." My face was as hot as the burning embers. He might not have been talking about that.

"Are you saying if I ask, you'll do it again?"

I choked on a shocked laugh. "You don't want to see that again."

"I assure you, Vienne. I very much do."

My breath caught in my throat. He couldn't be serious. I gawked at him and caught smoldering heat before he cleared his throat and gazed at his bottle.

No way.

No fucking way. He had to be reacting to something or someone else.

"You asked why I never married," he said gruffly, "but it's more that I don't want to be in a relationship. I wasn't going to ask a woman to regularly give up her career and her support network to move around the country with me and then I'd get deployed and she'd be alone anyway. I wasn't going to be that guy in my commander's office, telling him about my upcoming divorce. I've seen too many couples split. I know the odds. I *lived* the odds with Mama and Barns. But if you want to fuck around, I'm your guy—and I'm not Doctor-fucking-Jake."

Oh.

Oh. I hadn't been imagining things. He was interested. But he was like me—allergic to relationships. Only he was offering a whole lot less in the best way.

How did we enter this territory? Was he propositioning me, or saying in general, if one were to want a fuck-around guy?

I didn't know! And it didn't matter. He was officially a client. I'd taken myself off the market long before that. His admission would only make working together that much more treacherous. My end goal was the same. My economic needs outweighed my physical wants.

"So you're a monogamous fuck-around guy?" I kept

my tone light, but I couldn't keep a light tremor out of it. All the reasons why this conversation itself was a bad idea ran through my head and collided with my neglected sex drive, which thought it was nothing but a *great* plan.

"I am," he said with no waver in his voice whatsoever. "So keep that in mind."

א

The sound of metal thunking and large truck engines drowned out the impact wrenches of the repair shop across the street. The industrial disposal bin was being delivered early this morning. Construction garbage was one of the tasks I'd been able to arrange before I started working at the house with Austen.

I lay in bed wondering why the AC didn't seem to be working as well as it should. The windows were open, but the day was heating up. I should save as much cool air as I could. But then I'd have to get out of bed. Austen said he didn't want to start until ten, and since he was considerate in addition to being sexy, he probably only said that for me. Staying up late with him last night had been enlightening.

So keep that in mind.

My brain was having trouble hanging on to anything else but what he'd told me. The great big red flag that he'd spelled out—*I don't do relationships*—did not daunt me. I should have been planning how I was going to be nothing but professional after he dropped that bomb, but I was intrigued.

But if you want to fuck around, I'm your guy...

I didn't want a relationship either.

Yet I hadn't thought I wanted a relationship with

Jake, but I'd started getting hearts in my eyes. Deep down, I hadn't given up on the idea that I could find everything I wanted in one guy and that the man I found could also make me orgasm. I'd lost the forest for the climaxes with Jake.

Could I hold strong with Austen? He was even more dangerous. He possessed the emotional maturity Dave and Theo didn't. Austen was self-aware, and that trait was alluring. Too attractive. Just like him and his longish hair and his facial scruff. I'd succumb. I'd catch feelings and worse—hopes and dreams.

But he wasn't serious.

Was he?

A few notes of an old country song drifted through the window. I turned my head toward the light. A man was singing. He got to the chorus and his smooth voice grew louder, reaching through the space between our houses and caressing me from my ears to my toes.

Austen.

Did he have to have the voice of an angel too?

An angel who could get me naked in seconds.

I let my eyes drift closed and listened to him sing. Tingles spread through my body. I splayed my hand on my belly and crept it downward.

"Mom! Have you let Teddy out?" Catherine shouted from the other side of my bedroom door.

The singing cut off, and my eyes flew open. I sat up and straightened my tank top. Was I really going to masturbate to the voice of the man I'd be working with all day—for weeks?

"Mom?"

Quit thinking about Austen! "No, I figured he'd sleep late today too."

"All right. I'll do it." Her footsteps faded.

The singing didn't return. Disappointed, I rolled out of bed. I got dressed while staying clear of the window to keep from flashing him again, but I also recalled how he said he very much would like to be flashed again.

That man jumbled my brain and turned every nerve ending on high. Working with him would change how I felt. He was considerate, but I'd experienced Austen in small doses. We were going to be spending a lot of time together.

I rushed through getting ready, choosing jeans and a tank top so I didn't pit out in front of Austen from the get-go. While I made myself and Catherine breakfast, I brewed a giant pot of coffee and filled my biggest water bottle. When my daughter had eaten and was off to her camp, I went next door, my stomach flip-flopping.

Coworkers. Nothing but coworkers. No flings with the neighbor. If he'd been serious.

I knocked.

The door swung open. "Good morning," I said as if I hadn't intended to stroke one out to his voice less than an hour ago.

"Morning," he said with a rougher timbre than normal.

The rest of him was more rugged today too. Gone were the basketball shorts and loose T-shirts. He was wearing blue jeans with worn denim in the thighs and a rip across one knee. His black shirt was plastered to his chest, and he was smug about it. The tingles from earlier in the morning returned when the backward ball cap registered. Having his hair off his face made his cheekbones and square jaw more prominent. The yellow flecks were easier to see in the amber depths of his eyes. The country boy in him was loud and proud as if he needed to be more devastating.

He also looked rested and fresh, while the bags under my eyes needed their own coffee mug.

He stepped back to let me in. I dropped my tote bag full of the plans I had for him. I'd have to make some calls later, but if we could get the carpet hauled out to the bin, that'd be better.

"Ready to get started?" I asked much too brightly when I faced getting dirty and sweaty with a guy who'd only end up hotter after hours of manual labor.

"Lead the way, boss."

I liked it too much when he called me boss. Same with V. And Honey V.

For hours, we tore up the remaining carpet in the bedrooms. He'd consolidated all the old remnants and furniture in the rooms that now had bare hardwood. While I tore up dusty pads, he hauled out everything else.

All the work he'd done earlier this week was impressive. This renovation could go really quickly.

Disappointment curled through my belly. If we finished early, would he leave earlier? I'd go back to seeing him at big family gatherings. He'd chat with his brothers, and I'd be with my friends. We'd return to being acquaintances.

As if there was anything else for us.

I swiped my gritty forearm across my forehead. I'd braided my hair like Catherine usually did for volleyball, and my deodorant was still holding strong. I was covered in dust and dirt and had fought off one sneezing fit while Austen snickered and rewarded my efforts with that lazy grin of his.

Despite all that, today was awesome. I got to be part

of the face-lift in a house I'd admired since I was a kid. I could return some old farmhouse personality to a place that just looked like a run-down '90s remodel. I hadn't told my mom yet. She'd love to see the place, but I also didn't want her to witness how far it'd fallen.

Would she love what I'd done with it after the work was complete? Austen approved my ideas.

Would she claim I was being too simple with my suggestions? Some might disagree that a house with this much personality spoke for itself, but I felt this house needed a light touch. It didn't need intricate wallpaper or loud paint. Soft creams on the walls and restoring the wooden trim and floor to their glory would be stunning on its own. I was sure of it. But I also wasn't ready to hear criticism about it.

I propped my hands on my hips and walked from room to bare room. We had one more bedroom left, but I wasn't brave enough to step foot in it yet. It was *his*.

I found Austen in the middle of one of the other bedrooms with his arms held slightly apart from his body and his legs wide. My suspicions were confirmed—he looked better when his forearms were shiny from perspiration and the veins were bulging. He was nothing but power and muscle and a man musk that was equal parts sweat and smoked vetiver. Normally, he smelled like dry grass on a warm day. Now, he smelled like a hotbed of grass I wanted to curl up on.

"The floor is disappointing," he said, tapping the tip of his boot on it.

The boots did weird things to my hormones. My ovaries were reminding me that I was still of childbearing age and I should pick my man and get going if I still wanted babies.

Prickles spread down my back. That right there was why I should stay far away from Austen. If I was smart, I would quit and walk out and tell him he was a good neighbor and nothing more.

But I didn't move. I enjoyed today, and with Austen I didn't have the worry of proving myself, of being challenged with each suggestion. He respected my professional opinion in a way no one else had.

"The floors aren't bad." I scraped the floor with my athletic shoe. "The pine was never stained very dark, so it has the weathered look that'll be cool when it's cleaned up. I think the wood has a lot of character, but we can go over more stains to see what shade you like."

"It's not what I like but what you think the buyers will like."

The buyers. Yes. I had to wow people at the open house, and more than buyers would attend this one. Contractors would be interested in me. I'd send Jim an email, asking him if he'd like to let Dot know about the open house so she could look at my work.

More than my business was dependent on how well I did. So much of my pride rode on this project. I'd admired this house for years, and I wanted to do it justice. As for the floors, I wanted to keep the lightness in the wood to let the grain stand out, but this was not my house. I spun on my heel. "What about your bedroom? We can wait if you want to keep it comfortable to sleep in."

"We can rip 'er out," he said from right behind me. I jumped, and he chuckled. "I've slept in worse."

The man could be stealthy. I shot him a scowl and wandered into his room. I tried not to be nosy, but I clocked everything. His bed was neatly made with a plain gray comforter and two pillows. The nightstand was small and at the end of its lifespan, but he kept a short lamp and a clock on it. A box was open in the corner. Light-green camouflage fabric was visible, along with an American flag that was folded and framed. More boxes surrounded it.

His house was being renovated, but his bedroom still announced that he wasn't sticking around.

"Let me get these moved out." He started for the boxes, bending so his jeans tightened over his ass, those powerful thighs of his flexing.

"What's the flag for?"

He paused a moment. "We all got them when we returned from one of my deployments."

"Do you get one every time you go?"

"No." He closed the flaps of the box. "They mostly signify losing a service member or veteran, but after the last couple of decades, a lot of us have them from deployments."

The wall AC unit was blowing right on me, but I was mid–hot flash lusting at his forearm porn. He straightened, and I jerked my gaze off him to the window that faced my house. No wonder I'd heard him so clearly. I never noticed how closely our windows lined up. When I walked between our houses, I never paid attention to how much space was between the buildings. On the ground, it seemed like more than on the second level.

He was a couple of walls and a long jump away when I slept.

I also never thought of it that way when his brother had lived in the house.

"It's time for lunch." I tipped my head toward my

house. "I planned to have something with Catherine since she should be back at any time."

"No problem. I'll have all this moved when you get back." He disappeared into the hallway with his load.

"What about your lunch?" I asked when he returned.

"I'll have a quick sandwich." The corner of his mouth tipped up. "I eat fast. Hazard of the trade."

The tidbits he dropped about his life in the military weren't what I expected. He didn't mention factoids that would make him seem like a living action figure or a manly man, men of all men. Dave tilled the garden one time, and he boasted so proudly I wasn't sure I could get him to ever pick up his socks.

"It's all right," Austen said and scratched the back of his neck. My attention was not so discretely riveted. His chest was really that broad and muscular. "I'll be working evenings and weekends, but don't think I expect you to. I've got nothing better to do, and I kind of like having something to keep me busy right now."

He'd incorrectly read into my hesitation, but his sentiment was sweet. He wanted to make sure I knew he wasn't expecting me to work his hours. "Where are you moving after this?"

"LA. A couple buddies of mine are going to start a personal security company. I was the last to get out, and I wanted some time to acclimate to civilian life, so I asked for six months. I kicked around for a few months before moving into the house. I have to be out there the second week of August. Selling this place makes a good buy-in for the company."

He wasn't just moving, but he was going across the country. Investing in a new business. His hometown was almost three hours away. He'd be almost a three-day drive away. "Personal security?"

His expression turned almost sheepish. "Bodyguard shit."

I grimaced. "The ex-military bodyguard? Are you going to fall in love with the young starlet who hired you?"

He nodded. "After she does something to endanger her own life and I get shot." He swiped a finger across his shoulder. "A flesh wound, of course."

"Of course." I was laughing, but I could picture it. Austen was the type of guy to win anyone's trust and then their heart. "I'm sure you'll be excellent at it."

"Eh, it's a job. I knew I couldn't get out and start at the bottom of some gig when I'd been one of the ones in charge. Being my own boss makes sense."

"Including a quick flip of a house."

He took his hat off, smoothed a hand through his dark hair, and put the hat on the right way. "I missed working with my hands."

Instant desire kindled in my belly. I couldn't risk the conversation going into the same territory as last night. I'd never be able to play it cool. But I could play the fool really well.

"Okay." I clapped my hands to hide any awkwardness. "Are you sure I can't bring you anything back?"

"I've got food, Vienne." His smile was easy. "Don't worry about me."

I wasn't worried about him. I was worried about me around him.

Seven

AUSTEN

I was in the middle of wrenching a toilet out of the main-floor bathroom when the song on my phone blared out a ring through the Bluetooth speaker I had hooked up. I let it go. This toilet and I were having a reckoning.

Finally, it came free of the seal. I didn't let go but continued to carry it all the way through the house and out the front door. I'd hauled the tank out earlier. With a grunt, I heaved the porcelain into the construction waste bin Vienne had set up.

Overall, I'd been impressed with her. Other than being sexy and smart, she worked hard. Yesterday, we got more done than I thought possible for two people. She didn't complain, and I didn't recall the last time I'd smiled and laughed so much while on the job.

She wasn't willing to take me up on my offer to mess around. I shouldn't have said anything either. Maybe she hadn't thought I was serious.

I was.

My siblings might squawk at me for fucking around with Vienne, but a guy only lived once. I only lived in this house once. With Vienne as a neighbor once. No one would blame me for shooting my shot. Except for Aggie. And Cody. Wilder and Eliot might agree with them too.

Whatever. Better that Vienne acted like I never said anything.

Inside, I washed my hands in the sink that I'd be removing next. On my phone was a missed call from Johnson, one of the guys I was setting up the security company with. I should call him back.

I dried my hands.

Maybe later.

There was a knock at my door.

Was it Vienne telling me she had a boring weekend and could come over to help?

I opened the door to Wilder. He frowned. "Who were you expecting? You look like I stole your puppy and returned with a lizard."

"Your wife would be thrilled."

He grinned. "You mean the ex-wife I'm sleeping with."

"What are you going to do when you can't point that out anymore?"

"Tell everyone how my second wife looks like my first wife."

I chuckled. "You came too late. I already tore out the shitter."

"You pissing out the window or what?"

If I did that, the stream might hit Vienne's window. Not that I'd ever consider peeing in my yard that was surrounded by children. It was just that I thought about how close Vienne was a lot lately. "I'll be going to your house to use the bathroom. I'll just walk right in, so wear underwear."

"If you see my junk, you deserve it." He smirked. "Wanna go to Hummingbird's?"

My stomach growled. "Yes. Want to help me gut a bathroom?"

"Sutton's at the clinic, but lemme talk to her. Maybe she'll want to destroy someone else's property."

I stepped out and locked the door behind me. "She doesn't like seeing her brand-new clinic get demolished?"

"It's stressful. The business has hardly been open for two years, and we're already tearing it apart to expand. But she knows it's a good problem to have."

We walked down the sidewalk, our boot strikes syncing. A strong wind roared down the street, but the sun was high in the sky. A hot, windy day. I tucked my ball cap brim down to keep it from blowing off.

"I told Sutton I'd grab her a burger," Wilder said, "then I was driving by and remembered you're in town."

"Nice to know I'm first in your thoughts." I wasn't a priority to any of them, but his wife should be his top concern anyway.

"Not used to you actually being around for longer than a few days."

"Yep."

He peered at me. "And you're leaving soon."

"Right again."

"We're too boring for you."

"That's not it." I scoffed. "What would I do here? Get a deputy or highway patrol position and then never get to see my family?"

"You would," he argued, then grinned. "Just not on your own terms."

"Exactly."

"Isn't that what's going to happen with the company you're starting? You'll be living according to your clients' schedules."

"Maybe at first. Then we'll get some guys hired."

We reached the diner. Wilder and I settled into a booth. The AC was pumping out frigid air, but after my morning, I welcomed it. Wilder didn't bother with a menu. Most people who lived in Crocus Valley any length of time didn't need a menu.

Thelma appeared with a coffeepot and poured us each a cup without asking. "Same shit, different day, boys?"

"If you mean food, yes." I grinned. I had liked Thelma as soon as I'd met her. She reminded me of an old crusty sergeant major who'd seen it all but couldn't bring himself to retire. So he stuck around with his caustic attitude and imparted much-needed wisdom to the young folk.

"Same," Wilder said and slid the coffee in front of him. Neither of us were big coffee drinkers, but we'd never refuse Thelma's.

"Been out to spoil some babies?" I asked.

Thelma's lined face wrinkled deeper as she grinned. "Tova and the kids took me and Lana to Medora for a day. I was on baby Charlie duty while they explored the shops."

"Nice," Wilder said. "Sutton and I are going there to camp again over Labor Day."

"Good. You kids gotta keep getting out."

A thin snake of envy circled my chest. Day trips with family. Camping trips with significant others.

But I had a plan. A good one. Some guys retired and were lost. They lost themselves in their heads or got lost in the shuffle. As much as the military tried to ready us for the civilian world, it wasn't always a smooth transition. I refused to have issues. That was why I took a six-month break to acclimate to being Austen Knight from a small town in eastern Montana. I could be Austen Knight, a retired major living in a rural town in western North Dakota. Not a big jump.

I wasn't wearing my ball cap like it was my uniform hat like I'd seen a lot of guys do when they left the service. I wasn't replacing yes with "Hooah" or throwing acronyms around. I was proud of my service, but I was done. I was that kid from Buffalo Gully, and I had a job lined up. My very own company. Well, with three other guys. And yes, my schedule wouldn't be fully my own to dictate even after we hired more employees, but I had more freedom than in the last twenty years. I also didn't have too much. I wasn't going to end up roaming the country searching for that freedom like Mama had.

"Remember all the stories Mama would tell when she used to call?"

Wilder's brows notched up. "When she used to call?"

Okay, we'd had to get the stories through Aggie. Mama had been on a full man-hate ride and that had included her sons. All four of them. "She got a little wild."

"She abandoned us so she could get a little wild."

"Do you figure all that free time drove her a little crazy?"

He sat back, his hand around the plain white coffee

mug he hadn't taken a drink from. "Why bring Mama up now?"

"I don't know. I guess I'm in the same position she was in. Sort of."

"You got five kids somewhere we don't know about?"

I curled up the corner of my lip. "I'm not Barns."

He grunted. "None of us are. You'd never baby trap a woman. As for Mama?" He rubbed his chin, his brow furrowed. His hair had also gotten longer than he'd normally kept it when he worked as a deputy, and the scruff I only saw on weekends when we worked cattle or moved horses was a constant. We looked more alike than ever. "I think if she didn't have coping issues before she married Barns, she did when she left. And that's why she lived a little too wild."

"I tried to take a few months and just travel." Fuck if I knew why. Maybe to see what about it appealed to Mama? "I'd been around people for so long—"

"You wanted to find yourself. A little, what is that book? One of the dispatchers read it and gushed about it. *Eat, Pray, Love*?"

"I'm named after Jane Austen, jackass. Not whoever wrote that."

"So you went to—" He snapped his fingers, concentration written over his face. "England? France?"

"Didn't you ever read *Pride and Prejudice*?"

"Did you?"

"Yes. I read every Jane Austen book when I was deployed." Downtime could feel extra long on deployment, and maybe I'd been trying to connect with a mother who'd never cared to connect with me. I never got answers.

"*Little House on the Prairie*?" Wilder was named after Laura Ingalls Wilder.

"No. You have to read that."

"The fuck I do," he grumbled, then lifted a shoulder. "Maybe if we have kids."

"I'll be back to watch you read them their rights."

He flashed his teeth. "I'm not a cop anymore, but you'd better be back. Kind of nice having you around. Ever think you'll settle down?"

I didn't have time to bask in how he said he liked having me around. He hit me with the hard question. "Little old for that."

"I'm older than you and just getting married and planning kids."

I rolled my eyes. A burn smoldered in my gut. I should've ordered something besides a burger. Gutting a bathroom with heartburn all afternoon would suck. "Nope. Not for me." I'd had nowhere to settle down until my buddies called about the security company.

"I didn't think the military was, but you took to it."

"It was easier than dealing with Barns."

"Amen to that." He sat back when Thelma brought our food out. She gave me Wilder's hot beef melt, and Wilder got my burger.

We switched them after she left. She knew who ordered what; she just didn't care about the details.

"Anyway," Wilder said as he cut into his food, "don't discount yourself. Just because our parents sucked doesn't mean we have to be alone for life."

"Sure." I ignored the look he gave me and bit into my burger, glad his mouth was full too. I enjoyed the conversation, but I didn't need older-brother wisdom. Our lives took different paths, and he didn't understand mine.

When I was gone, he wouldn't think twice about it more than to update me on the happy events in his life.

Which reminded me. I had to call Johnson back when I returned to the house.

I'd be in California during the firepit parties and the s'mores roasting and when they gathered after cattle work. I'd get over it and make sure I took time off in the summer to come back.

I wasn't sure I'd forget about the night with Vienne and Catherine that flashed through my mind when Wilder said I didn't have to be alone.

Vienne

I stopped at the base of the escalator at the airport. Catherine had already checked in, and the security screening was upstairs. I held my arms out. Catherine slumped into me for a hug. Her peony-scented shampoo tickled my nose. She was definitely dressed like she was going to an athletic camp—shorts and a pink moisture-wicking shirt with black piping.

I was dressed similarly. I'd left my jewelry off, too, after a too-warm night. The air-conditioning unit had officially died, and I'd have to try to have someone out next week. With the heat this weekend, I'd be lucky if it was that soon.

"You know the drill," I said and pulled away. I stroked a hand over her braid like she was five. I'd never get used to sending her on a plane by herself. Thankfully, she took a direct flight to Denver.

"Text when I land, text when I'm in Dad's car, and call when I can." She gasped like she had forgotten something. "I should've gone to see Grandma and Grandpa before I left."

That was my bad. I didn't go out of my way to visit my parents. They loved Catherine. They were critical of me. "Sorry. We should've done it this weekend."

"They have AC."

"It'll be working before you're home, I promise."

She rolled her eyes but smiled. Then her grin dipped. "You think it's going to be different with the baby?"

Dave's wife of three years was perfect. She doted on Catherine without being false or smothering, and if she agreed with Dave on his child support nitpicking, she stayed out of it. I respected that. She was who he wanted.

I knew what I wanted. No one.

Yet Austen's lazy grin flashed through my head.

I shook away the stray thought. Back to Betti. "Hmm. She might start wearing leather and smoking and saying stuff like bruh." Betti would never be caught doing any of the three.

Catherine giggled. "Is bruh grammatically correct?" She gave me another quick hug. "Don't work too much."

"I'll be making the big bucks."

"And making people talk." She tipped her head and regarded me with eyes that were so much like her dad's. "It'll be okay. We know the truth, and everything else is BS."

Maybe no one would say a thing, and I'd get all offended no one thought I could land Austen. "Total BS," I reassured her. I shooed her toward the escalator. "Go, so you're not late."

"Promise me you'll have a hot girl summer."

"Absolutely—until the AC is fixed."

"Mo-om." She got on the escalator and held the rail. She looked back. "Have some fun. Go wild."

I waved at her while she ascended. The irony. My daughter told me to go wild when those days ended as soon as the second line appeared on the pregnancy test.

The drive back to Crocus Valley went fast. An odd cloud always followed me home from dropping my daughter off at the airport, and it was present today. When I got to town, I parked in front of my house. I had to change before I got to work.

Austen came out of the house carrying a couple bags of whatever he'd been destroying over the weekend. The basketball shorts were gone. He was wearing tattered cowboy boots, jeans that hugged his ass, and a red shirt that showed me all his muscles. The guy hadn't quit working, and I'd seen Sutton and Wilder helping him one day.

"You're not leaving me anything to do," I called.

"I have lots of hardwood for you, V." His easy grin sent the butterflies loose in my belly. "I should watch myself. You've barely started, and I'm harassing you."

"Are you telling me all you have is softwood?"

His smile widened. "We're going to find out how hard it is. On our hands and knees all day."

He wasn't kidding. "I'm bringing my knee pads over. I gotta get changed."

He turned serious. "How'd it go?"

"Good." I was going to leave it at that, but he looked at me like he cared about how I was doing after dropping my daughter off. "Then I remember she'll be gone for a month."

"Is it too early for a beer? The shade might be on the back porch."

I was tempted to sit with him and chill. It was a sweet offer. "Let me earn the beer first."

"Aw, V. The beer at my house is free. But we can save our Summer Sunset for the summer sunset."

I grinned and jogged to my house. Inside, I darted up the stairs. I nearly ripped my shirt off until I spotted the open window blinds. I'd closed the window itself to keep from heating the house more, but I'd left the shade up. If Austen was in his room, he'd get another show, only from the front this time.

Once upon a time, I might've been brave enough to risk it, but I was older now. More responsible. I'd been burned. And I'd told Catherine everything else would be BS. I didn't think I'd regret that promise.

Eight

AUSTEN

A week had passed since Vienne showed up after Catherine left for Denver. During lunch, she'd go home, and I'd make an unsatisfying sandwich, try to get my dick under control after seeing her bend, squat, and kneel in snug blue jeans all morning, then we worked all afternoon. Quitting time for Vienne was five. I shooed her out if it got too late. Catherine might not be in town, but I wasn't going to dominate Vienne's summer with stripping floors.

Instead, I got to peek out the windows at her playing with Teddy in the backyard and taking him on walks while I cleaned and repaired the upstairs floors. Once, I'd caught myself wondering what it'd be like to go on a walk with her. What would we talk about? Would we stop and chat with people we knew?

I missed parts of that community feeling. Those fleeting moments when I was in the army and I lived somewhere long enough to know my neighbors. When I'd get stopped by them when I was out working on my yard. By the time I reached that point of familiarity, I was packing my belongings to move.

Over the weekend, I'd continued low-key peeping on her while finishing the sanding of the hardwood.

This week, Vienne had been quieter. Monday was normal. We each split rooms to wash the dust off the floor and coat. Tuesday, she'd been quieter, and today, she'd hardly talked the rest of the day. There'd been one hushed conversation on the porch. I chalked it up to missing her kid. From what Catherine had said, she'd normally be returning this weekend.

Evening was approaching. I checked the time, after five. At this time last week, we'd been having a back-deck beer. Our neighbors had seen us coming and going all day. I'd told Sumi on the other side of the house about working with Vienne, and her husband had offered his plumbing services. I might have to take him up on some of it. The family behind us was gone, and Dobber was having fun racing Teddy up and down the back fence.

Twice, I'd seen Rudy crossing the street on his way to Hummingbird's. The third time, he caught me tossing a bag of trash, and he eagerly asked me what was going on. By now, the whole town should know Vienne was my interior designer.

It was quitting time for Vienne, but she had come downstairs to demolish the short wall that had been added in the '90s remodel. She'd keep hammering away, and I'd love to let her, but I also didn't want to take advantage of her. I was paying her for forty-hour work-weeks, and while I was paying her for the manual labor she was doing, the extra hours would add up.

A thud and tearing drywall made me jump. Vienne had wedged the sledgehammer in the partition wall by the main-level bathroom and braced her foot on the wall to tug on it.

I crossed to her, abandoning the cabinet I was ripping out. "Lemme get that."

"I got it," she said through clenched teeth.

"I know you do, Honey V, but you're running pretty hot today, and you're going to free that thing like She-Hulk. I don't want you to hurt yourself over whoever pissed you off."

She released the handle so fast she stumbled backward into me. I put my hands on her waist, and fuck, my body came alive, ignoring the lectures I'd given it since we began this project.

She clearly wasn't interested. She'd given me zero signs despite showing me paradise.

I let go and stepped back once I was sure she was steady. "Want to take it out on me?"

"No." She blew out a hard breath and pushed a few strands of hair that had escaped her braid out of her eyes. "It's my problem."

"I'm a good listener." And I liked when she opened up to me. Vienne was grounded. She could come off as flighty with her clattering jewelry and rolling energy, but she was smart, driven, and she knew what she wanted. I saw it in her plans for the house.

"No, it's nothing."

I went to the fridge. The new appliances were supposed to arrive closer to when I'd put the house on the market. We were stripping everything else out and would hopefully get the new cabinets in. They'd be in a new century, longer and in light oak, but with a classical taste.

I dug out a Summer Sunset. I'd stocked up on the stuff after we had a quick drink to talk about how the first day had gone, hoping that'd become a regular thing. I used the bottle opener from my pocket knife to take the top off. I held it out for her.

She let out a frustrated huff. "You outdo Dave on everything."

I was mid opening my beer and I paused. "Sorry?"

She kicked wall debris out of the way and took a swig. Another heavy breath eked out of her. "He's in accounting mode."

I worked over what that would mean. I was sure I'd heard the same complaints from soldiers over the years, but they'd never called it that. The "he" she mentioned must be Dave. "Let's sit on the deck. Then tell me what you mean." I walked out the back door so she wouldn't argue and go home instead.

The day was hot, but the shade was decent and the warm chairs soaked into a sore body. We'd been toiling away for days, and I hadn't done this type of labor since before I left home. I'd never been able to stop and enjoy a beer right whenever I wanted. A guy could get used to this. Hard work. Cold drink. Sexy woman.

"Dave latched on to the volleyball shoes, and now he wants a tally of everything I'm buying her with his child support."

Ah, yes. I'd been around many Daves. "And you can't tell him to fuck off, why?"

She pursed her lips. "Catherine, mostly."

"How does she handle him when he's like this, or doesn't she know?"

Vienne traced a finger over her beer label. "She knows, but she doesn't get it. She sees what I spend her money on, but she also doesn't know everything because she's not an adult paying adult bills. So telling him that I paid for the local volleyball clinic that cost a fraction of the one in Denver, and *still* paid half for Denver, lands on uncaring ears. But it's not just that." She took another drink.

I waited for her to elaborate, but she was glaring into her yard and at the puppy running around. Good thing Teddy couldn't take it personally.

"When he gets like that, I feel like the old Vienne," she finally said. "The girl who foolishly quit college thinking she'd have his support."

"Fuck him for letting that girl down."

She laughed. "Is that what you told your soldiers?"

"Sometimes."

Her smile faded. "He thinks I play around at running a business and coast off his underwhelming monthly check. He thinks that since he's remarried, he shouldn't have to pay as much, and he thinks..." She ran her lower lip through her teeth, her thumb flicking at the neck of the bottle. She didn't have jewelry to mess with. "He thinks that since he has a baby on the way, everything is about him again. Or rather, I think he fears everything no longer being about him, which is probably why he turned me down flat whenever I asked about having more."

And here he was, having the kids Vienne had wanted with a brand-new wife.

"How long have you been divorced?"

"The divorce went through four years ago, but I moved home five years ago when he said he wanted to end the marriage." Her thumb stroked the cool bottle faster.

The guy had had Vienne and a great girl like Catherine with him every day, supporting him, and he'd tossed them away. If I had someone like Vienne to come home to every day, I hoped I'd know how to not be a self-serving prick. "He's a selfish asshole."

"Pretty much." She gave an indignant sniff. "He always thought he was smarter than me. It was my fault I got pregnant and not his for failing Condoms 101. I live in Podunk, Nowhere, and I was raised on a ranch, so I must be dumber than fuck compared to his city ass." She made a disgusted noise. "I fed into it too. Thought I got myself a sophisticated guy."

"I can't blame you. When I look at me and my brothers and the guys we graduated with, I'm sure Crocus Valley was the same."

She shook her head, fire sparking the yellow flecks in her eyes. "You and your brothers were good guys even then, I'm sure of it. There's just a bigger variety of selfish assholes in bigger graduating classes. I came home because I was tired of the entitlement. Not just Dave's." She let her head hang over the back of her chair. "But the anonymity was nice. Everyone knowing my business here is hard to get used to. And when it backlashes on Catherine?" She shook her head.

"That part I get," I said softly.

She popped her head up and looked at me. "Yeah?"

"The Knights could make big news in Buffalo Gully. But we aren't talking about me."

She waved a hand. "I vented. I'm good. Dave is Dave, and I'll have to deal with him for the rest of Catherine's life. After she's eighteen, then I'll tell him to fuck off." She let out a gusty sigh. "Are you sure you weren't like an interrogator or something? I seem to spill my guts around you."

Her cheeks tinged pink. Was she remembering that morning I saw it all?

I never forgot. "I learned it was easier to let someone talk rather than throw my rank or position around."

She ran her lower lip through her teeth and considered her beer bottle. "Why are you moving so far away?"

My first retort was to ask her *Why, do you want me closer?* Something about this woman did it for me. I respected her. She was sexy as fuck. And she was easy to talk to. But she wasn't mine. "There's no reason not to."

"Four siblings and five nieces and nephews?"

Shit, was I an uncle of five already? Unless I was staying at Eliot's when someone slept over, I didn't have a lot to do with them. "They sort of forget I'm around. They're busy. I should've moved to Buffalo Gully and remodeled some shit there or done it for the ranch."

"But then that'd feel too much like returning to zero. To have never gone anywhere in the first place."

"Listen to you," I teased.

"In the words of Sutton, survey says...I was the same."

I laughed. I had noticed Sutton's tendency to repeat game show phrases.

"Eighteen-year-old me did not think thirty-year-old me would find herself raising a kid mostly on her own and trying to launch a business my ex didn't think was worth our time or effort. She certainly wouldn't think thirty-five-year-old me was still in the same position."

"What did eighteen-year-old you think?"

She gazed at the backyard while she thought, giving me a chance to study her profile. I tracked it all—the strong line of her nose, the delicate curve of her jaw, and the way her turquoise eyes caught everything. Guys might argue she was the common denominator when it came to

113

her exes, but after getting to know her, I thought she had shit taste.

She made a mistake with Dave and quit trusting her instincts when it came to men.

"Eighteen-year-old Vienne would have thought she would've played volleyball all through college, maybe did some coaching because damn, she loved that game. Then she would've been a career woman. Big money and an even bigger house." Her mouth curved up. "Maybe even an old farmhouse like the one she envisioned her mom talking about. What about eighteen-year-old you?"

"I'm doing it." At her questioning look, it was my turn to gaze across the yard and remember the aspirations of a kid who wanted more than what he had. "I guess the younger me would've thought the army life would've been more prestigious and less sweaty balls."

She chortled. "Do I want to know?"

"Add in sand when I was deployed and you can figure it out." I enjoyed her light smile. The way she lost all tension, tipped her head back, and her throat worked over the sound. I could picture her in that position—take out the humor and add in arousal and—

"Sweaty balls and sand were the only surprises?"

"The counseling. The mentoring. The babysitting. All that was unexpected. But for the most part, yeah. If you were to ask the me leaving home what he'd do after the military, I'd have guessed security or some shit."

"You never thought you'd settle back home?"

No. Never. Now that I was close to the place where I grew up and even closer to my siblings, I had thoughts. Crocus Valley wasn't Buffalo Gully. The towns were in different states, but they were less than three hours apart, yet there was a world of difference. Much of my family was happy here.

But I was a single guy. I could travel. I'd have time off. Probably. I'd do my thing, and my family would do theirs, moving on without me like they'd always done. "Living with Eliot, both of us bachelors and on the ranch? No thanks. Likewise, hanging out around all the happy couples sounds like a hoot." I shot her a sarcastic grin.

She giggled. "It's sickening, isn't it? So fucking happy."

"Awful." I grinned. "Don't get me wrong. I love seeing it. This weekend, we're all meeting at Cody's for the Fourth." I wouldn't have mentioned it, but I was confident Tova had invited her. With Catherine gone, Aggie, Tova, and Sutton would be rallying around Vienne.

"You and I can sit at the kiddie table."

"It's the funnest crowd at the party."

"Yeah," she said wistfully. "It is. Catherine is bummed she's going to miss it." She clenched her jaw. "She wasn't going to go to Denver until after the Fourth because of the party, but the camp is over the time she would've had with her dad." She polished off her beer when I thought she was going to mutter about Dave getting his way. But that was the thing about Vienne. She opened up, she got it out, and she moved on. I admired the trait. "Thanks for making me talk instead of demoing the wall. I might've taken out part of the ceiling if you hadn't stopped me."

She rose and stretched. Her lithe body turned long and sensual. All she was doing was raising her hands above her head. My gaze caught at her waistband, where her shirt threatened to sneak up and bare a strip of her abdomen.

"See you Sunday?"

I jerked my gaze up to her face. Her expression was neutral. Did she catch me staring?

Did she witness my lust? It didn't matter. We were nothing but neighbors with a working relationship. "Sunday, Honey V."

Vienne

I pushed up my glasses and peered out my bedroom window. Was Austen's window closed? Mine was as wide open as could be, but no wind carried cool relief in. I was stripped down to a tank top and underwear and was still too warm.

After being so wound up all week from simmering anger toward Dave, I needed to relax. An easier task when the room wasn't sweltering. The service rep could finally get here Tuesday after the holiday weekend. Everyone else's AC died before mine once the summer heat ramped up.

"Ugh." I twirled my hair up, got it off my neck, and flopped onto the bed, letting the strands splay over the pillow. The sheets were cool, but the feeling wouldn't last long. I tossed my glasses onto the nightstand.

The pent-up frustration on top of working side by side with Austen was getting to me, making me restless. I didn't want to flop around and get sweaty because I couldn't sleep. I was upset with my ex. I should be upset with the man next door. Having a beer on the deck with him all understanding and supporting, commiserating about living the single life around his wonderful siblings, hadn't helped cool me down physically. Being around Austen only increased a different sort of heat.

Sometimes, I caught him looking at me. I was never sure what it meant or if there was a meaning. He was leaving soon. Why would he want to start something with me and risk angering his family?

Why would he want to start something with me at all?

Dave was a decent-looking guy, but he was no Austen. He didn't have Austen's jawline or his broad chest and shoulders or those strong legs. Theo was in the same category as Dave, and while Jake was handsome, he wasn't the whole package either. Probably because I knew he was empty inside, just like Theo, and Dave could fit into that category.

It was bad enough being physically attracted to Austen. Liking him as a person and wishing my former relationships had possessed the same amount of self-awareness and maturity was downright lethal.

The man was sexy inside and out. I didn't just look forward to uncovering and restoring the beauty of that house and being able to enjoy some of the physical labor, but I sprinted across the lawn each morning because I got to do it all with Austen. Monday through Friday, it was us. A team.

He was going to Cody's for the Fourth. I wouldn't have to go the entire weekend without seeing his broad shoulders or that stubbled jaw.

I bet any girl he invited over would get air-conditioning and orgasms. A summer dream right there.

I wasn't that girl. Even if he offered, I was making

better decisions based on my past. I was maturing. How many times did I have to prove I was better off single?

But tonight, I was hot and horny and had a handsome neighbor who gave me a cold beer and listened to me moan about my ex.

I crept my hand down my stomach. His window was shut. Mine was open, and Catherine wasn't home. I wouldn't have to worry about her hearing the vibration or how loud I moaned. Energy would be released, and I would be able to fall asleep easier.

Win-win, right?

A steady throb between my legs had hounded me all week. Tonight, I'd do something about it. I got my little wand out of the nightstand and wiggled out of my underwear. I didn't need a lot of stimulation, but sometimes I missed that feeling of fullness. Theo had been intimidated by my vibrators, and I'd let him convince me they weren't needed. He should've been taking notes, and I shouldn't have tossed them, but I'd been fresh off a divorce and let another small man knock me down to his level.

Stroking a finger over my clit and testing the wetness, I let out a moan. God, that felt good. To be a little noisy. To not worry about anyone or anything intruding on my time. When I shut my eyes, my imagination went wild. It was Austen creating the heat around me. Austen in bed beside me, his weight solid next to me. My hot neighbor, who was sliding his finger through my seam to wet it—

No, Austen wouldn't need to. He'd make me soaked. I'd be so fucking wet all he had to do was whisper my name or that perplexing nickname of Honey V in my ear and I'd be toast. I'd be his, and he'd know what to do.

Another moan left me. He'd know what to do with his big fingers and his strong hands.

I spread my legs wider. I didn't need the vibrator when I had fantasies of Austen in my head. Dreams that were so real.

My breathing picked up, and I let the moans go as I imagined him moving over me, his heavy weight settling between my legs. He'd be huge. What I'd glimpsed in the loose fabric of his shorts was not wishful thinking, and more than muscles filled out his jeans.

A wave of pleasure washed over me, a different heat that I didn't mind. "Yes," I whispered.

He wouldn't shove into me but take his time filling me. He'd be intentionally slow and teasingly firm. He wouldn't randomly thrust, only caring about his pleasure. Oh no, my veteran handyman would get his pleasure from my arousal, from the way he pushed me toward a powerful climax.

I dipped two fingers inside me. The sensation helped my brain fill in exactly what Austen would feel like. "Yes," I said a little louder.

My hips were rolling and bucking against my hand. I kept steady pressure on my clit and thrust my fingers in and out. What usually took several minutes on my own now only needed a fraction of the time, thanks to Austen's smoky, vetiver scent. Fantasizing about how he'd feel catapulted me over the top.

"Yes." I gasped, so lost in my own touch I didn't even track what I was doing to myself. I reacted to my thoughts, to my assumptions, of what Austen would do. My climax bore down on me, and I arched against the mattress. My shirt rode up, and my peaked nipples strained for the ceiling as if Austen's mouth was poised to suck one pearly bud between his lips.

"Oh god," I groaned and dug into the mattress.

What if he was the one pumping in and out of me? What if it was his hands, his mouth, and his cock in me and not just phantom thoughts?

What if— My body couldn't take more speculation. I exploded quicker and stronger than I had since... I couldn't remember.

"Austen." His name left my lips in a breathy shout, not loud, but not as quiet as I would've done had I not been swept away.

I collapsed, my damp hand resting on my belly. My ragged breathing filled the air. I was alone. Just me. And I'd called out my neighbor's name while masturbating.

If I looked in the mirror, would I be flushed from embarrassment?

He wasn't just my neighbor. He was my best friend's brother. All my friends' brother. If I fucked around with him and got my heart broken, I couldn't make a clean break. I'd be hearing about him. No matter where he moved after he sold the house, I'd probably still see him when he visited.

My heart rate slowed to normal while I stared at the shadows on the ceiling. If imaginary sex with Austen was that powerful, I needed to make sure I stayed away from him. I couldn't handle tangible sex like that and walk away with my heart intact. Not if he was the one playing with my body. He was too decent of a guy but also as seemingly against commitment as I was. I'd be playing with fire.

The squeak of a screen door carried through the night, followed by the click of a door closing. My heart clambered into my throat. I sat straight up, yanking my shirt down. Shit.

Was that from his house? More importantly, was he going in or out?

Shit, shit, shit.

If he'd been outside, had he heard?

Oh, god. Panic turned to humiliation. He'd seen me in a pose in full daylight that only my gynecologist had ever witnessed. What if he knew I'd gotten off to thoughts of him?

I crept out of bed, snagging my glasses and pushing them on, and peered out the window, staying low. No lights were on in his house. I released a gusty breath and lay back down. He must've just gone outside. I could be fairly sure he didn't hear me. I was not going to ask him this time.

Nine

VIENNE

I settled Teddy in the backyard with food and water and put a new sleeping pad in his small doghouse. He and his little bladder would have to be outside while I was at the party. I was about to leave for Cody and Tova's when there was a knock. I wasn't expecting anyone.

When I opened the door, I was faced with a freshly showered Austen in a tight shirt like what he wore to work on the house and a nicer pair of worn jeans that loved his frame more than his other sets. His cowboy boots were also less scuffed but well used, and his Knight's Oil Wells ball cap was a different one than he used for work and he wasn't wearing it backward.

Heat curled through me, going straight for my face. I wished I wore my glasses to hide my flush. I could blame the lack of AC, but I'd been tormenting myself with whether he heard me or not the other night.

"Austen." His name came out husky, like I was ready to yank him in and strip him down.

I was, but that wasn't why he was here.

His gaze dropped down my body but lifted immediately, like my linen shorts, Birkenstock sandals, and loose pink shirt weren't what he fantasized about when he got himself off. "Wanna ride together?"

"Oh." No.

Yes, absolutely.

But...did he hear?

I was dying to know, terrified to find out, but I also wasn't going to make the mistake of asking. Ignorance was bliss. "Might as well. There'll be enough vehicles clogging their driveway."

"I'm nothing if not efficient."

I grabbed the bag with the bowl of pasta salad and the drinks I was bringing to add to the community cooler.

"Bacon ranch?" he asked, taking the bag from me so I could lock the dead bolt.

"You aren't more interested in the kind of beer I'm bringing?"

"I know you have a taste for cider, but I can buy that anywhere." He gestured for me to go down the porch. I'd have rather watched his long legs chew up the stairs, but I also couldn't ogle him like my eyeballs were starved for the sight of him. "I can't get your food anywhere."

He could get it anytime while he was around. I wasn't thinking about the food. *Naughty, Vienne.* "I can show you how to make the salad."

"Then you wouldn't be handling my bacon."

Laughing, I climbed into his pickup, grateful he had a way of putting me at ease when he had no clue what was going on in my head. His smell surrounded me in the cab, and I sank into the passenger seat. The interior was neat and clean. He kept his surroundings uncluttered like he was ready to pull stakes and move on from anything.

He kicked the pickup into drive.

"How do you like it here? What do you think of Crocus Valley?" I asked, watching the town I loved roll by. Sure, there were frustrations with living anywhere, especially when you'd been a precocious kid and you returned as a single mom. "I know you're not planning to stay, but compared to everywhere else you've been, what's it like?" Now I was prying like Catherine had done at the firepit.

He lifted a shoulder and draped his wrist over the steering wheel. "It takes number one. Like home but without the shitty memories."

"Really?"

He slid his gaze toward me, and my stomach flipped over the way his ball cap shaded his eyes. "Is it so surprising? I was never a city guy, but living around a big city was necessary. I went where I was told."

"I guess. You're going to LA willingly, so I assumed you preferred city life." We passed the grocery store. The little department store that was so small and packed with items that you took a display out trying to turn down the next lane. "It's just that a lot of people move away from North Dakota and shit talk it, but it always comes off as seeming like they're punching down to make themselves look stronger. And when out-of-staters move here..."

He snorted. "Everything's backward and uncultured. It's like that in Montana—in the Montana that's not by the ski resorts."

I nodded. "Again, it's like they're making themselves look better. Dave was bad about it, and he never lived here. He talked like he was so worldly. I got upset once and snapped at him. 'Sorry, Dave, but that Cancun resort we went to for our honeymoon was a tourist trap. You've never been in the real world outside of Denver.'"

"You told him that?" He was smiling, delighted I had spoken my mind. How refreshing.

"Yep, when I said I was moving home after the divorce. He didn't want fifty-fifty custody because his job was too important, and he didn't think our daughter should be raised by strangers. He threw a fit that Catherine would be raised in a town with one streetlight."

He glanced at me. "Crocus Valley doesn't have a streetlight."

"I know. He's a dumbass."

He laughed, a deep, pleasing sound. "Dave the dumbass."

I grinned. Austen's support meant a lot, and I didn't realize it until now. My parents were great, but they didn't understand why my marriage failed, not really. Yes, I'd had a part in the dissolution. The problem wasn't all Dave, but ultimately, we weren't compatible. The way I wanted to live wasn't how he wanted his wife to be, and he'd tried to bully me into place through the divorce process. He wanted subservient and doting, but those roles were suffocating. His new wife might fit better, and now that they were having a kid, well...hopefully, she'd handle giving up her identity better than I did.

A few minutes later, he was pulling into Cody and Tova's. The fence Austen had mentioned he'd helped them put up cut one pasture into two and butted up to the goat barn. Another new small shed was next to the barn.

The location of the cookouts had changed to the shop and the large cement pad in front of the building. If it was windy, we ate inside, but today, the sun baked the land with only a light breeze to take the edge off.

Cody had two grills and some tables and chairs were set up. Eliot was already by the grills, the most likely place for anyone to find him. Cody's older kids were playing with Ro in the grass. Aggie's husband, Ansen, stood off to the side, chatting with Wilder. Aggie and Tova were heading our way.

When I hopped out, Tova started for me, grinning. "Hey, you two. You made it."

She made it sound like we were a couple. I didn't hate it. Last night's lightning-fast climax proved I was good at pretending.

I gave her a hug. She was a little shorter than me but managed to appear tall with her long, wispy skirt and a loose camisole top.

Aggie playfully punched her brother in the shoulder. "I hope you didn't pick up Vienne just so she could drive your drunk ass home."

He grinned, his eyes twinkling. "Work smarter, not harder."

Flutters ignited in my belly. He was joking, and somehow, I knew he wasn't using me to be his designated driver. His casual attitude was a huge turn-on.

When did I become this girl?

He got my bag out of the back seat, and instead of handing it off, he carried it to the three coolers that were lined in front of the shop. He was considerate, playful, and didn't take himself seriously when he had every right to. I could lose myself with a guy like him. More reason to keep my fantasies to myself—and close the window next time.

"I can do that," I said, ditching my friends and trotting to catch up with him.

"I got it. Go visit." He started tucking the bottles of beer into the ice.

Gah, this man. I was going to be a puddle if he kept nonchalantly taking care of me. Dave had hardly unloaded the groceries. "Okay. Well, help yourself to a drink."

He grinned again. "I plan to."

Before I did something crazy like swoon at the way he cocked his head to see me beyond the brim of his hat, I approached Tova and Aggie. They were walking toward the house.

"Anything I can help with?" I asked when I caught up with them.

Aggie smirked. The breeze blew some of her curly hair into her face. She tucked the strands behind her ears. "You can help by giving me all the dirt on what it's like working with Austen."

Sexually frustrating. Enjoyable. The best job I'd ever done. "Good."

They both gave me sidelong looks.

"Seriously," I insisted, and we entered the house. Shivers broke out over my skin. Ah, a place with working central air. "He's been really mellow to work with. I know it's been a little more than a week, but he doesn't question me, and that's a relief. He does what I ask, and he puts in a ton of extra time when I'm not there."

"I'm not surprised he's not lazy, but has he hit on you?" Aggie's lips curved up. "That's what I'm really asking."

The chill of the house was chased away, and the heat returned. "N-no."

Tova gasped. "He so has."

"Who has what?" Sutton asked, rounding the wall of the hallway that led to the downstairs bathroom. She wore cowboy boots with her jean shorts, like Aggie, but her hair was caught back in a long braid. A smile brightened her face when she saw me. "Hey, Vienne."

"We're learning that Austen hit on Vienne," Aggie answered. "We're now trying to figure out if anything's happened."

Tova held up a hand. "Totally not our business. Yes, we're shameless and we want everyone to be having great sex like us."

"Uck." Aggie shuddered. "I mean, you go, girl, but still. Those are all my brothers you're talking about."

Tova and Sutton were transparent about how good in bed their spouses were. Maybe that was why I could clearly imagine how it'd be with Austen. The shivers from earlier danced down my spine. "Nothing's happened." I fought off a blush and failed. "And no, other than some teasing that's just Austen, he hasn't hit on me."

His words wound through my head. *So keep that in mind.*

"You want him to?" Sutton asked.

"N-no." I didn't have a stutter. I had a raging case of wanting their brother. "It doesn't matter."

Aggie put a hand out. "To be clear, he is treating you well? Not pressuring you or making you uncomfortable? Since he got a view to the wonderland."

"Wonderland." I snorted and shook my head. "He'd be the perfect man if he wasn't keeping his roots from ever touching the ground."

They stared at me. My lungs froze. Did I really say that? These girls were too good of friends, and I was too honest with them.

A smile played over Tova's lips. "Should we be asking Austen if you're treating him well or making him uncomfortable?"

"I'm not talking about me." My voice pitched up. "I'm not interested in starting anything with any man." I was a lying liar. I wanted to start something hot and end it with stars exploding behind my eyes from that man.

"Well, it's good to hear my brother isn't a creep," Aggie said, but sadness was in her eyes. "I just wish he wasn't afraid to settle, but our parents did a number on us. Anyway, we get him for a couple more months, so let's get the rest of the food and go party."

I helped carry out butter for the corn on the cob, another pasta salad that I was not going to see if Austen ate more of it than mine, and whipped cream for the mixed berries Tova had prepared.

Cody and Eliot loaded burgers and hot dogs on the food table, and we sat to eat. I ended up sitting next to Eliot and across from Austen. I'd been aware of him at Knight family get-togethers before. He'd been good-looking Austen. Nothing like now. I could tell his voice apart from his brothers' more acutely. I knew his different smiles. How he scratched the back of his neck when he was deciding what to work on next. The way he dressed for work, for fun, and just to hang out. I was *aware* of Austen.

"How's my brother as a customer?" Eliot asked, his broad shoulders not nearly as inviting as Austen's.

I pretended to think. Austen lifted a brow, but humor danced in his dark eyes.

"He does most of the work, so I can't complain."

"Lots of women complain," Eliot said.

"Complainin' they can't get enough of me," Austen retorted.

Eliot and I laughed and moved on to a discussion of the house and the changes we were making. My inner geek went overboard describing how the paint color would have a modern tone but complement the age of the house and how I was able to adhere to the rustic farmhouse look with the new cabinets.

Austen ate a lot of my salad, his jaw muscles bunching and flexing as he watched me. He didn't shut down my speech or underplay the changes we were making. If he did speak, it was to agree with me or elaborate on how my ideas were fitting. *Definitely better than anything I could come up with*, he'd said. That'd replay in my mind for a long time.

After we ate, I helped clean everything up. My salad was gone. Cody and Tova put out camp chairs that were more comfortable than the folding chairs we'd used for dinner. Austen was sitting next to me, not closely, but maybe nearer than we'd ordinarily be.

Eliot tapped Austen to help with fireworks.

Austen rose with a groan. "Can't I drink beer and watch you do all the work?"

"You're the one with experience blowing stuff up."

"What'd you think I did for twenty years?" Austen was incredulous.

Eliot rolled his eyes. "Blow shit up?"

"I wasn't a combat engineer. I was military police. I checked a lot of IDs."

He was playing it off, but the tightness around his jaw said he did a ton more than check IDs and was a little irritated his brothers didn't know more specifics. I knew exactly how he felt. I was the same with my mom.

"But you did blow shit up during your time."

Austen's lips flattened. "Everyone does in training."

Eliot's gotcha grin made him growl while the rest of us laughed. This lighthearted dynamic was missing from my in-laws. I had wanted Catherine to experience what I had with my cousins when I was growing up. Now, I wasn't super close to my brother; I swore his wife detested me, and I avoided my parents.

I was forever grateful to be included in the Knights' festivities.

Cody's oldest kid, Grayson, jogged toward them. "Can I help?"

Austen exchanged an *oh shit* look with Eliot.

"You clear that with your dad," Austen said. "He'll get mad at me, I'll kick his ass, then I'll be in trouble with Tova."

Grayson's mouth dropped open. "You can't beat Dad up."

Eliot held his hands up and walked away. "I'm not getting in the middle."

The guys all went to the end of the driveway. Grayson must've made a deal with his dad. Cody and Austen joined them.

Tova shook her head. "I'll never get over the idea of setting off fireworks right next to my house."

Aggie kicked one boot over the other. She had Tripp cradled in a sling on her chest. "We don't have to worry about forest fires eating up our state."

"How do your animals handle it?" I asked.

"The horses don't seem to care. I think all the animals are pretty desensitized to loud bangs after all the construction we've done on the indoor arena." She grinned at Sutton. "But I have my vet on call."

Sutton nodded. "Soon, there'll be another vet on call."

My excitement rose. Sutton and Wilder had a list of camping trips to take, and she wanted more flexibility to go to Bismarck if she needed fertility appointments. "You found someone?"

She nodded. "I wish they could start before my conference next week, but she's moving from Wyoming. She'll start at the end of July."

I grinned. "Right in time for you to get married."

"Re-mar-ried," Aggie sang. "I can't wait. I wish you'd let us throw a party."

"We already did the big wedding." Sutton's gaze dropped like she was embarrassed to have so much attention on her. "We'll have everyone over at our place the weekend after."

"Good enough."

The next couple of hours, we watched the fireworks show the guys put on. The kids played with sparklers. I missed Catherine. She would've loved this. I hoped her dad was helping her make memories with him.

When the spectacle was done, my belly filled with giddiness. I rode with Austen here; I'd ride back with him.

I got into his pickup, my stomach more riddled with nerves than for any date I'd been on. He did the same thing as when we arrived and took over my tote bag and loaded my empty bowl and leftover beer bottles into the back of the pickup.

"Thanks for getting that, but you didn't have to get the beer," I told him when he was setting the bag on the back seat. "Cody and Tova could've saved it for next time."

I got that panty-melting smile from him when he climbed into the driver's seat. "Then what are we going to drink on the porch at night?"

A warm glow ignited in my chest, terribly close to my heart. "My turn to supply the refreshments?"

Another grin that fused me into the seat and we were off. Fireworks dotted the dark sky around us. Closer to the ground, tiny pinpricks of light flared and went dark. He was turning onto the highway back to town when I gasped. "Fireflies!"

He pulled to the side of the road and leaned over. "Where?"

I pointed to little sparks lighting the air by the stop sign. "There."

"Cool." The dashboard lights shone on his grin. "There's another."

He kept his foot on the brake, and we watched the fireflies flicker along various points in the ditch. He seemed as enthralled as me. I hated to keep comparing Austen to my other relationships, but Dave and Theo would've been annoyed at my outburst. Jake would've used the stop to get me in the back seat. Austen was enjoying the fireflies with me.

"Thanks for stopping," I said.

"It's like a little bit of magic in the pasture," he murmured.

I turned to look at him. He leaned on the console, gazing out the window. The brim of his ball cap was down, and since it was dark out, his face was more concealed than ever. A tremble traced under my skin, swinging deeper and centering between my thighs. So damn handsome.

With a little turn of his head, he met my gaze. Our faces were closer than they'd ever been. "I should get you home. We've got an early morning tomorrow."

I was in a spell, hanging on his voice, his scent, his proximity. He looked away, put the pickup in gear, and turned onto the highway.

Disappointment had never been so heavy, so smothering. The night by the firepit must've been a fluke. A weak moment for him. We'd both clung to our senses like we should.

He pulled in front of his house and retrieved my bag before I did. I held my hand out, but he lifted his chin toward the house. "Go on. I'm programmed to walk the lady to the door."

Good thing he'd shown zero interest all day, or I'd get my hopes sky high before I reached the top step.

We didn't talk the whole way, surrounded by the sounds of the night and the dull bangs of fireworks going off around town.

"Well," I said as I unlocked the door. "Thank you for driving."

"No problem." He gave me the bag and I dug my keys out.

I pushed the door open and was about to step in when he said, "Hey, Vienne?"

Nerves fluttered through me. I wouldn't be strong enough to say no if he leaned in to kiss me. I wanted it too bad. I wanted to know what those lips felt like. That scruff.

"Yeah?" I asked, breathless.

He started to wander toward the stairs. My heart blinked out as quickly as a firefly.

"Have a good night. And leave your bedroom window open so I can hear you come with my name on your lips again. Even better if you let me watch."

Austen

Would she slam her window shut as soon as she crested the stairs? I'd said what I said and left her shocked with the front door hanging open, letting mosquitoes in the house. Then I'd gone into my house and went straight upstairs.

I had no idea how she reacted to knowing I'd heard everything last night. Every. Agonizing. Moan.

I gave her time to put Teddy to bed. Now, I perched at my open window in a dark room, like a kid waiting for Santa Claus. Fresh, humid air filtered in, and I didn't care if I was trying to cool off the whole neighborhood.

Would she do it?

The lights flipped off downstairs.

Was she taking her time on purpose? Did she believe me? All those moments I thought she was checking me out and then decided I was being ridiculous had vanished last night when I caught low moans and finally my name.

My goddamn *name*. I knew what a woman climaxing sounded like. I'd been hard enough to dent steel as soon as she finished that I'd had to go inside or risk being busted masturbating in my backyard.

The heat wrapped around me. I stripped my shirt off

and tossed it on the bed. I propped a hand on the window frame and waited.

A hallway light flicked on, then off. The bathroom light.

Goddammit, did I scare her off?

She wasn't going to sleep with you anyway, jackass.

But would she get herself off to me again? Or would she shut me out because working together wouldn't be the same after this? Would she quit my renovation?

She would be worth the risk. I just knew it.

A few minutes ticked by. How long before I was considered a pervert?

The bathroom light turned off. I tensed. Was the bedroom light next?

Wait, did I see movement in her bedroom?

She appeared, a shadowed form on the other side of the glass. I held my breath. We stared across at each other. Was she going to shut the window and flip the blinds closed?

Fuck, she was hot. Those dark glasses were sexy as fuck. She wore a light pair of thin underwear, and I could almost make out the outline of her pussy. Her tiny little tank top with spaghetti straps would tear so easily if I ripped the fabric off with my teeth.

Lust slammed into me, and my gut clenched. I'd been trying to tell myself there was nothing between us, that it couldn't go anywhere, and I'd been denying how fucking hard I got for this woman.

I gripped the wooden frame. My fingerprints would be in the damn thing. I didn't shift position, afraid the scrape of my boots on the bare wood flooring would startle her.

She opened her window and watched me, her chest

rising and falling. Her little tits would be a perfect mouthful. I could suck the whole thing into my mouth and tongue the nipple. My lips tingled with the imagined feel of her.

"What are we going to do, Honey V?" I growled low. Our neighbors didn't need to hear us. Anyone outside, lighting fireworks or walking between the houses, didn't need to witness what was for me, what was mine.

Her hair was still pulled back. The only movement I could make out in the glow of the streetlights was her pulling her lower lip between her teeth. Then she curled her fingers around the hem of her top and yanked it over her head.

"Jesus." My breath whooshed out of me. Creamy flesh with peaked tips. Perfect teardrops. My palms itched with the imaginary feel of her nipples rubbing against them. "Touch your tits for me."

She hesitated, but then she did as I ordered.

"Did you think about me the whole time last night?"

She nodded.

Fuck yes. I flicked the fly of my jeans open, shoved the zipper down, and freed my cock. I hissed at my own grip. I could picture her small hand wrapping around me, pumping and squeezing.

I couldn't see her eyes in detail, but the way she held her head, she was watching me stroke myself.

"I didn't think you heard." Her voice carried the distance, soft and shy but also needy.

"I heard it all. Every goddamn moan." This wasn't going to last. Jerking off in a different building than Vienne was enough to make me blow in seconds. "Put your hand on your pussy. Show me how you played with your clit."

My grip tightened, choking my dick, as she slid one hand down. Her fingers disappeared inside her underwear. I'd tell her to rip the damn things off, but I didn't want her to stop. She'd met me at the window. She'd taken her shirt off. Fear perched heavily on my shoulders that she'd come to her senses and realize we were crossing a line.

But then we'd already stepped over. No going back to not knowing the small full rounds of her tits or how her stomach sloped toward her hips. No erasing my memory of her hair off her shoulders and her body free of jewelry.

"Are you wet, V?"

"Yes." She gasped.

"Because of me?"

"Yes," she moaned, the muscles of her forearms flexing as she played with herself.

I had to release my hold on myself in order to stroke up, then down. Up, then down. "Are you close?"

"So close." She massaged her breast with her other hand. How hot was her skin? How soft? Was her clit soaked and swollen, begging for my touch?

"What are you imagining?" My grip on the window frame was the only reason I was still standing.

"That you're behind me. Doing this."

Christ, I wanted to be. Would she ever let me?

I couldn't think about the repercussions. We were too far into this private show for each other.

"I'd put my mouth on you." I didn't recognize myself. My voice was rougher, deeper, thick with arousal. "I'd suck your little clit into my mouth. I bet you're the perfect mix of sweet and salty."

The soft moan I'd heard last night came from her again. "Austen."

"There it is. Are you close, Honey V?"

"That name," she groaned.

If only she knew why I called her that.

Even uttering it made my balls tighten, jettisoning me toward climax. I was *not* coming before her. "Come for me."

She tipped her head back and rolled her nipple between her thumb and forefinger. She rubbed her clit harder, more frenzied. A tremble rolled over her body. Such an erotic fucking sight. My strokes were getting faster and more desperate, my release imminent.

"Now," I demanded.

"Austen!" Her body shook, her head back and her mouth open.

My orgasm hit as soon as hers did. Hot cum squirted into my hand. I couldn't release the window frame, or I'd hit my knees. She'd worry, and I was straining too hard to keep my eyes open and watch her finish coming.

I trembled, my cock oversensitized, my hand still wrapped around it. I'd made a mess I'd worry about later. How was Vienne?

Her shoulders rose and fell. She was breathing so loud I could hear her.

"Good girl," I said. I didn't want the night to end. I'd rather take her to bed and bury myself inside that wet pussy of hers. I'd like to wake up to her. Again and again.

How long would I get to experience her before I left?

The jolt of reality got to me, but I wasn't going to walk away and leave her confused. I pushed off the window, my stiff body protesting. My stay in Crocus Valley was as temporary as any other place I'd lived, but that didn't mean I wouldn't take what I could get. "Taste yourself for me."

Her movements were jerky, hesitant. But she raised her fingers to her mouth. I squinted, wishing I could see how pink her tongue was when she licked her fingertips.

A ragged groan left me. Not only were her tits perfect, but she did everything I asked. Desire kept that mind of hers from getting in the way. Same with the way she'd been treated in the past. She'd second-guess everything and try to forget. She'd distance herself and might even quit. I couldn't have that.

"Go to bed, Vienne." She stiffened so hard it was visible in the dark. "In the morning, if you start to question what we did, stop. We can pretend this never happened." I took my sticky hand off my still-hard cock and stuffed myself back in my pants. "And tomorrow night, meet me back here. I want to hear you come again."

꒦

Vienne

I stared at Austen's front door. After crawling into bed last night and staring at the ceiling, wondering if I ruined my biggest financial opportunity over a peep show, I still wasn't sure how to face the day.

We could pretend this didn't happen.

Could I?

I'd seen his dick. I'd seen him ejaculate. Could I pretend he didn't order me around until I orgasmed?

I had to try for two reasons. I needed this job. And I didn't want to be done with Austen.

I entered. He was at the island, drinking a protein shake, back in his work jeans, rough boots, and thin shirt.

"Morning, Honey V." His smile was lopsided, and the heat in his eyes wasn't completely smothered. Despite that, there was a tension that rode across his shoulders. "Ready to work?"

It was a loaded question. Was I going to pretend I wasn't going to meet him at the window so I could hear him tell me to put my finger on my clit again?

My heart rate angled up. A flush was crawling up my neck. How would I address what we'd done?

Hey, how'd you sleep?

On a scale of one to ten, how was your climax?

Should we play music tonight?

Acting like it was normal sounded the best. "I'm ready to work."

His smile widened. "Perfect."

Ten

VIENNE

I was out with the girls again. Thursday night. We'd already finished with darts, and I was trying to act normal, like tonight was any other night.

Pretend this never happened.

I could not. But I did. Every damn day. I woke up, went to work with Austen. We'd finished the upstairs hardwood and started on the main level. He talked about his family, and I'd pass on updates from Catherine and how she and her dad and his wife went boating.

And every damn night, I was at the window, watching him jerk off while he watched me masturbate at the sight of him.

Two days ago, my central air had been repaired. Yet before I went to bed, the window was open so I could hear Austen groan and growl and call me Honey V. Each time, I followed his instructions to the letter. I might be the one giving myself pleasure, but it was nice to be his puppet, to not be completely in charge of everything.

"Vienne?"

I jerked my gaze off my beer. Summer Sunset. The kind of beer we'd shared on the deck. "Sorry."

"Daydreaming about someone specific with that blush on your face?" Tova asked. Aggie's brows rose and Sutton tipped her head, her gaze brushing across my cheeks.

"Nope. Just wishful thinking." I playfully scowled. "Not about anyone specific."

I was very specific.

"How's work been?" Aggie asked.

"Good." Oddly relaxed and fun. We acted like we left work and didn't see each other until the next morning. "We're making good progress."

"I told you, you have to slow down, or he's going to leave sooner," Aggie said. "I like having him around. Cody does too, and not just because he's going to help cut hay this weekend."

"Wilder's taking him out tonight. I think he's also going to miss Austen when he leaves." Sutton opened her mouth to continue, then shut it and looked at her phone. "Oh. They're here."

The door to the bar opened, letting in evening light from outside and brightening the dim bar. Two tall figures stepped through. Wilder's gaze found Sutton right away and warmed. Austen was behind him, his hair falling over his forehead. He looked at me, and the corner of his mouth lifted.

I cinched my fingers around my beer. God, he looked good in his long-sleeved, button-down shirt with pale-yellow stripes and crisp blue jeans. Ruggedly dressed up. Wilder was the same, but my attention had never been drawn to him.

The guys crossed to us. My belly clenched and a quick, wistful thought passed through my head. What would it be like if I was his girl, and he walked toward me like Wilder was zoned in on Sutton?

"Oh, no," Aggie said with sweet sarcasm. "My brothers are going to make me go home so I don't get into trouble."

"We could never make you do anything," Wilder retorted, slipping an arm around Sutton and kissing her cheek.

Aggie shrugged. "True. I'd tell you two to get a room, but I know you have one and you use it."

A flush graced Sutton's cheeks. "A lot."

Tova snickered.

Wilder straightened. "I just came to say we're not crashing girls' night. Purple Petal was busy, and we didn't want to hog a table."

"The bar's big enough for all the Knights," Tova said. "Besides, it'll be nice to see a guy hit on Sutton and actually succeed."

"She still makes me work for it." Wilder grinned. "Ladies." He tipped his head and wandered away.

"I'd say not to enjoy yourselves too much, but where's the fun in that?" Austen's gaze lingered just a little longer on me before he followed Wilder.

"I saw that," Aggie murmured toward me.

I focused on my beer. "There's nothing to see."

"The energy that sparks between you two..." Tova shook her head, the dark hair in her bun bouncing. "It's like the Fourth of July all over again."

"What do you mean?" I played ignorant as best I could. Austen and I couldn't stay casual once friends and family were involved. Then we'd have to have a reason for what we were doing other than it felt really damn good. The nightly window rendezvous was a damn good stress release.

"You sure you're only working together?" Aggie's tone was innocent but also prodding.

I shrugged. "I'm not risking my reputation." I put it on the line every night this week. "I might have a chance to work with Jim again this winter on a big job for a client who would be an excellent launch pad. But she's sensitive about women around her work-from-home husband. I need that job."

Sutton frowned. "I hate that it's a problem. You two are adults."

"And he's your brother," I said to them. "I can't mess around with him and then make all your future family gatherings awkward." Like tonight—everything was normal. I treasured my friends, but I'd had enough people tell me what they thought of me and my relationship decisions over the years. No one knew about Austen, and that was the way I preferred it.

Aggie leaned on her elbows on the table. "But you are interested?"

The heat in my cheeks bloomed. "How could I not be?" I'd give her that.

Sutton cut her gaze toward the guys, who were thankfully far enough away to keep from overhearing. "That's exciting and depressing all at the same time."

"I can't believe he's leaving." Tova frowned. "Can't he set up a security company here?"

"Not enough Hollywood stars to protect," Aggie said.

"And all the oil-rich people conceal and carry their own protection," Sutton added.

I laughed. "If he was staying, that would definitely rule him out. No relationships. Remember? At least until I land that job and I'm finished with it."

"What if the right guy came along?" Sutton asked, a slight frown on her lips.

I shook my head. Men were not going to have too much influence on my confidence. "I don't want to find out one more guy isn't who I hoped he would be. It's too hard on me."

"I totally get that." Tova propped an elbow on the table. "It's scary even when he is the right guy."

The others nodded. I wanted to be cheered up. Yay, they agreed with me! Instead, I was more disheartened. What if I missed the right guy?

I mentally dismissed the question. I was not open to Mr. Wrong or Mr. Right. My daughter and my work were my priorities.

A group of bridesmaids piled into the bar. Aggie asked Sutton about her upcoming vows to Wilder. They were off the topic of me and Austen, and with no spotlight on me, my tension drained away. We chatted for a little longer. Customers came and went. I was aware of Austen and Wilder, and it was a struggle not to let my gaze land repeatedly on Austen.

Sutton glanced around. "Are there more women in here than usual?"

"Besides the wedding party, I think there's a family reunion in town," Tova answered. "A big one."

Two women sauntered in Wilder and Austen's direction. Sutton was in the middle of telling us about the conference she was going to when she cut off, her eyes turning to steel. I knew how she felt.

The women stopped by the guys' table. Neither were dressed like the girls at any family reunion I'd been to, with jean shorts that showed the curve of their asses and a low-cut, snug top. While I loved the sleeveless shirt of the blonde, jealousy ignited inside me. Her cleavage was in Austen's face. The redhead had on platform sandals, and they made her long legs look sinful.

Stomach acid clawed upward.

"I know Wilder's not going to be interested," Sutton whispered, "but I still want to jump them."

I caught myself before I said *me too*.

"He's not wearing his wedding ring yet either." Sutton sighed. "We're both waiting until we say our vows again."

Just then, Wilder tipped his beer toward our table. The blonde looked over her shoulder. Sutton held up her can of hard cider like she was clinking a cheers with him. The blonde's expression fell.

I was grinding my teeth together. Bypassing my usual hard cider had been a good choice. I'd have crushed the can by now.

I was about to look away, not willing to watch Austen take up what some other woman was so willing to offer when he raised his bottle in my direction. He'd ordered a Summer Sunset too.

My pulse fluttered, and I automatically lifted my bottle like Sutton had. The corner of Austen's mouth curled up.

"Nice," Aggie hissed next to me. She cupped her hand around her mouth. "Get a room!" she called.

The redhead's shoulders fell. She and the blonde smiled at the guys and walked away. They didn't look our way as they wove through the bar and back to their group.

I lifted a brow toward Austen. Did I look as relieved as I felt? He shrugged and dipped his head to indicate Wilder.

A tiny tendril of disappointment couldn't be helped. He was saying he was here to visit with his brother, not get laid.

"Thanks for saving him," Tova said, turning a speculative look my way. "But I can't help but wonder if it isn't wishful thinking on Austen's part."

"LA," was all I said, denying how damn relieved I was.

I didn't care why Austen rejected the redhead. All I cared was that he was back at the window tonight.

Vienne

It was that time. I was at home and pacing in front of my bedroom window in the dark. I'd left when my friends had. Wilder and Austen had stayed behind, and a part of me was afraid Austen had decided the redhead was a better option. He might get to be in the same room when she orgasmed. He'd have a partner who did more than watch him fist that magnificent erection.

Heat spread from my center out. What would he feel like inside me?

Why wasn't I finding out?

I hadn't undressed. I usually met Austen in my sleep top and underwear. Last night, I'd had my shirt off before I got in front of the glass. Tonight, my belly was in knots. Would he skip our usual session and hang out with Wilder? Find someone else?

My stomach rolled over, and I was back in that parking lot, seeing Jake minutes after he'd been with someone else. I shook my head, but the taste in my mouth was sour.

I tugged the hem of the loose navy top I had on with my linen shorts that went way below the curve of my ass. What would I look like in the booty shorts the redhead had on? Her fitted top? She had cleavage. I needed padding, lift, and a prayer to get cleavage.

The night Austen first told me to take off my shirt, I had wanted to run. My boobs weren't at my chin. They were small and, overall, uneventful. I had loved my lack of chesticles when I played volleyball. I hadn't had to worry about containment. My only mild concern was ripping a seam of my shorts in front of an audience. Then those years were done, and I hadn't thought about my breasts until now.

I hadn't been faced with attracting a guy with my assets, but the hunger that shone through the night from Austen had been intoxicating.

A light came on in the lower level of his house. He was home. Nerves flitted through my belly.

I worried my lower lip as the light blinked out. The house stayed dark, and my nerves vacillated from a flirtatious flutter to an anxious wiggle. Should I have left my contacts in? I liked crawling into bed after what he did and falling asleep to his imaginary arms around me. I didn't want to stop and take my contacts out.

I wasn't sure I'd be in the position to make that decision tonight.

He appeared, his shirt unbuttoned and in his jeans.

I couldn't see his expression, but he leaned into the screen. "Everything all right?"

Heat licked over my body. He was inspecting me, noting my clothing. More like the fact I was dressed. He could've been with another woman tonight. Had he turned her down for more reasons than being with his brother? "You didn't have to turn her down."

He propped his hands on the ledge of his window. The tails of his shirt hung down, and the rest of the fabric draped his chest in shadows. "No, I didn't," he agreed.

Hurt sawed through the walls of my chest. What had I expected for an answer?

"I could've seen how far she'd go, maybe even brought her here. I would've shut the blinds."

"Thank you," I said, suppressing my sarcasm. I had to hear what else he said.

"And then what? Tomorrow morning, we pretend nothing happened like usual and tomorrow night at ten thirty we meet back here?"

No. I would've kept my window and blinds closed.

He scratched the back of his head. "Sounds like something Doctor-fucking-Jake would do."

My lips twitched. "He'd probably tell you to just call him Jake."

"I like what we're doing, V. Do you?"

"But this is all we're doing." I sank to my knees and

folded my arms on the narrow ledge of my window. "It can't be satisfying for you."

He continued leaning over but adjusted his stance. "I can make you come from a different house. Don't underestimate how heady that power is."

I laughed. "Point taken."

"I like what we're doing, Vienne," he reiterated. "I'm not interested in being a career playboy. I'm almost forty. I was active duty for twenty years. I had my years to indiscriminately fuck around. I understand why you want things the way they are. You're not a random woman, and I prefer what we're doing over bringing a stranger home."

His words crashed into my foundation as much as they smoothed the dirt over. I both liked what I heard and wanted to cry. "I do bookkeeping for Rudy."

He gave his head a little shake. I pointed to the engine shop. "He owns that?"

"He owns five of those. But his kid and her husband are taking over, and I'll be out of that income at the end of the year. I have a chance to land a big job with the contractor I was working with when you hired me, but she's paranoid about having women in her house."

His nod was slow, like the full realization of what I'd told him at the street dance was sinking in. "I understand what's at stake for you."

I let his supportive tone wash over me. "All that to say, I like what we're doing too." Anything with Austen was better than nothing.

"Don't get me wrong—you want to be in the same room when we come, I'll be over there in a second."

I wanted to sprint over there and race to his bedroom, but I was already conflicted enough after seeing him get hit on. I smiled, but the anxiety was still circling my insides like a shark. "I'm gun-shy, and you're suffering the consequences."

"The only thing suffering the consequences is my laundry. I've had to wash clothes every night so there's not dried spunk lying around."

My giggles filled the night air. "Geez, Austen. File spunk under things I never thought I'd hear tonight."

His deep chuckle rumbled across the grass. I suddenly hated the distance between us. Yet I wasn't ready to strip and jump on that big dick of his. "Hey, Austen?"

"Yeah?"

"Can we have a beer on the deck?"

"Lucky for you, I brought a fresh six-pack home."

I smiled. A girl could fool herself that he stocked up in case I came over to talk on the deck after dark. I would be that girl.

"But, Vienne?"

"Yeah?"

"I won't touch you. I know you're not ready. But after we have our drink," he said, his tone was deep, rough, "I want you to put your feet on the patio table and make yourself climax under the stars."

Yes, please.

Austen

"That's it, baby. Ride it out." My voice was barely audible. We were closer than ever. I could touch her. I could feel how she shook through her peak. But I wouldn't.

That she was even over here after the dejected, uncertain picture she'd made in her window tonight was a miracle.

But she was on my back deck. My house light was off, and she was safely shadowed. To any neighbors who happened to peer out their windows at midnight on a Thursday night, we'd look like we were relaxing in the dark. She was facing my house, her place on her left, and me across the table to her right. Our empty beer bottles gleamed from distant houselights between us.

Her legs were relaxed open, her back delicately arched. Only I knew where her hand was. She'd placed her fingers exactly where I told her to.

Energy and lust vibrated through my body, zinging back and forth from the pulse in my throat to my groin. I was rooted to my chair only because I knew that touching her would break the spell.

She'd gone from taut to pliant—because of me. I had this much influence over her with nothing but my voice. If I could put my own fingertip on her clit, how quick would she orgasm? How powerful?

I nearly dropped to my knees and crawled to her. But goddammit, I was a man of my word. I'd stay where I was, and I'd enjoy the show.

A soft sigh left her, and she slumped in her seat. She rolled her head against the back of the chair to look at me. "Thank you. For the talk and for this." She started to move her hand.

"Stop."

She froze.

I leaned even farther forward than I was. "You don't have to come only once a night."

She blinked at me, but she didn't remove her hand

from her pants. A slow smile spread across my face. My muscles hurt to keep myself planted, but I wouldn't fucking move. She was getting off again, and I was getting a closer view than ever.

This position gave me hope that maybe soon she'd let me get my hands on her.

Eleven

AUSTEN

How long did the damn weekend have to be anyway? Vienne and I were back to window sessions. The backyard was too risky.

On Saturday, when I was done helping Cody cut hay, I worked on the trim upstairs. When that was done, I switched out the toilet. The sink would get replaced with a vanity sink, and the shower insert over the existing tub would get installed later this week, completing the upper level.

The main level was bare, and next week would be full of sanding. We'd do more with the baseboards and crown molding and install the new fixtures in the bathroom. But we'd finished the drywall on the partition Vienne had demoed. After the main-level floors and bathroom were done, then we'd replace the cabinets and appliances.

I could redo the basement, but the musty smell was a constant battle. It was better off as storage space. A "do what you want" space for the new owners. The rest of the renovations would sell the house.

My phone rang. I peeked at the caller. Johnson.

Too bad I wouldn't get to enjoy the results of all my hard work.

A twinge of disappointment was followed up by guilt. He texted a few days ago saying he'd send me information on workspaces to lease and to call him when I'd had a chance to review everything. I'd forgotten to call him. "Knight," I answered.

"You gettin' sick of me already?" He laughed.

I winced. I didn't mean to answer like I was sick of him. I had a lot on my mind. Mostly Vienne. "No, man. I'm in the middle of a reno."

"Roger. Did you look at the info for the office building Morales found?"

Shit. "I haven't had a chance to go through everything."

There was a beat of silence. "You still good with this plan?"

"Yeah, I'm just busy. I know it's a shitty excuse."

"As long as you don't say it's a girl, then we're good." He laughed like it was crazy I'd be distracted by a woman. In the past, it would've been unusual.

"No. It's the house. New kind of work, trying to time everything right. You know how it goes."

"That I do. Can you check it out by Monday? There are a couple of digital signatures we need. We've gotta move, or we're going to be working out of our cars when you get here."

Funny how Vienne could tell me what to do, but getting timelines from Johnson chafed. I wasn't on his schedule while I was in Crocus Valley.

But I was more than an investor. The security company was about more than me. So, yeah. I was on his schedule. "Will do."

When I hung up, I blew out a breath and tossed the phone on top of the fridge.

I was dressed in fresh but old clothes, my typical work stuff, ready to work my Sunday away installing the new vanity. Walking through the barren living room, a buzzing caught my attention. My phone. Dammit.

Was it Johnson again? If I ignored him, he might start getting worried about me and then the other guys would call me. They didn't have the cushion I did.

I retrieved my phone and dread vanished. Vienne. Wait. She never called. Alarm made me fumble the phone while answering. "V?"

"Hey, Austen. Sorry to bother you. Um, Teddy's limping and his foot's all bloody. Of course, Sutton is out of town, so I had to call Jake."

My grip should've crushed the phone. "Okay."

"I hate to impose, but he's coming over and...could you be here when he arrives?"

Hearing about Doctor-fucking-Jake's house calls bothered me. Going to Vienne's house didn't. "Be right over."

"He said he couldn't get here for an hour. He's on another call."

I was already out the door and walking across the lawn. "It's no problem."

I knocked on her door.

The other end got quiet. "Is that you?"

"Open the door and find out."

She disconnected, and when the door swung open, her expression was shocked but pleased. She was wearing jean shorts and an old shirt with a picture of a volleyball on it. Her hair was tossed on top of her head like I'd seen Catherine do. I liked this look on her.

I grinned. "How's the pup?"

"Whining, bloody toes, but still wants to play fetch."

"How can a dog with such short legs want to play fetch?"

"I had to buy special tennis balls that'll fit in his little mouth. Come in."

She led me to her mudroom. Teddy was inside, his butt wiggling and the toes of his front right paw bloody. "Do you know what happened?"

She dropped to her knees next to him and dug her fingers into the fur around his collar. "I think he chipped a claw down to the quick. Google makes it sound like he's going to die of a bone infection, and I got scared. Catherine would finish her childhood hating me if something happened to him."

"You're a good mom."

"I'm working on being a good dog mom. He'll be fine, right?"

I sat down with my back to the washer. Teddy wandered to me, his claws clicking. He sniffed my hands and arms, licking his tongue out like he was sampling various areas to get the full picture. "The point is that you don't know."

She pushed her glasses up and shoved her hair off her head. Her wrists were bracelet-free and she had no necklaces on. Small diamond studs glinted in her ears. "I keep his claws trimmed, but what if I could've done more? He's so little."

Worry was embedded in her eyes, and I couldn't stand it. I hated to see her fret about something she loved.

"When Mama was cooking one time, she had me at the table working on my math. Eliot was supposed to be doing flashcards or something. Now that I think about it, I was probably supposed to be helping him with his flash-cards." Her lips were curving up, and now that I was reaching the point of my story, I regretted opening my mouth. "Eliot got into the knife drawer. He'd handed Aggie a steak knife, and he was pretending to sword fight her. Mama lost her shit." Yeah. Not a happy story. "She was right there and hell still broke loose."

Compassion replaced much of the sadness, as if she read right through the moral and saw the problems underneath. "How old were you?"

"I was five. He was three, and Aggie was like one. Mama said I should've been paying attention."

"She lost her shit on you?"

"All of us. But she was terrified. I get it, but my point is that we're all tiny little beings with our own minds, even little puppies that want to play where they're going to get hurt."

She puffed a piece of hair out of her face. "He does love sniffing around those rocks. I'm considering digging every last one out." She picked at the hem of her shirt. "I've had my bad-mom moments with Catherine. It's hard when you're alone and feel like you have no support. I can't imagine five kids. You're all about two years apart, right? Bam, bam, bam?"

"Baby-trapping at its finest," I said grimly.

She recoiled. "Baby-trapping? She didn't want kids?"

"Not all of us. Definitely not beyond Wilder. Probably not beyond Cody." An ache started behind my rib cage. "'Five little burdens,' she used to say."

"Oh my god, Austen. That's awful."

The pain of the memory dulled, but embarrassment took over. I never talked to anyone about Mama. My siblings and I barely spoke of her. "I didn't come to take the attention off Teddy."

"It's okay to talk about it."

I didn't want to. But my fucking mouth wouldn't shut up. "I don't have many good memories of her. Or of Barns. Then Cody took over when she left. I was ten." My throat constricted. "Two days before my eleventh birthday."

"Austen," she breathed. "That's so..." She shook her head. "Your birthday must've been terrible that year. Does the day bother you?"

"My birthday didn't happen that year." Why couldn't I shut up? Her mouth dropped open. "Middle-kid syndrome gone wild." My joke fell flat.

"How often did that happen?"

"Only that one birthday."

"No, I meant middle-kid syndrome."

I wasn't getting into the traumas of my childhood more than I had. I'd left home for a reason, and it wasn't to revisit how I'd grown up. My siblings had moved on, and so could I. The summer day was gorgeous, and I was in Vienne's house. "Cody had a lot going on. It's fine."

"Austen."

"Why do you wear so many bracelets?"

She gave me a sheepish look and ran a hand up her arm as if she had at least five bracelets on. "I didn't wear much jewelry as a kid. I was outside on the ranch or playing whatever sport was in season. Then I settled into volleyball and didn't want my shit to get stolen in the locker room while I played. So once I was done..." Her mouth tightened, and regret flashed in her eyes. "They cheered me up. Then they annoyed Dave, and I was back to censoring what jewelry I wore."

"So after the divorce, you amped it up?"

She grinned, and I caught a glimpse of the energetic teen she must've been. "I did. Yes, it was partially to annoy Dave whenever we were in the same room, but now it's just because I like them. They make me happy, so I wear them. Catherine's given me charm bracelets, regular ones, and necklaces. They're kind of her thing to give me as a gift."

"The circle of life." She was a good mom. A mom who wanted her kid to feel special. My admiration for her grew.

"I told you something, so now it's your turn," she said.

"I already told you about my birthday. We're even." Spilling my guts was too easy, and I never thought I had many to spill.

"We could keep swapping."

I would like to learn more about her. A tempting offer. "The fallout of being the middle kid is that I got used to dealing with crap myself and moving on. No one was going to dote on me."

"Is that what you did in the military too?"

I shrugged. "If I needed to talk to a mentor or a professional, I did."

Her brows lifted, surprised. "Like a therapist?"

People were often surprised I was willing to seek help after a particularly hard deployment. A therapist also helped me verbalize why. "My dad put the onus of his issues on everyone around him. I wasn't going to be like that."

Her gaze softened. "You're a good man, Austen Knight."

I tried to be. "Good guys come in last."

"Do they?" Her question was full of curiosity. "Or do you narrowly miss someone who would take you for granted?"

"I think we get left alone." Which I was used to. Until Vienne. "About the same."

She gave my shoulder a small shove. "It is not. Good guys should come in first and last."

"Maybe the saying should be good guys make sure to come last."

I was enjoying her laugh when the doorbell rang. I disliked the disruption. I detested that it was Jake. Teddy's head lifted, and he trotted to the closed door.

"That must be him." She jumped up and nudged her way out of the mudroom without letting Teddy out.

Figured "Jake the Fucker" was early.

His voice reached me. "Hey, it's no issue. I'm around all weekend. I'll take a look and we can—"

The door opened, and his gaze landed on me. His expression went from chipper to dejected. "Oh. Uh, Austen, right?"

"Dr. Jake," I said, not bothering to keep the touch of smugness out of my voice.

Teddy was sniffing the vet's boots and jeans, which looked suspiciously clean for a guy who had supposedly been making a ranch call when Vienne had called. Since the smell of cologne was filling the room, I'd say I was right.

Did he think she made an excuse to call him over?

I rose and held my hand out.

His jaw was clenched as he shook it. "I forgot you two

were neighbors." He set a red, grungy bag down and kneeled by Teddy. "Let me take a look."

Vienne stepped around him and waited next to me. Her side brushed my arm, and I shifted closer. When we were working, I couldn't just linger. I was lingering now. If it suited her for Jake to think we were *together* together, who was I to argue?

I took it one step further and rested my arm behind her with my hand on the washing machine. On the outside, we looked like we were cuddling together while standing.

I didn't hate it. Vienne didn't put a stop to it.

Jake dug some items out of his kit. "Yep, he quicked himself, but it's not too deep. I'll give you some antibiotics, and he'll be good as gold."

When he stood, he brushed himself off. Yep, he'd dressed up to come over.

"I really appreciate you being able to make it out." Vienne folded her arms but didn't move away from me. "Sorry for the trouble."

Jake's smile was quick, his gaze clocking how closely I was standing next to a woman he was still interested in. "It's one of those things that's not an emergency until it is. You never know. It's been a busier weekend with Sutton out of town. I have to admit, it'll be nice when that new vet of hers starts." He adjusted his Dr. Jake's Vet Services ball cap. "So...you two...?"

I wasn't ready for him to ask directly. I scrambled for something to say that kept our nightly rendezvous secret but didn't make it seem like she'd invited me over because she feared she couldn't help herself when Jake was next to her.

"Oh, you know," Vienne said casually. "It's not something we have to classify. A busy career doesn't go well with labels and all that."

From the way chagrin flashed in Jake's eyes, I knew why Vienne had responded the way she had. He'd said the same thing to her.

Labels and all that? Jackass.

Yet...wasn't I more like him than her other exes? I wasn't promising commitment, just like Jake. We had a very sexual relationship too. But I was better to her than him. I had to be.

Jake's smile was tight. "Teddy should be good. He might bleed a little more, and if he continuously licks his paw, he'll have to wear the cone of shame until he heals."

Vienne walked the veterinarian out, and I waited in the mudroom. When she returned, she ushered Teddy to the back door.

"Come on, boy." She pushed the screen door open. "I'm sure you have to pee after all that excitement." She got Teddy down the stairs and let him play outside. I wandered into her kitchen. When she returned, she shut the back door and sagged against it. "Thanks for that."

"He came ready to treat more than a puppy."

She sighed and pushed her hair off her face. "I wouldn't have encouraged him. It was just nice not to have to stress about it."

"You never have to apologize for not wanting to be alone with a man. Good reply when he asked you about us."

She grinned. "You like that?"

There was a knock at her door.

"He must've forgotten something." She went through the house, and I stayed on her tail, far enough away to watch her hips sway.

The neighbor's dog started barking. Dobber. I had him to thank for that morning rear-end view of Vienne. I should toss some treats across the yard for him.

When Vienne opened the front door, it wasn't Jake on the other side. An older couple waited on the porch. The woman was slight, with light-brown hair heavily sewn with gray strands piled on top of her head. She was dressed like she could barrel race at a moment's notice, with a sleeveless tee and dusty blue jeans. The guy was the poster child for career ranchers. His eyes were pinched at the corners, and his skin was a ruddy tan thanks to years in the sun. He had a few brown sun spots dotting his face and neck, but with his long-sleeved, snap-button shirt, his arms were probably white as snow. He wore a multicolored woven belt and stood with a bowlegged stance that might be natural or a product of being raised on horseback.

"Oh, hi, Mom. Dad." Her voice was emotionless.

Surprise rose inside me. These were her parents? She was not excited to see them. A second perusal showed me the resemblance. Catherine looked a lot like her grandma, but she must have her dad's height since Vienne's mom was shorter than Vienne and her dad was several inches shorter than me.

"Vienne," her mom said warmly. She pulled a stiff Vienne in for a hug.

"Hey, kiddo," her dad said. "We came to have lunch at Hummingbird's but thought we'd stop by and see if you wanted to join us." His pale-blue gaze lit on me. "We didn't know you have company."

Where Vienne had fielded Jake's inquiry like a pro out for revenge, she clammed up in front of her parents.

I wasn't any more comfortable having her mom and

dad think we were fucking around before they even knew my name, so I stepped forward and stuck a hand out. "Austen Knight. I'm the neighbor she's working with."

"Oh, the heck." Her dad slapped his meaty paw against mine. I was a strong man, but his grasp could crush all my bones in one squeeze. "Dustin Wagner. This is my wife, Kayla. You're another Knight?"

I didn't have time to answer. Kayla skirted around Vienne and jerked me into a strong hug. I wasn't used to being manhandled by women.

"Nice to meet you." She drew out each word in a soothing way that made me think it really was nice to meet me.

"He came over to talk about his house." If Vienne wasn't careful, she'd sound like I was busted sneaking through her bedroom window, and her parents would know we were hiding something.

"She's been breaking a sweat with me," I added, having snuck through enough bedroom windows in my lifetime. "You'll have to come over and see all her hard work come to life."

Kayla's face lit up. Her eyes were a darker hazel and not as guarded as her daughter's. "Do you mind?"

"Mom."

"We never get to see you in action," Kayla argued, and Dustin bobbed his head.

"I work every day."

"Exactly," her mom said.

Vienne cocked her head, and I was glad I wasn't the only one who didn't seem to understand her mom's response.

I regretted opening a door Vienne didn't want to step through. I was figuring out how to tactfully rescind my offer when Vienne asked, "Are you sure you're okay showing them the place?"

I searched her gaze. She gave me a slight nod.

"No problem." I led them next door. Kayla oohed and aahed over the house that had been her inspiration for the house Vienne had grown up in. Then she stepped inside.

She covered her mouth. "I can't imagine what it must've looked like in here a century ago." Disappointment filled the look she gave Vienne. "You couldn't bring back the vintage style?" She shrugged. "I guess that takes a lot of research and expertise."

Hurt flickered through Vienne's expression. If I wasn't so experienced at keeping my distance from her, I'd wrap an arm around her.

"The old owner stripped out everything in the nineties," Vienne explained.

Dustin wandered around, tapping walls and peering into crevices.

Her mom shook her head. "I'm just saying...a little more intention and this house could be like a time capsule."

"I have to shoulder the blame." I jumped in, hating the wilt happening in Vienne's shoulders. We'd both put in a shit ton of work on the house. The upstairs was clean, simple but classy, and inviting. Definitely the nicest bedroom I'd ever slept in, and the home was no longer a drafty old farmhouse with no amenities. "Well, me and the previous owner. I thought it'd sell better with a nice blend of modern and older aesthetic."

"He made the right decision," Vienne added. "We made the right call for the house as it is today. People want the farmhouse style, not an actual museum replica."

Kayla glanced between us. She relaxed. "Of course. What the customer wants." She fluttered her hands. "What do I know? I'm just a simple ranch wife."

The sigh from Vienne was barely audible, but I caught it.

Dustin's boots hit the stripped-down floor as he walked toward us. "How about you have lunch with us, Austen? I'd love to hear more about what you're planning with this place."

And I'd love more insight into Vienne because after seeing her parents, the insecurity didn't just come from her exes. "Don't mind if I do."

###

Vienne

I was stuffed into a small booth with Austen's big body next to me. If standing close to him in the mudroom, practically tucked into his side, had been enough to rob me of breath, eating right beside him was downright intimate.

I rather liked touching him, having his body heat wrap around me and chase off the chill from the gale winds of the air-conditioning in Hummingbird's. I snuck peeks at Austen as he dipped fries in ketchup with his long, strong fingers that I'd had plenty of fantasies about. My peripheral vision was good enough that I could gawk at the lines bulging in the corner of his jaw when he chewed.

I'd come every night since the first window incident, but heat bloomed between my legs. I was turned on by my neighbor while out to eat with my parents in an old diner. The man was potent. Good thing he was fleeting. A girl might be tempted to throw out all her hard-earned sense.

The day had started with a vet emergency that brought Austen to the house instead of going the entire weekend without seeing him up close instead of in our respective windows—I could admit that now. Inviting Austen over so Jake wouldn't hit on me had seemed like an excellent reason at the time, but it hadn't been the root of my motivation. Yet it'd turned into Austen getting doted on by my mom and grilled like he was in an FBI inquisition by my dad.

Only Dad wasn't hounding Austen about his intentions with me or even about how well we worked together, which we did. Very well. No, Dad was all about Knight's Arabians and Cattle Company. He'd asked a little after the oil well side of the family business, and I didn't learn much more than what Aggie had described to me, but Dad was definitely geeking out over breeding, training, feeding, and caring for horses and cattle.

Mom listened just as avidly. I did too. I was raised on a cattle ranch, and I had done chores every morning. I helped move cattle, brand them, vaccinate them, haying and harvesting, and everything else involved. But I hadn't been obsessed with the lifestyle as much as my parents. I hadn't been interested in showing horses, doing 4-H for more than having been part of the fair every year, and I definitely wasn't interested in tying my income to cattle prices and hauling truckloads of animals to town.

I'd picked another finicky, pernicious career, thank you very much.

"You get out to Montana much?" Dad asked.

Austen shook his head. A tension built in his body that radiated toward me. "Not as much as I want to. I thought I'd be in Buffalo Gully more, bugging Eliot, but he has a couple more hired guys than he used to. He doesn't need me."

Yet Austen could've gone there anyway? Didn't he think Eliot would just want to see him?

What had Sutton said the other night? She'd told Wilder to take Austen out just because. Did his family only talk with him when they needed something? Otherwise, they forgot his birthday?

My parents could be smothering. Mom had zero faith or understanding about what I did. Shortly after I moved home, I'd started to feel like the pregnant college kid again, the girl who was treated like she shouldn't have made her own decisions. The girl who'd married a guy she hadn't thought about forever with until she got a positive line on a pregnancy test.

"You should come out," Mom said, leaning across the table to put her hand on his wrist.

Austen's brows knitted, and he looked at the contact like he didn't know what to do with a motherly touch.

"We've got a couple horses that could use riding," Dad added.

Mom patted the back of his hand and pulled away. "Oh, yes. Catherine's been so busy with her dance and volleyball she hasn't been out to exercise them. Her mother doesn't come out much more either."

Breathe, one, two, three...

How embarrassing. Was Mom worried about the horses losing all their rider training, or was she playing matchmaker? She'd been the one to tell me that hearing about me and Jake was embarrassing. That had been the kindest outburst.

First Theo and now Jake? You do realize you can't make Dave jealous when he doesn't live in the state?

I thought when you left for Denver, I wouldn't hear about your wild weekends anymore.

You do realize Catherine watches what you do, right? Do you want her following in your footsteps?

I had my own questions. Did Mom realize that Catherine and I could've visited and gone horseback riding but that I might have found more supportive people to hang out with?

How could I tell her I shouldn't bring Austen to their place because of how she treated me? How did I do it without making me the bad guy? It was a worry I didn't need. He wouldn't want to go anyway.

"I'd love to visit y'all," he said.

I gaped at him. His niceness was biting me in the ass.

He smirked at me. Incorrigible. "Whatdaya say, V? Care to do some trail riding this afternoon?"

Dad grinned. "Hell, I'll even pull out some food to grill."

"I have to confess, Mr. Wagner—"

"Dustin, please. We're not formal around here."

Austen's grin was quick and knowing. He'd been proper on purpose, like he wanted to win over my father and it was as easy as cherry pie for him. "I have to admit, Dustin, riding and grilling sound like a perfect afternoon."

My parents laughed. Of course, they loved him. Who wouldn't?

When Austen turned to me, the yellow in his eyes

twinkled. "How about it, boss? Mind if I don't get all the sanding done today?"

So tomorrow, I could watch his ass bent over all day? So I could see his powerful body go through the full range of motion while he got up and down from the floor? My libido had barely survived the upper level when I'd caught only bits of him working. "You're the one who's paying me."

All the extra work he was doing cut down my time on the job considerably. Probably his goal so he could leave sooner, and I wouldn't think about that.

His grin widened. "Then let's go riding."

"Oh, great. We'll invite Cullen over. Maybe Marly will feel up to coming." Mom rested her elbow on the tabletop and leaned toward Austen. "Did Vienne tell you she's going to be an aunt soon?"

"I think I recall something," Austen said, sparing me from a hurt and confused mom glare because, no, I hadn't said a thing. My parents' delirious excitement over my brother's new arrival this winter only sharpened hard feelings.

When I'd called her crying about Dave's decision to stop our family at one kid, she'd said *Maybe it's for the best, dear.*

Cullen was six years younger than me. His wife, Marly, was two years younger than him. But she was seven years older than I'd been when I got pregnant. She had an MBA and was a loan officer at the local credit union. She had "a good head on her shoulders" and was "so intelligent—did you know she has an MBA?"

I liked Marly well enough, but we'd never connected. There'd been no instant chemistry like I'd had with Aggie and Sutton and Tova. All were smart, level-headed women with good heads on their shoulders. So I didn't force it with my sister-in-law. Marly was polite enough to both me and Catherine, but that was the extent of it.

"A December baby," Mom gushed. "I can't wait. I'll get to be around for this one."

I stiffened. I'd been in Denver when Catherine was born, and Dave's family was a lot like Marly. I was nice enough, but I wasn't part of their network. I'd had little support outside of Dave, who didn't offer much, and that included from my own family.

"Congrats," Austen said before turning to me. "I have to get changed if I'm going to return to my roots today."

He was rescuing me. I took the lifeline. "Me too."

We slid out, promising my parents we'd be over in an hour. Austen and I walked the five blocks to our houses. I didn't offer much for conversation, and Austen let me mull over the visit.

"Thanks." I slowed my steps, not wanting the walk to end. "For covering for me."

"I know all about parents' digs that are meant to find weak spots. Barns was more blatant."

"I'm not close to Cullen. He made a comment once that he felt like an only child because I left home before he was twelve. Marly and I are more like acquaintances."

"Hard to be excited to be an aunt."

"Right? I'm happy for them, but I'm also dreading all the little comments. 'I'll get to be around for this one.'"

"I caught that." He flashed me a smile. "I've never had a baby, so the closest I can relate is all the forgotten birthdays."

"Austen, 'all the forgotten birthdays'? How many?"

"Officially, the one time. I shouldn't include when I

was an adult. My duty station changed so often it wasn't like they could keep track and send cards."

I squeezed his hand before I realized I had reached for him. I let go. "That sucks."

"It's not like giving birth alone."

"I wasn't alone. I had Dave whining about how uncomfortable he was in the hospital chair."

"A real pillar right there."

I chuckled. "It wasn't all bad. I didn't know any different at the time. It felt like life was supposed to be me and Dave against the world. If I look back, yeah, I could get really resentful about my former in-laws and my parents' lack of interest in Catherine's arrival, but I don't want to live like that. Which is probably why I've been keeping my distance."

"Gotcha." He walked me all the way to my house. "Meet out here in a half hour?"

"You don't have to go. I know you're on a timeline."

His gaze darkened like he hadn't thought of that. "Maybe I'll refigure how much I'm going to do before it's time to go. Your parents highlighted that I haven't seen Eliot like I should before I moved to LA."

"Whenever you need to go, let me know. If you're comfortable, you can always give me a key, and I'll work while you're gone."

His expression turned thoughtful. "Maybe I can sacrifice another weekend."

"You're the real boss. You can take a whole week."

The corner of his mouth tipped up. "I'm not going to be away from my window for an entire week, Honey V."

Twelve

AUSTEN

Being under the wide-open sky on the back of a horse felt good. Too right. Like coming home. I didn't know this horse from any other, but that was the perk of growing up breeding Arabians. I was used to climbing on the back of a new horse all the time.

Old memories were assaulting me left and right. Images of riding with my brothers when we were moving cattle. Open pastures and shallow ditches. Clear blue skies. Angry clouds and racing for home when we knew better.

I even remembered taking Aggie out when she'd had a shit day at school. Many of our days had felt oppressive and dull. All work and no play. But moments like this made me wonder if I was suppressing a lot of the good memories. There had to be more if one single horseback ride brought a rush of times I hadn't recalled in years, if ever.

The thoughts had been the only thing to take my mind off seeing Vienne as a cowgirl. She had plain brown cowboy boots that had seen plenty of work in their day. Her soft, worn jeans molded to her ass in a way her work jeans didn't even do, and her tank top was simpler, plainer than her dressier ones, and hugged her lean frame.

She even had on a tan felt cowboy hat.

Our horses didn't need us to tell them where to go. We had ridden around the fence line of their haying land and were now heading back. Tinkerbell, the bay she was on, and Ducky, mine, were content to walk next to each other straight for the barn. They knew the drill.

"I missed this," I told her.

She tipped her hat to glance at me. "Same." She focused ahead. "If I go, I have to take Catherine. She wasn't raised like me and isn't as knowledgeable about horses and riding. She's learning, but I'm also older and more aware of all the things that can go wrong. Mom thinks I'm shunning this way of life."

"When you're worried about your kid breaking her leg or her neck, it's a different experience."

"Right?" She shook her head. "I make Catherine wear a bike helmet when she rides, and I think my brother hemorrhaged the first time he saw. I even wear a helmet when I'm with her."

"Not today?"

She grinned. "Felt like being a rebel."

When we reached the barn, we slid off our mounts. I could've ridden all night, but as long as I got to hang with Vienne, I didn't mind that our time was up.

Dustin appeared out of the barn. "I've got them. You two go on in. Your mom wants Austen to meet Cullen."

Vienne frowned. "Are you sure? We can take care of the horses first."

"She's so stinkin' excited to have company." Dustin let out a good-natured laugh.

Vienne's brows lifted, then she narrowed her eyes. The sardonic twist of her lips said she didn't believe her mom was thrilled to have her around as much as me. "Let us at least put the saddles away."

After we stowed our gear and dusted ourselves off, we walked toward the house. The comforting smell of horse sweat seeped in. I missed that too. Would I be able to take time off to visit Eliot and help him at the ranch?

Maybe not for the first couple of years of the security firm.

Before a dark cloud descended on my perfectly nice day, I nudged her with my elbow. "Your mom's just as excited to have you visit."

"She's always more interested to hear about Aggie, Tova, and Sutton. To have a Knight over and be at the pinnacle of gossip?" She rolled her eyes. "She has to act quick before you move."

My skin suddenly felt like a million no-see-ums were biting at my flesh. Why was the idea I was transitory butting against my patience? Vienne and I weren't dating. We weren't messing around. We were neighbors and each other's private peep show. That was all.

Yet a new thought crept in... What if I wasn't always moving?

She squeezed my hand, but her touch gone before I could close my fingers around hers. She shot me a quick smile and jogged up the stairs to the deck along the back of the house. A sliding door opened into the attached kitchen and dining room.

In the house, voices filled the air. A deep voice that must be her brother. Women chatting. Vienne curled her hand around mine, and she towed me through a room stocked with homemade canned goods and winter gear.

Did she realize we were holding hands?

A warmth settled deep in my bones that felt so right my throat grew thick. I'd seen every inch of this woman from afar, but holding her hand left me tongue-tied.

The kitchen was on the other side. Conversation cut off. Kayla beamed. A pregnant woman who must be Marly was midword when she stopped with her mouth hanging open. The guy was close to my height and dressed much like me. He lifted his brows in the same way Vienne had done minutes ago. His eyes were a darker blue than his sister's, and his hair was more of a sandy blond.

"This is Austen," Kayla gushed. Her gaze dropped to our linked hands, and her smile widened.

Vienne yanked her grip off mine. I instantly missed her touch.

"Hey, Cullen. Marly. This is Austen. He hired me to help redesign the interior of the house next to mine that Mom loves so much."

Cullen narrowed his eyes and stuck his hand out to shake, his grip firm. I nodded toward Marly. She'd snapped her mouth shut, and her gaze jumped back and forth between me and Vienne.

"I'm going to go check on the grill." Kayla rushed to the sliding door and turned back with a grin. "You all just hang out and chat. When the oven beeps, get the potatoes out, please."

And she was gone.

Marly jerked a thumb over her shoulder. "I'm going to see if she needs a hand with anything."

I thought Vienne had downplayed how much distance was between her and Marly. I could thank sisters one, two, and three for befriending Vienne.

Cullen turned toward us, arms crossed. "I'm glad you moved on from Jake, Vienne, but what's this?"

I bristled. His attitude was out of place after hand-holding. I gauged Vienne's reaction, but I was tempted to say something. Only after growing up with four brothers and spending twenty years in the military I might not be that diplomatic.

She turned stiff next to me and put a hand on her hip. "Jake was none of your business."

Cullen grunted. "Jake was a bad idea, and you should've known it."

That was enough. Vienne had taken too much shit that I doubted Jake had to deal with. "I might be new here, but was everyone free to comment on all the women you dated before you met your wife?"

Cullen turned his appraising bright gaze toward me. "Excuse me?"

"I've only been in town for a couple of months, but how Vienne—and Catherine—have been treated about Jake pisses me off. Did she sign a waiver that said her dating life was open season? Does Dr. Jake have to explain his actions, or does everyone give him a pass because he has a big hairy set of balls?" I tensed. How badly had I stepped in it?

Her brother blinked at me. Irritation, anger, and then chagrin spread over his face. I relaxed. Finally, he looked at his sister. "Are his balls big and hairy?"

She screwed her mouth up and swatted Cullen's shoulder. "Shut up."

He danced backward, laughing and rubbing his shoulder. His smile dimmed, and he cleared his throat. "I'm sorry. He's right. You shouldn't have gotten crap for your epically bad taste. Did it affect Catherine?"

She nodded. "Kids at school. You know how it is."

He grimaced like he got it completely. "Well, I'm happy for you now." He lifted his chin at me. "You're already ahead of Jake in my book."

"Oh, no." Vienne waved her hands. "We're not dating. I can't date a client. People judge me too much based on who I date and not enough on how well I do my job."

She was correct but damn. Her instant denial was a hundred tiny paper cuts.

A sandy brow arched up. Cullen glanced between us. I folded my arms and gave him a tight smile. I knew what Vienne sounded like when she climaxed, but I'd hardly touched her.

"Sure," he said. "Not *dating*." He smirked like he was in on our secret, and I was afraid he'd guessed far too much. "Try telling that to Mom."

ॐ

Vienne

I didn't know what my brother was up to, and I wasn't sure how big of a grudge Marly had against me, but after tonight, I didn't doubt I was on her shit list.

I knew for a fact Marly hated campfires, but the fire

was her idea. Every time I turned around, my brother and his wife were throwing us together. Austen and I were a team for cornhole. We were a team for lawn darts. We were a team for axe throwing.

Each time I was paired with Austen, Mom floated on cloud nine.

Austen was having the time of his life. And to be honest, so was I.

He took the pressure from my family in stride. He even seemed to thrive on knowing that Cullen was messing with us on purpose.

It'd been ages since I had this much fun at home. Usually, I was tense, ready to absorb remarks about my decisions in life. I was busy defending my choices to Mom or trying to determine if Marly was naturally aloof or if she was just another person who didn't consider me good enough.

Tonight was completely different. I was flying high after Austen defended me. I'd been so wrapped up on defending and living with my decisions that I didn't think to point out the double standard.

"I have to run into the kitchen." I'd worked up a real thirst from the yard activities and from laughing.

I was closing the door behind me when it was nudged back open. Marly slipped through behind me.

"Oh, sorry," I said. Why did there have to be people I never did the right thing around? I'd closed the door in my pregnant sister-in-law's face.

"No worries. You know how pregnancy bladder is."

I chuckled, but inside, I was shocked. That was the most relatable thing she'd said to me.

"It's good to see you like this," Marly blurted out. She twisted her hands together and winced. Didn't she have to go to the bathroom, or was pregnancy bladder an excuse to corner me?

"Like what?" My instinct was to be insulted, but she'd said *good*, so...I was lost.

"Happy. I feel like..." She wound her hands around each other, and I was afraid she'd snap a bone. "Cullen talks about his wild older sister, and I've just never seen it, but tonight, I can see the fearless sister he grew up with. He said you were badass."

Oh. Emotion swelled in my throat. Cullen reminisced about me? A sense of loss echoed through me. I missed that girl sometimes. "I wasn't badass."

"Trust me." She smiled tentatively. "Compared to me, you were badass. I was doing extra math homework to keep from getting booted outside by my stepmom, but you were racing horses—"

"Not officially."

"—and herding cattle. He said you fixed cars and tractors too."

Aw, hell. Was that admiration in her eyes? I'd love to bond with her, but I didn't want to burst her bubble. "Cullen did all that too. Any kid who grows up like we did does."

"I know. It's just... I didn't see it in you until now."

"Oh." Now I wanted to wring my hands together. Was I really that different? I'd finished school with little support from my husband at the time. I also worked a bookkeeping job that was as fun as chewing marbles. For many of my weekend nights, I was buried in numbers. "I didn't mean to come off differently, but I guess I am different. Getting pregnant and married in college settled me down. I still have Catherine to think about, and I'd rather she was sliding across a gym floor with knee pads than, you know, making some of the mistakes I did."

Marly put her hand over her belly. "I hope this baby is braver than me."

Touched that she opened up to me, I wanted to ease her worry. "Brave comes in all forms." I thought that was something my family didn't understand. I didn't either until now. "You'll do fine. Cullen will be right there with you the whole time. I know he'll support you more than Dave ever helped me."

"I didn't like Dave." She gasped and covered her lips with her fingers.

Shock stole my words, then laughter bubbled up. "It's all right. As far as exes go, I could have worse, but I'm glad we're not married anymore." I wished I could tell the me from five years ago that. She would overflow with disbelief.

Marly tipped her head. "I never got the impression you liked me."

"Oh my god, I thought you couldn't stand me."

She laughed and dropped her head back. "I'm really awkward, Vienne. I don't know how I landed Cullen, but he kept coming into the bank. He was three loans deep before he actually asked me out. I quoted him an interest rate instead of saying yes."

Laughing with her, I marveled over how the day turned out. "I guess it's just because I'm on guard. Mom and Dad haven't understood all my choices."

She considered me, rolling her lips in like she was wondering how much she could say. "She loves you in the only way she knows how, but I don't think she knows how to relate to us. I think she's afraid we'll see her as a hillbilly housewife." Marly lifted a shoulder. "That's what she said when she had too much to drink after we announced we were expecting." She smoothed a hand over her stomach.

I would think about Mom later. If I dwelled on what Marly said, I'd feel guilty, and I was selfish enough not to want to ruin my high. "I'm really happy for you and Cullen."

A dimple indented her cheek when she smiled. "Thank you. I think Catherine is going to be an excellent cousin."

"She's in love already." Homesickness for my daughter hit. She would've had a blast tonight. Twice as much fun as usual with Austen here.

"There's really nothing between you and Austen?"

I laughed and waved my hand. "No. He's becoming a good friend, but no. There's nothing between us, and he's a client." My mind flashed to not having anything between us. No walls. No window screens. That night on the deck only increased my fantasies of having Austen's hands on me.

She squeezed my hand. "I'm glad you moved back. Now we can finally get to know each other." Her grin was shy. "I know you've been back for years, but I guess I was doing my version of quoting you an interest rate."

I was laughing when the sliding door opened and Austen stepped through. "I came to check on the womenfolk." He grinned, and my heart stumbled, banging against my rib cage. He was dusty from horseback riding and from the lawn games. He wasn't wearing his hat, but he'd pushed his hair all the way off his face, allowing me to get lost in his dark eyes. "Just kidding. Everyone wants another beer, and I'm here to ask Vienne if we're staying long enough that I can have another. We both have an early date with gutting a bathroom in the morning."

He was giving me an out. If I told him I was ready to go, he'd make it happen, and he'd probably blame himself, so he looked like the party pooper who called it a night and not me.

Why couldn't I have met him when I was twenty? Now we were both on our single lanes. A sense of loss filled me, and for what? We were two people on different paths, temporarily crossing until his house was done. The emptiness turned to sadness.

Enough of that. I was having fun tonight, and that was that. "Grab one for me too?"

His grin spread wider and there went my erratic pulse again. Marly's dimple spoiled the smile she was trying to hold back. She looked from him to me in a way that said *Are you sure you can't make an exception for this job? He might be worth it.*

I wasn't sure I had an honest answer for her.

Thirteen

AUSTEN

It was the Friday after hanging out with Vienne's family, and over the last week, we were nearly finished sanding and repairing the main floor. A new toilet, vanity, and storage closet were waiting to get installed in the main-floor bathroom and then we'd tile the shower. Progress was coming, and each day, I got a little less efficient. I took a few more breaks, and I quit earlier at night.

A big part of me didn't want the house renovations to be over.

Several minutes ago, Vienne had stepped outside to take a call from Dave. She'd skipped our nightly rendezvous last night, texting that Catherine had called. It had sounded more important than a normal check-in.

A restlessness had settled deep in my bones. Earlier this week, I'd signed the documents for leasing the office space in LA. My enthusiasm for the venture was waning. I should be gearing up to leave. Instead, I had cement on my boots. All week, I'd been trying to figure out what had changed.

There was one clear answer.

Did I want more from Vienne, or was I itching to leave? Since I was dragging my feet on completing the floor, maybe? We had painting and appliances and the bathroom. Then we'd be done, and I'd find an agent. I needed to schedule that open house for Vienne.

The front door opened and closed. Vienne's expression was tight, her shoulders rigid.

"Bad news?"

She sighed and looked around like she wanted to have a seat.

"Is it deck time?"

She smiled. "Have you got anything but water and beer to drink on the porch? It's too early to get shit-faced over shared parenting drama."

It wasn't too early, but Vienne drank recreationally. She didn't booze her problems away, and after seeing enough guys do that very thing, I wouldn't argue. "I happen to have Country Time lemonade mix in case I had nieces and nephews stop over." So it'd never been opened.

"Perfect."

"Go on out. Save me a seat."

Her half-hearted smile was better than the stressed line of her lips.

I found the mix and bonus, it wasn't expired. After mixing the powder with water, I added a ton of ice so we'd be refreshed while sitting outside on an eighty-five-degree day.

Vienne had her head resting on the back of the chair when I got outside. I handed her a glass and was about to set the pitcher on the table when she gulped her entire glass down until there was nothing left but ice.

Damn. I refilled her glass. "I've got more where that came from."

"Keep it coming," she said.

I took a swallow from my own glass. Cool and refreshing, but this wasn't the sweet flavor I wanted on my tongue. "Care to talk?"

"I told you Dave and his new wife are expecting?"

I nodded. The bigger family Vienne had wanted.

"Well, they're going to turn Catherine's room into the nursery."

"Ouch." Catherine had to feel like she was getting replaced. Like she was unwanted. I knew what that was like.

"Right? I can see that. You can see that. But Dave and Betti? I can't believe they were clueless."

"What was their reasoning?"

"Bigger room. More space for a rocker and a changing table." She gnawed into her lower lip. "They're arguing the logistics with her instead of just telling her they understand how it makes her feel and reassuring her that she's as much a part of their family as ever."

"And how did Famous Dave take it when you told him that?"

She smirked at me, but stress clouded her face. "You're going to be able to ask him that yourself."

"He's coming here?" I wanted to see the prick who fucked things up with Vienne. I also didn't want to meet him and be envious of a man who was so self-absorbed he let someone like Vienne go.

"He's coming here," she echoed. "The bright idea of Betti, who probably wants to nest without Dave whining about all the changes she's making. Father-daughter road trip. They canceled her flight home, and they're going to drive." She took another gulp.

"Betti's okay with him coming to stay in Crocus Valley where his ex is?" I'd seen similar scenarios fail over and over again.

She held up her glass. "Maybe I should've spiked it."

"I can make it happen."

"You can make a lot happen." She thunked her head back down. The shadow of the house blocked the sun so she could stare at the fluffy clouds in the sky without hurting her eyes. The glass was held loosely in her grip. "No. I'm not getting drunk over Dave. You know, I thought Marly acted like she was too good for me and it stung. That's because of in-laws and also because of Betti."

"Fuck your in-laws and Betti."

She laughed. "I keep telling myself that. She's not outright mean or insulting. There's just this general assumption I'm not a threat to her marriage." She stuck her hand up. "I'm not. Trust me, I'd never touch Dave again. But it's like she thinks it's because I can't compete with her. She's his perfect, gorgeous wife, and I'm the washed-up ex."

"You're an interior designer and sexy."

"Sure, stallion. Let's go with that."

I broke into laughter from both her nickname and her tone.

"She also graduated from an Ivy League school"—she talked over me—"and I have an online degree. Speaking of online, all my clothing is ordered online, and hers has designer labels. She's exactly what Dave wanted, and when he's here, I'll hear all about it. He'll complain there are no decent hotels in a place like Crocus Valley, and only the nonintellectuals would want to live in such a backward place. Ugh. I hate how condescending he is."

"When will that be?"

"A little over a week. They arrive a couple of nights after Sutton and Wilder's wedding celebration." She stretched her long legs out. She was wearing her work jeans and athletic shoes. We were both full of grit from sanding, but she could just as well be in a bikini.

Heat kindled in my gut, working its way lower.

She caught me watching her. Instead of looking away, I met her gaze, then stroked my attention back down her body.

"I'm tired of holding out," she said quietly.

I jerked my attention up to her determined face. My lust kicked in, but I tamped it down. I could take her glass, then take her hand, and lead her upstairs. Hell, I could take her against the wall, but a quick fuck right inside the door was only the tip of the iceberg of what I wanted to do with her.

But... She'd been through a roller coaster of emotions in the last twenty-four hours. She'd had good reasons for keeping us in separate buildings for our trysts. I couldn't let her backtrack on a whim. I wanted every part of her, but I could handle the need. Otherwise, I was afraid a rash decision would cost me all of her. "I want you, V. Don't doubt that. But I want you to take more time to consider what we'd be getting into."

The corners of her mouth pulled down. "I've considered it for weeks."

Exactly. And she'd kept her distance for weeks. "You're upset. Pissed at Dave and sex is a hell of an outlet. We've been able to hide what we're doing, and if you want to hide that we're going all the way, I think we can do it. But when I leave, even if no one finds out, you're going to know, and I think that'll be important to you. You can't go into that job you want with guilt."

Awareness dawned in her eyes like she'd forgotten that dream job. She let out a long-suffering sigh and tipped her head back. "How are you real?"

"I learned a lot about what not to do."

"And you don't want to do me," she murmured. She closed her eyes like another realization dawned on her.

"Vienne—"

She laughed and rose. "Well, thanks for talking me off the ledge," she said in a chipper voice I'd never heard her speak in. "See you Monday."

She took her glass into the house.

Whoa. When did she pivot from sounding grateful to radiating hurt and bitterness? I was doing this to keep from hurting her. I grabbed the pitcher and hurried after her. She set her cup by the sink, then her strides ate up the ready-to-stain floor toward the front door.

Goddammit. She was an even-keeled person. Whatever I did set her off. I wanted her to have time so we didn't ruin what we had going, but I'd ended up driving her away.

She couldn't leave upset and thinking I didn't want her. I didn't want to lose what we had at night, but I looked forward to our workdays too. I liked renovating next to her and seeing her passion for her work. I liked chatting about anything and everything.

"Hey." I jogged toward her, my boots echoing loudly in the stripped-down living room.

"Have a good week—"

I snagged her elbow and spun her toward me.

"Aust—"

I cupped her face in my hand and bent my head, but I stopped when my lips were a breath from hers. My restraint nearly broke, but I clenched every muscle to keep me in place. "I want to kiss you so damn bad."

"Do you need time to think?" she asked, her tone caustic.

"I said think about it, my upset Honey V. I'm not into taking advantage of emotionally distraught women."

She softened under my hold, but only slightly. "And how much time do I need to take?"

Five minutes? Ten seconds? No, I strove to be a good guy. I wasn't fucking this up and screwing her over so I could get some physical relief that wasn't by my own hand. "Tomorrow night." Saturday night wasn't a day she was usually over, and that seemed important right now. "Tomorrow night, if you still want to do this, we'll fucking do it."

I released her, missing the heat of her skin.

She didn't move. I didn't either. The sweet puff of her exhale caressed my mouth. Need vibrated through my body.

Her pupils were dilated, her nostrils slightly flared. She was as fucking turned on as me. "Okay, then. I'll think about it."

X

Vienne

Last night, I'd tumbled in a whirlwind of emotion after leaving Austen's. I'd been ready to strip down and climb on top of him. His rejection was both incredibly sweet and supportive, yet the burn of rejection had set in.

He'd been right to do what he did. A thoughtful man. And I'd thought the worst of him. Even after that, he'd given me time. I might've been more incensed, but I'd felt him shaking to keep from kissing me. So, when I got the text from Tova this morning, I saw my chance to start fresh. To think about it, like he'd said.

I knocked on Austen's door. It wasn't evening yet.

He opened the door, a brow arched and a lazy smile on his unshaven face and no shirt on his broad chest, showing his abs for days. He was back in his black basketball shorts. "It's not night yet," he purred.

I purposely rolled my eyes. "I was checking to see if you wanted to ride with me this time."

Confusion furrowed his brow. "Ride where?"

"Have you looked at your phone recently, or were you too busy being a shirtless god?"

"What? This old thing?" He brushed a hand down his chest and stomach. "I'll find my phone."

I waited on the porch. Safer for my libido here.

He returned and flashed the blank screen with an image of him in uniform with two other guys. A couple of the buddies he was going into business with? "What'd I miss?"

Oh, crap. Didn't Tova ask him too? "Uh...Tova said the kids want to have a water day, so she and Cody are taking them to the pool. Aggie's going with Ro, too, but not Tripp. Tova asked if any aunts or uncles could be an extra pair of hands."

I'd been so busy beaming about being an honorary aunt I didn't check to see if Austen was also on the thread. Horror cinched around my throat. I'd unintentionally hurt him. I'd highlighted how he was left out by his family.

Irritation made the back of my neck hot. Why wouldn't Tova add him? That wasn't like her.

He slipped his phone into his shorts pocket, his expression neutral. "Nope. Have fun though."

"Austen."

"Vienne, it's fine. I was heading out for a long run."

In the afternoon? "It's hot."

"I like to sweat."

Normally, heat would sift through my body, but not when he was covering his feelings. He'd been overlooked. I felt complicit. I would abandon the swim date to hang with him, but the determination on his face was carved from stone. Still, I'd try. "You can come anyway."

"They found enough aunts and uncles, and I've got my run to do." His smile didn't reach his eyes. "Have fun."

Shit. The pool wasn't far from the house, but now I didn't want to go. My swimsuit was on under my shirt and shorts, and I told them I'd be there in fifteen minutes. Ten minutes had already passed. Resolve filled Austen's face. He would go on his run and do his own thing like he'd been doing his whole life.

That wasn't good enough, but I didn't know what else to do. How could I help? I'd go and make sure the kids all had fun and stayed safe, but I'd also find out what happened. It wasn't like my friends to forget their loved ones.

I could still invite him. "We'll be at the pool for at least an hour, barring any meltdowns. Come cool down after your run."

He lifted a shoulder like he was shrugging off my "too

little, too late" invite. "Give the kids an extra squeeze from me." He stepped back and closed the door.

Dang.

I drove to the pool. How often did this happen to Austen and he didn't know? I wasn't invited to all the Knight gatherings. Some things were just for family, but Austen was family. My heart hurt for him and for that little boy who'd gotten skipped over on his birthday for something someone else did. That someone who should've been the one to make him feel special.

When I got out of my car, the sounds of happy kids screeching and heavy dives into the water filled the air. Across the small parking lot, Cody and Tova were unloading Charlie. The almost one-year-old was in a ruffled, little, yellow bikini with a pink sun hat that had a wide brim. Her chocolate curls were pulled back under the hat.

Tova's eyes brightened when she saw me. "Hey! Glad you could make it. Sutton and Wilder are joining us too."

"That's cool." Maybe I should stay out of it. The Knights weren't my family, but Austen had championed so much for me. "I stopped to see if Austen was coming, but he wasn't on the text, so he's going for a run."

"That's weird. Didn't I include him?" She frowned. "I'm not even sure I have his number. Cody usually contacts him."

Ivy clambered out. "Vienne! It's been forever." She threw herself against me, and I soaked up her theatrics. The Knight kids were always so dang happy to see me. Tova turned to finish digging out the swim bags. Cody came around to help, taking Charlie. And that was that. Austen was forgotten.

No wonder he wasn't attached to sticking around. He

loved his family, but he also buffered himself from them. Was he afraid to be hurt again?

Wasn't that what I was doing with my parents? Could they be just as clueless as Austen's siblings?

A pickup parked behind me. Aggie hopped out. "Hey, ladies and brother." Ansen wasn't with her. He must be at home with Tripp.

Sutton and Wilder pulled in. Sutton waved. I gave her a half-hearted wave back. These people had been so good about including me, but they weren't used to Austen being so close.

Yet he was and only for a short time.

Across the street, a tall man ran by, his strides long and his arms pumping. He had a ball cap on his head, sunglasses, and he was only wearing those shorts and had a holder for his phone around his biceps. If I was closer, I'd probably see the earbuds in his ears. No one else noticed him.

Pool time didn't sound so fun anymore, but I'd said I'd help. I had no idea how long Austen would be on his run.

I splashed around for an hour. There were more aunts and uncles than kids. Charlie didn't want anyone but her mom or dad. She was floating with Cody at the moment. Wilder paddled around with Ro. Tova, Aggie, Sutton, and I talked in the four-foot-deep part of the pool.

Movement caught the corner of my eye. Austen was trekking the same path back to his house.

"Oh, hey. Is that Austen?" Aggie waved.

Austen was looking straight ahead, like he was afraid to witness the fun being had without him.

"I forgot to include him," Tova said. Her dark brows

knitted together. "How awful is that? I'm a horrible third sister. I'm not used to having him in town."

"He's been here for months," I said gently, grateful they were aware. At the same time, what were they going to do about it?

"I like having him in town," Aggie said, "but this summer, I've really only seen him on the Fourth and at the bar that night."

"He helped us with fencing and haying." Tova's pink lips turned into a delicate frown. "Actually, unless it's one of our standard family gatherings, I think Austen's only ever been asked over to do some sort of chore. Not to actually, like, hang out. There was that night Wilder took him out." She frowned. "But like you said, he's been here for months. Once is not enough."

"He's going to be gone soon," I said as if it wasn't a mantra running through my head at least ten times a day. The phrase was both a reminder of what a bad idea getting involved with him would be but also a helpful suggestion of why a fling wouldn't be terrible.

I'd been resisting him for weeks, having secret window shows and telling myself it was enough to keep me from getting hurt. I would miss him when he moved. I would miss seeing him stroke himself in the window. I'd miss working with him.

When he left, I'd hurt anyway. I knew what I was getting into. Was I brave enough to follow through?

"Hey, um... I have to get going. I've got some samples to order."

Tova pulled me in for a hug, wet and cool from the water. "Thanks for coming."

I scurried up the ladder of the pool. I wove through parents and soggy children huddled around lawn chairs.

The concrete burned my feet, but I grabbed my bag from the pile the Knights had made and walked out without changing.

At the exit, I dug through my bag for my sandals and tossed them on the hot pavement. I slipped my feet into them and rushed to my car. The trip to my house took only minutes, but I didn't go to my door after I parked. I went to Austen's house and knocked.

He didn't answer.

I knocked again.

Nothing. My resolve didn't waver. I wanted this.

I tried the knob and it turned. A thrill traveled down my spine.

Did I dare?

The talk with Marly came back to me. *He said you were badass.*

How fearless could I be again? Brave enough to tell Austen exactly what I wanted?

I pushed the door open. Upstairs, the shower kicked on. If I was going to do this, I had to turn my brain off. I treaded through the living room, through the dining room, to the stairs. I jogged up the stairs, afraid I'd turn and run.

I faced another door. Breathe, one, two, three... Like I was having an out-of-body experience, I watched my hand rise and knock.

The water cut off.

"Austen? I don't need the full twenty-four hours."

Silence.

I squeezed my eyes closed. It'd figure, wouldn't it? I jumped off a cliff, and there was no guy at the bottom with a net to catch me. I was on my own and embarrassed. Again. My throat was going to close and slowly choke me, putting me out of my misery.

The door swung open. I sucked in a breath, desperate for air so I could survive to stare at the image in front of me. Austen was naked. He'd toweled off, but water dripped down his hair onto his neck. Droplets rolled through the dusting of hair down his chest. His cock was rising the longer we faced each other. His jaw was granite, but I couldn't tell why. Restraint? Hurt? Anger?

"We don't have much longer, and I'm tired of wasting time." I sounded breathless, needy.

He rubbed the back of his neck, his biceps flexed and his abs rippling. "You aren't taking advantage of a man who's a little emotionally raw right now, are you?"

"Does that man mind?"

Heat filled his eyes. "Do you really want to know why I call you Honey V?"

Fourteen

AUSTEN

Vienne in her swimsuit would be branded into my brain until the day I took my last breath. She wore one of those with a tank top that gave her perfect tits a boost and snug bottoms that curved around her pussy, covering all the best parts.

"Why?" she asked, breathless.

I stepped forward. "We'll get to that." Was I really going to do this? I told her to think about it. I wasn't in that different of a place than she was last night, but the last thing I wanted was her to tell me to take extra fucking time. No wonder she'd turned on me.

No, we were doing this. I'd finally get my hands on her.

I slid a strap off her shoulder. Then the other. My fingertips glided over her soft skin. I tugged her top down until her breasts popped free. Her breathing hitched. "I knew they'd be even better up close."

I kept her straps pinning her arms and palmed her cool breasts. Her skin warmed immediately under mine.

"Austen, I'm sorry."

I stopped kneading her flesh. "For what?"

"Wasting time."

"Honey V, we didn't waste it." All those nights in the window would continuously stream in my head. Nothing would come close to those visions, except for this, right now.

"I could've had you inside me."

My lust almost bowled me over. I would be inside of her. Soon.

"We'll make up for that." I skimmed my fingers down the plane of her stomach and rolled the waistband of her swim bottoms down. I stopped when I saw a short, thin scar. I traced it with my finger.

"C-section," she said. "Twenty hours of labor and her heart rate dropped and—" She grimaced. "My foreplay sucks."

I gave her a quick smile. "Don't ever apologize for your strength, Vienne. I happen to find it sexy."

"God, you say all the right things."

There was a hint of accusation in her voice, like this was part of my act. I could reassure her, but what would I say? I make sure I'm not the bad guy.

My cock throbbed, reminding me this wasn't the time to dissect my personal life. The woman I'd been daydreaming about for months was in my bathroom. We weren't in viewing-only mode.

I dropped her wet swim bottoms. They hit the floor, and she stepped out of them and her sandals. Then I drew her damp top over her head and let it fall by her other clothing. I got to be the one undressing her this time. Fuck. Yes.

Finally. Naked and within my reach. My fingertips tingled. My dick was obnoxiously swollen. All of me was eager. "You can't imagine what I've thought about doing to you."

She licked her pink tongue out again. "You better hurry so we can fit it all in."

I took her hand and drew her farther into the bathroom. "I don't have condoms in here, but I'm going to show you the honey V."

"Show me the— Oh."

I bent her over the edge of the tub. She caught her hands on the ledge. I was behind her, my pulse hammering through my erection. Her ass was in front of me, so inviting, so tempting. I bracketed her hips with my hands, and she moaned.

"Stay right here," I ordered. "Just like this."

She whined. Those sounds I'd had to strain to hear now so damn close. I lowered to my knees. She tensed. My face was right behind her butt, and she was exposed.

"No, baby. Don't move." I smoothed my hands over her ass. This was a show I couldn't get from a window. "That morning? When you lost your key?"

"Yeah?" She whimpered and rocked, just a little, against my hold.

I skimmed my fingers down the backs of her thighs. "I saw everything, and I've wondered just what you feel like, what you taste like, ever since. There's not one detail I've forgotten. I want to see it all again." I skated an index finger up the middle of her thigh and nudged her legs farther apart. She was resistant. "My ass is in your face?"

"Right where I want it." I used both hands to coax her open.

I brushed my index finger up her inner thigh. "This?" She was open to me, exposed, her pink flesh glistening. She was wet for me. Ready for this. A tremble traced through her. "And this?" I dragged the same finger up the inside of her other leg, only this time, when I reached the top, I slid my fingertip through her soaked seam. Her legs trembled. "Is the honey *V*."

She jerked, and her butt cheeks did the most perfect jiggle. "You've been calling me by a nickname you came up with about my pussy?"

A low laugh left me. "I'm going to keep calling you that. And each time, you're going to remember this."

I braced myself by gripping the outsides of her legs. Then I leaned forward and licked from the opening I couldn't wait to thrust into later down to her clit. Sweet. Like fucking honey. I could combust in a millisecond, but weeks of restraint were paying off now. The honey *V* was mine.

She groaned and one knee buckled. I held her until she righted herself.

"I didn't wait this long to let you fall." I resumed licking her.

Her legs quivered, but my hold was iron. "Austen."

She started rocking against my face, her self-consciousness gone. After all the nights I'd been watching her touch herself, I knew exactly what she liked—circles, not a lot of pressure, but no messing around. Vienne didn't want to play.

"I can't believe—" She gasped for breath.

I'd ask her what she couldn't believe, but my mouth was busy. After I gave her this orgasm, I'd get her on her back in my bed. I'd have her legs on my shoulders, and I'd be fingering her. She could be full of me while I got her off again with my tongue. I had to renew my determination to hold it together. My own climax was demanding its release.

The tremble in her legs grew stronger, her breathing quickened. If I wasn't worried about steadying her, I'd have a fist around my cock, but she was at the edge.

"I've never come this fast—" A long cry left her. Heat exploded on my tongue, and I lapped her up.

I was on the verge of coming. I'd gone long periods of time without being with someone, but waiting on Vienne felt like eternity had come and gone. And now, I could have her.

I kept licking until she sagged against the ledge of the tub and both knees gave out. I helped her sit and sat back on my heels. My erection thrust obnoxiously between us.

She blinked, looking over her shoulder, her eyes wide, stunned. "You made that seem easy."

"Making you come has been hard?" It never had been with me. My chest puffed out a little.

She nodded, her gaze dipping to my dick. Her cheeks were flushed, and her legs were folded like she was my very own mermaid. "I'm usually lucky to orgasm."

"Aw, baby. Luck has nothing to do with it. It's perseverance, consideration, and skill."

"You have all those."

"This time, *you* get to watch me make you come again."

Another owlish blink. "Twice?"

Had she been the only one to get herself off twice? Under my command? Well. I had even more ideas now. "If you want to stop there."

A nervous giggle escaped her. "Are you serious?"

"Does my cock look like it's joking?"

Her gaze dropped again. "No. It looks like it takes its job seriously."

There was a loud knock at the door. My stomach clenched, and some blood immediately rerouted to fuel my irritation. Who the hell was interrupting me when I finally got to taste paradise?

Vienne stiffened and moved to stand up but then froze like she realized she was buck naked.

"What do we do?" she whispered.

Wait for them to go the fuck away.

There was another knock, and Vienne drew in a sharp breath. She wouldn't be able to relax.

"I'll see who it is. Wait here."

"I don't have any clothes. Just my swimsuit."

I rose and helped her up. "Grab whatever you need out of my room."

She hugged her arms around herself before finally dropping her hands to her sides. She was self-conscious again. My cock was starting to flag, disliking her sudden anxiety.

The doorbell rang. Whoever it was wasn't leaving. What bad fucking timing.

"I don't want—" She chewed on the inside of her cheek. "I don't want to be busted."

I knew how she felt, yet the fact that she wanted to hide being with me hit like a blow below the belt. *This isn't about me, jackass.*

"I gotchu. Wait here." I didn't bother with a towel and stopped in my bedroom to get a fresh pair of shorts on.

The doorbell rang again. "Coming!"

I should've been coming so damn hard. I was close to having Vienne on her back in my bed with her legs over my shoulders, but some asshole suddenly wanted to talk.

Downstairs, I opened the door to Cody. His hair was damper than mine, and he wore board shorts and a half-dry T-shirt. He forgot me this morning, and he decided now's the time to be like *What's Austen up to?*

I was up to making her orgasm a second time, fucker. "Yeah?"

"Hello to you too."

"I was in the shower." Vienne's cries were fresh in my ears. The trip from my room to the door had helped abate the blood pumping through my erection. "I just got back from a run."

Ivy waved out the window from Cody's pickup. He'd parked between my house and Vienne's. "Hi, Uncle Austen!"

Grayson's greeting followed on the heels of hers.

"Hey, guys," I called. I couldn't see clearly, but it looked like Charlie's hands were flailing from her car seat between her brother and sister. I returned their waves.

Cody kept his dark gaze on me. "Tova doesn't have your number, so you didn't get the invite to go swimming. She feels like shit, and texting you didn't occur to me."

"Okay?" My response was curt, but my brain was scrambled from having Vienne at the tip of my tongue.

"Anyway, we're having everyone over tonight. Nothing big like the Fourth, just sandwiches and chitchat." Guilt gleamed in the depths of his irises.

"Is it a 'we forgot Austen again' party?" I would've been mildly annoyed yet touched any other time. What bad timing.

Lines winged out from the corners of his eyes as he inspected me. "It's a 'you're going to be gone again soon and we should get together while we can' party."

That didn't feel much better, but the party wasn't my priority. I loved my family, but I also was about to get laid—

"She's not answering," Tova yelled from somewhere. "But her car's out front."

"Is that my third sister?" I leaned out of the front door, and my stomach fell. Aw, hell. Tova was on Vienne's porch. They wanted to invite her tonight too.

I couldn't not go. I'd get peppered with questions about why. And if Vienne tried passing on the invite, my siblings were smart enough to put two and two together.

Just in case, I'd play it safe. "Didn't she swim too? Maybe she's in the shower."

Just not the one in her house.

Tova went down the porch stairs and walked toward the pickup. "I'll message her, but can you tell her if you see her? We were going to have an early dinner."

My prospects of spending the rest of the day with Vienne in bed were diminishing rapidly. My hopes sank like a stone. I'd gotten a taste of paradise and was being yanked away. "Will do."

"You coming?" Cody asked.

"Be there in an hour. What should I bring?"

"Your shining personality."

"Never leave home without it."

Cody peered over my shoulder, and my pulse jumped. Had Vienne come down the stairs? Didn't she realize someone could see straight through the house?

"You've done a lot of work."

Right. He had rented the place a couple years ago. "Yeah, it's coming right along."

Cody gave me an expectant look.

"You want a tour while your family waits in the car?" I'd love to show him around. I also wouldn't mind if they knew I was crazy about Vienne. But I knew Cody and the rest. They cared about Vienne, and they'd zero in on the fact I was leaving. I didn't care to argue about my time with Vienne when I could just be with her.

"Just thought I could take a poke around, but you're right. We've gotta go get the food ready, and Charlie's going to need a nap. See you in a few." He went to his ride, the kids calling their goodbyes to me.

Relief nearly made me sag. I'd never gotten busted sneaking a girl into the barracks when I was young and stupid, and I wasn't about to have it happen in my own house.

When he drove away, I went in search of Vienne. Would she be as disappointed in the change of plans as I was? My dick wanted to weep.

So goddamn close.

She was sitting on my bed, the only seat on the upper level. An old gray Knight's Arabians and Cattle Company shirt swamped her, and she had her hands folded together between her knees. Her pensive expression didn't bode well. Tova and Cody's visit spooked her.

I leaned against the bedroom doorframe. "You're invited to dinner at Cody and Tova's. They feel guilty about forgetting me."

She let out a small laugh. "I heard." She fell serious. "Are you okay?"

"I'm used to it."

She rose and crossed toward me. "Doesn't mean you're okay."

It had to. What could I change? When she stopped, I pulled her closer. "I'm not okay that we were interrupted."

She flattened her hands on my shoulders. "I was a little upset too. And now we have to go have sandwiches around everyone."

"I'd say we could fit something in, but I want to take my time with you." That was the truth. I'd waited too long to rush through our first time having sex.

She swept her thumbs over my skin. "Then, when we leave there, you come to my place."

My attention was riveted on her mouth and how her lips moved when she spoke. I'd buried my face in the most private part of her body, but I hadn't kissed her yet.

"Deal," I said before I captured those sweet lips. They were as soft and warm and sweet as the rest of her.

She didn't pull away but snaked her arms around my neck and stood on her tiptoes. She was responsive, just like she'd been before. Vienne was attention-starved. A woman who'd never been properly treasured by her partner, who'd never had her pleasure taken as seriously as his. Not by Dave, not by that Theo jackass, and not by Doctor-fucking-Jake.

I deepened the kiss, sweeping my tongue inside her mouth to stroke against hers. She whimpered, and I hugged her closer. I could do this for hours. I didn't track how long we kissed, standing in my bedroom doorway, making out, but I didn't want to let her go.

Eventually, she pulled away. Her lips were puffy, and her eyes glassy. "You're good at everything." She let out a nervous laugh. "I need to clean up and prepare myself to act normal at the party."

I was her secret. Normally, I wouldn't care. My relationships were short-lived. Fleeting. There was always an end date, and if not, PCSing—getting stationed somewhere else—would sever any lingering ties. I'd move and be forgotten.

I'd set up the same to happen with Vienne. It was for the best. If not for me, then for her. She wanted a guy to settle down with, someone she trusted to be by her side and treat her right. She might still want to give Catherine siblings.

I wasn't that guy. I didn't live a life conducive to a family, and my new career wouldn't be either. But I could show her what she deserved, and it'd stay just between us. Until she forgot me and moved on.

§

Vienne

Energy vibrated through my body while I chatted with Sutton. I ran my hand over the bracelets on my wrists. I'd loaded up after my shower. Ten bracelets. Almost getting busted by his family while I was still delirious with pleasure left me shaken and riddled with nerves. Getting through this impromptu get-together, knowing that afterward, Austen and I would finish what we started— well, I needed a few more bracelets to fidget with.

Nerves were building inside me like an impending storm. Outside, the sun was sinking in the clear sky. Inside, I was a needy mess. Austen gave me the quickest, most explosive orgasm ever, and I was supposed to pretend today was a normal weekend. That the entirety of my sexual experience wasn't just put to shame with one man's tongue?

I should win an Oscar. I had his whisker burn on my inner thighs, and I wasn't shouting that fact to the world.

I sat with Sutton on camp chairs outside the garage. Aggie was inside the house, changing Tripp and probably nursing him, and Tova had figured Charlie needed a change too.

The kids would be ready for bed shortly, and soon, it'd be time to go.

Excitement cartwheeled through my stomach.

My gaze strayed to Austen, standing as tall as two of his brothers and brother-in-law. He was wearing basketball shorts and a T-shirt, looking as sinful as if he was wearing a fitted tux. What had he looked like in his uniform?

We'd ridden together, acting like we usually did, like we were nothing more than neighbors and colleagues. Was having mind-blowing sex and moving on normal for him?

I could get scared off of continuing with Austen. The bathroom experience had been earth-shattering, but I had to know how amazing sex could be. After what happened in his bathroom, I wanted to know what not to settle for anymore.

How could a simple kiss scramble my brain? He'd held me and tasted me like I was a fine wine, like he was enjoying himself. Then he was content to stand and make out as if his erection wasn't hard and throbbing between us.

On Monday, we'd continue to work together and talk and joke. We might even share another beer on the deck.

Gah! Was he going to ruin a deck beer for me too?

Ro waved her chubby arms from her dad to Austen. His deep laugh drifted toward me. He took Ro in his arms and bobbed around with her. She giggled, her little teeth flashing and her tiny smile wide.

The flutters in my belly were different. Utter adoration for a guy who was good with kids. And longing. I had flashes of Dave and Catherine when she was a baby, but they were few and far between. We'd been so young and harried, and I'd chalked his distance up to that time in our life. Now, we were older. I knew my ex would be a better, more involved dad in his midthirties than when he was barely legal drinking age.

And I would watch from the sidelines, thinking about how my time had passed. I had a career I was building. A teen daughter who'd need me. And no man I could count on.

"Vienne?" Sutton's voice got through to me.

I blinked at my friend. She fiddled with the end of her braid and studied me. She had one bare leg crossed over the other, wearing a yellow sundress that must be one of Wilder's favorites from the way he was eyeing her legs from where he stood.

"Sorry?" How long had I spaced?

She shifted her gaze from me to the group of guys. She smiled at Wilder, and he gave her a heated look in return. Austen's back was to me, and I was hooked on his wide shoulders or I probably wouldn't have caught the exchange.

She glanced between me and Austen. "Something going on between you two." It wasn't a question.

I caught a strangled sound in my throat. "What?" I asked, my pitch high.

Sutton smirked. "I've been there—and you're the one who caught me."

"No, we're not—" Aggie and Tova hadn't come outside yet. Sutton had trusted me with her big secret of sneaking around with Wilder last year. I hadn't wanted anyone to know, but Sutton would understand. She'd been afraid the Knights would turn on her, and wasn't that part of my fear? That they wouldn't understand that I wanted to experience all of a Knight man's potency, then wave goodbye when he packed up to go?

Because at least when Austen left for California, it wasn't to move on to someone better than me. He'd had the plans before we started groping ourselves in the window. He was invested. Sort of like I was invested in landing the job with Jim to work on Dot's house. I needed the money.

If Austen was as devastating in the bedroom as I suspected, then it might help to have someone to talk to when he left. I could complain to Sutton when I went on a date with a guy and he just didn't measure up. I could also tell her that I'd miss doing the hands-on part of renovations I got to do with Austen. Jim would never allow me to leave the lane he thought an interior designer should stay in.

I'd never felt like I earned my hard-won degree more than in the last few weeks.

There was so much I wanted to talk about, and when Austen was gone, I would lose the one person I'd been telling everything to. Opening up to Sutton now might help me later. "We're having a bit of a fling."

"That's like being a little bit pregnant," she said dryly, but she wasn't surprised.

"We haven't...you know...*all the way.*"

"Is that how you had the birds and bees talk with Catherine?"

"I used proper anatomical terms." I scowled at her, but my lips twitched. "We haven't had *sex* yet, okay?"

She pursed her lips. "But more than the floors are getting buffed?"

"It's complicated— No. It's more weird." I didn't want to start on the window thing, and honestly, I'd probably take that tale to the grave. How would the explanation sound? *I played with myself, and he stroked himself and talked dirty, but it was like a balance between keeping the neighborhood from hearing but being loud enough for each other. And there was the one time on the back deck when he watched me finger myself in the dark. I had to be just as quiet.* No, the peep show was between me and Austen. "It's been a different path, but yes, we're going to have a full fling." Soon. Like, within hours. A thrum between my thighs reminded me that it wasn't soon enough.

Uncertainty rippled over Sutton's features. "He has no plans to stay," she warned.

"I know," I said, not liking the tendril of loss wrapping around my insides. Playing my fingers over my bracelets, I lowered my voice as much as possible. "That's why I'm doing it. I held off, afraid I'd fall for him, but now I'm afraid I wasted a lot of time not getting to experience what sex should be like. And he's not... He's not Jake."

"But you got attached to Jake when you knew better." Sutton sat forward, flicking the end of her braid.

"Austen, like the rest of his siblings, is one of the best guys I know. You're right; he's not like Jake. You might be okay when he leaves, but what about when he comes back to visit?" A furrow creased her brow. "What if he brings someone home?"

The urge to dry heave was strong. I swallowed. Hard. I wasn't interested in long term. I couldn't put those restraints on him. He was a good guy, and he deserved a lasting relationship if that was what he wanted. It wouldn't be with me. "What if I have someone too?" I chewed each word as it came out. They were wrong.

Sutton snuck another glance at the guys. The door in the garage banged open, and Tova came out. She passed us to hand Charlie off to Cody.

"I don't want anyone to know," I whispered.

"I won't tell. But..." She gave me a knowing look, a smile pulling her lips up. "It's kind of obvious, and it's not just the shared rides. You two have gotten way comfortable around each other since you've been working together."

"And you and Wilder were subtle?"

She grinned. "We were that one night in the theater."

I'd been so envious. Wilder had tracked down Sutton while she was on a double date with me, Jake, and his brother and had gotten her off in the middle of the movie theater without anyone knowing. To be fair, not many people filled the seats. I only caught her because I'd seen his pickup.

She had a guy care enough to race to another town and keep her from being with another man. And then she got to have good sex. Go on dates. They'd hid their fooling around, but yet they'd managed to go camping and get snowed in together.

Sounded like a dream. I was the one sneaking around now, and all I asked was that I was the only one he was fucking. The effort he had to make was to cross the yard to the house next door. But the emotional strides he'd made for me were unlike anything I'd ever experienced, and he made those seem like no exertion at all.

Aggie came outside next. She had Tripp in his car seat. "It's bedtime." As if her husband had supersonic hearing, he broke from the group and went to her.

Ansen took Tripp's carrier. "Stay and chat, Ags. I can rock him and lay him down."

So damn sweet. My heartstrings should be frayed. A doting husband and enthusiastic father? A dream come true, but my time had come and gone. I had accepted the fact.

Austen broke away, and it was like the sun's fading rays had a special shine for his long body. "We should let y'all get some rest tonight. You've had a busy day."

My breath caught. Time to go. Tonight's festivities wouldn't happen with two screens and twenty feet between us.

Sutton smirked at me when she waved goodbye. I worked harder to play it cool when my body was coming alive, flipping on light switches all over my skin, just waiting for Austen to blow all my fuses.

He drove to his house. We chatted about the evening, the kids, and what we'd each been talking about with our respective groups. If there was an award for compartmentalizing, we'd tie to win the top plaque.

He parked in front of his house. "You still want this?" His voice was a low rumble between us.

My hormones would revolt if I took any more time. "You promised me two more orgasms."

I got out and walked to the house, afraid to learn that he wasn't following me.

His body heat and smoky vetiver scent wrapped around me as he waited for me to unlock the house. The street was quiet. Hopefully no one saw him follow me to my doorstep. This was more than a friendly neighbor seeing me home.

"That was three during one session," he clarified.

Shock made me turn around. "I can't come three more—"

He maneuvered us in, kicked the door shut behind him, and crowded me against the wall. "You won't know if you don't try. Get those clothes off."

Arousal flooded my veins. The steady beat between my thighs amplified. Three more orgasms? He couldn't be serious. But if my nerves were light bulbs, I'd be a walking Christmas tree. *Please let him try*, my pussy begged.

I whipped my shirt off and threw it on the living room floor. My shorts and underwear came off next. He was undressed just as fast.

"Did you stay in your shorts and shirt so you could strip faster?" I asked as I undid my bra.

"Yep." He crept along the wall and closed my blinds. The mechanic shop across the street was closed, but we couldn't expose ourselves to any walkers out enjoying the beautiful evening.

I leaned out to watch his hard ass flex. His vein-lined erection really was impressive. I wasn't imagining it earlier, caught up in some lucid hallucination caused by intense pleasure.

He pinned me with his dark gaze. The lock of hair

over his forehead didn't soften him at all. "Get on the couch."

Tingles spread across my body. My nipples were rock hard and my knees trembled like they remembered how he commandeered my pleasure.

He fell in step behind me. My heart hammered as his heat surrounded me, comforted me, but also sank into all the places I needed to have his body on mine.

Before I could lie down, he reached around me and ripped the red-plaid throw blanket off the back of the couch and flipped it over the cushions. The man thought of everything. "Sit down and spread your legs."

I drew in a shaky breath. I would get a second orgasm for certain. Two that weren't given to me by me. I couldn't believe it, but I knew Austen could make it happen, and my body was primed and ready for him. When I sat, he kneeled in front of me.

A nervous laugh left me. "You won't be able to get on your knees anymore without me getting wet."

He grinned. "I'm going to like knowing what it does to you."

I thought he'd dip down, push my legs wide, and get to work. We'd already done foreplay hours ago. But he caught me up in another kiss, his fingers under my chin and his hand possessive on my thigh.

With steady pressure, he leaned me back until I was cradled by the cushions of the couch. He skated his fingers down my neck, over my chest, and stopped to cup a breast.

His big, warm hand with the roughened fingertips ignited all my nerve endings. Desire pounded through my veins, and I could come from the way he kissed a path down my neck until he got to the other nipple. He sucked the pearled tip into his mouth, and I arched into him.

I dug my fingers through his hair and widened my legs. He nibbled and licked and palmed my breasts until I was a writhing mess. He concentrated on my pleasure, and I wasn't sure I'd survive. My heart would slide into a coma from the onslaught. At the same time, my brain shouted *I knew it! I knew it could be like this.*

With the right guy.

He couldn't be the right man. Another wave of pleasure wiped out coherent thought.

"Austen." I sounded so damn whiny. "I need…"

He looked up at me from where he was licking his way down my belly. "What do you need?"

My hands were still twisted in his hair. "You." I needed him to get me through this maelstrom of arousal.

"You've got me all night."

The gut-wrenching thing was that I wanted him for so much more. I was greedy over the pleasure he was giving me, but it was Austen giving that pleasure. Austen, who made me feel supported and secure enough to do this with him. He knew what I was risking, and he'd made sure I wasn't being impulsive.

He laid slow, wet kisses along my abdomen until he reached my soaked middle.

One blanket was not going to be enough for what he did to me.

Hitching my legs onto his shoulders, he centered himself. "I'll never get tired of this sight." Then he devoured me.

"Austen!"

He tugged me to the edge to open me wider.

My legs were shaking. I had one hand fisted in his hair

and one grappling the blanket, trying to keep from flying off the couch, when he pushed a finger inside me. How could I be so sensitive? So ready to blow?

"Oh my god!" I needed both hands to anchor me to the blanket.

He withdrew his finger and slid a second one in with the next thrust.

An embarrassing whimper left me. He watched me try to hold myself together as he pumped slowly in and out. "You're so fucking wet, Honey V."

God, that nickname. Normally, I'd want to hide—my belly, my expressions, me... Not with him. I was comfortable and desperate.

"I'm going to watch you come. I didn't get to see it last time, but I got to fucking feel it." He started rubbing my clit with his thumb while moving his fingers in and out.

I was coiled so tight inside. He was my sole focus. I didn't see or feel anyone but him.

I feared the explosion. I was scared the unraveling would completely undo me. He'd already outshined all my previous experiences. He ruined me.

"You can come now." He added pressure with his thumb. "It's okay. I've got you."

With that, I shattered. Irrevocably. Completely. My muscles strained as I hit my peak and rode the wave of exhilaration so damn high I was going to blow the roof off the house.

"Austen!" My cries turned unintelligible as the shaking took over, and he didn't stop. He continued to play my body like the expert he was.

It wasn't until I sank against the cushions once again that he pulled his fingers out of me.

I blinked at him, trying to catch my breath, when he brought his fingers to his lips and sucked my juices off. That was straight-up fiction shit I didn't think actually happened. I wasn't a prude, but I had thought sex like this was a blatant fantasy.

He hummed his approval and smacked his lips. "We've got a problem, V." He reached his arms over my thighs, bracing himself against the cushions until he leaned over me.

My heart skittered out of my chest. "What?"

"My condoms are next door."

My relief was acute. That wasn't a problem. "Aren't soldiers supposed to be prepared?"

His chuckle vibrated through my body. "I am, but I have to run and get some."

I waved my hand toward my purse by the door. "I'm pretty sure I've still got some."

His smile was crooked and adorable but also so damn sexy. "That means I'm going to get inside you that much sooner."

He carefully set my feet on the floor and retrieved my purse. I got the condoms out, and he had it rolled on before I set my bag down.

"I like a girl who thinks ahead," he said as he climbed on top of me, steering me sideways so we lay lengthwise on the couch.

"I didn't want to argue when he 'forgot' to go to the store. That was how Catherine happened." I didn't regret my daughter, only the timing. I did regret my foreplay talk. This was worse than telling him about my labor when he was about to put his face in my pussy.

Anger flashed in Austen's eyes. "You've been with boys, V."

"I know." My mortification drained away. Of course, he took that in stride too. "You've shown me."

A self-satisfied smirk graced his face. "Let me show you again." He lifted my leg to the back of the couch. My other foot was pressed into his hip. He placed himself, and we both watched as he entered me, one slow inch at a time. I'd just orgasmed and everything was übersensitive, but he was perfect, hitting all the right spots, filling me the way my toys couldn't.

I had to hang on to his shoulders as the delicious feeling of fullness set in.

"Look at the greedy way your pussy takes me." He pulled out and slid back in.

"Yes."

"This is how it is supposed to be done, Vienne." He traced my C-section line. The way his fingertips danced over my skin gave my nerves a direct line to my spinal cord, sending shivers up my body instead of down, almost like he was intimately tickling me.

"Do that again." I thought the scar was numb, but he'd resuscitated all the sensations.

A light skim of his finger. More tingles. He was straight electricity. "And, Vienne?"

"Yeah?" I gasped, only able to concentrate because it was him. A marching band could stomp through the living room and I'd be intensely focused on Austen and what he was doing to me—twisting me into pleasure-filled knots that were going to fill each cell with ecstasy when they exploded.

"This is only the beginning of the next few weeks between us."

I groaned. I should've given in right away. I'd be better off not knowing that I had less than a month of utter orgasmic bliss on the table. "Wait—Catherine will be home in less than two weeks."

A quiver ran through his muscles as he held himself still. As much as I lost coherent thought when he touched me, I had to be a mom first. I couldn't put my physical pleasure—more like ecstasy—ahead of her well-being.

"Two weeks, then." His jaw hardened, carved from stone, but his hips bucked enough to make my eyes roll back. "But when I'm done with you, you're going to know exactly how a man should fuck you." He pulled out and shoved in, bracing himself with a hand on the back of the couch and the other on the edge so he didn't thrust me to the floor. Every time he buried himself to the hilt, it was like feeling full for the first time. I couldn't imagine ever growing used to it. "You're going to know precisely how a man should worship your body."

"Yes." I lightly scored his chest with my fingernails. The tight concentration of energy was happening again in my core, preparing to blow.

I was going to come again, just like that. He hadn't even climaxed once, and yet this was round two for me.

Lines of strain were etched in his face. He was holding back from finishing until I came again. This man was nothing short of amazing.

This might not be the three times he'd boasted about, but two orgasms were double what I'd had before.

"Austen." I couldn't tell him that what he was doing to me was too much and not enough at the same time.

"I've got you." He grabbed my hand and sucked the tip of my index finger into his mouth. My hand suddenly had a straight line of pleasure to my groin. I felt my pussy fluttering around him until my entire body was a quivering wreck.

Then he put my hand between us, my fingertip on my clit.

"Just hold it there." He bracketed me in with his arms and pumped into me.

The bump of the pad of my finger and his thrusts sent me over the edge. I arched back and the tidal wave of pleasure slammed over me. Just when I didn't think I could take more, he dipped his head and sucked a nipple into his mouth.

The flick of his tongue and the way he moved inside me left me speechless, yet hollering his name. He grunted and released my breast. "Fuck! V!"

Once, twice, he slammed into me, then he shook through his release. Watching him let go was an experience I'd never forget. His strength was in me and all around me as he lost control, but I'd never been safer or more treasured.

When he collapsed on top of me, I wrapped both legs around him and cradled him. I was gulping in lungfuls of air until my heart rate returned to normal.

He kept his head buried in the cushions beside mine.

"That was..." There were no words. If I wasn't so depleted after having my world rocked twice, I would be angry. I'd missed out on this? Was this type of sex normal?

There would be no one better. When Austen and I were done, I would embrace my career. Austen would help me launch my professional life with the completion of the renovations, and he'd be my one fearless memory. That time that solidified why going without was better than mediocre when it came to both the physical and emotional aspects of a relationship.

He lifted his head and pinned me with a predatory

gaze. "Do you have more condoms, or do I have to make a quick trip next door?"

"You mean, like, now?"

"I said three orgasms." His smile was downright dangerous. "I think I underestimated."

⌁

Austen

She was on top of me. We were in her bed, right next to the window that had dominated my thoughts for the last couple of weeks. Her tits jiggled as she rode me, taking her sweet time, learning what she liked and how she liked it. I'd had the worst of the edge taken off, and since this was our third time having full sex, I could let her play a little longer before I took over.

She planted her hands on my chest and rolled her hips. Damn, I wasn't going to last as long as I wanted.

Her hair fell over her shoulders, and her eyelids fluttered. "Does this feel good for you?"

"Watching you get off feels good for me. I'd be content like this for life." My joke landed heavy between us. Shit.

She held my gaze for a heartbeat longer before she let her eyes drift closed. "I think I might actually come again."

Relief poured through me. The idea of forever didn't sever this moment.

My thoughts were forgotten as her walls rippled around me, gripping my cock and not letting go.

A sharp inhale left her and then her eyelids flew open, her gaze astonished. "I'm coming."

I grinned and took hold of her hips. She bucked on top of me. As soon as her orgasm started, I flipped us both and let myself go. She continued to climax while I gritted my teeth through the onslaught of pleasure.

Goddamn, this woman was a fucking sex goddess. She had no idea what she did to me.

When the thunder between my ears abated, I didn't collapse on top of her like the first time on the couch. I could be more considerate.

I pulled out and rolled myself beside her. I stayed on my side and draped an arm over her stomach. She smiled at me, and we both lay still for a few moments.

Now that the worst of my desire was sated, the sense of being rebuffed came over me. She'd resisted this for weeks. Then I'd promised her until I left town, and she'd countered with a shorter timeline. Her reason was valid, and the past me would've never cared.

The current me, the guy who got to be with his family whenever he wanted and whose siblings planned a night just for me because I wasn't on the swimming thread, was starting to wonder...

She brushed her fingers over my forearm. "If you tell me we're going again, I might have to bow out."

I chuckled. "That's okay. You can just watch."

Her gaze flew to me, eyes wide.

I laughed. "Just kidding. I'd need a few hours."

"Oh."

We lay for a few more minutes. Drowsiness was taking over, and the bed was comfortable. I'd been wanting to be with her for so long I was just enjoying being with her.

She started fidgeting. A little wiggle at first. Then she crossed her ankles and uncrossed them.

I looked at her. "How are you doing?"

Indecision flitted across her face. "Good. I mean, great."

"Not a resounding confirmation of how tonight went."

She put a hand on my forearm and even that touch was enough to slap some awareness into my dick. "No, that's not what I meant. I guess we kept dancing around this moment that I never really thought of after."

"Like what?" My mind was foggy. I was sex stupid, or I'd be more attuned to what was fueling her anxiety.

"Well... We have to work in the morning. And, I mean, I have my bookkeeping job to catch up on."

She'd mentioned her other job in passing, but I'd forgotten my work wasn't her only job. I had all weekend, but she was a single mother with two jobs. "Right. You need rest." She didn't need me pawing at her all day.

I wanted to though.

"Yeah, and sometimes, Rudy catches up on orders on Sundays."

I had to scramble to remember who Rudy was. My desire gave way to hurt. She was still worried about being caught. Did I think the act of sex with me would overcome all her issues?

Did I think I was important enough for her to work around them? I knew better. "Right. We each have stuff to do. Like plan that open house." Or find a real estate agent. I should've done that a month ago, or say like, when I signed the leasing paperwork.

"Okay. Right. The open house." She nibbled on her lower lip. "Um, sorry? I feel like I'm kicking you out."

"Don't be." She kept her head through all this. Meanwhile, I was thinking about more than the next two weeks. I was thinking about how fucking amazing this would be to have for forever.

A scornful laugh caught in my throat, hurt immediately backing up behind it. I couldn't be a little boy who was hurt about not being included in the sleepover. She'd been transparent from the beginning. Hell, so had I. I had a job waiting for me. A company I'd helped form. Plans I'd thought about less and less as Vienne had claimed more mental space in my head. But we each had our own life. I was a little confused about the future I wanted for myself, and that wasn't her problem.

I kissed her and traced my fingers across her stomach. A shiver ran through her.

"Sleep tight." I climbed out of bed. I'd have to stop in the bathroom and take care of the condom and then sneak next door and hope no one was cruising town in the middle of a Sunday night while I snuck into my house.

"Austen?"

I was at the door. The upper level of this house was like mine, with only one bathroom unconnected to any bedrooms. "Yeah?" My hope surfaced. Had some of the same thoughts of forever been running through her head?

"Can you lock my front door when you go? You can just do the lock on the handle."

The question was a paring knife to my gut. Small but damaging. "Oh, yeah. Sure. See you tomorrow, V." I had to get my head straight. I was leaving. She didn't want me to stay tonight or beyond the renovations.

Fifteen

AUSTEN

Getting my dick sucked in the middle of a workday was always appreciated, but Vienne was going to ruin every single job from now through the rest of my life.

I tipped my head back, a groan resonating off the bare walls of the lower floor of my house. We didn't bother closing the blinds—didn't want to be suspicious in case any nosy Crocus Valley residents were peeking in as they walked by—but we were tucked into the corner. Ironically, the short wall we took out would've been the perfect concealment, but no one could see us. If a person was tall enough to look through the kitchen window, they'd see my back, my ass hanging out of my jeans, and Vienne on her knees in front of me.

I hissed at the exquisitely painful nip of her teeth. She gazed up at me, her cheeks hollowed and with wickedness dancing in her eyes.

I was in fucking trouble. She gave blow jobs like she

gave peep shows—with a dash of shyness but fully committed.

Sparks ignited at the base of my cock, warning of an impending boom. "I'm gonna come in that pretty mouth if you don't back away."

Challenge deepened the blue of her eyes, and she increased the suction.

Oh, fuck. My heart might stop if any more pleasure flooded my body. "Christ, I'm serious—"

She grabbed my ass cheeks and deep-throated me.

I flew into oblivion. "*Fuck.*"

I spilled inside of her, and she swallowed me down, continuing to suck and cup my balls. I slammed a hand on the wall to keep upright. I gently urged her to let up. "You're going to kill me, and I'll take us both out when I fall."

A different feeling wound through me that had nothing to do with the joking-not-joking warning I gave her. I was falling. Too hard and too fast. Vienne was fun. Practical. Ambitious. Tough. She wasn't a bullshitter, and I appreciated that part of her personality more than I could say.

When she was on her knees in front of me, it was easy to tumble all the way into a place I never thought I'd be.

She wiped off her mouth. God help me. This woman was a dream I didn't know I had.

I helped her up before tucking myself into my pants. "That was some amazing head," I said lightly before she sensed my emotions were more serious than usual.

Her grin was sultry. "Happy to be of service. Want some lemonade?"

I'd need to spike that lemonade to keep from pawing at her all afternoon. "It's lunchtime. We could go to

Hummingbird's and grab a bite." After eating there with her parents, she was more inclined to grab lunch out. We talked about the work we were doing when we ate.

"Give me a few minutes to let my flush go away, or Thelma's going to know what I was doing."

Before she'd dropped to her knees, I'd bent her over the island, burrowed my hand down the front of her pants and got her off.

Today was minor compared to the last week. Monday afternoon, we were sprawled on the floor of one of the extra bedrooms upstairs, naked and sated. Staining the main floor hadn't gotten done, that was for fucking sure. I was supposed to be in California soon. The messages from Johnson were coming fast and furious. He had a room ready for me in his apartment. I ignored how I'd be going from a big-ass house to being a roommate in a tiny apartment. I convinced myself I wouldn't care because I'd dive into the start-up. However, I'd be racing to get the job done here and put the house up for sale before I left.

I was losing time because we were too busy fucking.

Vienne was too responsive not to be with her every chance I got. I was humble enough to admit she made me feel like a god. The way her expression was stunned every time she came, how she looked at me like she couldn't believe I was real, got to a part of me I didn't know existed. Like I was needed. Wanted. If only for the short term.

While she was in the bathroom, I poured us both a glass of lemonade. When she came out, she smiled. Two bright pink spots were on her cheeks. I liked the look on her.

I handed her a glass. "You need this."

She downed the drink in seconds.

I chuckled. "Chug a few beers in your day?"

"In my way-too-early days. Otherwise, I was pregnant before I turned twenty-one."

"No partying after that?"

She shook her head. "I was okay with it. I did enough in high school."

"Didn't sway me. I had to make a conscious decision when I was in my early twenties. Did I want to miss opportunities because I was too hungover to care? That'd end up with me going back home and being under Barns's thumb. Or did I want to put some effort into my career? Then I could be independent of the Knight name and have more options outside of Buffalo Gully."

"I always thought Wilder was the only law enforcement sibling. Why wouldn't they talk about what you do? I mean, beyond being in the army."

"They don't understand it." After I'd come home a few times, my brothers had quit asking, and Aggie wasn't one to pry in the first place.

"What's not to understand?"

I lifted a shoulder. "The first couple of years, I was a gate guard. Not exactly scintillating. Then I was a lot like a beat cop, only I wasn't policing anyone my family knew, like Wilder did, which made the domestic dispute calls a little easier for me than they were for him. Once I got a little rank, I did patrols. But to them, to a lot of people, we're not real cops, and when we deploy and stuff, we don't do typical law enforcement things, so they think of MPs as general soldiers and not law enforcement."

"But you did MP stuff overseas?"

"Yep."

"How's it different?"

I'd had to explain my job to dates before, and I'd

always generalized what I did. Security. Working with local police. Training. But with Vienne, I went deeper. We were fooling around, but she wasn't superficial in my life. "You can think of it as a lot more security than law enforcement. We keep the rear area protected, do detention ops—you know, secure any prisoners. The guys I'm starting the security company with? Wentz, Johnson, and Morales? We used to do security ops for higher-ranking officials and route recon in Iraq. We went through some shit together."

"You're close with them." She lifted herself onto the island, the only countertop I'd left on until the new ones arrived. The cabinets were back-ordered for a week, pushing me ever closer to my go date.

I moved in front of her, wedging between her legs. My favorite place. "We came up with our business plan so many years ago, I'd forgotten it. I went the officer route, so my role changed. I was more involved in oversight and planning than actually in the trenches. I lost touch with them. Wentz got out first. Got divorced within the first year he was home. He needed a better job, so he called Johnson, who'd been out and divorced, not in that order, for years. Morales called me. Me and Morales were retiring within a year of each other. We decided to put our plan into action." It made sense. It still made sense.

But was it the right move?

What would I do for work if it wasn't?

"Worked out perfectly," Vienne said. "Would you have retired? Or did you need to retire?"

"I could've stayed in." I had planned to. I had nowhere else to go, and returning to the ranch full time hadn't been an option. While I loved Eliot, I didn't want to feel like the last twenty years didn't happen.

"Why didn't you?" She put her hands on top of mine that were flattened on her thighs. I didn't realize I was touching her.

Why didn't I? As soon as I'd learned I would get some inheritance free and clear from Barns without having to tie myself to the ranch or the oil well business, I waited out the rest of my time in the army. Before that, I thought I'd stay in until they kicked me out.

The inheritance hadn't changed my options, but the extra kick of money, not nearly what I would get if I was working for the ranch or oil well business, gave me an out for either option. I could afford to piss around for a while. I could enjoy not having mandatory morning PT or formations or bureaucratic bullshit. No more death by briefings. I could keep my own schedule.

Then Morales had called and reminded me of a brainstorming session that had given us something to think about other than being deployed. I'd half forgotten, but the conversation had imprinted on him and Wentz. They had remembered me. Considered me. Invited me.

I was honored.

I was due to leave the second week of August.

Yet, there was nowhere I wanted to be but in a house with no stained main-level floor, cabinets waiting to get ripped out, and a sexy woman on the countertop.

"We should go have lunch, or we're never going to get work done today." Humor laced her voice.

"Yeah. We should." I didn't want to work. "Or...we could go to the lake."

"The lake?" She laughed. "What would we do? I don't have a boat."

"I can go buy one." I wasn't usually impulsive with

my money, but I suddenly wanted to do something different. Because Vienne was different.

"A boat trailer?"

"I'll buy that too."

"Austen." Her smile faltered, and she smoothed a hand down the front of my shirt. "I enjoy what we're doing, I really do, but taking a work afternoon and going to the lake for a day?"

I was supposed to know what she meant. Our fling couldn't go beyond the respective walls of our houses, but couldn't we be more than coworkers in public? Didn't she consider me at least a friend? But that wasn't what others would see. "The gossip?"

"We're working very closely together. I'm still nervous about going for lunch. An afternoon at the lake is a bit... date-y, isn't it?"

She didn't want it to look like we were out on a date, or she didn't want to be out on a date with me?

Did the answer matter? Either way, she was saying no.

Disappointment kept a steady beat behind my sternum. I could tell myself her reason was of no consequence, but the dull ache said otherwise.

※

Vienne

The bar was louder than usual and more packed than when the family reunion had been in town. I recognized a few people. Hal from Hummingbird's. A friend of my dad's. Even my old gym teacher was out tonight. He grinned and waved when he saw me, always delighted when he saw former students. We'd had to bypass darts thanks to all the extra people and the tables shoved out of the way for karaoke.

"Are you going to sing?" Tova asked, looking at each one of us one by one.

"Absolutely not." Sutton shuddered. "I'd drive out half the bar."

Aggie's curls flew as she shook her head. "There's not enough alcohol."

That left me. I counted through my bracelets. Inhale, one, two, three. "Um...I don't usually join in." Unless I was with a giant group.

"Do it," Tova said. "I'm half tempted to tell Cody to come and sing. The first night I heard him play guitar—" Her face flushed, and she glanced at Aggie.

Aggie was in the middle of a gulp of water and she choked, squeezing her lips shut. She finally swallowed and laughed. "I don't want to know, do I?"

"Nope." Tova took a hasty drink from her can and failed to look innocent.

"Have Cody take the kids to my place." Aggie pushed her glass to the middle of the table. "I told Ansen I would be home to nurse, and my time is almost up. Get Cody and Wilder and Austen here."

"Does Austen sing?" Tova asked.

Was there a nonrevealing way to announce that I'd heard Austen can sing? *Hey, I had my windows open and I was attuned to everything Austen and he has the voice of a hot angel.* The girls had no idea just how entwined we were much of the day, and they definitely didn't know I'd been a master spy as a neighbor before we started our window meetings.

Aggie lifted a shoulder. "I've heard him belt out verses

here and there, but I've never heard him take on an entire song. Daddy wouldn't have tolerated him, or any of us, in choir."

"That must be why Cody learned guitar in college."

Aggie shrugged but also nodded. "I wouldn't be surprised. Eliot sings when he's working by himself and thinks no one can hear."

"Wilder can sing, but he'd never do it in public." Sutton stuck a finger in the air. "However, he'd love to give his brothers shit."

Aggie tapped out a message on her phone. "I'm letting Ansen know the plan in case the others go for it."

"I've got Wilder and Austen," Sutton said.

My belly did an excited flip. It was girls' night, but I also liked seeing all the sides to Austen. I liked getting to know the real him. I very much craved the way he touched me. How he growled in my ear when he came. A flush was creeping up on me. I forced my mind away from Austen, which was getting impossibly harder to do.

Tova was buried in her phone. "Oh no." Her shoulders slumped. "Charlie's not feeling good. She's super fussy. Cody thinks she's getting more teeth. He told me to stay with you guys, but I should get going too."

"It's hard to be out when your baby isn't feeling good," Aggie agreed and shifted her attention to Sutton. "Are we still on for the wedding party Sunday?"

Sutton became radiant as soon as the wedding was mentioned. "I'm happy to celebrate I'm a legit Knight again."

She and Wilder had said their vows last Monday. Aggie and Cody were their witnesses. Over the weekend, we would all celebrate.

Aggie squeezed Sutton's hand. "You always were." She slid off her stool, and Tova did the same.

After they said their goodbyes and left, Sutton set her gray gaze on me. She wiggled her phone. "Wilder and Austen can make it. Is that okay?"

"Why wouldn't it be?"

She leaned on her elbows over the table. "You've been awfully quiet tonight anytime Austen's been mentioned. I wasn't sure if the almost fling went all the way or fizzled out."

All. The. Way. Going to work and pretending I wasn't hot and bothered over him was tough. Being with him when we hadn't yet touched each other was a special form of restraint. But reverting to being nothing but neighbors who worked together was going to be hell when Catherine was back in town. My time messing around with Austen could be measured in hours.

"The almost fling definitely didn't fizzle," I finally answered. "But it will when Catherine's home. Dave's bringing her and staying for a few days."

Sutton's light brows tipped up. "He's staying?"

I nodded, dread dampening the foamy beer. "I'm glad for Catherine. When she calls, I can tell she's excited."

"But you're not?"

"I'm so not. If he comes as her dad, that'll be fine. If he comes as a pompous investment banker, then that's another story. Anyway, she's disappointed she won't be back in time for the wedding celebration."

Sutton's smile was understanding. "I've been missing her at all the get-togethers but it's fine. We'll have plenty more, and she can feed Sylvester whenever she wants."

I shuddered. I'd fed Sutton's bearded dragon meal worms and crickets when she was out of town, and I'd do it as often as she needed, but I was grateful I had a teen enthralled with Sylvester. "She'd like that."

The karaoke announcement went up, and the sounds of chairs scraping the floor filled the bar as people turned to watch those who sang. A few minutes later, Wilder and Austen walked in.

Just like before, Wilder entered first, his gaze going straight to Sutton. I held my breath until Austen came into view behind Wilder. He was already looking at me, dressed similarly to how he was the last time at the bar.

I smiled and gave him a wave. It looked like I was greeting both of them.

Wilder kissed Sutton and scooted the stool Tova had been sitting in closer to her.

"Hey, Vienne." Austen nodded toward Sutton. "Sutton, one of my three favorite sisters." When she rolled her eyes, he grinned. He sat, keeping the seat Aggie had used an inconspicuous distance away from mine, his eyes twinkling. "I hear we need to clear the air. Sutton and Wilder know?"

Panic climbed into my throat. Wilder knew? Of course he did. Sutton wasn't keeping secrets from him. Was Austen upset? Like I'd been talking about him behind his back?

Sutton grimaced, her gaze just as fraught as I felt. "I'm really sorry." She nudged her husband. "And he's supposed to be as secure as an armored car."

Wilder was unrepentant. "Doesn't mean I won't give my brother shit. It's not my fault he immediately confessed."

Austen shot him a sharp look. "You said it like you already knew."

"One of us has done more questioning in our law enforcement career," Wilder archly replied.

"I'm surprised you actually put us in the same category."

A troubled frown pulled at Wilder's lip. "Why wouldn't I?"

Austen only shrugged, but our discussions from earlier came back.

"I know our jobs differed a lot, but they were also really similar." Wilder grinned, and I was glad to hear him clarify his thoughts for Austen's sake. "But I looked better in my uniform."

"Sutton's opinion doesn't count," Austen countered.

The notes of a country song blasted out of the speakers, followed by the warbly notes of a woman who was laughing as much as she was singing.

Austen smothered his wince. We all did, but her energy made up for her off-key singing.

He got off his stool, and I thought he was signing up to do a song, but instead of crossing to put his name on the karaoke list, he bent to speak into my ear. "Sorry, I fessed up."

"Don't worry. I don't mind them knowing. They owe me for when I kept their sneaking-around secret." It took everything in me not to turn my face into his. I'd love nothing more than to feel his lips on mine. Instead, I shook my head. I'd been busted almost the same way. The prickles of people's gazes were on me. We were with Sutton and Wilder, but I couldn't make this look like a double date. Talk might get back to Jim.

Why did I care about what he or Dot thought?

Money. I had no job offers waiting for me. We didn't even have a date for the open house, which was supposed to garner me more job offers. I did have an end date for my bookkeeping income and for when the house had to be done.

The second week of August. The week after next.

Austen's gaze lowered to my beer. Summer Sunset. The flavor was good enough, but each time I drank it, I remembered our talks, and it made me want to have it again. It was becoming my go-to beer.

How much would I drink this fall?

He pushed away from the table. I didn't have to read lips to know he told the woman who'd been sing-giggling she'd done well. Her grin took over her face, and she gave her friends a *Did you see that hot guy talk to me?*

I feathered my fingers along my bracelets. Excitement rose like a birthday balloon. He'd be good. I knew it. I'd heard enough, and tonight, he had the soundtrack and a microphone.

"What's he going to sing?" Sutton asked Wilder.

"Something crazy," was his answer.

I turned in my chair to fully face the makeshift stage. Austen toed wires out of his way. There was no chance a drunk karaoke participant wouldn't trip on them by the end of the night.

He looked up. The glow of the poker machines, the neon alcohol signs on the wall, and two small lights shining in the direction of where the singer would stand were the only spotlights. A small screen with the lyrics was off to the side.

He winked in my direction, then grinned at the crowd, who was much more interested in him than the previous woman. I had never gotten the fangirl sensation before, but I'd throw my underwear at him after that wink.

The first notes started. Sutton's laugh was lost in the bar's roar. The song was Dolly Parton's "Jolene." I joined in with the laughter until Austen's voice rang out, then I was captivated. He tapped the toe of his shoe, keeping count as he sang. The man had done this a time or two.

Patrons whooped and hollered as he ran through the warnings to Jolene not to mess with his man. When he wrapped up, applause shook the room.

"No one's going to follow that," Wilder said.

"Wilder, get up here." Austen still had the microphone, and he continued to command the crowd.

"Nope." Wilder didn't speak loud enough to do more than read his lips, but his resolve was unmistakable.

Austen turned his gaze to Sutton, and she emphatically shook her head. His attention turned to me, and he grinned. "Vienne?" he purred into the microphone. The sound went straight to my clit like a physical stroke.

"Go on, Vienne!" someone shouted from the back, yanking me out of the way Austen's voice affected my body. I tried to find who was throwing me in front of the bus and found a friend of my dad's.

I wasn't as intentional as Sutton, but I shook my head, big groups only. I couldn't sing well enough to stand next to Austen.

"Can you nail a tune as well as you sledgehammer a wall?" Austen tried again.

I rolled my eyes.

"She can!" another man shouted. "I've heard her."

My old gym teacher. He'd have been to my choir performances in front of the school. I sang the national anthem at basketball games and football games, but I never did a solo. I was always with friends.

"Vi-enne," my gym teacher started chanting, holding his beer up. "Vi-enne. Vi-enne."

The crowd joined in. Damn. I slid off my stool before I knew I was moving.

I should've worn more bracelets.

Fear threatened to close my throat, but I caught my old gym teacher's eye. And my dad's friend. They were grinning, excited. They'd known me years ago. When I was ready for any challenge. When I didn't sit one out every time. When I didn't care what people said about me.

Finally, my gaze connected with Austen's. His grin was knowing. He'd asked Wilder and Sutton first to keep the crowd from knowing that he really wanted to get me up there alone with him.

He grinned and gestured for a second microphone. The DJ, a woman who wasn't far over the drinking age, with bleached hair, a nose barbell, each eyebrow pierced, and as many earrings as I had bracelets, tossed him one that was attached to one of the many wires. Austen handed the microphone to me.

I accepted it but kept it away from me. "I get to pick the song."

"It's already chosen." He got me right where he wanted me like he knew I always had a reason for not doing something like this.

Damn him for being sweet and tricky.

The lyrics popped on the screen just as the song started. Another Dolly Parton special. "9 to 5."

My giggle snuck out and grew worse as Austen started on the rapid-fire lyrics at the beginning. He and I were working together during the same hours. Was that the reason why he chose this song in particular? The chorus was coming up, and he waved his hand to get me to join him.

The humor took away my self-consciousness. I let loose like I was in the shower. Clapping drowned out our sound, and a familiar rush of adrenaline rushed through my veins. I'd missed this exhilaration, the freedom of pushing my boundaries.

When we were done and the applause died down, exhilaration pumped through me. I didn't even care when Austen asked the crowd if they minded if we did one more. And when Shania Twain's "Man! I Feel Like A Woman" started, I didn't miss the opening.

Austen was slowly giving me back a part of myself. He was helping me create fearless memories that would last long after he left.

Sixteen

AUSTEN

Last Thursday night after karaoke, we'd driven our vehicles back, parked in our respective spots in front of each of our houses, then I'd followed her into her house. I'd left two hours later, long before Rudy arrived at his shop to open the doors and send the sounds of an impact wrench down the street.

Today was Saturday, and we were celebrating Wilder and Sutton's marriage at their house. Eliot was in town tonight and had shoved Wilder away from his own grill, using the excuse that taking over was an early wedding present. His need to command the grill was likely due more to how he'd rather work than talk, and it didn't matter if he was surrounded by family.

Vienne had arrived and went straight for Sutton, Aggie, and Tova. I'd gotten a small, secret smile from her. I'd been able to keep from staring at her legs or the way her thighs curved under the hem of her shorts. I definitely didn't stare when the breeze picked up and pushed her loose cornflower-blue shorts against her side, highlighting the flare of her hips. I'd been a well-behaved man tonight, so none of the attendees would know I was thinking of Vienne naked.

I'd been through plenty of weddings. Hell, I'd been in tons of them between my siblings and the guys I'd served with. But this was the first time I wondered what it was like to plan for the future with a woman you couldn't quit thinking about.

Was it a relief to know she was swearing to be forever his? What was it like to talk about expanding the family? I was nearing four decades on this earth, and while I was a guy and could technically make babies until I hit my deathbed, what was it like for Wilder to strive for a family with Sutton? Or when Cody and Tova had talked about adding to Ivy and Grayson and juggling a blended family? Aggie and Ansen had decided to bang out kids in rapid succession because they'd lost ten years together, thanks to our dad.

Then there was me and Eliot. Did he have the same thoughts? Was that why he preferred to have something to do with his hands when he took over the grill? Because once these questions invaded your brain, you realized you were surrounded by the people answering them for themselves? I would be packing my bags in only a couple of weeks. Vienne had been excitedly talking about her daughter returning. She was moving on with her life, and I wasn't included.

The back of my neck grew hot, and I rubbed the spot like I'd gotten a sudden sunburn. My future was planned, and it didn't include a wife or kids.

And if it did...I was starting to see one woman's face. I

was starting to think about blended families with stepkids and—

Fuck's sake. I had to get off this line of thinking. What was the saying? That way lies madness?

I wandered toward Eliot. He moved hot dogs around to keep from charring them. Grayson detested over-cooked hot dogs and had a breakdown over them once after his mom had died. Eliot had been diligent about cooking them to perfection ever since.

I pointed to a black grill line. "You ruined it."

"Shut up, jackass. It's fine." He peered closer, and when I started laughing, he scowled at me. "Not funny. I'm not ruining their wedding celebration."

"If their divorce didn't ruin the wedding celebration, I think they're fine." Grayson was also less likely to have meltdowns these days.

"When are you leaving? I'm supposed to come back for another party."

"What party?"

He rolled his eyes toward me. "Your going-away party."

They were planning one? I thought I'd pack my bags, wake up, and drive out of town without being noticed. It was what I usually did unless Eliot was giving me a ride to the airport. But a party? That was a first. The center of my chest warmed. "I'm not sure I'm invited."

"Once, idiot. We forgot your birthday once. And we all know why. As shitty as it was, could you cut us some slack?"

I wasn't prepared for his venom, but I had to keep arguing out of principle. I wouldn't be a proper brother if I didn't. Besides, he was incorrect. "More than once."

"We sent texts." He smacked around a hot dog. "It's

not like you blow up my phone on holidays and birth-days. We usually have to hunt you down."

"I answer my phone."

"When you're in the field? Or when you're doing some of that strategy shit you do?"

He had a point. There had been times in my workday when I was without my phone.

I also hadn't done more than send a quick text on my siblings' big days. If I was coming home, then I would get them a present. Which wasn't much different than them.

Instant heartburn set in. It wasn't painful enough to apologize. "Fine, I'll come to my party. Quit begging."

He smirked, knowing I wouldn't admit he was right. "We'll just have it at your place?"

I loved my family, but they weren't trampling through a house before I asked someone to spend hundreds of thousands to buy it. "The house will be getting ready for sale."

"Cody said you weren't giving tours."

I scoffed. "Of course, you can come look at it. There's a lot of work that still needs to be done. Cabinets and countertops. I've only installed the island countertop so far. Light fixtures." I was supposed to wire those in last week. I might have to hire a painter. Or I could stay...

And bail on my buddies? I didn't like the thought of letting them down. They were counting not only on my investment but also on me as a body doing security. And yet...what was there here for me?

My gaze lifted to where the ladies stood chatting. Vienne was rimming her fingers around a charm bracelet.

He gave me a sidelong glance. "What've you been doing? Fucking around?"

"Shit takes time." Vienne was laughing at something Ivy told her. Ivy ran off and Vienne's eyes sparkled in the sun when she looked at Tova, still grinning.

Eliot flipped another burger. "That's how it is, huh?"

I yanked my focus off Vienne. "What are you talking about?"

"As if I didn't see that. You've literally been fucking around."

"No," I growled. One brother knowing was enough.

"No wonder you stayed away so long. You lie like shit."

"I have nothing to lie about." Instant guilt ignited under my heartburn.

Wilder came out of the house with a couple of bags of buns. He set them on the white tables he and Sutton had set up and crossed to us. "What'd Eliot do? You look salty as hell, Austen."

Eliot pointed at me with his metal spatula. "Do you know about him and Vienne?"

"How'd you find out?" Wilder asked.

Eliot barked out laughter that drew the attention of everyone.

"Shut it," I hissed. "Wilder, dammit." Eliot was chortling, and Wilder at least appeared remorseful.

"Shit, sorry," Wilder muttered.

"Like I couldn't see it for myself," Eliot countered.

Wilder nodded. "Once you know, you can't miss it."

"What the hell are you two blathering on about?" Crankiness spread through me. I didn't want to care that two brothers now knew. I didn't want to hide that I thought Vienne was amazing and I liked fucking her. The last part wouldn't be announced to the world, but if it wasn't for her reputation, I'd be fine with the world knowing we were a thing. For as long as it lasted. Or longer.

Which she didn't want.

"The way you look at her," Wilder said.

"How long you look at her," Eliot added. He brandished his spatula again. "You know, now that I think about it, he's always had a soft spot just for her."

My irritation increased. I did not act differently with her. "She's a good person."

Eliot grunted. "Definitely better than *'Sell My Shit When I'm Deployed'* girl."

"She didn't sell my stuff. She gave it to a buddy to store while I was gone." That ex had told me she put my belongings on Craigslist, and when I threatened to call the authorities, she spilled the truth. After her, I started storing my belongings at Eliot's when I had to leave for long periods of time.

"What about 'Sleep With My Battle Buddy' girl?" Wilder asked.

"Which one?" I asked, getting irritated. Vienne wouldn't have done any of that.

"What I don't get," Eliot said, flipping the remaining burgers, "is why it's a problem that we know. We like Vienne."

Not what I needed to hear weeks before I had to leave. "Catherine got a lot of crap at school about her mom and Jake."

"That's what Sutton said." Wilder shook his head. "All kinds of fucked up."

"Yeah, can you imagine if people in town found out she did more than work with me? She can't have gossip ruin her chances at running a business."

"I can see a lot of guys' partners telling them not to

work with her." Eliot picked off the hot dogs. "Small-town jealousy. She's an attractive, smart woman."

That small-town jealousy inconveniently reared its head. I didn't like my single brother noticing how sexy Vienne was. I'd be across the country in less than a month, and he'd be a convenient three hours away.

"Yeah, well. Keep your mouth shut. Her ex is coming on Monday and then we'll be nothing but client and interior designer." That damn heartburn. Did I have any Tums?

"She's doing way more than interior design for you." Eliot snickered when I glared at him. "I'm talking about the renovation. Get your mind out of the gutter."

My brain and body were happy to stay naked and in the gutter when it came to Vienne.

Cody came out of the house with Charlie in one arm. "That was a mega diaper load."

Ansen followed him out, with Ro sleeping against his shoulder.

"You sound proud," Wilder said.

Cody grinned. "I am." He glanced around my little brother group. "You guys are standing like you're afraid of the womenfolk."

Cody was the only brother who didn't know. I considered Ansen a brother, too, and he'd probably be less repentant than Eliot and Wilder. But if Cody learned about me and Vienne, he'd probably have opinions with a capital *O*.

Eliot snorted. "We're planning the next shindig at the ranch. You all in for working cattle and moving horses?"

Relief cooled the burn in my gut. Eliot had my back. I couldn't chance that Cody 2.0 still wouldn't try to talk sense into me or Vienne. I'd hate to leave the state irritated at him.

Worse, I'd hate to leave knowing one of my siblings had an issue with me and Vienne.

"I don't know how much help we'll be," my brother-in-law said, "but Aggie wants to make more of an effort to go for at least a day if we can't stay over."

"I have plenty of hands," Eliot said. "I need bodies for the party after."

I lived for cattle-working vacations. The only animals I had to police were of the four-legged variety, and they were more concerned with the juicy grass than self-destructing their personal lives and careers like the two-legged kind. I could hang out with my brothers and let the stress of my work slide off my shoulders until I boarded the flight back to my duty station.

Would I be able to arrange my new security job around cattle-working time?

A small voice in my head said that if I made a home in Crocus Valley, I'd have a lot more flexibility. I could still do some work for the family companies...or strike out on my own.

But I had to sell the house to get the income for my official investment. And Vienne needed the open house to propel her career.

I struggled to keep my gaze from straying in her direction.

Wilder stuffed his hands in his pockets. "If Sutton can't get time off, I'll help for a day or two. You in, Austen? We could ride together— Oh, wait. You'll be gone by then."

The back of my neck was getting so hot my shirt collar felt tight. "We'll be in the beginning phases of launching the security firm. I won't be able to get away."

"That's a cool thing you guys are doing," Cody said, shocking me. If he could be this laid-back about Vienne, I'd ask him about what I should do.

Wait— No plans were getting changed. I couldn't be changing the arrangement before I even talked to Vienne. "You'll never run out of business."

"Until some starlet steals your heart and then you're stuck protecting her forever," Ansen joked but sounded half-serious.

Eliot and Wilder monitored me like they were waiting for me to answer. When Vienne had made the joke, I had played it off, laughing with her. This time, no humor could be found.

My gut heaved. I didn't want a fucking starlet. I didn't want to date anyone I pulled security for. "My job is to fade into the background."

Cody nodded. "You'll be traveling according to their schedule. I'm sure your time off won't happen until you grow your firm, but then you'll have to work around your partners."

A knot was forming between my shoulder blades and spine. I must've pulled something hauling the old counters out.

I couldn't deny the freedom of the last few months had quickly become something I was used to. Seeing my brothers and Aggie regularly. My nieces and nephews. I didn't have to reintroduce myself each time I saw them until they were old enough to remember me.

I thought I'd need years to get used to being a civilian, to not live and die by meeting start times and training dates. Certainly, I'd miss the structure and the constant obligations. When I'd traveled those first few months after retirement, I'd done it partly to see what the allure was. Why had Mama left us for adventure? I hadn't found answers. Unlike her, I would've loved a steady place to call home. I might've thought retirement was a mistake, but I was doing a little of what Mama had— resisted putting down roots.

Then I'd bought the house and started fixing it up. I might've been a little restless until I started sleeping with Vienne. Talking to her. Having back-porch cold beers.

Those moments didn't feel like a mistake. They felt right. And I wasn't sure what to do about it now.

Vienne

Austen stretched his long legs out before him. We had a six-pack container between us with two beers left. The sun was still high in the sky, but the frogs and the crickets announced that we were in full evening. The wind had been strong today, but on the porch behind Austen's house, we were mostly untouched.

I shouldn't be having a deck beer with him on a Sunday. The neighbors might start wondering. They were probably already assuming, but seeing us together like this, more casual, wasn't good for the rumors.

I couldn't bring myself to care enough. I enjoyed these moments too much. Even Dobber was quiet as he watched us like he respected our dwindling time.

In my yard, Teddy was chasing after a white cabbage moth fluttering through the backyard. He was growing, but he was still a small little thing. Tomorrow, Catherine would give him so many hugs it'd be a miracle if she didn't squeeze all the air out of his little body.

"You're going to be sore tomorrow," I murmured, tipping my head back. My muscles ached in that contented way they sometimes did after a tough game or a brutal practice.

"I'll work through the stiffness with you in a little bit."

I cracked an eye open. "You have some stiffness of your own."

He adopted that lazy grin that made my stomach swoop and preen. "Want to find out?"

I grinned, but the thought I'd been ignoring inconveniently popped into my head, robbing me of the smile. "It'll be our last time together."

Catherine and Dave planned to stay in Rapid City tonight and do some sightseeing in the morning before driving the rest of the way to Crocus Valley. They'd arrive tomorrow evening.

The humor in his eyes dimmed. He worked his jaw back and forth like he was going to say something, but instead, he rose and grabbed our empty bottles of beer. He put them back in the box with two we didn't drink. His dark gaze was unreadable when he held his free hand out for me.

I slipped my fingers into his grip, for once not caring if any of our neighbors happened to be peeping out their window to see me following Austen into his house while holding hands.

Inside, he deposited the beer on the new butcher block island counter and led me to the stairs, where he stopped and pulled me into him.

I flattened my hands on his chest. "Are you okay?"

The corner of his mouth lifted. "I'm fine."

The serious look in his eyes would argue with the assessment. I slid my hands around the back of his neck and played with the silky strands of hair that usually curled from under his ball cap. Did I call him on his lie?

If he wanted to talk, he would. Austen didn't hold back, and some might think he was superficial, but he dealt with himself. After being raised by the type of dad he had, he refused to let others handle the burden.

That right there was a turn-on. So many different parts of this guy were a perfect fit, and this would be the last time I could enjoy them all in full. In the morning, we'd return to being business partners for a short while.

Then he'd be gone.

I rose on my tiptoes and pressed my lips to his. It wasn't a deep, smoldering kiss. More like a thank-you. Thank you for showing me what sex could be like and helping me reaffirm I was better alone than making do with less when it came to a relationship. Thank you for helping me find a long-buried part of myself I'd almost forgotten—that fearless Vienne who moved away from home to see what the world had to offer. He reminded me I was the girl who played with her whole heart out on the court until it'd gotten stomped on. I was the Vienne who was a little tired of not participating at all.

And thank you for understanding that this was it.

A tiny fissure formed in my heart, letting a thread of panic slip through. This couldn't be it. This couldn't be the end of the best thing I'd ever had.

He added pressure but didn't invade my mouth with his tongue, as if he sensed that this moment was more than frenzied sex.

Of course, he was the best thing I'd had. He was temporary. Any longer, and I'd only witness the downfall, the slow degradation that happened to every relationship I was in.

Eventually, he'd decide I wasn't enough, and his eye would turn to another. Part of the reason I'd been able to be myself, to return to Vienne Wagner before she became Vienne Ives, divorced single mom, was that he'd be gone before I experienced that all over again.

I pulled away and caught the indecision in his eyes.

He brushed his thumb against my bottom lip. "Can you spend the night?"

I nodded without thinking through the ramifications. His smile was slow, still a little subdued, but he picked me up. I automatically wrapped my legs around his waist.

He carried me up the stairs like I was nothing more than one of the packs he must've hefted around during his time in the army. He turned into his bedroom. The room was done and unadorned. His belongings were still in boxes and bins, but his bed was in the middle of the room like it was the centerpiece, the only item needed. And for us, it was.

He laid me in the middle and crawled over me.

I ran my hands over his shoulders and tugged his shirt off. "I can't get over how easily you carry me."

"I'll do it until..." He winced. "I guess that was it."

He said the last part like a question. I didn't want to dwell on how this would be the last time he undressed me or the last time I took his shirt off. The final time I could view him naked, or how I'd never get to feel him between my legs again once the sun rose.

So I whipped my shirt off and caught the smell of sweat and dust. "Ew. I need a shower." I did not exude masculine sweat like he did. I didn't smell like man and smoked vetiver when I worked all day.

"You know that's never stopped me." He wedged himself between my legs. "But we can shower together."

I grinned, biting my lower lip. We'd showered together before. In fact, we'd tested both of his new bathroom remodels, and I could gladly report that each one was spacious enough to accommodate several positions. "I think that'd be fun."

I trailed my fingers down his pecs. I liked this. His weight on top of me. We weren't really making out, but we were being flirty. We knew what was coming, but we also enjoyed just being together.

My heart skipped a beat, and my fingers faltered in their journey down his chest.

If he noticed, he didn't say anything. He dropped another kiss on my mouth, only this time, he swept his tongue in. I tasted the crisp beer and the unique flavor that was him.

"Vienne," he growled and dove back in.

I skimmed my hands around his sides and stroked his strong back, loving how his muscles rippled under my touch. He was rocking against me in the cradle my legs made for him.

Arousal built inside me, filling every crevice until I only knew him. Each time he shifted in a way that lined us up at my apex, I had a parallel sense of emptiness. I needed him inside me.

When he ground against me, I dug my nails into his back. I broke the kiss. "I'm going to need that shower."

The corner of his mouth tipped up, and he rolled off me. Instead of standing up, he turned me to face him.

I thought he couldn't wait, that he was all about

unshowered Vienne and getting dirtier before we got clean, but his expression made my inhale freeze. His eyes were troubled, and those perfect lips of his formed an uncertain line.

"Austen?" I thought of the worst thing he could tell me, but this was our last time. He couldn't break up with me when we were done when the sun rose.

"I thought I could do this, but I can't."

Alarm was a cold wave washing through my desire. "Do what?"

"Have sex and ignore what I want to talk to you about."

Talk? We'd chatted on the porch. Confusion mingled with the threat of panic that was ever present since fully acknowledging this would be our last time. "Okay?"

He unclenched his jaw. "I can't be with you knowing full well that what I say after might send you running."

My chest was growing tight like a belt was tightening around my lungs. I had flashbacks to facing Dave after he said he wanted to talk when he really meant to tell me our marriage was over.

I sucked in a slow breath. He wasn't Dave. Yet I couldn't shake the tension rippling through my muscles.

"Okay?" My vocabulary had apparently narrowed to one word.

Austen's jaw was a hunk of granite. He stroked his gaze over my face. My shirt was off, but I felt bare all over, completely stripped down in front of him. Like a spotlight shone on me when there were no lights on in the room, just the rays of the evening sun around the blinds.

"What if...I didn't leave?"

I blinked. "Didn't leave where?"

"Here," he said cautiously. "What if I stayed?"

"You'd stay here? In Crocus Valley?" One small soar of delight was taken down by the panic that bloomed to nuclear-cloud proportions. No.

No, no, no.

He couldn't stay. I couldn't watch him grow tired of me. I couldn't witness him realizing I wasn't fun Vienne, who could have sex at any time during the day but had to raise a kid and be a good role model. I could *not* hear him say he was moving on. "Why would you stay?"

His brows drew together and he swallowed, his Adam's apple working up and down. Was he...nervous? "For us."

"What about us?" I was nothing but a bag of inquiries. A parrot who asked redundant questions instead of asking him specifically what he meant. Us, as in, how can we keep fucking after Catherine comes home? Us, as in, how do I land that important job when people learn I'm officially with Austen? Us, as in, will I have to pick up more bookkeeping jobs because everyone will know I was fucking a client?

"I think you and I might have something that's worth exploring."

I let out a laugh and rolled up. "Worth exploring?" I pushed a hand through my tangled hair. I should've put it up, but I had wanted to look nicer than usual for my last day to fuck around with Austen. "And then what? You decide to nope out and move to California like you planned while I'm left trying to get clients who won't think I'll sleep with them, or—or with their husbands?"

I scrambled out of bed and started pacing. He sat up, his abs sinfully rippling while he leaned back on his hands.

"We had a good thing going," I accused.

"Yeah, we did. Really fucking good, Vienne. I like you. A lot."

I tossed a scowl his way and kept pacing. I liked him. A lot. Didn't he see that was the problem? "Austen, I can't—"

"I know you've been hurt before. I'm not those guys."

More dry laughter left me. No, he wasn't. He was so much more than those guys. He was better looking. He treated me better. He was funnier, handier, more thoughtful.

He could crush me.

The thought of being hurt again, humiliated, and having it be from Austen made a mushroom cloud of fear swell inside me. I struggled to draw in a breath. "I can't."

"You can't, or you don't want to?"

I didn't care for the accusation in his question or the way it made me defensive. "We had an arrangement." I threw my hands up, grateful I'd kept my bra on, or I'd look ridiculous right now. "And you want to change the rules? Nothing will affect you. Changing the rules will affect how *I* care for myself. I'm not just losing Rudy's account at the end of the year. I'm losing the equivalent of five." I *hated* doing bookwork, and I'd have to at least double what I was doing now. "It'll affect my daughter and what I can afford for her."

"I know. I'm not saying we rush out and announce we've been sleeping together all along. I can take you out. We can date. Properly."

I'd dated properly before and look how it turned out. I'd had to give up college. A sport I was passionate about. Fifteen years of my identity. I loved Catherine. She was hands down the best thing in my life. But if I could've chosen the timeline, I'd have picked differently. "A date?" Back and forth, I walked beyond the foot of the bed. The lick of his warm gaze heated my skin, but I was cold inside. "A date."

He could crush me. The line ran repeatedly through my head.

I'd already run back to Crocus Valley after one heartbreak. I had nowhere else to go. "This is my home."

He didn't reply. Did he understand what I meant?

"This is my home, Austen," I said, stronger this time. "If things don't work out between us, I'm rooted here. My daughter's rooted here until graduation. I can't just pick up and go. I have to face everyone." I flung my arm toward the window, and my boobs jiggled.

Count this as the first time I noticed them in an argument.

"You don't want to try." His disappointment was loud.

"I..." He didn't understand that I wanted him so badly that I couldn't try. I'd upheaved my life before, and I was still struggling. Just when I was gaining traction, getting stability for me and my kid, I couldn't yank the rug out from under me because I liked a guy.

But Austen wasn't just any guy. He wasn't Dave. He wasn't any of my exes. He was so much better. And he wanted to be with me.

What did I do?

I spun to make another trek across the foot of his bed. My gaze caught out the window and a screech left me. I dove for the floor. "Oh my god!"

Austen was off the bed and to the side of the window, in a crouch, peeking out. I had to be thankful for whatever training he had at the moment that he wasn't leering out with no shirt on.

"Is that—"

"Yes!" I scrambled for my shirt. The floor was smooth as hell, thanks to our efforts. "It's Catherine."

Dave had to be at the house too.

"Shit, shit, shit." I slipped the shirt over my head and smoothed down my hair. I jumped up, well away from the view. "Shit."

I ran down the steps and poked my head out the front door. My ex-husband was standing in the glow of my porch light outside my front door, his hands in the pockets of his khaki slacks. He had on a polo shirt, looking like he was ready for nine rounds of golf. His gleaming, light gold SUV with shiny chrome details was parked in front of my house.

He glanced over and did a double take. "Vienne?"

"Dave," I greeted. "What are you—"

Just then, Catherine darted out the door of the house. "Mom!" She flew across the yard. By the time I stepped out, she was racing up the steps, then flinging herself into me.

I laughed, my earlier fright and the conversation with Austen momentarily forgotten. I hugged Catherine and buried my head in her strawberry-smelling hair. I could squeeze her harder than I worried she'd hug Teddy. "Holy crap, have you gotten taller?"

She nodded, her strands tickling my nose. "Another inch. Now I'm taller than our middle hitter."

She pulled back and frowned at the door behind me. "What are you still doing here? I thought Austen didn't want you to work late."

"Yeah," Dave said, wandering over the grass like he

owned both properties, his hands still in his pockets. "She was worried when you didn't answer." His blue gaze drifted over Austen's house, more than mild curiosity in his gaze. "She didn't expect you to be *working* so late."

The censure in his voice made my hackles rise. My heart pounded against my ribs, but as long as they couldn't hear it, I played it cool. "I thought it'd be my last night to work since I wasn't expecting you until tomorrow."

Dave stopped at the bottom of the stairs. "She thought since you were just in Rapid City for a camping trip a few months ago, we could come here and she could spend more time"—distaste turned his lips down—"showing me around the rest of the week."

"Week?" I echoed faintly.

"Betti thought I might as well make some time of it. Once volleyball season starts, I know it's hard for Catherine to travel."

Harder for Dave to make it to a game for some reason. "Sure."

Catherine was peering through the screen door. "Wow. Are you almost done? Can I see?"

Giving a tour to my kid and my ex when I was just wrapped around Austen and then getting asked to get serious with him right before I had a meltdown didn't sound ideal right now. "I don't know—"

"Austen!" Catherine flung the door open, her fist shoved out.

"KitKat." Austen gave her an easy knuckle bump. He was wearing the same shirt I'd just torn off him, but he'd stuffed his work ball cap on backward. To mask the way I ruffled his hair? He didn't look at me but did the brochin-lift thing to Dave and stuck his hand out. "Hey, you must be Dave. Austen Knight."

Dave ascended the stairs and shook Austen's hand, the same curl of dislike on his lips. "Nice to meet you, Austen." His suspicious gaze shifted from Austen to me and back again.

"Can we see the inside?" Catherine asked, her smile wide. She was oblivious to the tension—between me and Austen, me and her dad, her dad and Austen. Lucky girl.

I played my fingers across my bracelets. "We should probably—"

"Those things still make a racket." The corner of Dave's mouth quirked. Not quite a sneer, but his distaste was apparent. I would've added more if I knew he was coming.

"I'd rather listen to those than a lot of other things." Austen sounded jovial enough, but his gaze was hard. He shifted his attention to Catherine, and his expression softened. "It's all right with me if it's okay with your mom."

I kept my smile as casual as possible. "Sure. Why not?"

I knew why not. While Austen gave the tour, I would only remember all the rooms and surfaces where I'd had sex with this man. I'd recall that I freaked out on him when he told me he wanted more. Even worse, I'd know the entire time we hadn't finished our conversation.

Seventeen

AUSTEN

Vienne must've died inside at least a thousand times. I had already led Catherine through the first floor. I waited by the island while she inspected the bathroom renovation. I deliberately blocked out any memories of Vienne naked or writhing under me. Even my irritation at her dick of an ex couldn't suppress the recollection of how her cries sounded bouncing off the walls. I was as cool as the spring Montana wind.

Dave either had resting unimpressed face or he was putting effort into his expression. If nothing else, shouldn't he get a kick out of Catherine's reaction? She'd babysat Ivy and Grayson in this house. Instead, the only change I'd witnessed was the anger when his gaze landed on the two remaining beers I'd set on the counter.

He knew what we'd been up to.

He'd probably guffaw to know what we'd actually been doing when he arrived.

"I can't *believe* you took down a wall." Catherine frantically waved her hands where the partition wall had been.

"I didn't. Your mom did." Vienne might've just ripped my heart out ten minutes ago, but I'd give credit where it was due.

"Seriously, Mom?" Catherine's eyes bugged out.

Vienne shrugged. "I've wielded a few sledgehammers in my day."

"Glad it wasn't me she was pissed at that day."

That broke through Dave's seeming disinterest. His gaze sharpened, and he looked at Vienne.

She avoided meeting his eyes. "Every girl should have a wall to knock down once in a while."

Vienne was about to shove her bracelets up and down her forearm, but she stopped and dropped her hand.

Goddamn Dave.

"What else did you do?" Catherine wandered to the back door, let out a shriek, and burst outside. "Teddy! I missed you."

"I think we lost her," I joked.

Vienne's lips begrudgingly lifted, only a little.

Dave's features formed into his mask. "I should check in at what they call a hotel in this town."

"They have openings?" Vienne asked.

He scoffed. "It's a Monday in the middle of nowhere North Dakota. Why wouldn't they?"

She clenched her jaw.

"Isn't there a lot of business traffic with the plants and the mine?" I asked Vienne. "I imagine that place is hopping."

Dave's expression turned flinty. "What is it you do?"

"I was military police for the last twenty years. I just

retired." I gave him a quick smile. His gaze hardened like he detested I had a legitimate answer. "Soon, I go to California. A few buddies and I are planning to open a security firm."

I lifted my attention off him to Vienne, but she was wandering to the back door. Presumably to watch Catherine but more likely to avoid me. The hurt from her panicked reaction to having me stay returned, sinking into a dull ache in my gut.

Our talk hadn't been finished, but there was nothing more to say. The entire conversation had been one big old nope. I didn't want to talk her into anything. Either she wanted me. Or she didn't.

I had asked her if she didn't even want to try, but her lack of response was enough. She'd spotted Catherine, but my answer was in the guarded way she stood. The regret in her eyes. The fear in her voice.

I wouldn't push her.

"Security for what?" Dave asked reluctantly, like he refused to be impressed but couldn't help his intrigue.

"Whatever there's a gap for us to fill, but mostly personal security. Johnson—one of the guys I'm doing this with—and I were on missions where we were basically bodyguards to high-ranking officers and visiting officials." Vienne was looking over her shoulder from her stance at the door. I might pour out a few more details to impress her. I didn't give a fuck about Dave. "We can also secure homes, buildings, and outdoor locations. It's easy enough to learn about civilian security systems. The rest is basically guard duty, which I've done plenty of in my day."

Dave lifted his chin to somehow look down his nose

at me. "Twenty years and all you'll have to show for it is being a bodyguard?"

Vienne made an indignant noise, but Dave paid her no mind.

That fucker. "I guess if I wanted to gloss over the hundreds of soldiers I've worked with and trained and mentored, the countless successful missions I've been a part of overseas and in CONUS—that means continental United States. Not long ago, I was just talking to Vienne about how I didn't realize how involved I'd be in soldiers' civilian lives either—helping them navigate trauma and personal struggles." I rubbed the back of my neck, pretending to be chill as hell when I was winding tighter. How long did Vienne have to deal with this asshole? "I don't need a medal to show what I've done." I smirked and summoned as much arrogance as possible. "Just kidding, I have a whole chest full of them. Anyway, I'll take being a bodyguard all day long over sitting behind a desk and groaning every time I stand up."

Dave flinched and played it off as a sniff. I suppressed a laugh. I couldn't be too cocky. I'd been known to let out a groan every now and then after getting up. More often, if I was honest. The higher in rank I had gotten, the more desk work I had seen. But in the name of belittling this jackass, I'd tell a fib.

I caught Vienne's gaze. She had her lips rolled in like she was fighting a giggle. She should fucking laugh in this dick's face.

Catherine burst through the door, her smile as wide as the house. "I missed him sooooo much. Dad, wanna meet Teddy?"

"Sure." Dave darted in her direction, putting as much distance between me and him as possible.

"I'll be right over," Vienne said to Catherine. "I need to talk to Austen really quick."

They were out the back door, and I was alone with Vienne. The heaviness from the way we'd left the topic of us landed between us.

"This can wait," I said quietly.

"Only because I'm dying to watch Dave try to jump that fence."

I chuckled but sobered quickly.

She twisted her hands together. "Austen..."

I shook my head. "It's fine. I understand. I really do. I'm not going to beg." I put my hands over my ball cap, lifted it off my head and stuffed it back down. "I'm leaving once the house is listed. If you want me to stay, you know where to find me."

"You'd just bail on your friends? Just like that?"

"For you? Yeah. I'd tell them I need some extra time." There was a lot I could do remotely to a point. I had to know if I needed to consider just how long I could stretch it first.

My statement didn't win her over. It made the furrow across her brow deeper and the stricken gleam in her eyes brighter. Fuck me.

"Hey," I stated gruffly, "don't worry about tomorrow. Catherine's obviously excited to be home." And I wouldn't mind a day to sulk in private. "The whole week even."

"The whole week?" she asked with more than a thread of disbelief and disappointment.

I nodded. "I can finish installing the cabinets tomorrow, then work on the countertops. The appliances will get delivered later next week." And then boom. Get it painted and on the market.

I had to find an agent first, especially if I wouldn't be here while the house was on the market, but it was a small town. All I had to do was stop into Hummingbird's and ask one of the guys that hung out for coffee all morning.

I could ask myself why I hadn't searched for someone already, but I chose to ignore that.

"You want to be done working with me." She hugged her arms around herself, her eyes shining. She looked so damn vulnerable, my heart cracked. I wanted to go to her.

I started to cross to her and stopped. If Dave and Catherine walked in, the consequences would land on Vienne. I didn't know Dave, but I knew enough guys like him. He'd take his negative moods out on Vienne, and she couldn't afford to have him bug her more than he did. "No, not at all. I want you to be comfortable when you're here. I don't want you to miss time with Catherine. Or Dave."

She shot me a *really?* look and I started chuckling. Her lips finally curved into a smile.

"Like I said, I'll be here. And we're good at pretending nothing happened between us."

※

Vienne

After the world's crappiest night's sleep, I took Austen up on his offer to skip work today. He'd have no issues getting the rest of the cabinets up. I would be a problem. I'd be fumbling screwdrivers and dropping levels.

How could he ask me for something real? He knew where I stood.

I wanted to be angry, but I was so damn sad. Maybe distraught was a better word.

I took a sip of my bitter black coffee. I rarely drank the stuff plain, but I'd curled onto the couch before I realized I had forgotten everything about my normal routine.

I was supposed to have gotten one last time with him. I was supposed to have closure. Instead, the hurt in my chest felt a lot like loss. It stung similarly to a broken heart, and god, if it was from just messing around with Austen, how shattered would the organ be when he dumped me later?

No, I'd made the right decision. But why did it have to be so painful?

Catherine curled up on the other side of the couch, saving me from my thoughts. She told me all about her camp and the road trip with her dad. She even talked a little about how giving up her bedroom scared her.

"I can't wait to show you everything I learned. I can do a couple of different swings now and my hits are..." She grinned wickedly.

"Deadly?" I asked, pride helping soothe the pesky pain in my chest.

"So deadly. The one coach that worked with me the most—she trained Big Ten players—said she could tell the dance has really helped." As Catherine chattered on, I soaked in every word, glad to have her home, glad to return to our normal.

The melancholy didn't abate. I had gotten a month of looking forward to the next project Austen and I had. We'd made stupid-fast progress, mostly because he'd spent so many extra hours toiling away, but he did it all according to my direction. He helped me achieve my vision for the house, which I was supposed to have designed with his interests in mind, but he'd given me full rein.

When would I get that next?

I had given up two bookkeeping clients to make sure I could be available for the farmhouse project, and now I'd have to find more.

My chest constricted. I didn't have more clients lined up. All that worry about messing around with Austen ruining the reputation of Designs by V, and I didn't have a packed schedule.

It was pretty damn empty, truth be told. Once he had the open house, I hoped my phone would flood with inquiries. I hoped I could provide for me and Catherine, and the need went beyond club sports. She'd be driving soon. Going to prom. College. Normal teen expenses, but also more than we had now. I did not want her decisions to be dependent solely on Dave and how much he was willing to go halfsies on.

Catherine checked her phone. "Oh! Dad's going to be here soon. I've gotta get ready." She jumped up and tugged her volleyball shorts down. She'd come down the stairs looking like she was walking straight to the gymnasium. Practices didn't start for a couple of weeks yet.

She ran upstairs to finish getting ready. I went to the kitchen and rinsed out my coffee cup, my gaze going out the window. Austen wasn't on the back deck, but I could see movement in the kitchen. He was lifting those cabinets with those big muscles of his, his body flexing and bending. I was missing the show.

I was dying to tell him about Catherine's experiences. How excited she was about her camp and how thrilled she was to work with the coaches she had. I'd love to complain about Dave and his attitude. I missed our morning catch-up after being apart for much of the night.

The doorbell rang. I fumbled my mug. I ripped my gaze off the window. How long had I been staring, trying to catch a glimpse of Austen?

I put the cup in the drying rack and answered the door. All my disappointment welled as I found a perfectly polished Dave on the doorstep. His brown hair, with no gray in sight, was combed to the side. He was wearing the same white-and-black golf shoes he had on yesterday, a similar pair of shorts, and a yellow, pin-striped polo shirt with the Ralph Lauren logo on the chest.

"Morning, Dave. She's almost done getting ready." I stepped away to let him in.

When he walked into the house, he didn't suck out all the air and leave me breathless like Austen. Dave compressed the air. Put me on edge.

"You're not working today?"

I would be doing some bookwork, both for my side hustle and to wrap up the farmhouse renovation. "Yes, but Austen said it was fine if Catherine wanted me along with you guys today."

"Austen," he uttered and toed the leg of the end table.

I dropped onto the couch but didn't offer him a seat.

"You and he a thing?" he asked, his gaze sliding slyly toward me as if he knew he wasn't being subtle and wanted me to call him on it.

"Why do you think that?" I didn't have the energy to tell him it was none of his business. He'd claim it was since my dating life affected Catherine, and he'd conveniently forget how he'd told me that his marrying Betti was none of my business.

He shoved his hands in his pockets. He at least stayed

where he was and didn't tower over me. "Do you normally work in a dark house with no lights on and drink beer with other clients?"

"Dave," I said with a sigh. I could make excuses. I could play off what I'd been doing last night with Austen. Instead, I went for the truth. Dave never liked when I was honest about how I felt. "I'm not interested in a relationship." The words stained my tongue like I was lying. "With the divorce and Theo and then…"

"I'm glad you're done with that Theo guy." He sniffed. "Catherine did not like that man."

"He wasn't bad to either of us." Ordinarily, I'd agree, but when it came to Dave, I was driven to defend my choices. "That'd take too much effort."

We both snickered.

Dave cleared his throat, and I just knew I wouldn't like what he had to say. "I don't want whatever's going on to affect Catherine."

I rubbed my temples. I should've had another cup of coffee instead of staring out the back window. "Did you feel compelled to discuss changing Catherine's bedroom to a nursery with me?"

"I don't get what—"

"That's the thing. You don't get it, Dave. You want to stand and lecture me about my dating life and how it might affect Catherine, but you didn't seem to have the same reservations about considering how a divorce might affect Catherine. Or marrying a woman only ten years older than her. Or expanding your family when she's old enough to remember our arguments about how you didn't want more kids and that was that." I crossed my arms. I looked like I was huddling on the couch in my shorts, T-shirt and bare feet, but for once, I wasn't backing down to keep the peace.

Dave was in my goddamn house, and I would defend it.

I didn't know what changed from how he'd questioned my choices with Theo, and then after the fact with Jake, but I didn't look too hard.

"Vienne, this isn't about—"

"Yes, it is." I didn't know what he was going to say, but I didn't care. "I feel like you're using Catherine as an excuse to question my lifestyle, but what you don't seem to get after all these years is that I'm the one continually sacrificing for her. Not you. I gave up college to care for our kid. I gave up my scholarship—"

"Which I had to help pay back."

I let out a long, weary exhale. "If you want to make this about you, just say so."

He recoiled. He opened his mouth to reply, then snapped it shut.

Shit, was that all I had to say all these years?

Footsteps pounded down the stairs. "Dad!" She flew into him for a hug.

These were the moments I knew I made the right choice, and I'd make the same ones all over again. The girl needed her dad. But she needed to see me not bend until I broke for a man like her dad.

His jaw was tight, and his hard gaze stayed on me, but he hugged her back. "Ready to get some breakfast, kiddo?"

Catherine had invited me to go to Bismarck to try out some new coffee shops and bakeries, but I had passed. Dave was probably just as relieved.

My daughter paused before going out the door. "We'll pick you up later?"

"Yes," I assured her. "You need to show me everything you learned."

Then she was out the door, taking Dave with her. I sagged, but the relief was fleeting as a sense of being lost took over.

I glanced at the wall that was closest to Austen's house. I could go help him for a couple hours until Catherine came back, but I couldn't bring myself to pretend nothing had happened between us. I'd be as likely to curl in a ball on the newly polished floor and cry.

Eighteen

AUSTEN

I did not peek out the window at ten thirty last night.

Maybe once.

Twice.

No more than three times.

Today, I hadn't looked out the window more than a million times. I saw Dave and Catherine drive away, but Vienne hadn't ventured to my house.

I hadn't expected her to. I told her to take the day off.

I might've hoped she would come over.

Why, after all these years, did I get hung up on the one woman who walled herself off from all the possibilities?

Stepping back, I studied my work. I'd been mounting cabinets like a robot all morning and through lunch. They were done. They were level. They needed a good cleaning, and I didn't have the will to dust a damn thing right now.

I went to the almost empty fridge and dug out materials for a sandwich.

Voices and closing car doors drifted in through the front screen door. Catherine and her dad.

Dave.

I couldn't picture Vienne falling for a guy like him. After meeting her sweet but overly critical mother, maybe I could. Dave was like a more callous version of her mom. Only where he nitpicked to make himself feel more powerful, Kayla actually wanted what was best for her daughter. She just didn't know how to express it.

Dave was a tame version of Barns. He picked up on others' weaknesses, and he poked at them for his own entertainment.

Or perhaps I was being overly critical of a guy Vienne had given up everything for, and I was a jealous asshole.

When I was done eating, I picked up all the protective wrapping that had been around the cabinets and the scraps of paper and wood. I used my boot to open the screen door and went to the bin to dump everything.

"Austen!" Catherine called.

I tensed, a muscle cramping behind my shoulder blade as I finished tossing everything in. I turned to find Vienne looking sexy as hell in a blue, oversized tank top and a black sports bra with tight-fitting shorts like Catherine wore. I was getting a glimpse of young athlete Vienne. Any other day, I'd imagine stripping her out of those clothes.

Wrong time, wrong place.

Dave was frowning on the other side of his daughter.

I brushed the back of my arm across my forehead. "Hey, KitKat."

"Wanna play volleyball with us?" Her face brightened more. "Then we can play two on two."

Vienne's eyes widened. She hadn't expected Catherine to ask me, or she wasn't planning on seeing me today? Being neighbors made it hard to avoid each other, which I had never minded. Today, it sucked.

Dave frowned and lifted his chin to look down his nose at me.

Because of that frown—and because I wanted to see Vienne in action, along with not wishing to disappoint Catherine—I made my decision. "Sure. Let me change."

The creases around Dave's eyes deepened, but interest lit in Vienne's eyes. My chest might've puffed out a little because of that.

"Where ya playing?" I asked before I got to the steps of my porch.

"The park on the other side of town," Catherine answered. "They have a sand court that's empty during the day."

"Y'all can go ahead. I'll change and run there." A grin spread across my face when I caught Dave's expression grow increasingly disgruntled. Was I showing off a little? Maybe.

As I took the steps up to my door, I heard Dave grumble. "'Y'all'? I thought he was from Montana."

"He's been all over the world, Dave," Vienne answered innocently. "You pick stuff up when you travel that much."

Her response wiped out the doldrums from the morning. She might not be able to top Dave on being oh-so sophisticated and worldly, but I was grateful she could use me to do it. I wasn't sure what it meant that she had, but I couldn't escape the flicker of hope it gave me.

When I showed up at the sand court, Catherine was demonstrating different hits. Vienne was by the net with three blue-and-white volleyballs at her bare feet. She'd toss a ball up, and Catherine would launch herself at it. Dave was on the other side, retrieving her hits. His feet were also bare, and his hair was mussed up, dulling the corporate-jerk vibe he gave off.

I jogged to the picnic table several yards away from the double nets. The temperature was in the mideighties with a few fluffy clouds in the sky, but I'd kept my shirt on to run here. I took it off. Sweat was starting to drip down the back of my neck, and I was only going to get sandier and sweatier.

"You're here!" Catherine caught the ball Vienne had just tossed. "Girls against guys? No—wait. That'd be unfair to have two volleyball players on the same team."

"It's been a long time for your mom." Dave chuckled. "I'll be on your team."

Vienne's lips thinned, but she stooped to pick up the balls. I set my water bottle and phone down, grateful not to have to play nice with Dave on the same team.

"You can serve first, Mom." Catherine tossed the ball to Vienne.

Vienne caught it and spun it in her hands, concentration written across her face. I took my place on the same side of the sandy court as her. The net vibrated in the breeze. Dave untucked his shirt and crouched into a ready position.

"Are you used to playing *Top Gun* style?" he asked, not quite a taunt.

I grinned. "The first movie or the second?"

He laughed good-naturedly. He might naturally be an ass, but he wasn't all bad. At least Catherine had gotten the best parts of him.

I peeked over my shoulder while Vienne served. She tossed the ball high and stepped into her hit. The ball flew over the net in a low arc. I'd seen her unrestrained, and that serve wasn't it. But what did I know about volleyball.

Catherine passed to Dave, who bumped it back to her, and she did what had to be one of her new moves, flying high in the air, snapping her body back, and slamming the ball over the net.

It flew off to my side, but Vienne dove and hit it. Nice. I set up high to give her time to recover. She jumped up and did a subdued version of the hit Catherine executed.

Was she rusty, or had Catherine learned some cool new move? My gut said Vienne was holding back. She was the Vienne I had moved next to. The aloof neighbor. The professional interior designer. Where was the Vienne who stripped floors and demolished walls?

This was the Vienne who shrank herself around her ex-husband to make life easier. I gritted my teeth together and tried to concentrate on the game.

We continued playing, all of us breathing heavily, trudging through the sand to get the balls. Each time Vienne served, she didn't jump serve like Catherine, but I had to assume that in her college days, she did. When she went to serve, she had the same intent look in her eye as her daughter, but each time, there was reserved energy coiled inside her.

Dave did not hold back when he served. More often than not, he went out of bounds, putting his all into it. Despite his unhinged efforts, we were neck and neck. I thought we would've won. Catherine was good, but my gut said Vienne was better.

It was Vienne's turn to serve, and I wasn't going to watch her lower her potential one more time.

"Water break, anyone?" I called. I had put my water bottle next to Vienne's. Longing tugged at my heart. I was used to seeing that damn thing around my house. I'd known those days were coming to an end, but I didn't fucking like it.

Dave went to his car. Catherine had set her water by a tree.

When I had Vienne to myself, I turned my back to them. "Why are you holding back?"

Her turquoise eyes widened. I was standing close to get that "lilacs in bloom" scent from her. She was warm and sweaty and just how I liked her, except for that cagey look in her eye. "What do you mean?"

"I mean, you could kill Dave with that ball, but you're not."

She stiffened. "Like he said, it's been a long time."

"The hell it has. Have you held out on Catherine too?"

Her brows drew together. "I practice with her at the level she needs."

"What if she needs to see how badass her mom is?"

Her gaze dropped from my face, and she chewed on the inside of her cheek. "I don't want to make her dad look bad in front of her."

"He doesn't seem to have the same problem."

"I'm not him," she snapped. "Maybe I'm sick of proving something to everyone." She took a long drink, her gaze darting around like she was tracking her ex and her kid.

I took a long drink to swallow my frustration, to give myself time to figure out how to build up the part of Vienne others had torn down. "You don't have to prove anything to anyone, not even yourself. But it's okay to be who you are, too, and if others have issues seeing how amazing you are—fuck 'em."

She blinked, but I set my bottle down and walked back to the sand.

The ball was waiting for Vienne to serve.

She picked up the ball and looked at me. I cocked a brow, and that mutinous mouth of hers formed a thin line. She served like she'd been doing the whole day.

Fuck's sake.

If she wasn't going to try for herself, why was I holding out hope for us?

Vienne

Austen's words burned into my skin like a brand. I was already marked so thoroughly by him I'd never forget Austen Knight. Yet his *But it's okay to be who you are too* ran through my mind on replay.

Dave got the last point, tipping it over the net to the left of Austen's admirable reach when he went for a block, winning the game for him and Catherine.

"Nice!" he yelled, belly-slamming Catherine. Then they high-fived and ran around their side of the court, cheering.

I smiled, but inside, I might have seethed. Just a little.

We could've won. Catherine was a good player, but

she was young. She'd only started doing extra camps and training. Her plays were improving, but my rusty skills were still superior. Yet how did I know if I didn't try?

Dave clapped Catherine on the back. "Your old man won against a veteran and a *collegiate* player."

My inhale was sharp. I'd instilled a healthy dose of good sportsmanship into my daughter, and I was watching her dad dismantle all my work.

Austen snuck a glance at me. So he'd heard the sarcasm too. Dave had never been to one of my games. He'd always meant to but claimed to never have time. And then I'd gotten pregnant and couldn't play.

I rolled my right shoulder. The joint was limber and loose. I rolled my left side.

Your old man won against a veteran and a collegiate *player.*

But it's okay to be who you are, too, and if others have issues seeing how amazing you are—fuck 'em.

I could still feel how I used to move. The height I was able to get. Like blocks clicking into place, it all came back. No, I couldn't jump as high as when I was nineteen. Not on a court and definitely not in sand. But the muscles in my arms twitched to do what I used to fucking love doing. And that was playing the game.

So, I was going to play the goddamn game.

I was going to give one hundred and ten percent like the old Vienne, and I'd show my daughter what her mother could do.

"Losers serve," Dave said and knuckle-bumped Catherine.

No way was that dick going to teach our daughter poor sportsmanship.

Austen started for the ball that sat in the sand not far from me.

"I got this," I said, stomping through the sand.

He narrowed his eyes at me, and I didn't miss the hope shining in the brown depths. I'd disappointed him enough in the last twenty-four hours. Time to show him what I could do.

I rolled the ball in my hands. Breathe in one, two, three, envision how the serve would go—

When had I quit that step? I'd kept the breathing, but I mostly used the technique to calm myself down. At some point in the last fifteen years, I'd quit visualizing. Once my future veered off course, I'd quit picturing the possibilities. I'd accommodated. Like I'd done for Dave.

"Doing okay?" Austen asked quietly.

I lifted my gaze to him, taking in his wide shoulders, the solid way he planted his feet in the sand, how his body vibrated with energy. He was ready to move. I'd been staring at the ball in my hands.

"I'm not sure yet," I said honestly. Then I charged forward two steps, tossing the ball in the air, launching up and slamming my right hand into it.

Dammit, I dropped my elbow, and the ball hit the top of the net. My heart rammed into my throat. That was what I got for showing off. A service error in front of my ex, my impressionable daughter, and a man I had a lot of respect for.

Then it tipped over the other side, leaving Dave and Catherine scrambling to reach it.

Catherine got the ball in the air, and the game was on. I raced around with Austen. Laughter bubbled out of me when each of us fumbled the ball, failing to rescue it. But dammit, around Austen, these small failures didn't feel personal.

His deep chuckle wound around me when we almost collided, going after the same return. I windmilled my arms and fell on my ass.

"You guys gotta talk," Catherine called in a nasal tone, mimicking something she heard way too often in the stands. We'd usually joke after her games about all the unhelpful things parents shouted out.

Austen's shadow fell over me, blocking out the hot sun and heating me up even more. He held his hand out. "Haven't we been talking enough?" he asked, giving me a wink.

For a blissful moment, I could pretend nothing had changed between us. I grabbed his hand with both of mine, and he yanked me up like I was made of cotton candy but looked at me like he wanted to lick every last strand of that cotton candy.

Dave served, adding more power than he needed. The ball should've been out of bounds, but Austen was tall enough to set it to me. I set it back and approached the net. He passed me the ball.

Muscle memory took over. I might be in sand, but I powered through and rose up as high as I could, flexing backward. Then I snapped my arm forward. Adrenaline and aggression fueled my decision midflight. I aimed the ball right at my smirking ex-husband.

The ball slammed into his gut, exactly where I'd aimed. He doubled over before toppling sideways with an oomph. "*Shit*," he groaned.

He wasn't expecting the speed or the power—and wasn't that an analogy for our marriage?

"Nice," Austen said under his breath. We exchanged a smile, and he looked away quickly. My happiness faltered.

"Whoa." Catherine's eyes were wide. She trotted to her dad. "Are you okay?" Without waiting for him to answer, she spun toward me, astonished. "Mom! I've never seen you do that!"

Pride rang through me. I should feel a little bad for downing Dave, but I couldn't bring myself to care. "You were too young to practice like that with me. I didn't want you getting hurt."

She shook her head. "I'm not too young now."

"You're right. I don't need to hold back anymore." The knowledge was a special freedom that made me feel lighter.

Dave's forehead pinched like he realized I was talking about more than volleyball.

"What the hell, Vienne?" He sat up and struggled to his feet. "Get some ball control."

"I had control the whole time."

Surprised, he met my gaze and realized I was serious. His face burned red. "Lucky hit for a red shirt," he mumbled.

Austen cocked a brow. He and my daughter were watching me.

I stiffened. Dave was not diminishing my skill in front of our kid anymore. "You didn't know me my freshman year, but I didn't red shirt the whole season. It's also not my fault you were too busy my sophomore year to come watch a game, or you'd know just what I was capable of." I held my hand up, triumphant. "Our serve."

Nineteen

VIENNE

The volleyball had carried me through the week to girls' night. The bar was busy. There was a fishing tournament in the area, and this place caught the overflow of anglers and summer tourists.

Tova, Sutton, Aggie, and I were squeezed into a corner around a high-top table. We had to shout to be heard.

"Wilder's coming here again with Austen," Sutton said, her gaze flicking to mine. "I swear he's not spying on us. It's just that we're usually busy together most nights, and this is the best bar in town to chat in. The Purple Petal is hosting tournament specials, so they can't go there."

I thought of the women approaching Austen the last time he was in here. The bar didn't have quite the single-lady crowd as last time, but there were some. And Austen was extremely attractive.

Working with him this week had been...a special form of hell. He'd pretended like we didn't know what each other's *O* face looked like. I'd done the same. There'd been minimal conversation beyond asking how Catherine was doing and if Dave was still in town.

He hadn't even called me V. Worse, he hadn't called me Honey V once since Sunday night.

Every time I looked at him, I saw a countdown. He'd never given a specific day he was leaving, but the house would be done next week. We'd paint and get the appliances in their spots and then...

"I'm going to miss having Austen around," Aggie said as if reading my mind. She shook her head, her frizzy curls going wild. "Ro just adores him, and I know Ansen feels better calling him for a hand than Cody since he's usually not so busy."

"And Austen doesn't question him as much as Cody." Tova grinned.

"My oldest brother's a little uptight," Aggie replied.

A smile played over Tova's lips, and she let out a dreamy sigh. "Yeah."

Aggie wrinkled her nose. "Gross."

Sutton snickered, and like she had a sixth sense, she looked over her shoulder just as the front door opened. A spear of light cut into the bar a moment before Wilder walked in. He was laughing at something Austen said.

Wilder's gaze found his wife's almost immediately. A stab of envy pierced my chest wall. They were such a sweet couple.

Then there was Austen. He glanced around the table, nodding at everyone, giving me no more time than the others.

Oh, god, that hurt. A shearing sensation occurred in my chest, like my heart was literally getting ripped in two.

This feeling reaffirmed I made the right choice. If his rebuff affected me this much when we hadn't really been an item, then I'd be a pile of ash if he broke things off later.

But why did I feel nothing but doubt and indecision? And fear?

I tried to concentrate on what the others were saying, but my mind mulled over Austen. I noticed all the people who noticed him as he chatted with Wilder. There was a woman around my age with a fresh blowout in her long brown tresses. She was wearing nicer clothing than I was like she came straight from an office. I looked like I came directly from a kid's summer day at the park.

I'd practiced volleyball in the backyard after dinner with Catherine before I came here. I was still in a loose gray T-shirt and my pink athletic shorts.

The girl had tight white capri-length pants paired with wedge heels and a loose, blue-striped top. Summery. Professional. Yet sexy.

I wasn't the only one who noticed. She seemed to know a few people, but I'd never seen her around before. I wouldn't pay attention to her, but her furtive glances in Austen's direction were disconcerting.

"Vienne?" Sutton asked.

I jerked my gaze off the stranger, grateful I wasn't busted staring at Austen. "Sorry, what?"

"How's the Dave situation?" Sutton asked. "For real?"

When we'd all arrived, they'd asked about Catherine right away. A little about Dave, but we hadn't been ready to deep dive into our private lives.

"Honestly," I said, "it's been cathartic. I was letting him treat me like twenty-year-old Vienne, who was so enamored with the finance major that she was willing to overlook what an ass he was. He's been the Dave who's okay with others giving up their life so he can be cozy in his. Now, I'm not letting him get away with it. It feels good."

Catherine and Dave hung out together while I was working, and in the evenings, Dave claimed to need to catch up on work. But when we crossed paths, his typical little digs at me that had slowly eroded my confidence were no longer tolerated. He was getting tongue-tied around me.

Good.

I told the girls about volleyball. I credited Austen with the encouragement. Sutton's gaze sharpened on me, but she didn't ask further questions.

"From everything you've told us, I don't like Dave," Aggie said, her smile smug, "but I would've loved to have seen that."

"I don't think he's going to play volleyball with me any time in the future." Austen and I had easily won the game I'd nailed Dave in. Against Dave's wishes, Catherine had begged for a third game. Austen and I had taken that one too. She'd been delighted to see me play at my full potential, and it didn't matter how much my skills dulled over the years. "He leaves tomorrow, and next week, she starts practice."

"I hate that you went through a divorce," Sutton said, sympathy pouring out of her. She was the only other one who knew what the process and emotions were like, but she did remarry her ex. We didn't have parallel experiences. "But I'm glad you're able to surround yourself with people who can build you up instead of tear you down."

"Me too." This time, I couldn't stop my gaze from veering toward Austen. I didn't miss how he'd made sure to point out all the work I'd done on the house—in front of Dave. Austen had encouraged me to put my whole self out there, even if it meant rocking the boat with Dave. I'd needed to, for me and for my daughter.

"I'm so grateful for all of you." I played with the bracelets at my wrist and tore my gaze off the handsome man with his hair falling over his forehead and his chiseled jaw that smiled so easily.

Had I made a mistake? Was missing him like this worth putting off impending heartbreak?

"If I knew what was waiting for me in North Dakota, I would've moved years ago," Tova said, then she frowned. "Wait a minute."

Aggie chortled. "Then you would've been hit on by every single straight man in this bar and not one of them would've been Cody."

"Right." Tova's grin was sheepish. Cody had only moved to Crocus Valley shortly before Tova arrived. Go back too far, and he would've been married. "Everything happens on its own timeline, and my love life and motherhood journey were definitely not meant to happen earlier."

Sutton nodded. "I hope my motherhood journey is still to come." She traced through a droplet of moisture left behind by her glass of draft beer.

I almost said, *Me too*, but I started coughing again. I was in my midthirties. My daughter was in high school. I'd given up that dream long ago.

Because Dave hadn't wanted it.

I was saved from dwelling on my gut reaction to having more kids when I saw Wilder and Austen scoot out of the booth.

Wilder swaggered over to Sutton. She glanced over, as ever attuned to his proximity and could sense when he was getting closer.

"Hey, ladies." He had to lean in to speak loud enough for us to hear.

Austen stopped next to him. He didn't look at me and patted Wilder on the shoulder. "I'm gonna get going. Call me with the dates, and I'll make it work."

"Will do," Wilder answered. Neither of them elaborated on what they were discussing, and no one else seemed curious. Did everyone else know what they were talking about? Was I the only one out because I wasn't part of the family?

Ugh, any more of the burning in my chest and I'd have to stock up on heartburn relief.

Behind Wilder, I could see Austen walk by the bar. The attractive woman swallowed and smoothed her hands down her impeccable pants. Before he passed her, she tapped on his shoulder.

I strove not to stare and pay attention to what Wilder was saying about the expansion of Sutton's animal clinic, but I couldn't take my focus off the way Austen stopped, cocked his head to hear what she said, then nodded and moved closer to her at the bar. Then she held her hand out and he took it, his easy grin slipping into place.

My stomach sank. He was happy to talk to her. There was no stilted politeness like when he was hit on the last time he was here.

The friend of the woman grinned at him, then at her, and scooted over. He propped a hand on the bar and one on his hip, his head tipped down. The woman talked, her hands animated.

If I was honest with myself, their interaction didn't look like the typical flirt-fest going on in bars, but my brain refused to think of another reason a sexy woman would talk to a devastating man. They looked good together. Him with the plain blue jeans that didn't have jeweled pockets like some of the men in the place, a clean green polo, and his cowboy boots. Her with her casual corporate look.

She'd say something, and he'd answer. She was turned on her stool, facing him. He wasn't in her face, but he was close. They had to be able to hear each other but also...

The burn in my throat grew hotter, and another one ignited behind my eyes.

I couldn't watch. "I've gotta get going."

Sutton cut off. I hadn't heard what she'd been saying, and I was a shitty friend, but I had to leave. "Are you okay?" she asked.

"I was practicing with Catherine before I came here." I slid off my stool. "I think I need to get into pajamas and put an ice pack on my head. Too much sun."

They all nodded, but their expressions said they would've pressed for more if Wilder hadn't been around.

I pushed through the crowd, rude as hell, but I only had eyes for the exit. And when I felt that familiar heat stroke between my shoulder blades, I knew Austen was watching me.

I rapidly blinked away tears. How unfair was it that I was just admiring how attuned Sutton was to Wilder when I was the same with Austen and it was all for nothing?

Austen

I leaned against the island, watching the front door like I'd done every morning since I'd started this damn project and knew Vienne would be arriving. This morning, I dreaded her arrival as much as I anticipated it.

I wanted to see her, but I didn't want to see her expression when she heard the news. The rest of the week had been enlightening, and after Tuesday and Wednesday, I'd come to a difficult conclusion. Last night had solidified my decision.

Leilani, the woman I met at the bar last night, came out of the bathroom, her gaze stroking over the doorframe from the floor to the ceiling. "Very nice."

Her long brown hair was neatly curled and hung over her back. She looked like she had a good night's sleep. Mine was shit.

"I can call you later—"

There was a familiar rap at the door. Vienne's perfunctory knock.

My pulse kicked up, always too damn excited to see her. Like a kid at Halloween, wondering what treat I'd get from the other side of the door, I was excited about which pair of jeans she'd be wearing. The ones with a tiny rip at the corner of a back pocket where I caught the color underwear she was wearing. Or the ones that had faded spots over her thighs and at the hips.

"Excuse me." I went to the door. Leilani stayed in the kitchen, wandering around.

"Morning," I said, drinking her in. She was wearing

the jeans with the tiny hole. Lust punched low in my gut. Amazing after all the frustrated ejaculations I had last night.

"Morning." She looked like she left the "good" off her greeting for a reason. Dark circles rimmed under her eyes, and her shoulders were hunched. I only got a little pleasure thinking she was getting the same lackluster sleep I was.

Her gaze lifted over my shoulder, and she jerked as if a live wire clapped her on the back. "Oh. Oh my god. I'm sorry." She backed up a step. Her throat worked as she swallowed hard. "I didn't realize you had company."

She blinked rapidly. I was about to ask if she was okay when the reason for her stiff and stunned reaction dawned on me.

If Vienne wasn't the reason I felt like recycled dog shit, I'd explain everything immediately. Instead, all I gave her was, "Leilani came over. Do you know her?"

She shook her head, and anguish drifted through her features. Her eyes misted over.

Aw, hell. Shame branded my skin. If Vienne was acting like this now, then why had she acted like a goddamn acquaintance all week instead of someone I knew intimately inside and out?

Her cool attitude all week was the reason I was torn in two this morning. "She's a real estate agent," I explained.

Vienne sniffed and swallowed. "How convenient."

I almost laughed, but my frustration smoldered too hot. I glanced to make sure Leilani hadn't snuck up on me. "Honey V, the only thing my dick is seeing is my right hand." While she was blinking at my statement, I stepped into the house and held the door open for her. "She introduced herself last night, and she's here this morning to meet with both of us. Leilani," I called over my shoulder. "I'd like to introduce you to my interior designer, who's also into carpentry."

Leilani popped into the opening between the living room, dining room and kitchen. Her smile was wide. "Hi! Vienne, right?"

Vienne nodded, but she hadn't entered the house yet.

"Come on in, V." I enjoyed the way she was trying to smother her jealousy.

She jerked her bright gaze to me. She finally walked in, her steps wooden. "Hi," she said robotically.

Leilani crossed to us, her hand stuck out. "I'm Leilani Yager. I'm new to the area." She enthusiastically pumped Vienne's hand. When Leilani let go, Vienne's arm dropped, lifeless.

I kept my smile to myself. I'd been fucking lonely and miserable all week. I'd soaked it up that Vienne might be feeling the same. Then I got upset.

It didn't have to be this way. If we felt the same about each other, why was I leaving?

Leilani wandered through the living room, chatting with her hands flying like last night when she'd explained herself to me. "I was out with a colleague, and she pointed out Austen. Said that rumor had it he was fixing up the house to sell, but she hadn't heard that he was working with an agent. She encouraged me to introduce myself." She stopped and faced us. "My boyfriend and I moved to town months ago, and getting my name out there has been a challenge."

Vienne lifted her chin in an *ahh, I see* move when the word "boyfriend" slipped from Leilani's lips.

"Austen was kind enough not to chase me away." She did a three-sixty spin, her gaze on the ceiling. "I heard how bad the first remodel was. I'm impressed with how well you brought back the ambience of a farmhouse." She walked forward a few steps and did another turn. "You enter and you're hit with the farmhouse vibe, but then you walk around and it's all modern. A nice compromise."

"Thank you." Vienne pushed a hand through her hair, pausing with her hand on her head. "Sorry, I'm a little out of it this morning. Headache."

"Oh, no problem." Leilani's smile was sheepish. "I've been told I talk a lot."

"No, it's not that. Embrace your chattiness. Hell with everyone else."

Leilani's eyes flared, but her grin spread wider. "Why, thank you. My boyfriend says the same thing. Except he swears more." She dug in the tote bag hanging off her shoulder. Brandishing a business card, she handed it to Vienne. "I'd love to get your contact information. Austen's been filling me in on everything you guys have done. And in a short time. Impressive."

"Austen did a lot of the work in the evenings and on weekends," Vienne mumbled, still unable to take compliments.

Leilani fluttered her fingers at the floor and the walls. "The simplicity, though. You stripped out the fake and let the real bones shine through. Others might've come in here and heavy-handedly ripped out original material to replace it with what they think the time period should look like. Sure, it might look good, but it's not the house that was built. No, this is old farmhouse made good. I walked in and thought, now, this place was built in the 1920s. Only I wouldn't have to pump my own water for that amazing bathtub. Anyway." She clutched the straps of her tote. "I'll call you later when I gather some market comparisons, and we can set a time for the open house. And yes, absolutely, once we get a key box set up, I'll do everything, and you don't even have to step foot back inside once you leave town next week. I can let the painters in and everything if Vienne's unable to."

Vienne's head spun toward me. My stomach dropped. Last night, I had wondered why she left before the others until I saw her face when she spotted Leilani. She must've seen us talking and ditched the bar, upset. And now, I had to tell her I was leaving town sooner than expected.

⅄

Vienne

It was hard to believe I only drank one beer last night. I woke up with a pounding headache and scratchy eyes from crying.

I was confused. How could I have been so torn up over Austen talking to another woman that I went home and sobbed into my pillow so Catherine wouldn't hear? I was supposed to be saving myself from the pain, yet when I saw the gorgeous woman hanging out in his kitchen, I almost started wailing again.

Fuck me.

Now he was leaving and I'd *known* it, but the reality hit me hard.

What the hell did I do?

Leilani had left shortly after the bomb was dropped that Austen was leaving. Her floral perfume lingered in the air. My nose wanted to revolt. Sure, she smelled nice, but my brain did not like another woman's smell in this house.

I pressed my fingers to my temples. "When are you leaving?"

His pause went on longer than expected, amplifying the dread pooling in my belly. "Today."

My legs wanted to give out, but there was nothing to sit on in the living room. I couldn't have heard him correctly. "Today?"

I was supposed to have time. My thoughts were still a jumbled mess.

He winced at my high pitch. "Sorry, it was too late to call you last night." I would've been up. "But Eliot got ahold of Wilder. One of his employees has a family emergency, and another's out for sick leave. He could use a hand. Wilder can help for a couple of days, but he and Sutton have appointments with the fertility specialist in Bismarck."

Right. Sutton had talked about that last night while I'd been absorbed in Austen.

Austen shrugged and folded his arms across his chest. He at least looked sorry to have disappointed me.

"Anyway, after I met Leilani, I told her I might not get everything done in the house before I leave and I need it listed, and she offered to help let workers in to finish. I don't even need to be here for the open house. She might have questions, and since you're both the interior designer and the neighbor...I'll pay you for any extra time, of course."

"That's fine." Nothing was fine. He wasn't going to be at the open house? This was it? The last thing I was worried about was my job when I should've been prepared. I knew today was coming, but...I hadn't prepared myself for the reality.

I hadn't been approached with inquiries, and I wasn't prepared to not have Austen be my neighbor anymore.

"Don't worry about it," I murmured.

"If you don't want to, I can ask Wilder. This kind of stuff is up Cody's uptight alley. I can talk to him."

A small smile lifted my lips. I didn't know the uptight version of Cody I kept hearing mentioned. Tova kept him loose in ways I'd be jealous of if I thought too hard. Because Austen was a lot like my own Tova, only he was leaving. Today.

He said I had until he left to change my mind and ask him to stay, but then he pulled an UNO card and would be gone sooner. And I'd waited too long.

Twenty

AUSTEN

The day was hot, and wind had sandblasted me in the face with dirt the whole time I did groundwork with a three-year-old Arabian. I took my hat off as I stomped toward the main house. Twenty years later, I was back in the same bedroom I'd grown up in.

The house was different. Eliot had remodeled the place to be tastefully modern instead of sorely out of date with animal heads all over the walls. I understood why hunters wanted to mount their hunting accomplishments, but I didn't want an elk staring me down when I was sawing through my Eggos for breakfast.

The ram's head had been the worst, mounted in the living room and silently judging me for sitting around and watching TV. None of us had hunted rams, and Barns had never told us where he got the damn thing. Eliot had said it was the first to go. He'd kept his bedroom, too, leaving the main bedroom that our father used to sleep in empty. No one wanted to claim that space.

I took off my cowboy hat and slapped it against my leg. Any dust that puffed up was instantly carried away. My hair got ruffled by the wind gusts, but my sweat-soaked strands needed to be dried.

I stepped through the door into the garage. The door was almost yanked from my hand. I fumbled with the doorknob and slammed it shut. "Goddamn wind."

"You're cranky."

I barked out a "Fuck!" I found Eliot with a brow lifted, staring at me from the workbench lining the front of the usually empty garage. He was reading some sort of instructions. Something was always broken on the ranch. "Warn a guy, will ya?" I roared.

"Why? You got PTSD?"

He was partially serious. I scowled at him. "Not every vet has PTSD."

"How'd you escape it?"

I swatted my hat against my thigh again. The sun streaming through the garage window let in enough light to see the dust billowing off the brim. "I don't know, but I also went to therapy."

His second brow notched up. "Seriously?"

"Yep," I muttered. Why did everyone find it surprising? "But overall, I would've been fine. I can't tell you why some people have issues and some don't." I stuffed my hat on my head, or I'd keep thwapping the shit out of it against my leg. Eliot had been right. I was fucking cranky. "I have a buddy who hates driving through parking lots. He gets all jumpy and loses his temper. Another guy who got out ten years ago still has issues with fireworks, but another one of my friends will spend thousands on them and load up the back of his pickup for the Fourth. They'd been on many of the same missions."

Eliot shrugged. "I believe you that you're doing okay, but what the hell is going on?"

I leaned against the riding lawn mower. Not once while I was growing up had the garage ever had a vehicle in it after Mama walked out. The place was our workshop and storage.

I could play obtuse and ask him what he meant, but I was in a crap mental space. I told Vienne I was leaving— for fucking good—and she'd been stunned. But that was it.

I was leaving. She knew what that meant. And she'd told me she'd help Leilani if needed and watch the house while I was gone. Then, she'd walked out of the place and out of my life.

Part of me had hoped she'd bring up that we hadn't had our last time together. Maybe we should take advantage of an empty house and... I'd been left hurt and disappointed. "I told Vienne I wanted more."

Surprise lit his face. He tossed the instructions on top of the workbench. "Let's grab a beer before we launch into this conversation."

"As long as we don't drink it on the deck."

His look turned measuring. I wasn't going to tell him why having a cold beer on the back deck would only complete the self-pity circle I was building.

"Too windy anyway," he said and sauntered inside.

I walked behind him through the laundry room. The soft smell of detergent barely drowned out the horse-sweat smell that covered me. In the kitchen, Eliot opened the stainless steel door to the fridge and withdrew two longnecks. He took the tops off and slid one across the counter.

It wasn't a Summer Sunset.

Instead of being relieved, I grew saltier. I tossed my hat onto a recliner in the living room as I passed by and flopped onto a stool at the island.

Eliot stood across from me like he was ready to restock my beer. "I take it since you're here and I'm supposed to bring you to the airport in a week that she said no."

"Her loser exes have ruined my chances."

He took a long drink, his gaze on me. "*They* ruined *your* chances?"

My mood darkened. "What's that supposed to mean?" I didn't let him answer. "I was a goddamn gentleman. I treat the women I date right—you know I do. Just like I know you do."

"Because we're not Barns."

I nodded, sullen, ignoring my beer.

"So, what was her reasoning?" he asked.

"First, it was that she didn't want Catherine to get any backlash or for it to hurt her business reputation. Then, it was because she was done with relationships. She doesn't trust me. She doesn't want to trust me," I amended.

"You wined her and dined her and—" He stopped when I shook my head.

"I tried to take her out. She wouldn't even go to lunch. Only once, I sort of pretended we were together because I was getting hit on at the bar—in front of her." My frustration was boiling over, ramping up my temperature. I sucked half my bottle of beer down.

It wasn't as good as Summer Sunset, dammit.

"You two were just fucking, and when you said you wanted more, she said no?" He snorted.

I glared at him. "We were doing more than fucking."

"Like what?"

"Working on the house." Having cold beer on the back deck.

He chuckled and shook his head. "God help the women of the world. There's going to be a mob after you."

"Asshole."

His smile grew wider. He polished off his beer, went to the fridge, and set two more cold ones on the counter. "You really liked her."

I glowered at my beer.

"And just like that, you're giving up."

I turned my glare back to him. My expression was going to freeze this way. "She doesn't want more."

"Do you know what she's scared of?"

I lifted a shoulder and polished off my first beer. For good measure, I took a drink of the second one. My blood was still hot. Damn Eliot for pointing out how little I tried. "I don't know. Her dick of an ex-husband decided he didn't want more kids and didn't like her nagging him to man up and think about more than himself, so he asked for a divorce. Now he's married and expecting a kid."

"Ouch."

I nodded. "And there's that one guy—"

"What the hell was his name?"

I shook my head. Theo, but I wasn't saying the asshat's name.

Eliot screwed his face up. "I think I met him once and thought cardboard would be more exciting. I couldn't figure out what Vienne saw in him. Did she end it?"

She'd told me things in private I didn't care to share with Eliot. I wasn't going to be the scorned lover who hurt the girl any way possible. I was better than that. "They weren't on the same page. She was too strong for him."

"I'm noticing a trend. What about Jake?"

I didn't bother to ask how he knew she'd been sleeping with Jake. Eliot was around Crocus Valley a lot more than me. He'd be in the know way more than I would once I got to California. The dark cloud over my head turned black. "He was still fucking everyone he could, and she decided she wasn't willing to be one of many."

His nod was knowing. "Sort of on trend. Dr. Jake wants to do who he wants when he wants, and he doesn't want anyone to tell him not to." He tapped his fingers on the island, his forehead furrowed. "She's worried you're going to do the same—leave her behind when she interferes with your fun."

I wasn't like them. "I don't know how else to prove myself."

He let out a snort. "Leaving ain't the answer."

Anger swept through me as hot as a grass fire in this wind. "She doesn't want me," I said tightly.

He pointed at me with the neck of his beer. "She does, but she's afraid you're going to up and leave her when you're done with her. Which..." He tilted his head from one side to the other. "You kind of have."

The grass fire inside me turned into an inferno. "What the fuck, Eliot? Am I supposed to tell the guys who are counting on me to start a business with them,

'Sorry, I can't. I have to stalk a woman who doesn't want me.'?"

"I can't answer that, man." He was an infuriating jackass. "But it sounds like you had one leg out the door the whole time you and her were"—he cocked his damn brow again—"*seeing* each other."

"I told her I'd stay if she wanted me to."

"Sure." He drained his second beer, but he didn't retrieve another. "That's why you left even earlier than planned, and you're not even going back for the open house."

He didn't understand. It'd be easier on both me and Vienne if I wasn't at the open house. I sucked down the rest of my beer. The cool liquid could just as well have been battery acid. My throat burned, and my stomach was churning up a storm.

"Look, we're all goddamn gentlemen. You, me, Cody, Wilder. We made sure of it after what we grew up with. Cody married Meg and was too honorable to admit he wasn't happy, and she was too stubborn to do the same, but that's a moot point now. The Cody who married Tova is a totally different guy and more like the brother we both had when we were kids. Then there's Wilder. You think that's the same Wilder who married Sutton the second time as the first time?" Numb, I shook my head. "And then there's us. You and I haven't been in a meaningful relationship in...ever."

The look he gave me dared me to say differently. I couldn't.

"I'm the nice guy." Women didn't want nice guys, but the excuse sounded weak.

He clenched his teeth and sucked in a breath. "So am

I. I'm so damn nice, and it's easy because I make sure I don't get too attached to anyone."

"Then they can't leave like Mama," I mumbled.

"Survey says— Fuck, sorry. I've been around Sutton a lot since I helped Wilder build the vet clinic addition. But, yeah. Our parents fucked us up."

I didn't see how being a decent man could ruin a relationship. Eliot's words weren't getting through to me, but...they'd stuck. What he said was swirling through my brain, insisting on being heard. I made sure I treated my dates right, so when they walked away, I couldn't say it was my fault.

"I'm supposed to be in California at the end of next week."

"Yep," he said.

"We've put in a lot of planning."

"I'm sure you have." He went to the fridge.

"They're counting on my investment. They'll need me to work and bring in money like the rest of them."

Instead of coming back with a beer, he had a log of summer sausage. After slamming it on the counter, he dug around for a knife. "Is that what you want?"

"For what?"

He rolled his eyes as if saying, *Seriously, dumbass?* "You want to guard people and buildings, and then when you retire, you'll be a beach bum?"

I ground my jaw back and forth. The slab of summer sausage was slapped onto a paper towel and set in front of me. As I worked through a response, Eliot dug out some crackers, cream cheese, and jalapeño jelly. My stomach chose that moment to rumble like it wanted to point out that I did not have heartburn, that nothing was wrong with my gut.

My heart was hurting.

"I don't care about being alone for the rest of my life." Fucking liar.

Eliot gave me a stare that said the same thing. He dropped his gaze and spread cream cheese on a Ritz. "Me either."

His wooden tone said otherwise.

I sighed and scrubbed my hands over my face. "I want Vienne, and I don't fucking care if she wants to do nothing but work and then work some more after Catherine graduates. I don't care if she wants five more kids and she wants them before she turns forty."

My stomach knotted itself.

"I got one question."

"Only one?" I asked like a sarcastic dick.

He put a dollop of jelly on his cracker. Instead of adding summer sausage, he popped the whole thing in his mouth. The muscles in his jaw flexed. He was making me wait. Jackass.

When he swallowed, he started on another cracker. So help me—

"When you gave Vienne the proposition," he finally said, "did you consider what you'd do if she said she wanted you to stay? Because if the answer is that you would've asked the guys to give you a few more months, that sounds a lot like you were waiting to give yourself an out."

I was planning to do exactly that. "I was giving her an out."

He picked up another cracker and the butter knife. "Sure about that?"

No. I wasn't.

Twenty-One

VIENNE

Marly brushed her hand over her baby belly, and tears nearly sprang into my eyes. I spun toward the counter to continue loading dishes into the dishwasher.

Mom had invited me and Catherine over for dinner. We'd eaten already. I was doing dishes and attempting to forget the disappointment in her eyes when I told her that Austen probably wouldn't be back in Crocus Valley anytime soon.

"Ugh. I have to pee again," Marly grumbled. "I'll be right back."

I brushed my hair out of my face and frowned when some strands tangled in my damp fingers. Mom opened the sliding door and stepped in.

"Don't worry about it," I said to Marly. "Go put your feet up."

"Yes, yes." Mom peeked out the door. "Catherine's

talked Dustin into starting s'mores early." She chuckled. "That girl and her s'mores."

"Are you sure?" Marly arched her back. "I think my ankles are swelling."

Another beat of jealousy went through me. When did I get all envious of pregnant women? Since before I'd shut off a part of my brain after Dave made his announcement. I'd relied on the same detachment I'd used around pregnant women and happy little families, even around my closest friends and family. Now, that part of my mind had cracked open.

"Go relax, Marly," I said, hiding the swell of emotions. "I'm almost done."

Marly flashed us each a smile and disappeared down the hallway.

"I'm so glad you two are getting on now," Mom said.

I didn't bother playing dumb. The discomfort between me and Marly was gone. "Yeah, she's cool."

I started the dishwasher and straightened to tackle the rest of the dishes. Catherine had been so excited to see the horses that she'd dragged my dad and brother out for a horseback ride after dinner. She must've lobbied for a firepit the whole time.

Mom grabbed a dish towel and positioned herself next to me.

"You cooked, Mom. I can get this." I wasn't feeling terribly social either. That was the main reason I was doing dishes in the first place, and I didn't need to be critiqued on them.

"I wanted to chat with you a little." She gave the dish towel a flick. "Since you don't come over just to visit."

I dumped a pan into the soapy water. "Because I don't want to get criticized for all my life choices."

Her stare weighed on me. I realized what I'd said. More like how bluntly I'd said it. Twenty years drained away, and I was a petulant teen arguing with my mom.

Marly came out of the hallway and scurried outside with a smile, hopefully oblivious to the tension between me and Mom.

Letting out a breath, I put my hands on the edge of the sink. "I'm not Cullen, and I'm not Marly."

"No, you're not. I've never said I wished you were like either one."

"No, but you made sure to tell me whenever I fucked up." The confusion in her voice made me lash out.

She didn't flinch at my cussing. I was a damn adult, but I didn't usually swear around Mom.

"You felt like I was criticizing you?" she asked quietly.

I gave her a side-eye. Her expression was dismayed. I grabbed a cloth and scrubbed the scalloped potato dish like it wronged me in another life. "I get it, Mom. I messed up a full-ride scholarship."

"Are you calling Catherine a mistake?" Her tone was more questioning, keeping my defensiveness from rising higher.

"Of course not. The timing was not good, and if I'm to be honest, I should've known the guy wasn't right."

"Tell me about it," she grumbled.

I tossed the dishcloth into the water with a plop, fed up with another one of many of her comments.

She held her hands up. "I knew what you saw in him. I tried to make him feel welcome, and it was hard." She sniffed. "He's an arrogant prick."

I barked out a laugh. "Yes. He is."

"It's just that...you changed when you went to

college, and I didn't know if it was the school or having a baby or the Dave."

The Dave. What an appropriate name to refer to him as.

"You wanted to get away and experience life and the world," she continued, "but then you stayed home. Quit school. You didn't quit Catherine, and I'm terribly proud of you for that. But you also didn't let us in."

I scrubbed a particularly baked-on area that I'd normally let soak, but it was nice to have something to do with my hands for this tough conversation. All my bracelets were on the counter. "I didn't want to hear it."

"You never did." She sighed. "Bullheaded. Just like me, sometimes. I guess that's why I gave you space. I was really happy when you moved home though."

I whipped my head toward her. "You were? I thought it was just another sign I gave up."

"You did give up, Vienne." She held my stunned stare, daring me to challenge her, and I had nothing. "You gave up on yourself when you had Catherine. There was no reason you had to quit school. Maybe not even the team." I opened my mouth to argue, and she put her palm toward me. "We won't know, but my point is you never asked for help. I could tell you weren't happy, but you never talked to me, and if it was something I did, fine. I'll own it. I'm a lot like my mother, I guess. Pointing out flaws, hoping that'll open a person up when it only shuts them down."

Yeah, that was exactly what had happened.

She wound the dish towel in her hands. "Lord help me; I celebrated when you broke up with Theo."

"He ended it." God, that felt good to admit. Like it

was no longer my burden to bear. "He thought I had too much attitude."

Pride shone from her eyes. "That's the Vienne I know."

"You weren't very nice about Jake."

"Why would I be? I know he's a guy who wouldn't treat you right." Her look dared me to argue. I could not.

"I know. I thought I was ready for it."

"And you weren't. Because, my dear, it's obvious you want more out of life, and I'm tired of seeing you lessen yourself for weak men."

I couldn't even be surprised that Mom had pointed out the same thing Austen had at volleyball because I was tired of it too. I was so damn tired of not feeling like myself. The one person who brought out the real Vienne was gone. "Austen wanted more out of me and him."

She folded her arms and leaned a hip against the counter, facing me. It was time I admitted the baked-on scalloped potato had come off several moments ago. I rinsed the dish, ignoring her proximity.

"I thought there was nothing going on between the two of you," she said in a gotcha tone.

"It was an arrangement. After what happened with Jake, it was supposed to spare my reputation and save Catherine from hearing about it."

"You didn't want more?"

"I wanted everything," I whispered. I pushed the back of my wrist against my forehead. My throat grew thick, and I fought back tears. This was the first time I admitted what I wanted plainly while acknowledging the fear that went with it.

Without the fear, I could feel how deeply I wanted to be with Austen. How happy I'd been with him. How safe

I'd felt. I could tell that seeing him leave hurt me more than being scared ever did.

"You were afraid you'd get hurt again?"

I nodded, sniffling. "He's the best guy I ever dated. You know he made sure to highlight everything I did in the house to Dave? And to his hot real estate agent? While I was seething with jealousy, losing sleep over seeing him talk to her, he was boasting about how good I was. And that was after I'd told him no."

"Oh, Vienne."

"And he encouraged me to knock the shit out of Dave with a volleyball."

Mom's brows rose. "Oh? I'd have liked to have seen that."

I huffed out a laugh. "Catherine did, and I think it was important that she saw me do it. Don't worry, she doesn't know it was intentional."

Mom's smile was faint. "You were such a fearless kid, Vienne. I'm seeing more of the Vienne who wasn't afraid to whip through chores, practice long hours at volleyball, and move away for school in a city that has as many people as our entire state. I'm sorry for being critical, but watching my girl fade wasn't fun for me. Could you imagine seeing Catherine go through that?"

Thinking of Catherine's light dimming broke my damn heart and the possibility that it'd happen because of a guy made me nearly feral. "Low blow, Mom."

She wasn't repentant. "What are you going to do about Austen?"

"He's gone. I'm too late."

She inhaled slowly, studying me. Then she turned and grabbed her dish towel. "The Vienne I raised wouldn't let something like that stop her. Maybe you've gotta ask for help."

Asking for help sucked. Instead of being in the bar, I'd asked the girls if we could meet at my house around the firepit. Catherine was practicing with some of her friends at the same park where we'd played with her dad and Austen.

I got the fire going before the girls arrived. Each step involved remembering when Catherine had invited Austen over. I especially dwelled on how we'd chatted after she'd gone inside. Talking with him was easy. Being myself around him was difficult and simple at the same time. He'd seen the real Vienne, and that was scary. He'd watched her decimate a useless wall with a sledgehammer. And he had left.

He hadn't left until I'd made it absolutely clear I would not be pursuing more with him.

If that had been me, I'd have been devastated. As it was, his absence demolished me.

Sutton played her fingers over her long braid. I should've grown my hair longer to do that. I wouldn't need the bracelets I'd been constantly fidgeting with tonight.

"Everything's looking good so far," she announced. "On the baby front. Wilder's swimmers are normal. I have a little bit more testing, but so far, the doctor hasn't found any reason why we shouldn't move forward." Her grin was hesitant. "I'm trying not to get excited."

"You waited for the right time," Aggie assured her. "I know you regret not doing this earlier."

"I had my reasons, but now that we're in it, I do wish I'd looked into everything earlier." She smiled wider. "It's really nice not to worry about having Wilder there with me. I still can't believe it. Every single appointment."

"I'm happy for you two," Tova said.

Aggie and I nodded. The slight detachment was back. I was happy for Sutton. Scared for her. Nervous. But also, like her, I had regrets too. So damn many. After talking to Mom, they'd bloomed exponentially. Which was why I'd asked my friends to gather somewhere more private.

Tova peeked back at the house, then sat forward, an elbow on her knee and her chin in her hand. "Okay, spill it. Why'd you want us here?"

Was my anxiousness rolling off me in palpable waves? I rolled my lips in and stared into the crackling flames. "I messed up with Austen."

Aggie's brows drew together. Same with Tova. Sympathy filled Sutton's expression.

"We were messing around."

Aggie pounded her thigh. "I knew it!" Her startled gaze darted toward the house. "Does Catherine know?" When I shook my head, a smug look filled her features. "I told Ansen that I thought there was more between you two than friendship."

"I was clearly clueless," Tova said, shocked.

"It's okay," Aggie replied. "You didn't grow up with Austen. I've never seen him hover over someone like he does Vienne."

My throat wanted to close up again. He no longer hovered. I swallowed the regret down, but it wouldn't stay.

"What happened?" Sutton asked.

Aggie narrowed her eyes. "You knew?"

Tova's mouth dropped open. "I'm so out of touch." She turned her wide blue eyes toward me. "I didn't even catch a hint. I'm so sorry."

Her concern helped bring me out of my *I fucked up* loop. "I'm glad we weren't as obvious as Aggie started making me fear." I explained to them how Austen and I had an arrangement. The window play was left out. I stumbled over how I'd turned Austen down when he told me he'd stay if I wanted him to.

"He offered to stay?" Awe filled Aggie's voice, and I felt worse.

I nodded, miserable. "I'm sorry I didn't say anything. I didn't want it to get weird between us if Austen and I didn't turn out." We hadn't worked—because of me—and I'd take weird over the way my heart hurt every time I thought about him, which was a lot. Tears poked the backs of my eyes. "I was so scared."

"I imagine." Understanding filled Tova's voice. "I remember how closed off Catherine was when I started working for Cody. You didn't want to disrupt the progress she's made integrating into Crocus Valley."

Appreciation for my friends' understanding grew. "It's not just that. I've been trying so hard to get established as an interior designer in the community. I've been so cautious and afraid for my reputation. And I'm tired of it. I'm sick of having to appease people and prove that I'm what they want. You know what? I don't fucking care if I get that job. I did damn good work on Austen's place, and I've made it this long. I shouldn't have let the fear control my decisions." I should've done like Mom said and asked for help. I knew people in the community. I had more contacts than guys like Jim, who refused to see me as grown-up Vienne. I messed up so bad. "Now

Austen's gone. He's not even painting the house himself. Hired it out so he could leave sooner."

Sutton chewed her lower lip. "He's only in Buffalo Gully. He's not in California yet. And..." Her hands played up and down her braid like it was a musical instrument. "I think he might be open to hearing that you really want to be with him."

I was about to scoff. How would she know? But then I recalled Austen saying that Wilder and Eliot knew about us. Had Eliot said something to Wilder, who then mentioned it to Sutton, because why wouldn't he? I wanted the small-town gossip to work in my favor.

"What have you heard?" I asked.

Aggie threw her hands up. "Was I out of the loop again?"

Sutton winced. "I'm sorry. I guessed about Austen and Vienne, and I told Wilder, and then Eliot tricked him into slipping. And maybe I've heard from Wilder, who heard from Eliot that Austen has been a cranky mess over Vienne."

"Sounds like my brothers. And they both likely delighted in keeping it from Cody."

"Do I get to be the one to break all of this to Cody?" When I nodded, Tova's grin said she was unashamed.

The three focused back on me. Austen was feeling as awful as me? Should that give me hope?

"How serious are you about getting him back and keeping him?" Aggie asked. She was more solemn than I'd seen her outside of her rescue. Austen was her brother, and she wasn't going to help me if I was waffling about my feelings.

"I really think he's everything I've ever wanted, and as much as I'd like to sprint into the house and tell you guys to forget everything, I'm more scared of not trying. The last week has sucked. I was heartbroken after my divorce, devastated, but I didn't have this sense of..." I thumped the middle of my chest. "Panic? This regret is different. Stronger. Before, I regretted how much I wasted on a marriage that went nowhere. The regret was aimed at the past. Not the future. If that makes sense."

They nodded. I'd forever be grateful for their support.

Aggie leaned over and grabbed her water bottle. "Well, that settles it. We should go." She rose.

Startled, I stood too. Did I drive her off? Not only did I ruin things with Austen, Aggie was upset with me. I wasn't sure what I'd said, but I'd ruined it.

Tova and Sutton exchanged looks, but they started gathering their phones and keys.

Aggie faced me, her gunmetal-gray water bottle with AKA Rescue emblazoned on the front clutched between her hands. "We can't figure out a game plan until you talk to Catherine."

Twenty-Two

AUSTEN

I hopped in the side-by-side and wished it was more than a blue-collar golf cart. No AC. Barely any protection from the wind. And somehow, the roof of the rinky-dink cab was never in the right place to block the sun.

I waved at the two guys left working in the stables as I drove off toward the main house. Eliot was…somewhere. He was working the cattle side of the operation today. I'd have to find him soon to discuss our plans.

My stomach twisted itself into a second knot as if I hadn't been fighting a case of nerves for the last week. I'd had a lot to think about. A lot to arrange.

I was almost to the shop closest to the house. Normally, I'd park the side-by-side next to the building for chores in the morning, but I blew past it. The dust cloud I kicked up was blowing away, and I was about to get out when I saw someone wander around the side of the house.

A woman was playing with the multitude of bracelets at her wrist, wearing the cowboy boots and jeans I'd seen her in only once before. Her hair was back in a ponytail and blowing to the side, thanks to the wind. A sight I hadn't seen for almost two weeks.

Vienne.

I stopped and jumped out of the side-by-side so fast I nearly face-planted on the gravel. The skittering of rocks as I jogged toward her caught her attention, and she stopped. She gave a little wave, then twisted her fingers together.

I was gaining ground. She stood in place. The indecision in her expression was growing clearer. She was here and wasn't sure she should be.

All I could think about was hot damn. She was here.

It was a sign.

I drank her in with each step, my euphoria rising. The anxiety in my stomach dissipated, and all I could feel was a swelling in my chest right around my heart.

"Hey, Austen." She stopped wringing her hands and went back to fiddling with the bracelets. She had on several necklaces. The woman was nervous. "I'm sorry to just stop in like this."

Only feet to go. Her eyes widened when I didn't slow down. Somehow, my cowboy hat stayed on.

"I'm not." I cupped a hand around the back of her neck, another around her waist and pulled her in for a kiss.

Her lips parted a millisecond before my mouth was on hers. She tasted like sweet sunshine. Fucking heaven.

She curled her fingers into my shirt. I was sweaty and dusty and I probably smelled like I'd been born and raised in a stable.

I pulled away and brushed a lock of hair out of her face. "Sorry, I'm all dirty, and you're here looking like my very own Cowgirl Barbie to play with."

Wide, stunned turquoise eyes gaped at me. "You don't hate me?"

Confusion crowded my thoughts. "I'd never hate you."

"You left so abruptly, and you're not coming to the open house."

"I'll be there." I feathered the backs of my fingers over her cheek. I kept her close to me with my other arm around her.

"You will?" Surprise made her irises brighter. God, she had beautiful eyes. I wanted to gaze into them forever.

"I'm moving back in."

She leaned back like she had to get a better look at me. Her fingers were still buried in the fabric of my shirt. "Into the house you're selling?"

"It's no longer for sale. There's this girl next door. I have to win her heart."

"But California—"

"Is canceled."

She blinked at me. "I came here to ask you to stay," she said shyly.

I grinned so wide my cheeks ached. "Yes."

A giggle erupted from her. "That was easier than I thought." She sighed and rested her head on my chest. "I've been so stressed." Popping her head back up, she pinned me in her stare. "Are you sure? Your business—"

I cupped her chin and silenced her with a kiss. "Isn't what I want to be when I grow up. I'll figure that part out, but I know who I want to be with, and that's the most important."

"You quit your job—"

"Technically, I haven't started yet."

"—and you're not selling?"

"That girl I'm crazy about? She loves that place."

She stroked across my shoulders. "Oh, Austen."

"And I'm crazy about her. And her kid. Not her ex-husband, but I think we can tolerate each other. I don't think he'll be playing volleyball with us again though."

She tipped the brim of my hat up. "You really are serious. You canceled on California? For me?"

"For you." Her disbelief told me I did the right thing. I was still an investor, just not as big of one as I would've been. I promised to help brainstorm names for them to approach and offer the fourth position to, but I was confident they'd figure it out. They'd have to because I was staying in Crocus Valley. "I want you, Honey V. I want to go to sleep with you and wake up to you. I want to remind you to put your glasses on when your eyes get scratchy in contacts. I want to watch you push those damn things up your nose like you're some sort of sexy librarian fantasy come to life. I want everything. I want to cheer on Catherine at her games with you. I want to be with you at her dance performances and when she graduates. You're my future, and I finally realized you're worth risking rejection over."

Understanding swam in her eyes. "I can't believe... What about the open house? Leilani never said the sale was canceled when I talked to her yesterday." She frowned. "Although I thought she was being cagey about something."

"How can the town see the work you do if I don't let anyone in to see it?"

Her mouth dropped open. "You're doing the open house for me?"

"I'd do anything for you." I pressed another kiss against her lips, loving how she instantly melted into me. I pulled away before I lost myself in her and carried her back to the shop so I could find a quiet corner. "I told her she could show it, explain that I decided not to sell, but the town would know I planned to use her as my agent, so hopefully, she'll get more leads."

"Austen, you're too good to be true." She traced her hands over my shoulders. The look in her bright eyes went from joyous to unsure. Her breath hitched. "I'm terrified."

I knew she would be, and my leaving hadn't helped fill her with confidence I'd always be there. But she was here. She'd come to tell me she wanted me to stay. The dedication I felt toward this woman filled every nook and cranny of my heart. "Then it'll be my job for the rest of our lives to make sure you feel safe with me, that you trust me."

"God, you're perfect." She threw her arms around me and buried her face in my shoulder. "I missed you so much."

"I missed you," I murmured against her hair. "I fucking love you too."

She tipped her head to look at me again, awe filling her gaze. "I came here prepared to beg. To apologize and tell you how sorry I was that it took me so long to realize I messed up, and you're telling me you love me? I'm crazy in love with you, Austen. I'm falling harder and harder each time you open your mouth."

A tremble racked her body. She was scared, like she'd said.

I picked her up. She curled right into me. Good. She'd have to get used to me randomly sweeping her off her feet for decades to come. "Wait until I get my mouth *on* you."

⚜

Vienne

He carried me into the house. I clung to him, afraid I'd wake up and I'd still be reeling from my stress. I could barely sleep last night, but I was determined to drive to the Knight ranch and declare my love for a man I had barely known at the beginning of summer. And I had.

His boots crunched against the gravel, grounding me to the moment. My mind spun.

He was staying. He was moving in permanently, and he wanted me with him. He wanted me and Catherine. She wasn't an inconvenient reality in order to date me, and she wasn't someone I needed to keep Austen a secret from.

When it came to Austen, I had Catherine's full support.

Go get him, Mom. You deserve to be happy, and he makes you happy. Then we can do more firepits, and he can help me practice when you're busy.

He might be hauling me inside to have sex, but I couldn't ignore the stark beauty surrounding us. Miles of gently rolling land with short peaks in the distance. When I'd driven in, I'd seen a winding river and a valley dotted with cattle I could only assume were part of the Knights' stock.

"This place is beautiful."

He continued to carry me like I was a treasured sack of potatoes—I might be lumpy, but he was ready to devour me. "You want a ranch of your own?"

"I'll take the farmhouse."

"It's yours—and Catherine's and Teddy's." He rounded the side of the house and pushed through a garage door.

I didn't have time to soak in the house he'd grown up in before he took us down a long hallway and turned into a small room. The decor was plain, with tasteful pictures of horses on the wall, quality wooden furniture, and soft tones. Comfortable and mature.

"Is this the bedroom you grew up in?"

"Yeah, and you want to know what else?" He laid me on the bed, took off his hat, and set it on the dresser behind him. Then he leaned over me.

I stuffed my hands through his warm strands, loosening them from the mold the hat made. "What?"

"I've never had a girl in this room."

The joy that spread through me was shameful. He hadn't lived here for over two decades, but my heart didn't care. I tugged his head down to mine. He only gave me a quick kiss before pulling back and yanking my boots off.

"We'll make out later. I need to be in you now."

Desire welled inside me, making my belly quiver. "I was so upset about not getting one last time with you."

"This is only the first of many, Honey V."

He shed his shirt, and my breath caught like it always did when faced with his wall of muscles, but more because of what he said. The first of many. I'd only been with him when I was thinking about the inevitable end.

For once, I got to consider that there would be no end. That Austen and I would work. And we'd be happy.

The last of my fears drained away. I trusted this man. I trusted him with me, with my heart, and with everything I cared about. He'd already proven himself in every facet.

"I can't wait," I said breathlessly.

His smile was lopsided, genuine, and everything about Austen I fell for. The man melted me from the inside out.

He continued to undress us. My shirt was next, and while I worked on getting my bra off, he was sliding my pants down. Finally, he stripped his boots and jeans off, and our clothing was in a pile on the floor.

His erection jutted proudly. I didn't have time to admire his body while the heat inside me crowded into each cell, amping up my arousal until I was ready to explode.

He prowled over me, and I was flat beneath him, widening my legs to cradle him. His mouth was on me, nibbling down my neck, and he skated his hand down my side. I'd missed this. The two weeks without him had stretched longer than the months living next to him.

Then he stopped, his head coming up. "I don't... Fuck. I don't have protection. It's packed in one of my boxes."

Instead of being a cold splash dousing my desire, I warmed even more. He'd left thinking we were done, but he wasn't prepared to fuck around. He'd never know how much that meant.

As for the topic at hand, this was a talk we needed to have eventually. "Do you think...do you think we need it? After..." I didn't want to say another man's name while

Austen was naked and on top of me. "After I was humiliated, I got all checked out."

"V, I'm not worried about that part."

A cloud passed over his expression, and I reveled in
how he was incensed for me. "I did the same after I
retired. The only thing we need to discuss is kids."

He was on me, but he held his weight off me like he
was afraid our close and naked proximity would influence
my decision.

I wrapped my legs around him, lining our centers up.
His hard length was only one rock of my hips away from
being in the perfect spot to get myself off with no pene-
tration. If the topic wasn't so serious, I'd toss the conversation out the window and continue what we were doing.

"Do you want more kids, Vienne?" he asked, his voice
a low rumble.

Did I? I had for so many years. Had the time passed?
"I...don't know. I'd given up thinking I'd have more, and
I've been on birth control for a long time." I chewed my
lower lip. I was exposed in more than one way. He was
staring into my soul, telling me he'd be willing to grant
me any wish. "Do you?"

He dropped his head to nibble along my collarbone.
"I want what you want. You want five more kids, we'll get
started ASAP. You want one more—got it. None?
Catherine's it, then."

My old friend fear came back, clogging my throat.
"Can I think about it?"

"Of course."

For how long? Would I put it off a month? Until next
year? When Catherine was moving out for college?

Fuck this. I didn't drive all the way to Buffalo Gully
to throw myself at Austen—granted, that hadn't been

needed—only to flake out on what I really wanted in life. "You know what? Yes. I want to try for more kids, and it's going to take some time to wrap my head around the concept of trying for and maybe having a baby, but yes. Let's do it."

The lazy grin was back. "You know what that means?" He nudged my legs farther apart. "You're going to wear my ring on your finger. I'll get you a silicone one, of course, for when you're sledgehammering walls down." He adjusted his hips and pushed inside, filling me in one smooth move. "I want everyone to know you're mine."

I let out a groan and rocked against him. How did I think this wasn't worth risking a little heartbreak for? "Are you proposing with your dick in me?"

He pulled out and thrust back in. My eyelids fluttered as pleasure exploded from where we were connected.

"I'm not above using what I've got to sway your decision." He pumped in and out, twining his fingers through mine and pinning our hands above my head. "Whaddya say, Honey V? You gonna marry me?"

"Yes!" My exclamation had nothing to do with the building climax inside me. That was the volume. I never thought I'd marry again. Never thought I'd consider it, but with Austen, the answer was easy.

"Fuck." He grunted. "I'm going to come too damn soon. Been without this pussy too damn long."

"It's been two weeks." I gasped.

"Too damn long."

He changed his angle, grinding into me, hitting all the right spots, propelling us both to a simultaneous explosion. I shattered. He held my hands down, and he controlled the rest of my body. I was his to continue plunging into until he went rigid, his thrusts shortening.

"Fuck, V."

My cries bounced off the walls, mixing with his growls and grunts. His hold on my hands loosened. I wrapped my arms around him, and we lay there for several moments, catching our breath. I reveled in our reconnection.

There was a knock on the door. I barked out a cry, and my pulse jackhammered. It'd been almost twenty years since I'd been busted with a boy by my parents, but the feeling was the same.

Austen lifted his head, his expression irritated. "Fuck off!"

"That'd better be Vienne in there, or you're an asshole," Eliot called.

Fiery heat filled my face, but I was pleased Eliot was on my side. "Hi, Eliot. Sorry for, uh, not calling first."

"No need," he replied through the door. "You're always welcome. Especially if you're getting this cocksucker to stick around for a while."

"I'm sticking something alright," Austen murmured.

I suppressed a giggle.

"And, Vienne?" Eliot had moved from the other side of the door.

I caught Austen's eye, confused. Eliot sounded serious. "Yeah?"

"I didn't know you grew up ranching. I can expect you and Catherine to be out helping move cattle and horses this fall, right?"

I grinned. I could hear Catherine's squeals when I told her we'd be going to the Knight ranch to help with fall work. "Catherine would love it."

"Good. I pay in steak, beer, and jokes."

"You aren't funny, idiot," Austen said.

"I'm hilarious. I'm also going over books with Banks in the shop and then I'm heading to town, so you two love bunnies can fuck away."

Eliot's footsteps, the ones he must've muffled to sneak up on us, faded away.

Austen slid his hand down my body, massaged my ass, and rocked against me. "Do you have to get back tonight?"

I shook my head. "Catherine's staying with a friend. She'll be at the open house."

"Well then, we'd better get going while you can be nice and loud."

Twenty-Three

VIENNE

Only a few people continued to meander through the house. The open house was a success. Leilani had been cornered by several prospective clients during the four-hour window. I'd been one of them. Catherine was thrilled to move next door. We'd be staying in town, practically at the same address, and she thought her future stepdad was the coolest. She'd introduced him to all her friends who'd stopped in.

So many people had showed today. We got a ton of lookie-loos and several people who were disappointed to learn the house was off the market but were happy to learn Austen was staying. Mostly, I received a ton of compliments on the appearance.

Austen was chatting with an older couple who'd been friendly with a set of previous owners. I wandered into the kitchen.

Jim strode over. He always reminded me of my dad. "Good work, kid."

My pride was on the upswing when an older woman appeared behind him. Dot Bentwood. She lifted her chin and looked down at me. "I agree. You used a light touch and brought out the natural beauty."

My ego stayed in check. There was something in her tone that had a *but* effect. "Thank you."

She glanced around, her eagle gaze bouncing off the few people left until it landed on Austen. "Austen Knight owns the house?"

"Yes. He's not selling." That'd been the most common question today. *Was he selling?* I'd been happy to say no.

"He hired you, correct? Independently."

"Yes." I knew where this was heading, but I didn't have to explain myself.

Her lips turned down. "Hmph."

I didn't cringe or cower. "I'm happy to discuss anything about the renovations with you."

She glanced at Austen again. He looked over and gave me an indulgent smile. I grinned back at him, unashamed and so damn glad we weren't hiding.

"I see," she said. She turned to Jim, giving me her shoulder. "I'm not interested in her *work*."

I bristled but held my pleasant expression. "That's okay. I don't take jobs with clients who judge me based on my personal life—or my past. Thanks for coming."

Dot huffed and stalked off. My biggest potential paycheck to date was walking away, and I didn't care. I would be fine. Whatever expenses Catherine had, I was making sure Dave paid half.

Jim's bushy brows popped. "Damn. It's going to be a

long winter working for her," he muttered. "Thanks for not throwing me under the bus."

I knew what he meant. I could've told Dot I wasn't interested in fucking her husband, and she might've fired Jim for telling me about her worries. I'd said what I had to say, and it was cathartic.

He clapped me on the shoulder and swaggered out the door.

Leilani came toward me, a giant smile on her face. We'd met her boyfriend, and he thanked us for giving Leilani a chance. I was happy to give her the boost I'd wished for in my career. "This was *great*. I think you're going to get so many calls to refinish hardwood floors."

The floors had turned out really nice for two rookies who'd never messed with hardwood before. "They'd have to talk to Austen. He did most of the backbreaking work."

A strong arm wrapped around me. "Oh no. Don't shove off all the recognition. I would've still been sanding this damn place if it hadn't been for you."

Pride beamed out of me. "You did a ton of work off-hours."

He shrugged but tucked me into his side. We'd driven back this morning, and it'd been a whirlwind day. His family was coming later. They didn't want to clog up the open house. A fire with s'mores, a happy puppy with short legs getting used to his new yard, and my guy.

My guy.

"Well, if you ever want to start your own business, I think you'll get a lot of word of mouth from today." She smiled at me. "I expect you to get tons of calls." She wiggled a finger between us. "Maybe you two should team up."

Austen's gaze landed on me. Leilani's phone buzzed and she excused herself to answer it.

I met his stare. "Are you thinking of hanging a shingle? Becoming a handyman? A carpenter? A—"

"A sexy interior designer's bitch?"

I laughed, but he only smiled. His eyes were serious.

"Oh. You'd want to— I thought you'd look at law enforcement jobs or something."

He shook his head. "I'm done with that line of work. I got rather fond of making my own hours. So whadya say? Want to flip houses?"

I was an interior designer. I wasn't the idea guy—I made the clients' ideas happen and look damn good. But...I couldn't deny how much I liked getting my hands dirty. Setting my own schedule. Having my own contractor at my beck and call. I loved the idea of working with Austen, of controlling the work that came to me. I could take on projects that didn't need Austen to vet me to everyone in town. I would only have to do my own company's books.

The more I thought about it, the better the option seemed. There was one major problem. "I can't just go buy a house."

"You already have one, boss."

Oh. Excitement kindled in my belly. I did have a house I would have to sell. A house I hadn't had time or money to plug into for the last five years. "You really want to do this?"

"Hell yeah."

I was about to jump into his arms when Leilani returned.

"The open house is officially over. I saw that last person out when my call was done." She clapped her hands. "I'll just wrap up everything here and clean up the kitchen."

"Don't bother," I said. "We're having company." I didn't technically live in the house yet, but those words felt good coming off my tongue.

"Twist my arm." She grinned. "When do you want to meet about your house?"

I glanced at Austen again. "We might have to shift the timeline. My new business partner and I might do renovations before we sell."

Delight lit the real estate agent's gaze. "Are you two really teaming up?" She squealed. "That place will get snatched up. It's cute already, and with your eye, it'll only be better."

After a few minutes of discussing ideas, Leilani left.

Austen faced me. He was wearing the same clothing he'd worn to the bar the first night, but my fingers itched to unbutton his shirt. It was a sin to cover that chest.

"You don't have to do this if you don't want to," he said. "You can just hire me for every job, and I promise I won't try to get you naked in houses we don't own."

I laughed as heat flushed my body. He'd worn me out last night and once more this morning, but here I was, ready to go.

His gaze turned solemn and he faced me. "Don't make the decision today. You built your business, and I'm not coming in and taking over. I can do anything. I can even be a bum for a while, thanks to my retirement and inheritance."

I was still building a reputation, but since I was independent in a small town, my opportunities were limited. If I worked with Austen, I would have more variety, and we could branch out in a way I couldn't as a single mom.

He could work in a neighboring town, and I'd do office work if it was a day I had to be close for Catherine.

With what Austen was saying...I'd be fully in charge of the projects we took. I liked the sound of that.

"I'll think about it." I knew my answer, but he wouldn't accept it until he thought I'd mulled it over for a few days.

"Good." He stepped back, reached into his pocket, and withdrew something I couldn't see.

Then he dropped to a knee and presented a beautiful, square-cut diamond ring.

I gasped, my hands flying to my mouth. We'd just talked about this last night. Naked and in bed. We'd been mostly naked and in bed since we'd discussed our future together.

"When did you have time to get a ring?" Astonishment rang in my voice.

"V, I went out and bought this the day Eliot made me see how dense I was being. I planned to come back here and win you over, no matter how long it took, and I wanted to be ready for the day." He tucked his hand in his pocket, still on his knee, and brandished another ring, this one a light-gray silicone ring.

He had already bought the rings?

He really meant to stay—for me. His entire family was in the area, but he was still here because of me.

"I have this too." He held the rings with one hand and dug in his back pocket. He withdrew a simple silver bracelet, one that'd be perfect to run my fingers over. "It's Montana silver."

The rings were amazing enough. But no one other than Catherine had ever given me a bracelet.

Instead of bitching about my jewelry, he bought me more. "Oh, god, Austen. Yes, of course."

He took my hand and gingerly pushed my ring on. "I wasn't sure on the size, but I described every part of you to the lady at the jewelry store."

The fit was perfect.

He rose and lifted me in his arms, my feet dangling off the floor. I liked being his sack of potatoes. I kissed him hard. As if it was possible to communicate everything I was feeling through the press of his lips on mine.

This man. He was more than I could've asked for. Everything I'd ever wanted.

"Knock, knock," Aggie called from outside the front door.

Austen didn't let me go. "I'm kissing my fiancée," he called.

"Are you kissing her with clothes on?" Cody asked, his voice carrying across the empty room. "We can get the fire going, but I don't want to see your ass."

"This is how it's going to be, isn't it?" Austen asked me. "My family cockblocking me at random times?"

"That's how it's been for us since the beginning. Why change what's worked?"

He hooked his hand through mine, and we opened the door to all the people who'd become my family.

Epilogue

AUSTEN

Nine years later...

"Is Catherine getting there before us?" I asked, my arm draped over the steering wheel of the pickup. I might be looking fifty in the eye in a couple of years, but I was as giddy as a kid at Christmas for this trip.

I always looked forward to my whole family getting together. Nuclear family, extended family, I didn't care. I'd missed so many gatherings during my time in the army that I made sure I was at every single one now. But this was a big Knight family camping trip. I was towing a pull-behind camper, and Teddy was in his kennel strapped in the bed of the pickup with his favorite toys and a bed that was plusher than mine.

"She's staying with friends tonight, getting up to no

good in Deadwood." Vienne was in the passenger seat, working on her laptop.

We'd been partners—in and out of the bedroom—since we'd gotten married. She'd been my wife for nine years, and we'd been buying houses to flip for nine years. Sometimes, she'd wade in the renovations with me, and sometimes, she'd do the office and admin work. No matter what, she was the mastermind of the details and design. I was the grunt work, and that suited both of us fine.

"When can I see KitKat?" Our seven-year-old daughter, Francine, kicked her legs against the seat. If she didn't dominate the court in volleyball, we'd all be surprised. Catherine had been giving her toy volleyballs since she was born. She was a coach now, and we had family games when Catherine came back to Crocus Valley for visits.

I thought her brother, Harrison, older by a year, would be interested, but he preferred to get into Daddy's tools. There'd been more than one patch job on the walls after he got loose with a hammer.

"You'll see her when she gets there," Harrison uttered. If there was a smart-ass gene, my son got it, and Vienne claimed it was from me.

I couldn't argue.

I could also empathize with my mama's struggles. I couldn't imagine raising three more of him at the same time. She'd been young when she started having kids, and Barns had been controlling. Didn't make what she did right, but I was eternally grateful to have Vienne at my side.

After being a bachelor for a good two decades, I never would've thought I'd be a dad taking my family on a weekend camping trip to hike and fish and sightsee, but I'd done it several times since I'd married Vienne.

We'd also made trips to LA to visit my buddies. I was still a silent investor in their thriving security company. There were no hard feelings, and all our families loved hanging out.

"Ooh, I'll have to show you this place when we're all set up at the campsite." Vienne wiggled in her seat, and it was all I could do to keep my eyes on the road. I had precious cargo but also I couldn't get enough of Vienne's ass. "It's an old farmhouse on five acres. The house is... It'd be a big project, but with summer coming, we'd have good weather to do the outside work."

"Any interest from buyers, boss?"

"Maybe for the land, but the house is rough. I emailed Leilani, and she said it has good bones."

We'd become some of Leilani's top clients. I hadn't been sure how much work Vienne and I could do once we opened the doors to our joint venture. The community might be small, but older homes that needed a good face-lift were more common than one would've thought. We'd had all the work we wanted over the years, but we hadn't needed to hustle, thanks to my other income. I just enjoyed watching Vienne work. She loved her job, and she loved being a mom. I was the lucky bastard who got to witness all sides of her.

She fiddled with a thin gold chain around her neck. I got her a bracelet and necklace for every birthday and Christmas. Seeing her wear the things I got her, to run her fingers over them daily, satisfied the caveman part of my brain. She was mine. She had my gifts on her.

"Are we hiking tonight?" Francine asked. She tossed her book down. She wasn't antsy like her brother. He took after his mom, but she was fearless, also like her mom.

"We can hike around the campground, but all your cousins are going to be there too."

"Yes!" Harrison kicked the back of my seat for the hundredth time. I didn't have to look behind me to see that all his fidget toys were scattered across the back seat.

Vienne closed her laptop and looked out the window. Tall trees lined both sides of the winding roads, rising high on the rocks and cliffs. "I can't believe it's been so long since we've been out here."

"Only this time, you're not going to be so dismayed to hear I'm your new neighbor."

The last time I'd been camping in the Black Hills was after Wilder won Sutton back for good. I'd announced that I retired and bought the house next to Vienne, the one we still lived in. Everyone had been excited but her.

"It wasn't personal." She grinned, her turquoise eyes sparkling. "I swear. Although having a hot neighbor who's the brother of all my friends stressed me out a little."

"Then I hired you."

"And I turned you down."

I laughed. "The audacity too. After I'd seen it all?"

"What did you see, Daddy?" Francine asked.

After having been in the army for so long, I should be used to having ears everywhere. Raising kids was a lot like being in charge of a bunch of newly enlisted privates. "My honey V."

Vienne smirked. "I don't turn you down anymore."

"Nope. I make sure of it." I made sure she had nothing to fear when it came to me. Same with our kids, including Catherine, who traveled the country coaching volleyball and didn't come home nearly enough for her old stepdad.

"I'm really looking forward to this," Vienne said. "But I seem to look forward to anything that has to do with you."

"Like I said, I make sure of it, Honey V."

A few hours later, we were pulling into the campground. I followed the directions to the campsite next to Sutton and Wilder. When I found it and spotted it decked out in colorful balloons and streamers all over the picnic table at the site, I glanced at Vienne.

"You did it again?"

"Happy birthday, Daddy!" both kids cried from the back seat.

I chuckled and slowed to a stop. Sutton and Wilder were waving from several feet away, and their boys, Alex and Drew, were jumping up and down. My kids were going to vibrate out of their seats.

Ever since Vienne came into my life, my birthdays were a big deal. Her mom, whom I called Mama K, liked to help plan the celebrations. I also made sure to do more than message my siblings on their big days. Then there were the kids, the nieces, and the nephews. I'd had a lot of celebrating to do since I'd retired from the army.

Once we had the camper in place and the pickup parked, I cornered Vienne in the kitchen of the camper. The kids were outside playing. "You had something to show me?"

Her ass was pressed against the mini counter, and she wrapped her arms around me. "It was for work."

"You know how I like to mix work and pleasure."

She giggled. "I think we have two kids to show for

how you don't let some remodeling interfere with pleasure."

I kissed my wife. I never tired of getting my mouth on her. "Nothing will get between us—except for the dog and the kids." I kissed down her neck. "Did you bring everything for your bacon ranch salad?"

Her smile was saucy. "I've got everything you want."

"You gave me everything I could ever want. And I love you, Mrs. Knight."

"I'd say that was my favorite name you call me, but I really like when you remind me how you came up with Honey V."

"Mm... I think you've forgotten again, and since the kids are playing—go get on your hands and knees, wife."

———

Eliot is the last single Knight brother. He thinks he's going to stay that way until he overhears his sister-in-law's new employee Lily name him as her new fiancé. Then he learns the single mom has to get married or she'll lose her house. He's a guy who wants to do the right thing. In this case, it might be to say "I do" in An Endless Memory.

You're invited to another Knight wedding! You can find Austen and Vienne tying the knot when you sign up for my newsletter at mariejohnstonwriter.com.

About the Author

Marie Johnston writes paranormal and contemporary romance and has collected several awards in both genres. Before she was a writer, she was a microbiologist. Depending on the situation, she can be oddly unconcerned about germs or weirdly phobic. She's also a licensed medical technician and has worked as a public health microbiologist and as a lab tech in hospital and clinic labs. Marie's been a volunteer EMT, a college instructor, a security guard, a phlebotomist, a hotel clerk, and a coffee pourer in a bingo hall. All fodder for a writer!! She has four kids, cats, and a corgie.

mariejohnstonwriter.com

Follow me: